m∠r

ꓕ

THE TINNER'S DAUGHTER

Also by Rosemary Aitken

The Girl From Penvarris

THE
TINNER'S DAUGHTER

Rosemary Aitken

ORION

Copyright © 1996 by Rosemary Aitken

All rights reserved

The right of Rosemary Aitken to be identified as the author of
this work has been asserted by her in accordance with
the Copyright, Designs and Patents Act 1988.

First published in Great Britain in 1996 by
Orion
An imprint of Orion Books Ltd
Orion House, 5 Upper St Martin's Lane, London WC2H 9EA

A CIP catalogue record for this book is available
from the British Library

ISBN 1 85797 637 1

Typeset by Deltatype Ltd, Ellesmere Port, Cheshire
Printed in Great Britain by

For George and Gwen,
who made this possible.

PART ONE : 1899

CHAPTER ONE

By the time Carrie left for school that Thursday morning, the storm was already brewing. The September wind, which only yesterday had been a playful thing, tickling the laughing waves down in Penvarris bay, this morning was a savage creature, flattening the late corn in Crowdie's fields, and buffeting the single row of terraced houses cowering in the valley.

Carrie opened the front door, and at once a gust of wind whipped her legs and billowed her petticoats to her waist. 'My lor',' she said, turning to her mother, who was standing behind her in the warmth of the narrow passage. 'If it's like this down here in the Terrace, there's going to be some gale up on the top of the hill. I told you it was no good me wearing that bonnet, it'll be blown half way to the Scillies before you can say knife.'

But her mother only laughed. 'Carrie girl,' she said, 'it isn't a bit of good you carrying on. You'll be thirteen next week – a grown-up woman, near enough. If you are going into Penzance this afternoon to see after that position, then you are going to wear a hat and look a bit respectable, or my name's not Cissie Tremble.'

Carrie grinned. 'Well, 'tisn't either! You ask Miss Maythorne!' That was daring, and Carrie knew it, but it was also true. Mother was christened Annie, but as the only girl among seven brothers she had become 'Cissie' from the start; and as for Miss Maythorne, she still called Mother 'Hoskins', as though it was still 1880, and Mother was a girl again in service, and not a married woman with a daughter of her own.

'Cheeky monkey,' Mother said, but she was smiling. 'Now stand still and let me put this bonnet on you, or you'll be late for school!' And Carrie had to submit to having the loathsome thing tied under her chin, and tucked under the hood of her cloak. 'Now then,' Mother stood back to survey her handiwork, 'that looks something like. Now don't forget,

Crowdie's coming at four sharp with his cart to pick us up, so make sure you come home a bit lively. Good thing it's market day, and he's going in to pick up his boy, or we'd have had a sorry walk this weather.'

Carrie nodded. She had seen Crowdie's boy earlier, driving the cows in to the cattle market in Penzance. The farmer's cart would be a welcome luxury: the walk to Penzance was two miles or more across fields – longer if you went on the roads to save your boots, which Mother would have insisted on. And then there was the walk back. There was a horse-bus, but that cost money, so it was out of the question unless this wind brought real rain with it.

Which it might, Carrie thought suddenly. The clouds were already piling angrily in the sky. It was worth a try.

'You sure about this bonnet?' she said. 'Looks as if it might rain. Spoil the ribbons.'

'And if it turns sunny it will fade them, I suppose,' her Mother said, laughing. 'Get on with you, Carrie! And mind you're a good girl at school.' She handed her daughter the little parcel of books and pasty, gave her a hasty kiss and bundled her out of the door. 'And you just be thankful to Miss Maythorne. She's been some good to you!'

Carrie sighed and set off, across the road and over the stile. Thankful! Well, she was thankful, mostly. Miss Maythorne had been good – to all of them. Almost twenty years since Mother had left her service, but Miss Maythorne had never forgotten 'Hoskins'. Every Christmas there was a parcel for them all – good things too, with a lot of wear left in them. Vests for Father, left from old Mr Maythorne. Dresses for Mother to wear, or to cut down for Carrie. Once, even, a good woollen coat, which Mother still wore. And for Carrie there were other things too – neat brown boots, which hardly pinched a bit, and a pair of white gloves, only a little stained, which she kept for Sundays and which made her feel like a real lady. Yes, truly, Carrie was grateful.

But then there were the hats. There were two of them, and they were the bane of Carrie's life. Great buckets of things, fat and pink, all flounces and flowers like Miss Maythorne herself. Too folderol for Mother, but they would come in for Carrie. The smaller one, with the feathers, had been to chapel once or twice, but Carrie had always managed to avoid the larger one with its swathes of ribbons and rosebuds. Until now.

She had reached the top of the field by this time, and as she clambered over the top stile, the full force of the wind tore at her, blowing her hood back, and snatching the bonnet from her head. 'Dang the thing,' she muttered, clutching at the offending millinery, which was threatening to

4

throttle her in its ribbons. She glanced back down the hill. Here, behind Crowdie's wall, she was out of sight of the Terrace.

For a moment she hesitated, and then, with sudden decision, she tore at the knot. There was a hole in the stone wall nearby, the 'secret box' where she and her friend Katie Warren from next door used to leave treasures and letters when they were small. It was the work of a moment to bundle up the bonnet and stuff it into the crevice. It would be safe there, she told herself, from wind and rain, and she could pick it up on her way home.

'There!' she said to herself, and her heart was so light that she picked up her petticoats and ran all the way to the school. Even so, the wind was so fierce that it slowed her progress, and she only just had time to straighten her skirts and her wayward hair and walk demurely through the gate marked 'Girls' before Miss Bevan came out with the big bell, and it was time to go in and sit with the others at a high desk, and struggle with sums and copy-books and the dates of the Kings of England.

And already, outside, the first heavy drops of rain were falling.

The storm was rising fast by the time Seth Tremble, Carrie's father, came home from the mine. It was raining hard, and the wind drove the drops horizontal into his face, but he hardly noticed. He went slowly down the lane, the memory of the morning weighing heavier than his boots, though they were water-sodden and his feet squelched as he walked. He came down the paddock and let himself in through the back gate, his legs mechanical as tin-stamps, lift and fall, lift and fall.

He stopped at the door to take off his streaming footwear, and saw his wife through the window. She was ironing, with the loose-block from the iron hot and hissing on the fire, and as he watched, she lifted it carefully with the firetongs and slipped it into place in the back of the heavy iron. Then she busied herself with a piece of old sheet, spreading it between the iron-sole and the garment 'to catch the scorch', and splashing water on the shirt-front to dampen it.

'I am washed,' he heard her sing, 'I am washed in the blood of the Lamb!' Despite himself he felt his mood lift, and he found himself smiling. Trust Cissie to find a hymn to match the occasion. He stood a moment, only half-sheltered by the porch of the door, as she went about her task, wiggling the toe of the iron between the bone buttons in time to the twiddly bits, oblivious to his presence.

He loved to see her like this: busy, contented, cheerful. 'She'll do,' he had said, twenty years ago when he first saw her – no beauty, even then, but a kind, honest, open face, and a no-nonsense air that pleased him from the start. He courted her from that day on, and never regretted it – though folks had clicked their tongues, and predicted that no good would ever come of it, a girl of eighteen and a man nearly twice her age.

Well, more fools they! Only one thing had marred their happiness. He had wanted sons, but there had only ever been Carrie – and that after years of trying.

He saw her turn to look at the big clock on the mantelpiece, between the china dogs and the statue of Dick Turpin on horseback. Watching the time, then, waiting for him to come. There would be something hot for him, as there always was, and the ironing would be folded up and put away in deference to his presence. And what would she say when she heard his news? The need to tell Cissie was almost the worst part of it all.

Well, standing here would pickle no pilchards. He put his hands softly on the handle. 'I'm home then!'

She turned with a little start, set the iron down at once, and lifted the heavy kettle onto the stove. 'My dear Seth! Whatever are you like? I knew how it would be, as soon as I saw the rain set in. Out in all this weather, and with your chest, too.'

He glanced down at himself, seeing what she saw: his coat soaked through and his shirt clemmed to his back like a second skin. Even as he stood there, his stockinged feet were making little damp patches on the rag-mat, where his boots had let in water.

He avoided her gaze. 'Now then, Cissie, don't you start. A man's got to get home somehow. And of course I've been in the rain with my chest, I can't leave it behind in the "dry" with my working clothes, can I?'

It made her smile, as his fooling always did, and she said, in a softened tone, 'A "dry" it's supposed to be, with all them steam pipes to dry out your things. You might as well have got changed in a "wet", the state you're in! Look at you standing there, giving off puffs of steam like a railway engine.' And indeed he did look rather like it, with the vapour rising from him in the heat of the room.

Seth said nothing, but began to cough again, that dry, racking cough that kept him awake nights.

'Oh, take those wet things off, do!' Cissie cried. 'Put on your red flannel while I dry these off a bit over the fire. There's a drop of soup set by, so drink that and see if we can't get some warmth into your bones.'

He pretended to protest at the notion of wearing his nightshirt in the middle of the day, but he was soaked to the bone and apart from his chapel clothes he had nothing else. So ten minutes later found him sitting on the wooden settle by the hearth, with a cup of steaming soup in his hands, and a blanket ironed and wrapped hot around his feet for comfort.

'It's only a pity you were on the early shift,' his wife said. She had already ironed the worst of the wet out of his clothes, and, sure enough, was now bundling everything away. 'If you had gone down lunchtime, like you belong to do, you'd have missed all this.'

Seth sipped his soup. 'Mind,' he said, 'I knew there was a storm brewing. We were down on the deep level, out under the sea, and you hear it – the stones shifting in the water. Always a sign of a storm, that is.'

Cissie tutted. 'I don't like to think of you out there, under the seabed like that. You know what happened out at Wheal Owles a year or two back. Hit the wrong seam and half the Atlantic poured in, and all they poor miners drowned.'

Seth shook his head sadly. 'Engineer's fault that was, not the men's. Made a mistake on the chart.' He sighed, not so much for the memory as for the news he had to give Cissie. 'Still, it won't be a question of being down there much longer, my handsome. Captain Tregorran, the mine captain, came to see me today.'

He saw her stop rolling the dampened sheet she held in her hands, and stand as still as a statue. She didn't look at him as she said carefully, 'And?'

But her eyes betrayed her. She already knew what he was going to say. That cough of his: not all the camphor oil and goosegrease in the world could disguise the fact that it was no ordinary cough, no autumn cold, to be shaken off with hot blackcurrant and wool next to the skin. This was the miner's sickness, phthisis they called it, borne of the up-country mines of his youth, filling his lungs with dust and grit so that his spittle grew grey with it. One day that grey would be streaked with red. And not even the doctors, with their fomentations and poultices could help him then.

'And?' she said again.

Seth set down his soup-can with a clatter. 'And Captain Tregorran said what we both knew anyhow, Cissie. Eddie Goodbody had just set off a charge before we came down, and the smoke and dust hadn't cleared altogether. It got on my chest, somehow, and I couldn't breathe. Coughing something chronic. I'm sorry, Cissie girl, I did my best to keep it from him, but it wasn't a bit of good. Can't expect a Captain to keep a man on down the levels if he can't pull his weight. He's moving me up, next week, help the blacksmith with the horses. Nothing skilled, mind. And he'll find me a place with the carpenter next time one comes vacant. Knew I'd done a bit of woodworking, one time, when I was young.'

Cissie breathed out, very slowly, and resumed rolling the sheet. She said gruffly, 'Well, it'll save me a power of work, washdays. Always supposing you don't come home smelling of horse-muck.'

She understood! Another woman might have grumbled. Sympathised even. He could not have borne that. She knew, without a word being spoken, that Captain Tregorran had been good to him. Found him a surface job right off, and never made it look like charity. He got up then, and came over to her, ridiculous in his night-shirt and bare feet in daylight. He took her by the shoulders and turned her to face him.

'It won't be the money I was getting, Cissie girl.' If she knew what it had cost him to say that! 'Not the same money, by any means.'

She gave him a little firm smile. 'Well, there's more to life than money, Seth Tremble. And it's to be hoped we'll have a little coming in from Carrie very soon. I'm taking her to see after that job this afternoon. Nice respectable family. Tobacconists. Miss Maythorne put in a word for her.'

Seth released her shoulders. 'Why you want to go with her, weather like this, I'll never know. Great girl like that, she's big enough to look after herself.' But they were idle words, and they both knew it. If Miss Maythorne had recommended Carrie, it was because she was Hoskins' daughter. Cissie would be expected to present the girl in person for an interview.

'You spoil that girl,' he said gruffly, as though his gawky, impulsive, laughing-eyed daughter was not the moon and stars in his own universe.

Cissie smiled. 'I'll just make sure she gets there respectable. And I can drop in and get a few things at the market while I'm there.'

'You'll have a job, then, getting her there respectable this weather. Look what a state I came home in, and I wasn't out in it more than half an hour. There's worse jobs than mining when it comes to weather. You should have seen that fishing boat out past Penvarris Head on the way home.'

Cissie said sharply, 'How's that then?'

'Tossing around like a cork, it was, and the water coming down on them in torrents. French, by the look of them.' Everyone knew the French boats by their sails – not the rich red-brown of Cornish luggers, but a deeper, sadder brown, from the different bark the sail-tanners used. 'Be some fight to get her in tonight. You talk about me being down under the sea, Cissie, but I'd a sight rather be under it than on top of it, weather like this.'

Cissie turned to her husband, her hands on her hips. 'And you stood there watching in all that rain, like a great gummock? Seth Tremble, you haven't got the brains you were born with.'

He grinned. In all their troubles, she still thought firstly of him. 'Yes, she'll do,' he thought, with gratitude. Somehow, blacksmith's boy or no blacksmith's boy, they would survive. Aloud, he said, 'Knew my wife would make a fuss of me when I got home.' He put a playful hand on her waist.

'Get out of it, you daft thing!' she said, but she was laughing, and there was still half an hour before Crowdie came.

Carrie had a moment of panic when she came out of the school gate. Mother and Crowdie were already there, waiting with the cart. No chance, now, to collect her bonnet.

'Couldn't let you walk in all this rain,' Mother said, arranging a leather bag for her to sit on and draping shawls and sacking "to save the worst of the wet". 'Not when you want to make a good impression. You'd be over your boots in mud before you got halfway home.' She gave Carrie an appraising glance. 'Left your bonnet in there, out of the rain, have you?' She smiled. 'Perhaps you were right, at that!'

And that was all. Carrie could hardly believe her good fortune, but nothing further was said about hats, all the way to Penzance. Instead, Crowdie grumbled the whole journey about the weather. Ruin the corn, he said, and he'd be lucky to get any hay for the horses.

'Too late now, anyroad,' he said dolefully. 'Should have got that field in weeks ago, but it didn't seem to want to ripen. Good thing I've only got a field or two down to cereals – not like they poor fellows up east. One good rainstorm, and they're half ruined, poor souls.'

Carrie stole a sideways look at him from under her makeshift sacking hat. She had always thought of Crowdie as someone rolling in plenty: milk and eggs and winter broccoli. It hadn't occurred to her that farmers, too, counted their pennies and worried at the weather.

A trickle of cold water ran down her forehead and into her eyes, and she huddled up closer to the pile of empty wooden boxes which Crowdie had heaped up as a makeshift shelter against the weather. At least, she told herself, pulling the warm sacking around herself against the chill of the wind, they would arrive like ladies, without having their petticoats sodden to the knees, and their boots covered in mud to the ankles.

Crowdie was as good as gold, too, taking them right to the end of the street. He swung round, rain dripping from his leather hat and jerkin, to help them to the pavement. 'Here you are then. Victoria Road. Well, I'll be looking for you around six then. Fishmarket at Newlyn do you? I'm meeting my boy there, and going to pick up a stone of fish while I'm about it.'

'That'll do grand,' Mother said. 'Bit of fresh herring would do Seth good.'

'Right then,' Crowdie said. 'And good luck to you, Carrie my lover. You dry your hair and face off a bit, you'll look as good as new.' And with a 'Heigh up, Bess!' he was off, the cart rattling down the street.

9

The pavement was slippery with wet, but they found the house without difficulty. Albert Villas. One house, not two, in spite of its name. It was tall and grey, with thin bay windows overlooking the street, and a narrow front door up a small flight of steps. It looked, Carrie thought, as if the house was pursing its lips and squinting down at you with a disapproving air.

'Let's have a look at you,' Mother said, when they reached the safety of the porch. Then there was a rearranging of skirts and shawls, Mother produced a rough towel and rubbed Carrie's hair – in bunches today, not pigtails, in honour of the occasion – and scrubbed her face glowing. She was just retying the ribbons, with a satisfied 'There now!' when the door suddenly opened, and there stood a small, apologetic girl in apron and cap.

'We've come about the position,' Mother said, hastily stuffing her possessions into her bag, and tucking her own damp locks back into her bun.

'Mrs Tucker saw you come,' the girl said. 'You better come in.'

Miss Maythorne had told them about Mrs Tucker, but to Carrie's surprise there were two women in the room, sitting on either side of the fireplace. As the door opened, they rose to their feet together, like a pair of marionettes pulled by a single string, so exactly in time that Carrie was hard put to it not to giggle.

It was hard to imagine that two people could be at once so alike, and so completely different. They were sisters, that was plain to see. The same height and build, the same pale, freckled skin, the same sandy-red hair piled into identical topknots above their little round, snub-nosed faces. But there the resemblance stopped. One seemed to have been upholstered into her dark-green dress; everything about her was firmly and fiercely buttoned, from the soles of her feet to her tight mouth and her little boiled buttons of eyes. The other, though a substantial lady too, seemed a thing of wisps by contrast. Her eyes, the same faded blue as her sister's, were mild and vague, and her burgundy dress, though of an identical pattern, seemed somehow haphazard, as though she had been bundled into by some passing wind, and might just as easily be blown out of it again.

'I'm Cissie Tremble,' Mother said, by way of explanation. 'Cissie Hoskins as was. Miss Maythorne said that you were wanting a kitchen maid, and you were expecting us, I think.'

The wispy one said 'Aahh,' as though she might have been thinking of summoning tea, but Button-eyes motioned Carrie into the middle of the room and then suggested that Mother might like to take a walk and come back in an hour.

'Or I'll meet you down the fishmarket,' Carrie said, and wondered if she shouldn't have. But it seemed to do no harm. Mother smiled and left – pleased to be out of the place, Carrie thought – and Button-eyes (who introduced herself not as Mrs Tucker at all, but Miss Limmon) pursed her lips and nodded. 'Well, you have initiative, I'll say that for you.'

Mrs Tucker smiled wispily.

There followed a barrage of questions, mostly from Miss Limmon. Had Carrie been in service before? Was she frightened of hard work? Did she drink? Did she have followers? Did she expect to be allowed time off for fairs and frippery? Was she strong and healthy?

Carrie, who had been answering 'No, ma'am,' like an automaton, changed it to 'Yes, ma'am,' just in time for the last question, and the interview seemed to be over.

Mrs Tucker rang the bell, saying to her sister, 'She'll suit very well, do you think, Emily?'

And Miss Limmon said, 'Oh, I daresay, but we shouldn't rush into these things. She'd better drop by tomorrow at the same time, and we'll let her know.'

Drop by! And outside the storm was still rising! And then they would only 'let her know'. Her heart was in her boots as the door opened, and the maid came in, answering the summons.

'You can show this girl out . . .' Miss Limmon began, but her sister interrupted.

'Oh, I think she should see Edward, don't you? He'll be here in ten minutes. Meantime, she can have a look around. Dolly here can show her the kitchen and where she'll be sleeping.'

'*If* we decide to keep her!' Miss Limmon said, with a sniff. 'Well, I suppose if you must consult Edward on everything, you must. Don't mind me! Give her a guided tour, Dolly, do!'

'And give the child some tea,' Mrs Tucker put in, and Carrie found herself outside in the passage, staring blankly at the closed door.

'You all right, are you?' said a little voice at her side.

Carrie jumped. She had been so lost in her own thoughts that she had half forgotten Dolly. 'It's that Miss Limmon,' she said. 'Can't decide if they want me, so I'm to call back tomorrow. Take me half a day, and in this weather too! Why can't she say no and have done? That's what she wants to say, that's clear.'

Dolly led the way down the back stairs, into a smell of damp and onions. 'I wouldn't worry about Miss Limmon,' she said. 'It's Mr Tucker will say yes or no, and Mrs Tucker's taken a liking to you.' She pushed open the kitchen door. 'Now, you come in and sit down there and I'm sure Mrs Rowe will give you a cup of tea. Mrs Rowe, this is Carrie.'

Mrs Rowe, a beefy woman with a square red face, turned from the saucepan she was tending and waved a ladle in the air. 'Come to join us, have you, my dear? Well another pair of hands is always welcome – though what Mrs Tucker wants with an extra maid in a house this size, I'm sure I don't know. It's that Miss Limmon, I reckon – heard the chemist next door has got two maids now, so we must have them. Still, Dolly and I won't say no to a bit of help, will we, my lover?'

Dolly grinned. 'Especially not with the new century coming up in a month or two – Mrs Tucker is already making good plans for the biggest dinner you ever saw. And then it won't be half good enough for Miss Limmon.'

'Well, this is how it is,' Mrs Rowe, said, pouring strong tea into a cup and pushing it across the deal table towards Carrie. 'Kitchen maid they said, but there will be upstairs work too. You start at six . . .' She went on, outlining the duties of the new maid.

Carrie winced as she listened. Not at the chores so much, though the hours were long – she had never been afraid of hard work, and she had helped Mother ever since she could hold a duster. It was the remembering to say 'Yes, sir. No, sir', the walking politely, the watching skirts and elbows near fragile cups and saucers, that filled her with alarm.

She said as much to Dolly a few minutes later, as they looked into the little attic bedroom with its bare floor and two iron bedsteads. 'When Miss Maythorne talked about this, I never thought about working above stairs. Specially not around Miss Limmon – one look from her and I'd turn all fingers and thumbs. Miss Limmon! Miss Lemon, more like.'

Dolly laughed. It surprised Carrie – she hadn't intended to be funny – but Dolly's laugh was so irrepressible that she found herself laughing too.

'No,' she protested, with a giggle. 'I mean it. My father is always saying so. "Carrie, my dear girl, you'd make a better carthorse than a maiden!" I'm forever clattering down the stairs, or closing the door too loudly behind me. If I'm to work upstairs I need some stout, hearty farmer's wife, with china to match.'

Dolly laughed again. 'I hope you do come,' she said, ' 'cause this is where you'll be sleeping. And you'll have me for company.'

' 'Tisn't up to me,' Carrie retorted, remembering Miss Limmon.

Dolly smiled. 'Oh, Miss Tucker wants to have you, or I wouldn't be sent to show you round like this. Only she can't stand up to Miss Limmon.' She giggled. 'Miss Lemon! But Mr Tucker'll be home in a moment, and we'll see what he has to say. I'll put in a word for you myself, if you like.'

Carrie looked at the girl in amazement. 'You can't!'

Dolly gave a knowing little laugh. 'Can't I though? We'll see about that.

There's more than one way to skin a cat. Listen, there he is now. I've taken a liking to you, so say if you want this position, and it's yours, or my name's not Dolly Boas.' She reached over and squeezed Carrie's hand. 'Do say yes, Carrie. We should have some larks!'

'Well . . . of course, if they'll have me!' Carrie said, and Dolly was off down the stairs like a shot.

Carrie loitered in the shadows above, close enough to see a large man with moustaches come into the entrance-hall, in a fluster of coats and hats and gloves and gaiters. Dolly went forward to assist him, and Carrie heard him say, 'Did that girl come about the post Emily was so keen on?'

And Dolly's voice, very polite. 'Yes sir, she's here now. Ten miles or more there and back in the rain, and Miss Limmon says she's to come again tomorrow, but I think Mrs Tucker would take her now, and save the journey.'

'Would she now?' Mr Tucker said, and there was the sound of the parlour door closing.

Dolly came to the foot of the stairs and beckoned, and Carrie came slowly down. But she had hardly set foot in the passage before the door opened again and Mr Tucker appeared. He looked, Carrie thought, rather like the Prince of Wales in the photographs. Confused, she dropped him a curtsy, painfully aware of skirts and hair still damp from her drenching.

'So you're Carrie,' Mr Tucker said. He had a deep voice, but gentle. Carrie stole a look at him. He was smiling. 'Seems you are to join the household. Monday week then, at eight sharp, and mind you are on time. I gather my sister-in-law has told you the terms.'

And that was that. She could hardly believe it, and she almost ran the half-mile or so to Newlyn and the fishmarket. 'Almost' ran, because by now the rain the rain was sheeting so hard that Carrie was forced to keep her head down and mind her footing in the wet. She longed to be under the shelter of Crowdie's sacks and on her way home to fire and supper.

It was worse in the fish yard. The pavement, always slippery with scales and blood, was like sheet ice in the rain. And there was no sign of Mother! And then she saw her, one of a little crowd of people huddled in the shelter of the shed, gazing out in the direction of the sea. Carrie made her way over, turning up her nose at the stench of fish. 'I got the job, Mother. Whatever's to do?'

Her mother turned. 'Some poor fellow out there in trouble, so they say. Lost half his mast, or some such thing.'

Carrie followed the eyes of the crowd, but she could see nothing, only the grey tossing of the sea and the white clouds of foam under the angry sky. A wave, lifted by the wind, reared up against the harbour wall and smashed down in a hail of foam – hard, cold drops that sent the watchers scattering.

'My stars!' Mother said. 'Let's get off home before we have to swim. There's Crowdie now!' She set off towards the cart lurching towards them.

Carrie followed, but the idea of the stricken fishing-boat still haunted her, and she turned back, trying to get a glimpse of it. As she did so she cannoned into someone, and a pair of startled hands grasped her shoulders to steady her. She looked up, to find a young man staring at her in surprise.

A tall, lanky, awkward young man, with a good-natured smile. Carrie flushed, embarrassed at having effectively walked into his arms. 'Had a good look?' she enquired pertly, to cover her confusion. 'You'll know me another time!'

And she was up and on the cart beside Mother before he had time to reply.

CHAPTER TWO

Ernie watched the retreating figure out of sight. 'Know me again!' Cheeky monkey! Well, he would know her again, too. Not that he was likely to come back to Penzance in a hurry.

He shouldn't be here now by rights. He should be up at the St Blurzey china-clay pits the other side of St Austell, working. Or turning off home, more like, at this time of night. He had worked a night-shift, once – when the engineers had struck a terrible wet seam, and they had to work twenty-four hours, shift about – but it was rare they wanted a toolboy, nights. Mostly the end of the day would see him going up to the dry to take off his clay-sodden clothes and the wooden-soled 'streamer's boots' Da had given him, and home to his supper.

But not tonight.

It was all the fault of this rain, he told himself crossly. It had come on to rain at the pit just after lunch: hard, driving rain that threatened to wash the clay out of the levels without human help. He had known then what would happen.

It happened every time there was a new man in the pit. First real wet day, they'd send the toolboy out for all the makings and brew up a 'join' – cocoa so thick you could cut it with a knife. And it was up to the new man to pay for it – hand over his first day's pay to the foreman, and if he didn't do it civil, they'd hang him by his boots from the crook-beam till he paid up. 'Shoeing the colt,' they called it.

And now Vince Whittaker had come to the pit. Year or two older than Ernie, and had worked on other pits, but he wasn't actually a family man, so he was fair game. The pit captains had been waiting for a good rainstorm to find an excuse. Well, today they had it.

There was a whip-round first because the money Vince had from his first payday wasn't enough to pay for everyone. Then Ernie was sent off, all the way to Bugle, the nearest town, for cocoa and sugar, milk and cream and eggs, and some trouble it had been to carry it all back.

Then it was all put in the huge works' pitcher, and Ernie was sent off again to fetch water, to be boiled and added to the sticky mass. Dick Clarance, Ernie's cousin, was a pit captain, and he stirred it himself, using his hickory stick – the one he used for packing straw into his boots and around his feet, to keep them dry in the damp of the clay-diggings. Dick made a good thick cocoa, always did, best in the works. They never got to 'shoe' Vince Whittaker though – he'd paid up like a lamb.

Ernie was enjoying himself, though he wouldn't have been sorry to see the new man refuse, and be hung upside down by his ankle-boots. Not that he had anything against the fellow, except his job. It should have been Ernie out there, working on the overburthen. Couldn't expect to be working skilled, not to start with: not a hose-man, washing the clay-slurry from the cliff, or a streamer, standing in the running water breaking up the clay and rock – but a trammer, shifting the useless overburthen to the tips, Ernie could have done that. Would have done too, if a more skilled man hadn't come by looking for work just when the post came up vacant.

Then Ernie would have been a proper clay-miner instead of still a humble toolboy after eighteen months at the pit. Why, Ernie's Da had been a toolboy – kettleboy, they called them – when he was no more than ten years old. And here was Ernie, fourteen and a half, and still not doing a man's job. True, he had been given a rise twice, and was taking home elevenpence a day. More than grown men earned, some places. All the same, it rankled being passed over, and Dick Clarance's cocoa tasted all the sweeter for being at Vince's expense.

And then the work's manager, Mr Borglaise, came in about the parcel.

If the men had been working, he would have gone himself on his horse, he said, but since they weren't cutting clay somebody could be spared to go down the station and collect it. It was Ernie's job, of course. Fetching and carrying, bringing water for crib and dinner, taking the tools to the blacksmith, anything that needed a stout pair of legs. There was a parcel should have come on the afternoon train. Important papers from London, and Ernie was sent off, in his walking clothes, to go down to St Austell and pick up the packet.

That was bad enough. Rain was lashing down and the wind howling round the tops of china-clay waste and lifting the whitish water from the puddles to hurl into face and eyes. Even the lakes on the settling pits had lost their unreal blue colour, and looked sullen and grey. By the time he had walked the three miles to St Austell he was soaked to the skin.

The parcel was not there. One of the porters remembered seeing it, in the guard's van of the down train.

'Thought it was funny,' he said. 'Addressed to Mr Borglaise, St Blurzey's China, Penzance. But I didn't know but that there was another pit out St Just way with the same name. No, my handsome, Penzance, that's where it will be. You want to go down there and fetch it?'

'Haven't got the fare,' Ernie said, with a sinking heart. He could see what was coming. A long walk back to the clay-works, only to be sent back to catch the next train.

'Don't you worry about that,' the station master said. 'I know Mr Borglaise. I'll put it down to the pit, and he can sort it out some other time.'

Ernie hesitated. Should he go back and ask? Or should he take the offer and board the train? He thought about the long wet walk, and chose the train. He could walk over to Newlyn while he was there, and buy his mother some fresh fish. Threepenn'orth of sprats would make a tasty tea.

Only, of course, the parcel wasn't at Penzance. The station master had realised the mistake, and put the parcel on the next train back. It would be at St Austell by this time.

So here was Ernie, with a ticket in his pocket which Mr Borglaise would have to pay for, a smelly packet of fish in his hand, and another half an hour to wait for his train. And Mr Borglaise still hadn't got his parcel. Ernie would get the blame for it, too – though he'd been trailing around in the wind and rain while the others were enjoying their bit of join in the dry of the sheds.

And now, there was this bit of a girl walking slam-bang into him one minute, not looking where she was going, and answering him back the next. Sauce!

Another solid wall of foam reared up over the harbour wall and crashed down in cloud of spray, drenching everything for yards around. Ernie turned tail and fled back across the promenade towards the shelter of Penzance station.

All in all, it had not been a successful day.

Crash!

The wave lifted the fishing boat and smashed her down with a force that shuddered her timbers.

The man they called Philippe Diavezour braced himself on his pitching deck, wiped the salt from his face with a weary arm, and peered anxiously upwards, blinking through the flying foam and sheeting rain. The splinted spar that held the top of the sail clear of the masthead. Would it hold?

Crash! Another wave took her and tipped her, and although the extra length of the bowsprit had been shipped inboard, she buried her nose in the roller, threatening to broach.

'*Kaoh!*' Jacques, the oldest crewman swore under his breath in Breton, as he and Ramon struggled to lash down the last of the nets and pots, leaning into the wind, one hand for the ship and one for themselves, while the *Plougastel* heaved and reared. 'Loeiz. Lend a hand here!'

But the boy clinging to the foot of the mast did not even turn his head. He crouched there, shoulders heaving, half dead from fright and *mal de mer*.

'*Kaoh!*' Jacques cursed again, '*Laoz Diavezour!*' He cast a furious look in the direction of the ship's master. Philippe, still wrestling with the tiller, caught the look.

He knew what they said. *Laoz Diavezour*. Filthy foreigner – although he had been born in Plougastel and his father before him. Outsider, he was still – the crazy 'foreign' landowner, and his crazy foreign boat. They would not sail with him – only 'mad' Ramon, drinking himself to a stupor at every port, and Jacques, from Marseille, an outsider himself.

Perhaps, he thought, gazing at his ruined rigging with eyes that squinted through wind and rain, perhaps he *was* crazy, giving up the solid security of the *manoir* – a housekeeper, a life of crops and cows – for this! Pitching about in white water off a foreign coast, in an ancient boat.

Grandfather's boat. Philippe had learned to handle it as a boy – loved the feel of the tiller in his hands, the tug of the sails to his helm, the cream of the wake on the water. The old man had taught him everything he knew – the lore, the seacraft, even his outlandish language and the tales of his youth. And Philippe had loved it, as he loved the man. But Mother had always fretted, and after that dreadful night when the sea had claimed one of the old man's sons and three of her own she had forbidden Philippe ever to go again. So the boat had been brought home, into dry storage: and Grandfather too, away from the sea, dried out and withered and died.

And Philippe had put the sea behind him. Until last year . . . but no, he would not think of that. Eved. His wife. Her brown eyes and pointed face, her long-legged coltish grace. That was what crazed him, if crazy he was. Love and grief and loss. Eved. Dead, struggling to bring their son into the world. In one short hour he had lost them both – the wife he cherished, the son he had longed for. By his own act of love he had killed her, yet she danced before him, in his dreams, night after restless night. It was worse, by day. Not so much that the *manoir* seemed empty without her – her absence was like a presence, filling the house: her books upon the table, her perfume in the air. And so he had had the *Plougastel* refettled, and come back to the sea, trying to lose himself in action, to forget.

Crash! Another great shudder, almost wrenching the tiller from his hands. The boat wallowed, refusing to answer, and he fought her like a wrestler, until the sweat prickled under his drenched jersey and oilskins.

'Come on!' he muttered through gritted teeth, and then, as the two men forward flung themselves on the lashing, wayward thing which had been a sail, the *Plougastel* did wallow around, her decks awash, to lunge petulantly head to wind.

Philippe brushed the spray and rain from his streaming face, and peered up at his straining mast. Suddenly he gave a shout. 'Loeiz! Look out! The sail! Move!'

At the masthead the sail hung crooked from the broken spar, flogging like a whip in the wind. The boy lifted his head slowly, looked from the splintered wood to Philippe, and back again, but he did not move.

Philippe lashed the tiller hastily, and began to stumble forward down the slippery deck.

'Loeiz!' This time it was Ramon, the boy's father, and his voice was a roar. 'Obey the *maître*! Get back! That sail will break loose!'

And even as he spoke, it happened. It was nobody's fault. No-one could have done more than his crew. They had achieved miracles. Lowered forty foot of swaying, solid topmast in the teeth of the gale. Sweated and sworn at the bowsprit, bringing the heavy, slippery baulk back inboard, so that the bow did not bury itself in every breaker. Struggled with the dead weight of the canvas sails, reefing them hard in record time.

Even when the gaff had gone, half an hour earlier, they had contrived somehow, lashing an oar in place to hold the top of the sail out and away from the mast. Miracles!

Crash! This time it was too much. The makeshift gaff had already cracked, and now it splintered like matchwood in the gale. The heavy sail, taking the full force of the wind, broke free at one corner and whipped viciously across the deck, a lethal combination of canvas, rope and wood.

And the boy, Ramon's boy, there in its path, frozen motionless with fright.

Philippe flung himself forward, covering Loeiz with his body. He felt the boy hit the deck, heard his grunt of fear and surprise, and then a flying wooden block caught him savagely on the shoulder, and it was his own voice crying out in pain while the world misted in front of him.

After a moment, he opened his eyes.

Jacques and Ramon had hurled themselves bodily upon the sail, but it was still billowing and heaving around them, as the wind caught the torn ends and ballooned it into a live thing. It was like fighting a whale on the pitching deck.

And losing. They were strong men, but wiry, and their combined weight was no match for that convulsing mass. Another moment and he would lose the sail. Or a man. Or both.

'Kaoh!' he cursed, and then he was with them, slithering across a deck which crashed and heaved under his boots, and flinging himself full-length on the plunging canvas. The sail was heavy with water and stiff with salt, but the wind lifted it like thistledown, and brought it down again with a vicious snap. The flying rope and splintered wood curled again into a giant cat-o'-nine-tails.

'Cut it loose!' he hollered, using the Breton patois. He felt, rather than saw, Ramon roll forward. There was the flash of a gutting knife, and the splintered spar collapsed onto the deck, smothering them in heavy folds of wet canvas.

Philippe heaved himself up again and flung his body down on the bellying sail beneath him. He felt the air escape from it with a sharp tearing sound. A seam had gone, splitting the sail from luff to leach.

But it was enough. Ramon, in his turn, rolled himself sideways, grabbing a handful of rope and sail, and then they had it – an awkward, unlovely, unseamanlike bundle, but a sail again. Jacques was already lashing it down roughly among the tangle of nets and floats on the foredeck. *Plougastel* settled into a steady, plunging motion, her demon quelled.

Philippe stood up, panting, gasping for breath, blood streaming from his arm, and made his way back across the streaming, littered deck. He unlashed the tiller. The men staggered to their feet.

'*Porhel!*' old Jacques said, and spat over the rail.

Philippe smiled grimly. 'Swine, Jacques? Me, or the weather?' But he knew better. It was the *Plougastel* herself the man was cursing. *Plougastel*, with her strange, foreign rig. Grandfather's ship – built to his design, like a Brixham smack, and not a 'proper' Breton trawler. Waiting for him, fixed and fitted, in Brixham harbour that night all those years ago, when Grandfather had sailed the *Ocky Tar* in and sailed *Plougastel* out again, her lockers full of banknotes and silver, under the very noses of the preventative men. Not a moment too soon, to hear Grandfather tell it – they were within a whistle of catching him, and that would have meant losing his ship, or having it cut in half, if they hadn't hanged or deported him for a smuggler. What would he have thought, the old man, seeing his grandson out here, fighting a storm at sea? And off Cornwall, too – the land the old man had never been able to return to, though he spoke of it often. Philippe fingered the watch chain and key around his neck under the oiled wool of his jersey.

Well, it would be Newlyn tonight. Driven to it, by the storm. Perhaps he would try to find them, that family Grandfather had always spoken of. Trezayle. The men would grumble and fret. Blame him, as they had always blamed him, because he was an incomer, with incomer's ways.

What would they say of him, later, in the inns of Newlyn? That he had half killed them with his outlandish gaff, just as his brothers had drowned long ago? No matter that they had perished trying to save a neighbour from the wild seas. No matter that a dozen other ships had foundered in that same storm. No matter for any of that – the tongues still wagged. And today would set them wagging again. The Curse of the Diavezours, the villagers would say. What do you expect if you sail with one of them?

They had said the same when Ginette, his frail and red-haired Breton mother, had died of fever. Said it when the storms stripped the roof from his father's *manoir*, or flattened the apple trees in his orchard. Said it when Father died, and when Eved . . . He wrenched his thoughts savagely back to the present.

What of poor Loeiz there, inching to his feet, his face whiter than cod's belly, and shivering from head to foot like a mackerel on a line? What would he make of this, his first working voyage? The Curse of the Diavezours? He had seen it all. Broken rigging. The crack of canvas. Green water. Blood. The stuff nightmares were made of.

Yet they had come through. Grandfather could be proud, he thought grimly. Many a grizzled Breton sailor would have shown less seamanship than the '*laoz Diavezour*' tonight.

'Man those ropes there,' he shouted, lifting his voice over the wail of the wind. 'Sheet her in on the port side.' They sprang to his orders, grumbling. Always grumbling, but they were his men still – as they had been in storm and calm, reefing sails or hauling in the wriggling catch and the dead weight of the nets, roughened hands working the rough and water-heavy ropes. He felt a little surge of pride.

'Loeiz!'

The boy looked up at him, afraid of a blow, a curse. '*Maître?*'

'Come down here. Hold the tiller, so.'

The boy looked at him, speechless.

'Can you hold her? It's not easy, with just the foresail.'

The tiller was bigger than he was, but the boy nodded, his eyes very bright.

'We'll make a fisherman of you yet.'

Ramon came slithering down the pitching deck, and stopped, looking from the boy at the tiller to Philippe, who was pressing a wad of cloth into his shoulder to stop the bleeding. He hesitated.

Philippe said brusquely, 'What is it, sailor? You wanted something?'

Ramon hesitated again, and then, with a slow grin, shook his head.

'Then get that Breton flag hoisted,' Philippe said, 'and stand by to warp her in! We've got a catch to land.'

And so, creaking and wallowing under the weight of the gale, the *Plougastel* limped slowly towards Newlyn. The boy at the tiller stood very straight and proud, almost as if the captain were not behind him, with his hand, too, on the helm.

When Carrie awoke the next morning, the storm was over. A feeble sun was shining through the bedroom window, lighting the yellow satin squares in the patchwork (one of Miss Maythorpe's dresses, useless to wear, but still pressed into service) as though they were made of sunshine themselves.

Carrie swung her feet out of bed, leaned forward, still in her nightshirt, so that her elbows were on the windowsill, and looked out. There was a squally breeze blowing even now, and the morning was cold, but there were breaks in the cloud, so that you could see the sky – a thin, high, watery blue, as if the colour had been washed out of it in the storm. Everything had the same rinsed look – the hill, the thicket of fierce little trees, the back paddock with Crowdie's scruffy pony, and Mrs Goodbody's two goats. How familiar it all was. The backs of the little houses, all built alike as pins, yet you could tell who lived where, Carrie thought, from the gardens. Apple trees and vegetables, chickens and geese, wheelbarrows, fuel-piles, tumbledown sheds and waterbutts, and even – at the very end of the Terrace – Liza Trembath's pig, pink and baleful under a stumpy tree.

She must have seen these same things thousands of times, every day of her life. Impossible to imagine that in a few short days she would wake to different sights, in a different room, without Mother's cheerful rag rugs, the lopsided washstand, and the framed cross-stitch tract that Grandmother Tremble had made when she was a girl. How would it feel to get up with only grey roofs and grey pavements to look at – and worse, to live in a street of strangers? In Penvarris she had known everyone since her birth, and those who weren't friends were family, like disagreeable old Bert Hoskins, or the houseful of cousins who had lived down the way.

But it was already changing. The last cousin had just married and moved with her husband to America. Even Katie Warren, the girl next door, who had been Carrie's friend and companion all her young days, was different now. Obliged to leave school early when her mother died, and help keep house for the family, including the new baby, under the forbidding eye of an ancient, bony aunt. Only able to sneak away for an hour of an evening, under the pretence of helping Carrie with her homework.

She picked up her hairbrush and, leaning forward so that her brown hair fell over her shoulders, began to brush, methodically, as she had been taught. How often she and Katie had brushed each other's hair! She would miss Katie. And Katie would miss her too.

As if in answer to her thoughts, the back door of the neighbouring house opened and a pretty, dark-haired girl came out, carrying a great wicker basket and a bag of gypsy pegs. Katie Warren! Out already with the washing, and on a Friday too – but with a small baby there was always washing, and drying it would have been a sorry business yesterday, with all that rain.

Carrie pushed open the window and called softly, 'Hey, Katie! Some storm, wasn't it?'

The girl, who was moving the wooden strut to lower the line, glanced up and smiled.

'Went for that position, yesterday,' Carrie said. 'You know. With Mr Tucker – keeps the tobacconist's in Causewayhead.'

Katie put down the washing basket and motioned 'Shh!', putting her finger to her lips and nodding towards the house. Carrie understood. If the aunt caught them chattering there would be trouble. Would it be the same for her when she went to work next week? Afraid to have a cheerful word to her friends? Except that she wouldn't have any friends to chatter to.

'All right?' Katie's face, rather than her voice, asked the question.

Carrie made a little gesture of triumph, and Katie gave a silent cheer. 'You?' Carrie pointed at Katie and raised her eyebrows.

Katie gestured towards the house and made a grimace of such doleful despair that Carrie laughed aloud. Katie stopped, in the act of pegging out a piece of sheet used as a nappy for the baby. 'Think I'll get a position. Then I could get away!' she mouthed.

'You should try it!' Carrie mimed the words with exaggerated care, but Katie only looked puzzled. Carrie tried again and then, struck by a sudden idea, seized her old school slate which was lying on the washstand.

'You . . . should . . . try . . . it!' she wrote carefully, taking pains to reverse the letters. Katie, after all, was looking at it the other way. Then she stood up and held the slate to the window.

Katie put down her pegs and stared at it, perplexed, for a moment, then burst out laughing. 'You great goose,' she called aloud. 'What did you write it backwards for? I'm not in a mirror.'

'Nor you are!' Carrie said, suddenly convulsed with laughter, and they were both giggling helplessly when a voice interrupted them.

'What you doing out there? You get on with your work and let Carrie get to school!' Katie's aunt, black as a broomstick, was standing in the doorway.

Katie hoisted the line upright and fled back into the house with the empty basket. Carrie closed the window slowly.

She had always envied Katie for her brains and her looks – those bouncing black curls and blue eyes. Beside her, Carrie's own lanky limbs and brown mousy waves had always seemed so dull.

'Nonsense, Carrie,' Katie had said once. 'You've got a lovely face. Lively, as if you were always laughing. And those great brown eyes. Hundreds of girls would give their eye teeth for them.'

'Well, some sight they'd look then – four eyes and all gummy!' Carrie had retorted, and made them both laugh. All the same, she had always been a little envious of Katie Warren – until now.

Maybe, after all, going into service with Mrs Tucker wouldn't be all that bad. There was always Dolly, and her day off.

She was still thoughtful as she dressed and went down to breakfast.

'Now, here's your note to Miss Bevan. And a bit of something for your lunch. Mind you bring that bonnet home, when you come,' Mother said.

Carrie stopped by the crevice in the wall on her way to the schoolroom, and what she saw filled her with dismay. The 'secret box' had been no match for the wind and rain, and the bonnet was a sorry sight, the straw sagging, the ribbons and rosebuds spattered and sodden. My lor'! Whatever would Mother say!

She stood for a moment holding the damp, dishevelled thing in her hand, until she heard whistling behind her. Crowdie coming over the stile! She stuffed the hat roughly back into its hiding place, and walked quickly on. She would have to worry about it on the way home.

Down the hill and across the stream, and so, for the last time, to school.

CHAPTER THREE

Ernie came out of the count-house fuming. He had expected Mr Borglaise to tear him off a strip, so that had been no surprise. In fact, he'd got off lightly there; Da had been sure that Mr Borglaise would stop the price of the ticket out of his wages.

No, what rankled with Ernie was the second ticking-off he'd had, from Dick Clarance. All right, so the man was a pit captain and he'd a right to tell his men what for, but he needn't have done it so public, in front of the whole shift, and to his own cousin too.

And now Ernie had been sent on the two jobs he hated most – carrying a load of picks and boryers for sharpening and repair, and fetching the ale for the men working down the new adit.

Taking the gear to the smithy was bad enough; the metal was dirty, heavy and awkward. Dick Clarance had decided that there wasn't a barrow to be spared, so Ernie would have to manhandle the lot the mile or more across the workings to the blacksmith's shop. The whole pile would have to be scrubbed off, in a bucket of freezing water, because old Fred, the smith, swore that clay and granite dust got into the heated metal and weakened it. Then there would be a long hot wait, shifting from one foot to another and dodging the sparks from the anvil, until it was time to carry them back again. And however quick you were, there was always someone to say it should have been quicker – though there was nothing for it but to wait for Old Fred to finish. He always took his time, besides.

But fetching the ale was ten times worse. Many of the younger toolboys liked it – dipping their fingers into the top of the slopping jug, or even stopping to sip a bit: 'No-one'll notice a drop gone in all this lot!' Made them feel like men, perhaps. But Ernie hated it. The tavern was twice as far as the smithy for one thing, and they always sent him with the biggest jug because he was older. The slippery weight of it, when it was full, seemed to increase with every yard, so that you didn't know how to hold it, and the ale foamed and splashed as you walked, threatening to slop over the lip and spill itself on the uneven road. And the smell! There would be no need to have a Band of Hope and a Temperance League, Ernie felt, if every man-jack on the pit had to carry four gallons of ale three miles or more every day, breathing in that sweet sickly smell at every step, and on an empty stomach, too.

Still, it was what a toolboy was paid for. He looked over to where the men were working, real work – digging clay, or tending the slurry in the settling pits. He scowled. Why couldn't Dick Clarance have found him a useful job to do, like oiling the cogs of the water-wheel?

'What's up with you then? Lost a shilling and found sixpence?' It was Vince Whittaker, coming from the nearest clay-drift, with a wagon of waste to be trammed to the spoil-heap.

Ernie shifted the load he was carrying, so that the broken boryer stopped digging a hole in his shoulder-blade, and scowled more fiercely than ever. The last thing he wanted was Vince Whittaker for company. If it wasn't for Vince, it might have been him there, pushing the wagon, a proper part of the team.

'Fed up with the way they treated you, I should think,' Vince said. 'And no wonder. You were only going for his blooming parcel, when's all said.'

'Wasn't my fault,' Ernie said, surprised into speech by this unexpected sympathy.

'Course it wasn't,' Vince said. 'Stands to reason. Have it all their own way, these bosses. Think they own you body and soul. Well, time will come, they'll have another think coming. You mark my words. Still, you better get off, before you drop something. Why they couldn't put that lot in a barrow for you, I'll never know.'

'Wasn't one spare,' Ernie said.

'Don't talk daft,' Vince said, voicing the thought which Ernie had secretly been nursing all morning. 'Place this size, and there isn't a spare barrow? No, they've done it on purpose, teach you a lesson. Spiteful, I call it. Good lad like you too.' He gave Ernie a grin, and put his shoulder to the wagon again. 'We should stick together, you and I. See you lunchtime, maybe?'

Really, Ernie thought, as he struggled under his awkward bundle towards Old Fred's smithy, he had been a little too ready to judge Vince Whittaker. He didn't seem a bad fellow, after all.

Carrie bent her head to her slate again, frowning with effort. She was not a quick scholar, for all she had won the Standard Five attendance prize only a month before. Brain quicker than her hand, Miss Bevan said, and a tongue quicker than either. Still, this was botany, which she loved. The life-cycle of a dandelion. Miss Bevan had modern views, and believed in teaching more than the three Rs, even for girls.

'Right!' Miss Bevan's voice cut across her thoughts. 'You can finish the sentence you are writing and sit up straight with your hands folded. And put that tongue away, Carrie Tremble – it's your slate pencil you are writing with, not your tongue. And sit up straight, do, instead of lounging about like a farmboy! I do declare, my girl. You'll never make a lady!' But there was amusement in her voice.

Still, Miss Bevan's scolding was nothing to what was waiting for her at home over that bonnet, she thought to herself, as she wrote 'the cycle is concluded' in her best copperplate, and sat up straighter than the blackboard pointer, arms folded across her chest.

'And good luck to you, Carrie. I hope you are happy in your new post,' Miss Bevan said, a few minutes later, as Carrie collected her cape from the hook and glanced around the schoolroom for the last time. The map of the world with the British Empire marked out in red. The Sermon on the Mount picture, curling in the sun. The Readers for the Young in a faded row on the shelf.

She sighed. 'Thank you, Miss Bevan. I hope so too.' And the school door shut behind her, and there was no going back.

She walked home sedately, head held high, shoulders back. She almost hoped that she might meet a neighbour, walking to Penzance, or on the way to the graveyard to lay a bunch of wild flowers, so that she could say, casually, 'I've left school now, and I'm going into service, Monday.'

For a moment she thought she might be lucky. There was somebody in the top field, but after she looked for a moment, she realised that it was nobody she knew. Odd! You didn't often see strangers in Penvarris. She squinted against the sun, craning her neck to see better.

A man and a lad – a skinny lad a little smaller than herself. They were oddly dressed, both of them, in the striped blue-and-white Breton jumpers which she always associated with onion sellers. But that man was no 'oniony', hawking his wares in long strings from his shoulders or cycle. There were no onions, for one thing, but it was more than that. He wore a seaman's cap instead of a beret, his boots were fisherman's boots, and his lithe, loose movements and tanned rugged face suggested the same story.

From that fishing boat then! But what were they doing all the way over here at Penvarris? And, worse than that, she realised with dawning horror, what was that perched on the wall?

The boy had a pile of stones at his feet, and was deliberately taking aim at something he had set up as a target – a sorry pink object, its ribbons flapping in the breeze. Her bonnet!

'Hey! What do you think you are doing? That's mine. You put it back!' The words were out before Carrie had time to think, and she was already running full pelt across the field towards the two strangers, all thoughts of dignity forgotten, before reason dawned.

It was no earthly good to holler at them in English! They were furriners, and fishermen at that – knowing less, probably, than the onion-sellers, and they had little enough English, some of them.

But her shout had some effect, at least. The boy stopped his stone-throwing, and the man picked up the bonnet and came towards her, carrying it, dripping and dirty, at arm's length. Carrie faltered to a standstill and eyed him nervously. Suddenly this encounter with two strange sailors from another country made her feel uneasy.

The man was speaking, courteous and concerned. 'This is yours?'

Carrie was more than astonished, she was thunderstruck. There was an accent, certainly, behind the words – but he spoke so well, so easily, that she wondered for a moment if she had been wrong in her assumptions.

'I'm sorry,' the man said. 'My English is a little – what can I say – rusty. But this bonnet. You said, I think, that it was yours?'

Carrie was still too startled to make any sensible reply, but she nodded dumbly.

'This is a pity,' the man said, looking at the bonnet.

It was a pity, too. It had looked wretched enough this morning, damp, dirty and bedraggled, but now the straw was pitted and split where the muddy stones had struck it, and one ribbon was torn away, unravelling the rosebuds.

The enormity of it struck her, and Carrie felt the tears of panic rise in her eyes and trickle helplessly down her cheeks. She could never hide the damage from Mother and Miss Maythorne now.

The Frenchman was looking at her keenly. 'You loved this hat?'

She shook her head. 'I hated it,' she muttered, through her tears.

He said something to the boy in his own language, and then he turned to her again. 'I think,' he said gravely, 'I did not understand.'

She looked up at him. He was still gazing at her intently. Carrie knew that look – as if he were trying to learn her off by heart, like the life-cycle of a butterfly. His eyes were deeply, glitteringly blue against the tanned skin of his face, and, suddenly, in their depths there was the suspicion of a smile. It *was* ridiculous, on the face of it, crying over the ruination of a hat which you hated. She flushed.

'Someone gave it me, but I hid it. My mother will be angry.'

'Ah!' he said gravely. 'And why did you hate it so?'

'It's so ugly,' she burst out. 'All those flowers and frills!'

He held it aloft, examining it, and she thought that he would do something frightful – jam it on her head, or throw it into the stream. But instead he nodded. 'Yes,' he said, 'it is very ugly.'

He pronounced it 'urg–lee' and it made her say, without thinking, 'You speak good English.' She had almost forgotten, in the last few moments, that she was talking to a Frenchman.

He smiled. 'I should,' he said. 'My grandfather was English. Cornish. He was a fisherman, born in St Just. I have been there, this afternoon – to try to find my family.'

'With your son?'

He laughed then, a deep amused chuckle. 'Loeiz is not my son. He is the son of one of my crewmen. But he preferred to come with me, to try to find my grandfather's birthplace, than to stay with the boat this afternoon. Poor Loeiz had enough of fishing boats yesterday – today he prefers the dry land.'

Carrie thought of the pounding seas she had seen in Mount's Bay the night before. Loeiz had her sympathy. 'Was the boat damaged much?' she said.

The man shrugged. It made him seem suddenly very French. 'We are waiting for a new spar,' he said. 'It will take several days to arrive. Then we must repair the sail. Already we have pumped out the boat and tidied below decks.'

Carrie nodded. It sounded important, though she had no real idea what it meant.

'But,' the Frenchman said, 'it is not so easy, I think, to repair your hat!'

'No,' Carrie said, suddenly recollecting. 'And there's no time, either. There's my mother now!'

Mother was climbing over the stile, carefully balancing a big flat basket. Carrie knew what that meant. Blackberries. She might have guessed Mother would be out this afternoon, before it was October, and the 'devil touched the berries'. Well, it couldn't be helped. Mother hadn't seen the hat yet, but it could only be a matter of minutes now. She took a deep breath, and squared herself for trouble.

The Frenchman looked at Mother, and then at Carrie. 'It was very ugly,' he said slowly, and to Carrie's astonishment he dropped the bonnet, deliberately, into a deep muddy puddle, and planted his heavy foot firmly upon it. By the time Mother had glanced in their direction, he was holding it up, crushed and sodden, the imprint of his foot etched into the ribbons.

'Oh, mam'zelle,' she heard him say, as Mother approached. 'A thousand pardons. I have treaden upon your 'at.' His accent, Carrie noticed, had become suddenly very peculiar. She glanced at him, and to her amazement one blue eye flickered into a wink.

Mother was with them in an instant, and the Frenchman was all apologies. His clumsy feet, he explained. The young mam'zelle had put down her hat for a moment, a puff of wind, and *zut*! see how he had crushed it. And into the puddle too.

Mother was all of a flutter, charmed by his attentions. 'Well,' she said at last, 'it don't signify so much. Carrie's got another bonnet, and she never did like this one. I wouldn't put it past Carrie to have put it there on purpose for you to tread on.'

Carrie couldn't meet his eyes, and looked away. The young boy was standing by the wall, staring at them both. He hadn't understood a word, she realised, but he must have seen the trick that was played.

'Well, Carrie, what do you say? This gentleman, Mr . . .'

'Diavezour,' the Frenchman said.

'Yes, well, this gentleman has offered to bring us some herring tomorrow to make up for the hat. I call that handsome. And I'm sure you'd a sight rather have a herring supper than that bonnet. So you say thank you, and give me a hand home with these blackberries.'

'Thank you,' Carrie said. 'Thank you very much.' The blue eyes were looking at her very shrewdly, and she turned her head, hardly knowing whether to laugh or cry with relief. 'I'll never forget you for this,' she added softly, as Mother turned back to the stile to pick up the blackberry basket. 'Never.'

Eved! It had been his first thought when he saw the girl running across the fields towards then.

Eved! So like! The same long-limbed coltishness, the same oval face, even – when she tossed back her hair as she ran and it tumbled loose, freed from its ribbons – the same glossy mane of golden-brown waves.

So like. For a moment it had almost stopped his heart with a wild irrational hope – but of course this was not Eved. Eved had been a woman; this was a girl – he could see it when she came closer – a mere child, though she was tall and slender. But there was something of Eved, too, in the brown eyes that brimmed with tears over that ridiculous bonnet: though the mischievous smile and the shining eyes as she thanked him had been all her own.

He looked over the stile, towards the house in the valley where she and her mother had gone, and where he had promised to deliver a bonnet's-worth of fish tomorrow. He would see her again, then. Was it wise? She reminded him so sharply of his loss. Well, he shrugged, it was too late now. The girl had raised the ghost again: that ghost he had come so far and battled so long to banish.

Was that why he had yielded to impulse and trodden on the bedraggled thing? For Eved? Of course it was. He was almost ashamed to own it, even to himself. Not for the real Eved, of course, but for this unknown child, because she looked like his wife.

He gave himself a little shake. The girl had smiled. A huge, bemused, delighted, grateful grin. And brown, laughing eyes. No, really, not like Eved at all. And yet the girl gave warmth to his memory of the day.

It had not begun well. They seemed to have walked for miles, he and Loeiz, and he had almost given up hope of finding Grandfather's birthplace altogether. Up the hill from Newlyn, and across the fields to St Just – too far to come for the 'chase of a wild goose', Loeiz grumbled.

Philippe himself was beginning to believe that his memory of Grandfather's tales had deceived him. This St Just, he found, was not at all the little fishing-village he had imagined. This was instead a small town, with a market square and church tower: not a harbour at all, but set among the high fields of the cliff-top farms, where lean cows and donkeys grazed on the thin grass, amidst crops laid flatter than his own rigging by the recent storms.

A strange place indeed for a smuggler to hail from. And when he learned, from a plump countrywoman with a basket (who stared on hearing his accent, as though he had descended from the moon) that there was another St Just further east, 'on a river, so they do say', he was all but convinced he had come to the wrong place.

Yet there were things that made him doubt. The names they had passed on the way. Pendeen. Botallack. The Cobb valley leading down to the sea, where the little tin-stream wound between the valley walls. Surely Grandfather had spoken of that?

He went back into the town and asked again: in shops, on corners, even in the tavern. Most looked at him with suspicion and shook their heads, although when he asked a gaggle of old men sitting on a seat by the pump, one of them gazed at him thoughtfully with rheumy eyes and said, 'Trezayle? Belonged to be a family of that name round here once. Drownded, I believe. Or moved away. One or other. Or was that the Curnows?'

It was the butcher's boy who told him at last. 'Yes, mister. Used to be a big family of them – now there is only the old lady left. Not in the town, mind – mile or two down the road. Big grey house up on the cliffs on your left.'

And it was. A solid, gentleman's house of grey granite set back up a curving drive between stone pillars and the ruins of a garden. Not at all what he had expected. He stood hesitating. This air of faded gentility, surely this was not the home of the dour old salt who had been his grandfather? But having come so far, he walked up and rang the bell.

The door was opened by a housemaid, a little, frail lady in a uniform of faded stuff. She looked, he thought, as though she might have had the outfit as a girl, and grown old along with it.

She was startled by his greeting, and hovered for a moment gazing from him to Loeiz as though she had forgotten quite what to do with visitors, if they ever came, but at last she showed him into the parlour and went off to find the mistress.

Philippe looked around, uncomfortable and out of place. Loeiz, clearly, was feeling the same. He shuffled uncomfortably from foot to foot, gazing miserably at the dusty velvet of the curtains, the worn pile of the Chinese carpet, the dulled mahogany of the chairs. There had been expensive taste in this house, Philippe thought, and money, once, to indulge it. Not a smuggler's home, surely? This could not possibly be the place.

And then Miss Trezayle came in. There seemed more than a generation between them. She was dainty, and grey, with round eyes and sudden tripping movements like a little bird. Indeed, when she took his hand between hers, and held her head on one side, nodding, to look at him, she reminded him powerfully of a sparrow tapping for worms. But he had only to glance at the blue eyes and the firm jut of the little chin to know that he had come, after all, to the right house.

'Uncle Will's boy?' she said sharply, as she sent the bewildered maid for English tea. 'How do I know that?'

And he had shown her the watch-chain, and the heavy key on it, and the fob with a lock of Grandfather's hair, and she had listened to him, absorbed, while Loeiz ate himself nauseous on little dainty cakes of singularly sticky sweetness.

'Leave the key with me, cousin – I suppose I must call you cousin, though your grandfather was my uncle,' she said. 'I think I know what it belongs to. And if I do, then you must call again, and we will open it together. Now, you must tell me about yourself, and your family – everything that happened since Uncle Will left this house. Everything, from the beginning. Is this your son?'

And he had done so, finding it amazingly simple to talk. How Grandfather had fled from the preventative men, and taken his fortune to

Brittany. How he had bought the *manoir*, married a wife and raised four sons of his own, before the Curse of the Diavezours took one of his boys and three of his grandsons. How Mother had feared and loathed the sea, and Father had turned his back on it, living as a landed man all his life. About Eved, and how he himself had shut the *manoir* after her death – shut it up, all but a few rooms in the care of a housekeeper – and gone back to Grandfather's boat, the wild sea, and the wind.

'And there she is now, alas,' he said mournfully, 'tied up in Newlyn harbour for want of a spar and a sail, while I am visiting chandlers and fitters and writing letters to this one and that – and all the time the year is passing and we are missing the fish.'

She looked at him appraisingly. 'But surely, with the *manoir* . . . ?' She left the rest unsaid. 'You have money', she meant.

He smiled, a sad wry smile. 'You see, cousin, the Diavezours have never trusted their money to the banks – not since Grandfather's time. And my money is all in francs. I can get it, but it will take time, and I am not known to the bankers. I am in the wrong country here. And this one –' he gestured towards Loeiz, who was stuffing the last iced strawberry bun into his mouth '– will eat me out of all Grandfather's fortune. A greater appetite than Mattie Trezalye that Grandfather used to speak of.'

She looked at him then, a sharp look, so like his grandfather that he almost exclaimed loud. 'Mathilda? You have heard of her? What other tales did your grandfather tell? But no! You must come back, since you are to be so long in harbour. Come back and take a meal with me, Monsieur . . . How do you call yourself, you say?'

'Diavezour,' he said. 'It means "different from us". It's what they called us, back in Brittany, so it became a name. As well, perhaps. Who could believe in a Frenchman named Trezayle?'

She laughed. 'You look like a Trezayle to me. Tuesday then? Luncheon. There is . . . there are some people I should like you to meet.'

He was dismayed. 'My dear Miss Trezayle . . .'

She protested. 'Adeline! Since you claim I am your cousin, cousin!'

'Well, then, cousin, you must understand. I have been at sea, and fishing too, in a storm.' He had not dressed smart, like a landsman, since Eved died. 'I have no clothes fit for luncheon with a lady.'

She smiled. 'But I have. Uncle Will – your grandfather – left a great wardrobe of clothes when he went. They have never been moved. You are much like him, in build as well as manner. And there are some of my brother's too, if Uncle Will's are a little old-fashioned. We shall find something to fit you, never fear.'

33

'Perhaps that is the key,' he said. 'The wardrobe?' She had kept the key, and said no more about it. He had thought of asking for it back.

She smiled, meaningfully, he thought. 'Perhaps. We shall see on Tuesday. Shall you bring the boy?'

He shook his head. 'You are most kind. But no. He has no English, and besides, there are others in the crew.'

She nodded her bird–like head. 'I think it is better, so. There may be . . . family matters. Tuesday then.'

And so it was settled. He had half regretted it, till now. But it made an additional excuse, he told himself. Not an excuse, a reason. Tomorrow he must come back, with that basket of herring. And Tuesday he would come this way to visit his cousin.

Perhaps, once more, he might get a glimpse of her. The girl with the bonnet. The ghost of Eved.

CHAPTER FOUR

The smell of frying sprats reached Ernie as soon as he opened the door of Buglers on Saturday night.

The cottage was always called 'Buglers', though the other cottages in St Burzey Row had proper names like 'Holly Tree' and 'Ivy Cottage'. Called after a soldier boy who went to Sebastopol, so Da said, but Ma only laughed and said it was people that came from Bugle, more like. She was probably right, but Ernie preferred his father's version. When he was younger he used to lie awake at night dreaming of it – the flags and the bands and the horses and the guns. He even went so far as to look for Sebastopol on the globe in the schoolroom, but he couldn't make sense of it. Russia looked to be bigger than France and England put together, and that couldn't be right.

He took off his boots, stamping them to save tramping white marks onto Mother's floors, hung his coat in the passage and jammed his cap into his trouser pocket. He had changed up at the dry, of course, before he left the pit, but the clay dust got everywhere and even his clean clothes were full of it.

He opened the kitchen door and a wave of warmth rushed out to meet him, heavy with fish and onions. Mother had marinated a few sprats for a second supper.

'There you are then, Ernie,' Ma said, already ladling a generous spoonful onto a wedge of bread. 'Wondered wherever you were to.'

Ernie muttered something, and shuffled into his seat behind the table. Time enough for explanations later. Ma would likely not be pleased to hear what had kept him – half an hour in the Tinner's Arms with Vince Whittaker. Dick Clarance had seen them, so Ma would have to be told, sooner or later. But in the meantime, there were the sprats.

'Haven't made you pit captain yet, then, boy?' That was Linny May, grinning toothlessly from her chair by the fire. She said the same thing every day, in the same satisfied tone, pursing her horrible hollow lips into a crinkled smile. She had a set of teeth, purchased from a pedlar at St Austell fair, but she refused to wear them. They rubbed her mouth, she said, and she only put them in to chew.

Linny May was Ma's mother, otherwise, Ernie thought, even Ma would not have put up with her. There was a picture on the landing, taken in a studio when Ma's father was alive. Ernie often looked at it and tried to imagine Linny May in that imposing figure with the lace collar, and the dark hair piled up on her head under the large hat. But it was impossible. Linny May today was a small, sour, crumpled woman, with a face whiter than clay dust, spiderwebbed with wrinkles and crowned by a huge white cap. Ernie had only once seen her without her head-dress, and the effect of the pink scalp shining through a dozen wisps of yellow-white hair was so horrible it had haunted him for weeks.

Even in the picture, though, there was a knowing glint in Linny May's eyes. It was there now, as she said again, 'I said, they haven't made you a pit captain yet, then? You want to stand up for yourself a bit more, young Ernie. There's Dick Clarance giving himself airs, and you no better than a errand boy. You want to tell him what for – or get yourself off to Canada, like those two older brothers of yours.'

'Leave the boy alone,' Da said. 'He does well enough.' He was sitting on the wooden settle against the wall, his clay pipe wedged between his knees while he stuffed it with his Old Salt tobacco. Ernie could remember a time, just, when Da had two arms like anybody else, but that was before the accident at the pit, when the driveshaft had splintered and the plumb-bob had whipped up and taken Sam Clarance's right arm with it, clean as a whistle, at the shoulder.

Ernie threw his father a grateful glance, and Da gave him a wink in reply. They were together in this – both a disappointment to Linny May. Her father had been Captain before he died, and it seemed to Ernie that she never let anyone forget it – although she had only been a bal-girl herself, cleaning clay blocks in the linhay. That is where she had got her name, 'Linny May', to distinguish her from her cousin 'Dairy May', who had been butter-girl on a farm.

'Like father, like son,' Linny May said, with a sniff, and then Ma gave her a piece of hevva cake to eat, so she had to put her teeth in.

Ma did that sometimes when Linny May started in on Da. It wasn't Da's fault he'd had to give up the clayworking. Not a nice job, sweeping up after the horses in the streets, but he was paid. Twice, sometimes. There were hotel-keepers who would pay him to sweep the yard, and then he would take the sacks of manure in his handcart and sell them to the gardeners around St Austell.

Ernie took a mouthful of his sprats, his cheeks burning. Why couldn't Linny May understand? Lots of men wouldn't have had the gumption to find another job at all, one-handed. But Da wouldn't be beaten. Even invented his own muck-catcher: a strip of wood nailed to a flattened piece of tin from an old can. Da would strap it to the side of his boot, so that when he shovelled the muck against it, the tin scoop trapped it. It made his boots come home stinking, so he had to leave them in the privy, but he had got so adept at it that he could pick up more muck in an hour with one hand than other men could shovel with two.

Ernie shot a look at Linny May, dunking her hevva cake in her hot sugary tea, and mumbling between her false teeth. Tell his cousin what for, eh? Well, he might at that. That would show her. Vince Whittaker had said the same thing.

'You stand up for yourself,' Vince had said. 'Tell Dick Clarance you've been kettleboy long enough and ask for a proper job, or you'll go to another pit. Plenty of people would be glad to have you. Just because he's your cousin, you don't have to stay and work for him, earning a pittance.'

And Ernie had nodded, sipping gingerly at the sickly bitter-sweet foam of the ale. He hadn't wanted it, but he'd have looked a fool in front of Vince Whittaker else. Drank it, too, though the taste turned his stomach.

The memory of it made him feel queasy now. He pushed away the remains of the sprats. 'Like father, like son?' he said, standing up suddenly. 'Perhaps you're right, Linny May. Da wouldn't let himself be beat, and I won't either. You wait and see.'

He would have liked to make a dignified exit, but there was nowhere to go. 'I'll be in the privy,' he said, 'if anyone wants me!'

He jammed his cap on his head and walked out of the room.

Seth Tremble, too, was eating fish.

He pushed aside his plate with a satisfied sigh. 'Nice drop of herring, that,' he said, wiping his mouth politely with the back of his hand. Wouldn't do to be seen all buttery in front of Carrie, and her going into service with respectable folk. 'Where'd you say you got it?'

His wife turned from the fire, the kettle hissing in her hand. 'That Frenchman I was telling you about,' she said, filling the heavy teapot, which had been on the hearth. 'Came round with them this morning, and spent an hour talking to Carrie and me. Turned out nice, he was too. Proper shirt and collar, and a good frock-coat like a gentleman. Never would have dared say a word about that bonnet if he'd been dressed like that yesterday.'

Seth glanced at Carrie, still mopping her plate with a bread-crust, and winked up at his wife. 'Come to something, hasn't it, when we get gen'lemen calling at the Terrace after Carrie, all dressed to kill. Though I'd sooner it was a proper Cornishman, Carrie, instead of this Frenchman of yours.'

Carrie looked up sharply. 'He's not *my* Frenchman! He trod on that silly bonnet, that's all.'

Seth looked at her. She was flushing with embarrassment, her cheeks pink and her eyes flashing with protest. It would not be long, he thought with a pang, before this teasing would be in good earnest, and some young man with his face scrubbed and his boots polished for the occasion would be knocking at the door asking for Carrie. Not even this door, perhaps, when Carrie was working in Penzance. Suddenly his joking seemed less comic than before.

He said, more gruffly than he meant, 'Just as well, too, or I might have something to say about it!' Two pairs of startled eyes turned towards him, and he said, to cover the moment, 'This furrin fish is all very well, but it isn't a patch on Cornish herring.'

'You liked it well enough a moment ago . . .' Carrie began.

Cissie caught his eye. 'Bad enough the child grown up and going to the town, without having gentlemen calling, eh Seth!' Drat the woman, she had read his thoughts as if they were written on his forehead. 'Anyhow,' she went on, 'come the day after tomorrow, Carrie won't have time for followers, even if she'd a mind to. She'll have her hands full with her new position – that Miss Limmon won't stand for any nonsense. And if you don't drink up that cup of tea, Seth Tremble, and let me get on with mending the child's skirt, it'll be the Sabbath and she'll have nothing fit to wear.'

Seth swallowed the hot sweet liquid gratefully, and stood up from the table. 'Getting stuff ready for her to go, are 'ee?'

Cissie nodded, already busy with cups and saucers. 'Bound to. And Carrie, you can give me a hand with this cloam.'

'Well, then,' he said. 'I got something out in the shed to give her. I meant it for her birthday, but now's as good a moment as any.'

Carrie put down the pile of plates she was carrying to stare at him in amazement. 'For me?'

'Isn't much,' he said, suddenly overcome with embarrassment. 'Not like they wooden dolls I used to make when you were young.'

'Don't you take any notice of your father,' Cissie said. 'Been down that shed half the day when he's had the chance. And woe betide anyone who went near. Something nice, I'll be bound.'

He wished she hadn't said that. It made it harder, somehow. But there was nothing for it. He would have to fetch it now.

Even then, when he got to the shed, he hesitated. It was only a little thing, no bigger than his hand, but it had cost him many hours in the making. He held the box for a moment, looking at the tiny dovetails, the polished wood of the lid and sides. Yes, it was a pretty thing.

He wrapped it tenderly in the piece of blue sugar-paper he had saved for the purpose, and carried it carefully back into the house. They were waiting for him, too curious to carry on working until they had seen what he had made.

Carrie took it, carefully as though it were a bird's egg and might break in her hands, and unwrapped it with trembling fingers. She was as pleased and excited, he thought with a little rush of pride, as when she was a child and he had made the boy and girl dolls, and the little stool and sweeping-brush from the pieces of driftwood collected from the bay.

'It's a proper box, with little hinges and a hook to close it and all!' Carrie exclaimed. She looked up at him, eyes shining with tears.

'Well, open it!' he said, ashamed to feel a pricking in his own eyes.

She did so, unlatching the delicate hook and pushing the lid upwards with a forefinger. 'Oh, look, he's made a message in it – all little bits of wood inlaid.'

'Markingtree,' Seth said. 'That's what it's called. 'Tisn't perfect, mind. Lift up the bottom then.'

She looked at him enquiringly, and he showed how to pull the little ribbon, and lift the bottom of the box to reveal the tiny cavity within. 'For your treasures,' he said.

'There's a treasure already in it,' Carrie laughed, showing her mother the farthing piece.

'Don't spend it all at once, now,' he teased.

'That's some lovely box, Seth,' Cissie said, as proud of it as he was himself.

'It is,' Carrie said. 'I'm that thrilled . . .'

He cut her short. 'What does it say, then?'

Carrie read the words, tracing the inlay with a finger. ' "Silence is golden." You meant that for me. You're always saying my tongue moved quicker'n my brain.' She looked up, her face aflame with laughter and delight.

'Well, mind you heed it then! I don't want thankin',' he said gruffly, and went out to the garden before she could say any more.

But they all of them knew that there was another message in that little box, not written in words.

Carrie hardly slept on Sunday night, she was so nervous, but once she got to Penzance – walking in the crisp October dawn, startling the field-mice in the corn-stubble, and tasting the salty little breeze from the sea – there was so much to do that there was no time for anxiety. Mrs Rowe had decided that an extra pair of hands gave an opportunity for what she called a 'good clean-out', before the preparations for the end-of-century party, and Carrie found herself in the centre of a whirlwind of activity.

It began with the kitchen knives, dozens of them. Rusty ones to be stuck for an hour into a great pot of garden soil, then rubbed with a damp cloth dipped in ashes, and scoured clean. Then Mrs Rowe showed her how to rub the blades with mutton fat, and wrap them in brown paper to prevent them rusting again. It was a wonder to Carrie how anyone could want a knife that was put away in a drawer and used only once or twice in a twelve-month, but Mrs Rowe puffed herself up like a turkey-cock and said that of course any cook worth her salt would need a special knife for poultry, and another again for game, and a filleter for rabbit, and so on through a great long list that lasted for minutes.

Carrie, who had given up listening, said, 'Yes Mrs Rowe,' and went off to clean the ivory handles of the dining knives with a slice of lemon.

After that there were saucepans to be polished, and then all the knives had to be sharpened, in a strange little machine where you turned the handle. Carrie was fascinated, turning the handle with such a will that Mrs Rowe had to come and stop her, before she sharpened the blades clean away.

Then Dolly came down to the kitchen and it was time to help Mrs Rowe with the luncheon, which Dolly served; and by the time Mrs Rowe set their own meal before them, Carrie felt that she had already been working for a lifetime. The bowl of hot vegetable broth seemed doubly delicious because it provided an opportunity to sit idle while you ate it. By and by Dolly came downstairs with the plates from upstairs, and Mrs Rowe let them eat the leavings: a whole slice of meat which had been cut and left untouched, and three broken carrots in a dish. Leavings, indeed! At home Mother would have added a potato and onions and made a meal for the three of them!

After lunch it was back to the 'clean-out'. This time Mrs Rowe sent her to Mr Tucker's bedroom, since the family were out for the afternoon, and the room had wanted doing since the spring, she said.

Carrie felt odd, going into a gentleman's room. It was a very masculine room, too, with heavy mahogany furniture, and ebony-backed brushes and mirrors on the wash-stand. There were pictures, too, on the wall. A woman facing the other way but without a stitch on, and one of a lady tying on a shoe, her skirt hitched up over her ankle in a way that made Carrie's cheeks burn. And in the master's bedroom too! Just as well Miss Limmon wasn't here to see them. Carrie turned her attention to the job in hand.

The beds had been made, once, but everything had to be taken out while Carrie cleaned the dust from the bed-springs with a dry mop, and then a damp one; and sponged the brass bedstead with a paraffin cloth, and washed down the paint with vinegar and water. Indeed by the time she had finished, what with the paraffin and the vinegar and the methylated spirits for the long mirror, not even the beeswax could disguise the smell, and Dolly and Carrie had to open all the windows and put a saucer of hot water in the room, with a cloth in it, soaked in oil of lavender. It would freshen the air, Mrs Rowe said, and get rid of the flies into the bargain – and indeed, by the time Carrie went up to turn the bed down there were a dozen of them drowned in the sweet-smelling liquid.

It was a close thing, getting the room back to rights before the family returned, but with Dolly's help she managed somehow. It was difficult to see that her efforts had made any difference – the room had looked spotless before she began – but Mrs Rowe seemed delighted, and talked of having a go at the other bedrooms when the opportunity arose. Carrie's heart sank. She had not had an idle minute all day – how had the Tuckers ever managed without her?

Even after dinner it was not over. There were dishes to be washed, firing to be fetched, beds to be turned and warmed, and the breakfast room to be prepared for morning. It was Dolly's duty to serve the supper, and as soon as she was able Carrie took herself upstairs to bed. She was already washed and in her nightdress when Dolly came into the room.

'My stars,' Carrie said, when she saw her. 'I was never so busy in my life.'

Dolly smiled, shaking off her cap and letting her hair tumble down on her thin neck. 'Don't you worry, my lover. That's just Mrs Rowe's way. She'll turn the place upside down for a week or so, so you won't have time to breathe, near enough. There's always a host of things to be seen to before the winter, and now you're here they might as well be done. And she can't have you seen above stairs without a uniform. Besides, it'll give her something to say to Miss Limmon when she wants to know what you're up to – there'll be a list as long as your arm. Give it a week or two though, when the cleaning's over, and you've got your dresses – you'll find yourself upstairs, helping me, I shouldn't be surprised. They'll never manage this party without you, come December, that's for certain sure.'

She tipped cold water from the washjug into the enamel basin on the washstand, and splashed her face with it. 'You aren't sorry you came, are you?' She emptied the water into the slops bucket and towelled herself dry.

Carrie thought for a moment, of knives and the paraffin and the cleaning. And then she thought of Father coughing his days out in the blacksmith's shop, and the wage that she could take home at the week's end. Those few shillings would make a big difference to Mother now.

'No,' she said, pulling the cotton eiderdown firmly under her chin. 'No. Not sorry at all.'

CHAPTER FIVE

She was like Grandfather. He could see it in the way she lifted her head and nodded, a quick, sharp nod of approval, when he was shown in.

'You see,' she said, to the tall, thin ghost of a man who was sitting in the easy chair by the fire, and struggling to his feet as Philippe entered. 'My brother Walter, to the life. Philippe, this is Mr Tavy, my solicitor. James, this is Philippe Trezayle. Calls himself . . .'

'Diavezour,' Philippe finished for her. 'How do you do?'

The solicitor looked at him grimly. 'A likeness, certainly. But my client . . . Miss Trezayle is too easily led by enthusiasm. You have, I suppose, some proof that you are who you claim to be?'

Philippe stared at him. 'Proof?'

'Documents? A will? Something?'

Philippe shook his head. 'Nothing in my possession,' he said. 'And very little in France. It is not necessary. But there must be records. Not baptism, we were of the wrong persuasion – outsiders again, you see – but marriages, I suppose so. And, I suppose, there is the boat. It might be proved, I imagine, that it was built for Grandfather, and there are those who would swear it has been in our family ever since. It was a legend, you see – the curse of the Diavezours. My crew were brave to sail with me. They would vouch for me, I suppose. But what is this about? Documents? Why?'

'You realise,' James Tavy said, 'that there may be a considerable sum?'

'A sum?'

'You see?' Adeline said. 'And he had the watch–chain. It is in the photograph, there.' She nodded towards an ancient daguerreotype standing on the mantelshelf.

Philippe took up the picture and looked at it. 'No,' he said sadly. 'No.

43

There is some mistake. That is not my grandfather. Rather like him –
especially around the eyes – perhaps we are related after all. But
Grandfather was a much bigger man – dark-haired, like me, and a wider
face. I am sorry to have imposed on you.' He was sorry, too, he realised. He
had not known, until that moment, how much he had wanted to find a
family. 'Your Uncle Will is not my grandfather, after all.'

But Adeline was clapping her hands. 'You see! James! I told you so. That
is not Uncle Will – that is my father, Philip. You were called for him, I'm
sure you were. What do you say, James Tavy?'

The solicitor sat back, folding his arms. 'Well, it seems likely, I'll agree. I
will look into the records you speak of, M. Diavezour, and if they prove
satisfactory, then Adeline shall have her way. She proposes, you know, that
you should come into everything.'

Philippe gazed at her thunderstruck.

'Not quite everything,' she said, with a little laugh. 'There are one or
two minor legacies. But the house and contents. There is no-one else, you
know. All dead, the Trezayles – except you and I, cousin. The curse of the
what-do-you-calls. And not until I am dead, of course – and I propose to
keep you waiting as long as possible.'

Philippe laughed. He liked her immensely. 'I have one house,' he said,
slowly, 'shut up and unused. What should I do with two?'

She twinkled at him. 'That is for your conscience. For myself, I should
hate to find the place shuttered and sold to strangers. Now about this sail
and spar your require . . .'

He forestalled her. 'I would not presume.'

'My dear man, what earthly difference does it make? It will all come to
you in the end.'

And it was Tavy who said, 'The matter is not legally settled, yet,
Adeline. But we might, I suppose, give him the chest.'

'The chest?'

Adeline nodded. 'That key belongs to Uncle Will's sea chest. It was
never opened – no-one could open it, without the key. My father, I think,
hid it when the customs men came looking, and it has been in the attic ever
since. I asked James to come here before I gave the chest to you.'

It was hard to open it. The lock was heavy with disuse and it was fully an
hour, and an oilcan, later before the lock yielded and the lid eased open.

Philippe held his breath. He did not at all know what he was expecting.
Pirate treasure? Jewels? Coins? Gold? It was none of these things. In the
chest were six silver flagons, beautifully chased.

'Brandy,' Tavy said, and opened one of the flasks. A faint odour of
alcohol wafted up to them. 'Empty, I fear.'

Philippe laughed. 'Grandfather would have taken care that he left no brandy behind him – if he had to carry it in his stomach! So! The treasure chest proves to hold little treasure.'

But Tavy was looking at the silver flagons with interest. 'I don't know. These would have some value, in themselves. This is good silver. Not a fortune, but a substantial sum.'

'Enough for a spar, perhaps, and a sail?' Adeline said with a smile. 'Leave it to me, cousin. I will have these sold, and in the meantime, James shall give you a draught on my account for what you require. You can pay me later. And now, Marie will be chafing, mourning the ruination of an excellent lunch! We should have sat to table half an hour ago.'

He could not well refuse, and the draught was drawn up, before she sent him back to Newlyn as the light was fading, riding in her own carriage.

'You can pay me,' she said, 'by coming again on Thursday, and by visiting me whenever you are in port.'

So on Thursday he went again, and they talked like old friends. They walked in the grounds – fallen into neglect, Adeline said, since the death of her brother. Philippe had laid a new garden at the *manoir* ('foreign nonsense,' the villagers had said) and he was soon discussing Adeline's plans for a rhododendron garden. He was so absorbed in debating the fertilising merits of seaweed that he stayed far too late, and then on his homeward route across the cliffs, he met the bonnet-girl, hurrying home.

When she saw him her eyes lit up, and she talked a long time – tales about her new position as a maid, which made him chuckle. One way and another, it was past four before he strode down the quay.

He was whistling as he stepped aboard the *Plougastel* – but as soon as he went down the steps into the dark little cabin, the sound died on his lips.

It was cramped enough at the best of times; four bunks with their lockers under, a table and four seats, and it was often festooned with drying clothes and oilskins. But this was different.

A great hunk of canvas, too heavy for a man to carry, had been tossed willy-nilly into the middle of the cabin. Ramon was beyond, in the gallery, from where splashing sounds were emerging. Scrubbing himself down, no doubt, while they were in port and there was fresh water to do it. There was little room for such refinements while the *Plougastel* was at sea: sanitary arrangements were simply 'bucket and chuck it', as an English sailor had once said.

Philippe surveyed the solid pile of thick brown canvas with a frown. The new mainsail, and the new towing sail. His cousin had conjured them from the riggers sooner than he would have believed possible. 'Ramon! Why isn't this on deck, or in the sail-locker?'

Ramon's slurred voice came from beyond the bulkhead. '*Laoz Saoz!*' He came carefully to the opening.

Philippe could not suppress a smile. 'Filthy English!' The canvas had been dumped here in exasperation, he guessed. Ramon could be wilfully unhelpful when he chose. And, judging by his deliberate actions and slurred speech, he had been at some waterside inn for an hour or two. Nothing made Ramon more unhelpful than a little too much to drink.

He said, 'Where's Jacques?'

Ramon tossed his head. '*Kaoh!* Went off with Loeiz hours ago – no head for drinking, that man.'

So that was it. Jacques had taken the boy into the town when his father had settled down to drinking. It came of having the crew sitting idle. He had kept them busy for many days, mending the trawl nets, scrubbing the fish tanks, washing the decks free of salt and scales, but he could not hold them for ever. It was his own fault, he supposed, setting off again to see his cousin.

'So you thought you would have a bath?' Philippe said.

Ramon shrugged his soapy shoulders. 'Until that *laoz* Jacques arrives, we cannot move this. It passes the time!'

'Jacques is back!' came a voice from behind them. 'And your son with him. And the new spar, too. So be careful who you call a *laoz*, my friend!'

It took them a hour, all of them, sweating and straining to lift the sails and lug them painfully back to the deck – not the weight so much (properly stowed, even the huge towing sail could be hoisted from the sail-locker with ease), but the impossibility of finding a purchase on the loose canvas in that confined space.

But at last it was on deck, and the new spar with it. Ramon rigged on the towing sail, twisting the vicious iron spirals around the forestay as though his life depended upon it. Jacques and Loeiz dealt with the new spar and the other sail.

'Right,' Philippe said. 'Warp her out.' There were a dozen men on the breakwater to pull the ship clear and out past to the harbour entrance. 'Now,' he said, his voice strong and clear as the tiller rose to his hand, 'hoist that main. Loeiz, you stand by to hand those ropes.'

They went, each man to his station, and miraculously, as the new canvas inched upwards their spirits lifted with it, inch by inch. The sullen look lifted from Ramon's face, Jacques hummed as he winched the sail higher, and even Loeiz, hanking in the mooring-ropes, managed a cheerful smile.

Jacques looked up at the proud new sheet of canvas. 'Take a few herring to pay for that.'

Philippe laughed. 'Didn't I tell you I had found my family?'

Jacques raised a grey and bushy brow. 'There is money, then?'

'Enough for a new sail, at any rate.' He said no more. Only, a little later, as the *Plougastel* passed Land's End, he glanced to shoreward. It was too far to be sure, but he thought he glimpsed the dingy black of an ancient brougham on the clifftop: and was there, over towards Penvarris, a running girl with the grace of a young colt? A man could always hope.

He dipped the new sail in salute, and sailed on into the November night.

Ernie was waiting for Linny May to say it from the moment he walked into Buglers.

She was sitting by the fire, stuffing a ticking case with feathers, and she didn't look up as he came in. It was a job she often did, to help Ma make a few extra pence from the geese and ducks. 'Not too old to be useful, so I should hope!' She plucked them too, sometimes, to Ernie's relief – he hated doing it, a fiddling thankless task, till the quills caught your fingers and the little feathers got up your nose. The sight of all that pale pimpled goose-flesh, besides, was enough to put you off poultry for life.

Linny May was frowning over it now, plunging handfuls of feathers into the pillow, while the air around her was white with strands of down.

'There you are then,' Ma said, coming in from the front passage with her arms full of ticking. 'Early for once, aren't you? You sit down there a minute and I'll soon make you a drop of tea. There's a bit of jam pasty too, you can have, and there's boiled eggs for tea, but I shan't be cooking them till your Da's home.'

He was bursting with his news, sitting on his chair with his hands pressed between his knees, as if by squashing them together he could stop the words from escaping. The women were too busy with their task to notice.

Da did though. 'You look pleased with yourself, young Ernie. Had a good day, have you?' They were his first words as he came through the door.

And then, at last, she said it. 'Haven't made you up to pit captain, yet, I suppose?' She had finished her sack of feathers, and was brushing the white strands from her skirt with a finger dipped in lick.

He said, with a little swagger, 'Not yet. Start tramming clay-spoil tomorrow, though.'

Ma put down the egg-saucepan and looked at him in surprise. 'You never are?'

'Spoke to Dick Clarance about it this morning. Said if he didn't, I'd find another pit.'

'You never!' Ma said again. 'Shouldn't talk to him like that, boy. You got a job, you be glad of it.'

'Well,' he said, defiantly, 'didn't do no harm, did it?' He was rather disappointed. He had hoped she would praise him for his nerve. 'Vince Whittaker said it wouldn't do no harm, and it didn't.'

'Whittaker?' That was Da's voice, very sober and concerned. 'Is that Ralph Whittaker's boy from Roche? You want to be careful of him, Ernie lad. His father was one of those led the clay strike a year or two back – got mixed up with some socialist writing-man from Penzance – and his son's no better, by the sound of him. Thought you were fed up with him, anyroad, on account of he got the job on the overburthen that you wanted yourself.'

'Well, so he did,' Ernie muttered. 'But now I've got a proper job too, so there's no harm done. They're cutting a new shaft tomorrow, and I'll be shifting spoil instead of carting tools like a schoolboy.'

'Well,' his father said, 'the money'll be useful, no doubt of that. But you watch out for the company you keep. Have you down the Tinner's Arms, next, filling your head with ale and politics.'

Ernie flushed, wondering if Dick Clarance had already been speaking to Da. His moment of triumph had been less than he expected.

But later, when the woman came to get her pillows, he heard Ma saying, 'And my son Ernie, been a kettleboy down at the clayworks, but he's starting tramming in the morning.'

Then Linny May, 'Told that Dick Clarance what for, too. Stood up for himself good and proper. Make something of himself, he will, that Ernie. Takes after my side of the family, of course. Always did.'

And Da, catching Ernie's eye, gave him a cheerful wink.

Dolly had been right. Now that Carrie had sorted out her uniform, and the 'clean-up' had been done to Mrs Rowe's satisfaction, life was settling into a more orderly routine, despite the big party looming on the horizon.

It was strange somehow. When Carrie put on the pink-and-white striped dress with her apron and cap, she felt like a proper housemaid suddenly, instead of a great schoolgirl, all arms and legs. And once she looked respectable, she was allowed upstairs and even waited at table.

The first time it happened it took her by surprise. She had been in the house six weeks or so when Mrs Tucker suddenly summoned her, first thing. Carrie crept upstairs with her heart in her mouth.

Mrs Tucker was sitting on a stool by the dressing stand, in a woollen wrap, brushing her hair, while Dolly laid out her clothes on the bed. When she saw Carrie, she took her tortoiseshell combs out of her mouth and said, 'Now Carrie.' She scraped most of her hair into its flyaway bun, and looked at herself in the mirror. 'It is Carrie, isn't it?'

Carrie did not know if she should say 'Yes Mrs Tucker' or 'Yes ma'am', so she hesitated.

Mrs Tucker turned to face her. 'My dear girl, you mustn't be afraid of me! Nothing is the matter. Mrs Rowe says you are a good worker. It is only that I'd like you to learn to serve at table. We shall need you on New Year's Eve for the party, and it's never too soon to learn. You can start with breakfast this morning, and Dolly will show you how.'

Carrie went back to the kitchen in a daze. Serving at the New Year Party! There were to be eighteen people. Miss Maythorne was coming and all! Supposing she should drop something, or stand on the wrong side, or forget to pass the plates. And starting today! She would make a mess of it at breakfast, she was sure of that.

But she need not have worried, for there was little to do, once the table had been laid with a crisp new cloth, the cutlery and a white china plate with gingham napkin at each place. A big silver bowl of porridge was set on the sideboard, followed by a platter of scrambled eggs, and everyone simply helped themselves. Carrie and Dolly had only to stand by and remove the dirty dishes, and then to bring up the toast, tea and marmalade on a tray. It kept them busy, but it was not half the ordeal she had expected.

Even so it would have been easier without Miss Limmon, who folded her lips in a disapproving manner when she saw Carrie, and kept up a monologue all through the meal about the undesirability of having the kitchen staff waiting at table. She interrupted herself only to demand the cream or the butter or the salt, but Dolly had laid the table and it was all to hand.

Mrs Tucker said nothing, but smiled vaguely, until Mr Tucker, who had hidden himself behind the paper for most of the meal, suddenly looked over the top of it and said mildly, 'My dear Emily, if you are desirous of hiring another parlour maid, feel free to do so. Only it will be at your charge, naturally.'

At that Miss Limmon turned a sullen red and lasped into silence. It was a wonder she could eat, Carrie thought, with her lips drawn so tight.

'I've heard of pursed lips,' she said to Dolly, as they carried the dirty dishes back to the kitchen, 'but now I know why. Just like a purse they looked, pulled up tight with a drawstring.'

Dolly laughed so much she dropped the sugar-basin, and Carrie spent half an hour on her hands and knees sweeping up the grains so that they didn't 'walk into the carpet'.

'If you two are going to make work,' Mrs Rowe said severely, 'I shall have to keep you apart. Carrie, you take this kettle and do the washing-up. The wooden tub, mind, for the best china, or you'll have it all chipped; and you can boil a bit of soda in those saucepans, too. I seem to have "caught" everything this morning.'

So Carrie turned to her dishwashing and her blackened pans and Dolly went upstairs to make beds and light the fires. But Carrie was not downhearted. She had quite enjoyed her little session above stairs. Perhaps the New Century Party would not be quite the ordeal she had expected.

She was reminded of the party later, too, when she was dusting the skirting-boards in the passage. The two sisters came down, on their way to take a walk. They stopped at the hallstand to take their gloves, and hats.

'We might take a turn into town,' Carrie heard Mrs Tucker say, 'and look for some fancies to give at the party. I could ask Mrs Rowe to do it, but you never know what she might choose.'

And Miss Limmon. 'Well, you must do as you think, Lorna, but it seems to me an unnecessary expense. Eighteen guests and a present for each? It could run to quite ten guineas. And such people. Whyever Edward must invite an auctioneer! And that dreadful woman who paints! Why couldn't we have been content to have Miss Maythorne, dear Adeline and one or two real friends?'

'Edward is quite a collector of paintings, in his way,' Lorna said, 'and I suppose he may invite anyone he chooses. Anyway, Emily, you would not wish us to seem niggardly, since the chemist and his wife are coming.'

'Well!' Miss Limmon's voice was sharp. 'As long as it is clearly understood that there is no such present forthcoming from me. If Papa had not left me so short of money, I might have thought differently.'

That was awkward. Carrie had been thinking of standing upright and revealing her presence, but now that old Lemon-Pips had started talking about money, it would never do to let herself be seen. She crouched lower in the shadows and peered nervously through the bottom of the banisters.

But worse was to follow. 'Did you hear,' Miss Limmon demanded, 'the way Edward spoke to me at breakfast about that maid!'

Carrie could see her through the banisters, jamming a hatpin fiercely into her burgundy hat, as though Mr Tucker were hiding inside it. Mrs Tucker, adjusting a veil (worthy of Miss Maythorne, Carrie thought) over her grey bonnet, murmured something in reply.

'Well, I don't think you should allow him to speak to me like that,' Miss Limmon said. 'In front of the servants, too.'

'My dear Emily,' Mrs Tucker's voice was mild as ever, 'Edward will do exactly as he pleases at his own breakfast table.'

And as they left, Miss Limmon – carrying a great burgundy umbrella with a duck for a handle – had a face the colour of her ribbons.

Odd, Carrie thought. Just because you had cream on your porridge and servants to serve it didn't mean you had money of your own, or any say in the running of your affairs. No wonder old Lemon-pips was as sour as limes. She finished her dusting in a thoughtful frame of mind.

CHAPTER SIX

It was late December, and the sea-mist was blown to tatters by an Atlantic wind.

Seth was glad to get down the mine, out of the wind and into the familiar warm of the levels. Same temperature, summer or winter. He went down the pit on one of the big kibble-buckets, lowered by the steam-whim. He would as soon have used the ladders, as he had done for thirty years, but old Hobson the blacksmith was a stoutish man with no head for heights, and couldn't be doing with half an hour climbing before he started work, and twice that when he'd finished to get up to ground again.

Besides, there was all the gear to carry. Hammers and nails and pliers and files for the hooves. The horseshoes were made already, of course, fashioned in the forge before they ever set off and only heated again for the shoeing. Knew the horses by name, old Hobson did, and could make a shoe to fit any one of them by eye alone.

It was Black Jess today, proper little horror of a filly, only been down a month or two and never really got accustomed to the blackness – though they kept the horses in darkness for a fortnight or more before they took them under, and again when they brought them up, blindfold, at the end of their working lives. She'd cast a shoe down on the tenth level, half a mile underground, pulling a tram of tinstone up to the grizzly for riddling.

Jim Goodbody, who had been leading her, was all for having her sent up to grass for good and all. 'Never make a pit-horse, that one. Too skittish by half. And as for trying to ride the tram behind her, you can forget that. Kick you halfway to kingdom come, and break your arm into the bargain. And if you try to lead her she bites your behind. No, take her up and sell her, that's what I say, before she takes a piece out of somebody good and proper.'

But in Hobson's hands she stood as still as a statue, only rolling her eyes and showing her teeth a little as he worked. Seth stood by, handing tools and holding the hurricane lamp. Old Hobson swore he couldn't see to work by candlelight, and pretended not to believe that the tinners mined all day by the light of the tallow candles on their felt hats, with a bunch of replacements hanging like pale yellow fingers from their canvas shirts. Seth himself preferred the candles: they 'read the air', he always said – guttering a warning if the air was thin at the end of a level, or if the smoke from blasting was hanging invisible above your head.

But no, Old Hobson would have his oil-lamp, with its glass screen, and a garish light it gave too, making the lips of the men look pink and moist against the red dust on their faces and the glittering whiteness of their eyes. Poor horse had to be blindfolded, of course. That much light would disturb her, and some game it was tying the black scarf around her eyes in the narrow confines of the level.

Hobson had finished now, and Black Jess was led away, skittering and fretful, while they collected their tools.

'Make sure we haven't left anything,' Hobson said, and Seth lifted the light high, his eyes searching the rough stone floor of the level. As he did so, a fit of coughing took him. Old Hobson turned away, busying himself with his bits and pieces, pretending not to notice, as Seth leaned against the damp, dusty granite of the wall, bent double, gasped and spluttered and spat. At last he pulled himself upright.

'Are we ready? All right?' Old Hobson said, as though Seth had been searching for lost nails all this time, and Seth said, 'Yes,' and prepared to follow him back to the whim and be winched back to surface.

But it was not all right, and Seth knew it. The harsh light of the hurricane lamp had shown him what he feared to see – flecks of fresh red in the spittle at his feet.

Well, he would not tell Cissie yet. Time enough to trouble her when he was getting past working.

Yet it had hit him, like a physical blow, and all afternoon the knowledge of it sapped his strength. Old Hobson noticed it. 'Some cold you got there, Seth lad. You get off home sharpish tonight and have a hot salt bath. Nothing like it for breaking up a cough. Or rub a bit of camphorated lard on your chest.'

If Hobson had noticed that something was amiss, Seth would never hide it from Cissie. Better to play the invalid – take Hobson's advice and let her worry about him having caught a cold. That way she need not know the truth, at least for a little while.

So, when the shift was over, he went home to his bed. He loitered on the way, his spirits lower than his boots, and as he looked over the cliffs towards Penzance, he glimpsed a figure in the distance, striding along the path. So that Frenchman was back! Once or twice, since that basket of herring, Carrie had come in on her half-day, saying that the boat was in harbour, and she'd met the man walking on the cliffs. Walked part way home with her, too, more than once, and Cissie had given him a cup of tea.

Seth frowned. He didn't altogether care for it. Cissie seemed to think there was no harm – nice enough fellow, she said, and a gentleman too, in spite of the fishing-boat. Just being kind to the child, and glad of a bit of company in a strange country. Seth sighed. Cissie was probably right – she usually was – but all the same . . . Gentleman he might be, but he was a foreigner: and Carrie was no longer a child. Lots of girls, in Seth's young day, were married when they weren't much older than Carrie. He had thought, though, that the fishing season was over and it had all come to a natural end. And here the fellow was again. As if a man hadn't enough problems!

A fit of coughing took him, and he shook his head sadly. He went back to the Terrace, and to bed, with a piece of paper soaked in saltpetre burning in a saucer beside him. Cissie was out, sitting with a woman in childbed, but when she came home and found him she was all concern.

'My dear Seth, why ever didn't you send up for me? Here, let me rub a hot iron over those sheets and get a bit of warmth into you. And let me see your tongue. Are you sickening for something?'

He took a sip of the hot honey and lemon she had brought him in an enamel mug. 'Yes,' he said slowly, 'reckon perhaps I am.' For a moment words failed him, and then he forced himself to smile. 'But bring me another cup of that concoction, and I'll be as right as rain tomorrow.'

And, as far as anyone else could see, he was.

Philippe bounded up the cliff path, his cheeks aglow in the cold winter sunshine, and a little smile of anticipation on his lips. Thursday. Her day off. He would be likely to find her – he had learned that over the past few months. On Thursdays she went to Penvarris to visit her parents, and it was surprising how often he found himself in Newlyn Harbour on Wednesday night.

There was nothing in it, of course. The girl amused him, that was all, like the younger sister he had never had. And the parents were charming. 'Salt of the earth,' Adeline would have called them. Though he had never, in fact, mentioned them to Adeline.

He did not altogether know why. There was nothing to be ashamed of. Loeiz had ruined the girl's bonnet, and he had befriended the family. There was nothing in that. In fact it gave him pleasure to think that here, in the country of his forefathers, there were people who knew him, friends of his own. This little household, with its cheerful kettle always on the hearth, seemed to symbolise that permanence – that sense of being in one's rightful place – which he had always yearned for. They did not own land, of course. Rather, they seemed to belong to *it*. The idea warmed his heart.

And there was more than that. The girl amused him. She had a freshness, an enthusiasm which made him smile. And a wicked tongue, too. She would caper beside him on the path, and do little imitations of her employer.

'Do you know what happened today? I was cleaning the grates, and I had all the brushes and black-polish and cloths and that, and I was trying to take it all in at once, save myself another trip downstairs, and I dropped a brush in the hall. Well, Old Button-eyes came out and glared at me.' Carrie did a glare that would have curdled milk, and made him laugh. 'And Button-eyes says, "That's far too much to carry, Carrie!" Like a poem, see. Well, Dolly was with her, so I said, "I'll put some of it down, down, before it comes to 'arm, marm!" And Dolly laughed so much I thought she'd burst something, and Old Button-eyes got so mad she stopped twopence out of my wages. For impudence, she said.' The girl looked downcast. 'Shame that is, I could have done with it for Christmas. Bought something a bit special to take home – Father's a bit poorly.'

'Wouldn't your employer understand?' Philippe said, but he knew the answer. He would not have tolerated such talk from a servant himself.

She made a face. 'You don't know Old Button-eyes.' She pulled herself in, and pinched up her lips like a dried plum.

He laughed. 'Who is this "Button-eyes" lady, anyway?'

Carrie glanced at him impishly with laughing eyes. 'I'm not telling. You won't tell me about your family out St Just, I'm not telling about her. Only fair, that is.'

She was teasing him. But it was true. Some instinct had held him back from mentioning the name Trezayle. She might know the name – his family had obviously been quite notable in the area. And he had a distinct impression that, if she classed him as landowner, she would be less open with him. Of course he was well-dressed now, to visit Adeline, but Carrie — he was sure — saw him simply as a fisherman in fancy clothes.

But it wasn't chiefly that, he acknowledged to himself. Mostly, it was that he did not wish Adeline to hear of this. What would she think of him, laughing and gossiping with a kitchen maid on the cliffs, as though he were a butcher's boy?

'How come you got relations in St Just anyway? I never heard of anybody out there called Dia — whatever it is.'

'Diavezour.'

'Di-va-sor.' She stumbled over the word.

He had to smile. 'Not Divazor! Diavezour. You make it sound like "Dinosaur". You know what that is?' She shook her head. 'Old, old creatures that used to live thousands of years ago — that's what they think, but nobody knows very much about them. They've found bones in lots of places. Some in France, I believe.'

She looked at him, teasing. 'There you are then, I was right all the time. You *are* Mr Dinosaur. You are an old, old creature and lived in France and nobody knows anything about you. That's what I shall call you.'

He shook his head and laughed. 'Serves me right for teasing you! But I will tell you about my family in France, if you like!'

And he had told her. Not about the *manoir*, of course — that would have made him a landowner again. But about his life. About Grandfather. About Eved, their courtship, their marriage — even, at last, about that dreadful day when he had lost her, and his son, and his hopes and dreams in one agonised hour. 'I couldn't help her,' he said, 'and it was my fault. I would rather have died myself — anything, to save her that. I did die, I think, a little. At all events, I stopped living.'

He stopped, confused. He was a fool, talking like this to a mere child. She would make some silly joke, imitate him to that maid-friend of hers. But she was looking at him seriously.

'Hard, that was,' she said, at last. 'I don't know. I'm not very good at things like that. But strikes me, you being miserable — doesn't bring her back, does it? Seems to me she'd have wanted for you to be happy, if you could. Not like some. There's Bert Hoskins, mother's cousin, on the Terrace. Nice enough once, by all accounts, but after his wife died, he turned meaner than an old sow. Grieving, so Father says.'

He glanced at her, grateful for the understanding between them. It was almost embarrassing. He had said too much. She seemed to feel it too.

'I'm not saying you are an old sow, mind,' she said, and the moment was over. 'Here, see that tree? My father could jump over that when he was a boy.'

'He couldn't!' Philippe changed the subject gratefully. 'That's a big tree for Penvarris, four foot or more, and your father isn't a big man.'

She grinned at him. 'Well, it was a smaller tree when he was a boy.'

And Philippe had pretended to chase her up the cliff-path, like the child she was.

He smiled at the recollection. He had grown fond of his bonnet-girl. But today although he had timed his walk carefully, there was no sign of her. He was disappointed. Embarrassed too. He had brought two good turbot, wrapped in a paper parcel, and he had planned to give them to her – to make up for the lost twopence, and give her 'something a bit special' to take home. He had thought of lobster, or crab, but had settled on the turbot as easier to carry. And now she wasn't here. He could hardly visit Adeline with a couple of wrapped turbot dangling from a string.

Well, he would visit the cottage. Mrs Tremble would be pleased to see him, and glad of the fish too, no doubt. And then at least, Carrie would know that he had called. He squared his shoulders and knocked boldly on the door, aware of the glances of the neighbours from behind their windows.

Mrs Tremble opened the door, and he found himself being ushered into the warmth of the tiny kitchen, full of the hot, spicy steam of baking.

'Here's Monsieur . . . here's that French gentleman come to bring us a drop of fish, Seth.' She gestured towards her husband, who was sitting behind the table nursing a cup of something hot and steaming, and giving off a smell of camphor. 'My husband's home early today. Third time this week. Got a bit of a cough he can't seem to be rid off. Here, I'll put the kettle on and make a drop of tea. This hevva cake'll be ready in no time. You will have some, won't you? Bit of a thank you for that handsome fish.'

And her husband, struggling to his feet, said, 'Yes, stop and have a cup o' tea. I'm just going down the shed, see if the glue's dry. While you're waiting, come out with me, see what I've been making. You're a practical man, see what you think of this.'

He led the way out of the back door. Philippe followed, a little puzzled. He had met Carrie's father only once before, and felt, somehow, that the man was rather reserved with him. But this invitation was pressing enough.

He went into the shed. Seth had been working on a stool, and the shed was littered with evidences of his work. The glue was drier than a bone.

There was a long silence.

'That's a fine stool,' Philippe said, not knowing what else to offer.

'Good as I can make it,' the man agreed.

'You are a craftsman.'

Seth Tremble shook his head. 'I like it here, that's all. Here, working in my own shed. Reckon a man is always happiest when he sticks to where he belongs.' He was looking at a piece of wood, turning it over and over in his hands.

The message was for him, Philippe knew. 'You mean, I don't belong here, and I should go away? Back where I came from? Back to France?'

Seth looked at him with troubled eyes, but his voice had a gentle firmness as he said, 'I aren't saying that, exactly. Carrie says you got family here, and the cliffs are free – you got as good a right to walk on them as anyone, better'n some, maybe. But walking on them so you meet up with our Carrie, that's a bit different, isn't it?'

'But there's nothing . . . I mean, I didn't intend . . . There isn't . . .'

Seth looked at him steadily. 'I aren't saying there is. My wife says you're a nice fellow, and I put a lot of store on what she thinks. And I daresay you didn't intend anything more than kindness. But what about Carrie, that's the question. Thinks a lot of you, she does. Too much for my thinking.'

Philippe shifted uncomfortably. 'I think a lot of Carrie, too,' he said.

Seth was still holding him with his eyes. 'And what does that mean, exactly? You weren't thinking to marry her, I'll be bound.'

'Marry her!' Philippe was dumbfounded. 'But she's a child.'

'She'll be fourteen, October,' Seth said. 'Plenty of girls got married that age round here when I was young. She's old enough to be looking out.'

'But Carrie doesn't . . .'

'No,' Seth said. 'I don't believe she does. Nor you either. So there's no harm done. You go your way and leave her go hers, and you can think kindly of each other as long as you please.'

Philippe said, feeling a prickle of affronted pride, 'You are telling me to keep away from her, because she's young?' What did the man think he was?

Seth met his gaze. ' 'Tisn't only that, is it? Even if she was nineteen, twenty, what then? Gentleman like you, would you want to court a kitchen maid? A tin-miner's daughter? And our Carrie always gives her heart before she uses her head. No, like I say, better off where we belong.'

Philippe said nothing. He was taken aback, appalled, but some part of him had to acknowledge that the man was right. Why else had he been so anxious to disguise his Cornish name? Why had he said nothing to Adeline?

'Thing is,' Seth said, turning away and picking up a piece of turned wood which would be a stool-leg, 'it's been noticed, besides. Wife's cousin, Bert Hoskins, said something to me yesterday.'

'I see.'

Carrie would find it hard to bear the criticism of the Terrace. Seth Tremble was right, he thought suddenly. He had been thoughtless. Careless. Thinking only of himself. 'That is unfortunate. I thought of her only as a child. She reminds me, you see, of my wife.'

Seth nodded, a slow grin forming. 'She said so. I can see, mind, how that would happen. If I met someone looked like Cissie when she was gone, I'd be wanting to look at her and all. I can see how a man could do it.'

It was generous. Philippe said awkwardly, 'And I can see that it might cause gossip, my walking with a young girl on the cliffs.'

Seth looked at him. 'Cissie said you were a real nice fellow. Reckon she was right, at that. See this, did you?' He showed Philippe a drawing of a little box. 'Made it for Carrie.'

It was a way of closing the subject, but Philippe said, 'I'll drink the tea and then go. I'll leave the fish. Will you tell her I brought them?'

Seth smiled. 'I'll tell her it's an old Breton custom. That's what I told Bert Hoskins. Here, there's Cissie calling us in for our tea. Did you see what I wrote in the box? All in markingtree, it was. Took me hours.' He showed Philippe the sketchy drawing.

'Silence is Golden.' It was a message – and Philippe understood. Nothing was to be said to Cissie or Carrie about this conversation.

Philippe drank his tea and left, pleading his engagement with Adeline. He had been a fool, he told himself angrily. To have to be warned off by the girl's father! Well, it was easily dealt with. He would not speak to the girl again. But he would miss her. Those conversations on the cliffs. Those dancing eyes. That gawky, laughing figure.

But what was he thinking of! He set himself assiduously to remember Eved, and arrived at Adeline's in an appropriately chastened frame of mind.

It was Friday night, the 29th of December, past eleven, and Carrie was sitting up in bed hugging her knees, and listening to the wind howling around the chimneypots. Dolly was undressing, chattering the while.

'My life, Carrie, I thought we should never be done for the night! Looks well, though, doesn't it? Better'n a hotel.'

Carrie nodded. The kitchen was groaning with pies and galantines, jellies and puddings, cakes and comfits, and she herself had spent half the afternoon clarifying stock for the soup. 'Can't see how a hotel would want half the food,' she said. 'Fills me up looking at it. And we had Christmas, only last week. Just as well it only happens once a century – it'll take them a hundred years to work up an appetite again, after all that.'

Dolly laughed, slipping her petticoats around her ankles. 'We shan't stop for the day, tomorrow. Just as well New Year's Eve is a Sunday, so it's only a "quiet" do – till midnight, anyhow.'

'It is something, though, isn't it?' Carrie said. 'The twentieth century. Think of that!'

'I am thinking,' Dolly replied. 'There's a man going round the town with a big placard, saying it'll be the end of the world. Midnight Sunday, sharp, he says.'

Carrie groaned. 'Don't say that – they aren't sitting down to supper till after midnight, and we shall have made all that food for nothing.'

Dolly giggled. 'Eighteen of them, mind – though how we're going to seat them all, I still don't know. Mrs Rowe says there are to be card tables set out, and all sorts, with candles and name-places shaped like swans. Mrs Tucker is doing them herself, mind, so it won't be down to us if they turn out looking like seagulls. And there's to be forfeits and games – though if you ask me they'll all end up sitting on each other's laps, or taking turns with the chairs like they do down our house.'

Carrie grinned. She never tired of hearing stories about Dolly's home in Newlyn – there seemed to be hundreds of brothers and sisters. 'However do you manage?' she said. 'All the girls in one bed and the boys in the other?'

Dolly laughed. 'Father says he has a system. Sends the youngest ones to bed, and when they're sound asleep, rolls them out and props them in the corner to make room for the next lot.'

Carrie chuckled, but all the same she was curious. She had never in all her life shared a bed with anyone, except Katie Warren from next door once or twice, and that was a treat, not a nightly necessity. Sixteen people in three beds sounded mighty uncomfortable, even if the men were out fishing half the night, and the older girls were working in the fishmarket and slept shifts.

'Trouble is,' Dolly said, lifting her arms to drop her nightgown over her head, 'Denbal's four now, and my mother's that scared she'll – you know – fall for another one, she won't go near my father when he comes home. Almost drives him to drink, but the dear knows what would happen with winter coming, if there was another mouth to feed.'

Carrie nodded, though this sort of intimate talk always turned her cheeks scarlet. Her own parents were glad of the little extra she could bring home – how much more must Dolly's wages matter? She had already watched how Dolly always set aside some of her own supper, to take it home on her day off. 'Make a bit of tea for someone,' she would say briskly, slipping it into her basket.

'Payday tomorrow,' Carrie said, her fingers almost itching at the thought of it. It wasn't handsome, half a crown a week and all found, but she was only a kitchen maid, and on probation too. Lots of folk were worse off. Sometimes the men on the seine-nets earned less than that, Dolly said.

'You'll get your full pay tomorrow, then,' Dolly said, and Carrie nodded. The first month or two, of course, Mrs Tucker had stopped sixpence or so to pay for the uniform – though the aprons and the cap were provided free. But tomorrow she would have it all. Two and sixpence in her pocket every week, and with her food and rent provided, it was all her own. Even if she gave Mother two shillings, she would still have sixpence to spend on pies from the street-vendors, or trinkets from the pedlars. A shilling or two would buy clothes, even, from the tallyman or the sixpenny arcade.

'Mrs Tucker said it might be two and nine after Easter,' Carrie said. 'Three shillings after a year if I really suit. That's twelve guineas a year, near enough. Think what you could buy with twelve guineas! I saw real lace camisoles in the town last week – nine and three! I could save up and buy one in a month or so! If I wasn't sending money home, that is.'

Dolly was climbing into bed now, shivering at the damp cold of the calico sheets. 'Lace camisoles! If you had any sense you'd be saving your sixpences for a length of good flannelette, this weather. I swear if you put a mirror in this bed it'd come out misty, for all I try and air it.'

Putting an edge of glass in the bed was one of Mrs Rowe's peculiarities – if the sheets were damp, she said, the glass would cloud. Dolly was under strict instructions always to leave the warming pans in Mr and Mrs Tucker's beds until the mirror came out clear – though Mrs Rowe wasn't so particular about Miss Limmon's.

'Never mind,' Carrie said. 'If you lie in one place it will soon warm up round you.'

She was reaching for the candle when a bell sounded in the hall outside.

'Darn it,' Dolly said, climbing out of bed again. 'That's Mr Tucker wanting his warm milk.'

'I'll get it,' Carrie said. Dolly would have stopped her, but she threw a shawl over her shoulders and went to the kitchen. The hot milk was warming in a saucepan, and she poured it into the cup and carried it to the room. It seemed strange, in the candlelight, heavy with mahogany and the smell of bay rum. And the pictures, which had confused her by daylight, were more than she could look at with Mr Tucker lying there.

'Bring it here,' he said, giving her a warm smile. 'That's a good girl.'

She put the cup on the bedside table and stood for a moment, hesitating. Mr Tucker seemed to be staring at the floor. 'Will that be all, sir?'

He looked up. She would have sworn he coloured a little. 'Yes, lovely. Thank you.'

She went out, strangely confused, and shut the door softly behind her. When she got back to the attic, Dolly was looking at her anxiously. 'All right?'

Carrie frowned. 'Couldn't he have it before we went to bed?' she asked.

' 'Tisn't that,' Dolly said. 'It's just . . . No, well, it wouldn't be the same, that's all.'

For a moment Carrie stared at her, aghast. 'What do you mean . . . He doesn't . . . ?' She trailed off, a cold disquiet trickling down her spine. She had heard of employers who 'took advantage', though she had only a hazy idea what it meant, when it came to people. Animals, of course, she had known about all her life.

Dolly laughed. 'Mr Tucker? Don't be so daft. No, he doesn't do anything. Well . . . not exactly *do*.' She broke off, confused.

'What then?'

'It's . . . It's just, looking. At your feet. Didn't you notice? He always rings when you've gone to bed, and first I couldn't make out why he did it. And then one night I went up in my stockings, because it was a perishing night, and he, well . . .' She giggled suddenly. 'It's stupid, really. He asked me to go away and take them off. And then I realised. Every time I went, he was staring at my feet.'

'Your *feet*?!'

'I know,' Dolly said. 'And when he realised that I knew, he gave me two shillings not to tell Mrs Tucker. So then I knew it was odd. But he doesn't do any harm, not really. And he's as nice as anything the rest of the time.'

Carrie looked at her feet, white and bony with a chilblain on one toe. Two shillings to look at them. It made her feel peculiar, unclean almost, and at the same time she wanted to laugh. Would she, she wondered, dare to tell M. Dinosaur this, the next time she bumped into him on the cliff-path? She hadn't seen him for a week or two. 'Your feet!' she said again.

Dolly met her eye, and this time they burst into giggles together. 'Everyone's out tomorrow night, and there's the party New Year,' Dolly said. 'So he'll have to wait till next century before he can gawp at your feet again. Anyway, you'll know another time.'

'There won't be another time,' Carrie retorted. 'He won't catch me again. I'll go to bed with my boots on.'

And for most of the time she worked for the Tuckers, that is exactly what she did.

PART TWO : 1901

CHAPTER ONE

Another Christmas had come and gone.

The new year had 'come in bitter', as Dolly said, and even now, more than a fortnight later, the morning air was raw. Carrie got out of bed and dressed quickly, glad of the new woollen stockings which Mrs Tucker had given her as part of her Christmas box. Even Miss Limmon's handmade 'mitts' – strange crabbed affairs in tight brown wool, which threatened to cut off the circulation at your wrists and knuckles – were not to be scoffed at, when the insides of the attic windows were sheeted with frost, and your breath came in little steaming puffs on the bedroom air.

She looked over at Dolly, pulling on her clothes by the washstand.

'I'm like Joseph, with this here coat of many colours!' Dolly said, indicating the stripes on her home-made undervest. Her mother had knitted it up out of two outgrown cardigans of the baby's, but she had run out of wool, and the top half of the back was made from odds and ends in all sorts of colours. The worst of it, Carrie thought, was that Dolly's skin was pink where the rough wool rubbed and itched. She thought of her own soft camisole, mended but neat, and mentally blessed Miss Maythorne.

'Never mind, it'll be warm downstairs,' Carrie said. 'And besides, it's a third Thursday.'

A third Thursday was Carrie's favourite day of the month. Not only because it *was* Thursday, her half-day, but also because on the third Thursday, regular as clockwork, Miss Limmon went to visit her friend Miss Adeline. Not just a simple call, with tea and muffins, but a proper visit, lasting a whole weekend. It wasn't fitting, Carrie thought, to be so delighted at the prospect of three whole days without Miss Limmon, but the whole household felt it. Even the smoky old grate in the dining-room seemed to know, and drew sweeter when Carrie swept and lit it ready for breakfast.

Breakfast on one of Miss Limmon's visiting days was a fraught affair. As well as her usual strictures on the crispness of the toast and the tartness of the marmalade, Miss Limmon had the carriage to worry about. Miss Adeline always sent her own, an ancient black brougham drawn by a dusty black horse of equal antiquity, and driven by an elderly coachman in a fusty green frock-coat and a high hat like an undertaker.

Dolly and Carrie had to be sent to the window every ten minutes to watch for it, until it arrived (as it always did) on the stroke of ten. Then there was such a coming and going, such a fetching and carrying of reticules and valises, that you would think Miss Limmon was provisioning an expedition to Australia, and not going a few miles to St Just. Even then she usually contrived to leave something upstairs, and one of the girls had to be sent for it, while the coachman waited. This morning it was her white muff.

'I believe Old Button-eyes does it on purpose,' Carrie muttered, as she passed Dolly on the stairs. 'She couldn't carry on like this if she went on the horse-bus, like anybody else.'

'On purpose? Course she does! Wants all the neighbours to see her going off in a private carriage, and the coachman with his brass buttons and all. And her muff's on the chair in the dining-room, I saw her put it there before she went downstairs.'

Carrie fetched it down, and the coach lurched away. Carrie watched it out of sight around the corner, with the coachman sitting straight as a lamp-post, with his long whip upright, even taller and thinner than he was.

'Well,' she said, as she let herself back into the kitchen. 'There's Miss Limmon gone, off to find fault with Miss Adeline. How those two ever come to be friends is more than I can see.'

Miss Adeline was a favourite in the Albert Street household. Of course, she had been Mrs Limmon's friend, first off, but when the mother died she had continued to be friends with Mrs Tucker and Miss Limmon – everyone knew that. What nobody could fathom was why she seemed to have a particular fondness for Miss Limmon, expect perhaps that she, too, was lonely and anyway, as Mrs Rowe was fond of saying, 'opposite poles attract'.

Miss Adeline came to tea regularly on the first Tuesday – the day she came to Penzance to see to her affairs – and in the spring she came for two or three weeks and stayed while her house was spring-cleaned, because, she said, she could not stand the smell of distemper and carbolic. She was a tiny, neat woman: kindly, too, and always left something for the servants, although she was known to be very particular on the subjects of boot-polish and boiled eggs.

'Poor Miss Adeline,' Mrs Rowe agreed. 'Still, her loss is our gain. Now then Dolly, it's half past ten gone, and us standing here with nothing done. You go on up and do the bedrooms – give Miss Limmon's room a real going-over, mind, while she's away. And you, Carrie, you can give me a hand with this here rabbit I'm going to boil for Mr Tucker's dinner.'

Carrie sighed. Trussing a rabbit was not a job she enjoyed, though she had helped Mother do it many a time. Why would people who could afford good beef and mutton choose to eat rabbit, she wondered, as she hung it by its back leg and eased the furry skin down and away. And why, oh why did Mr Tucker insist on having his rabbit served all of a piece, with the tail and ears left on? Skinning them was a right game, and it was almost twelve before she had removed the eyes and stomach, rinsed it a dozen times, and had it neatly stuffed and sewn ready for boiling.

Mrs Rowe, who had kept a watchful eye on the preparation, was pleased. 'You're coming on there, Carrie. That's a neat job. Make a cook one day, my girl, I shouldn't wonder. Now, there's a bit of bubble and squeak set by for your meal, so you eat that and when you've finished with the lunch upstairs you can get off home. And if you look a bit lively, you can take them carrots back to the greengrocer on your way. Mr Tregorran should have known better than to send them up – they're that wizened they're not fit to feed to the horses. If it hadn't been for that Miss Limmon and her fuss, I'd have looked them over when the boy brought them.'

Carrie smiled. Mrs Rowe lived in a continual state of friendly warfare with the fruiterer over the produce, and it was a rare week when she didn't find something to quarrel over, to bring the errand boy toiling back up the hill with replacements on his handcart. Mind, Carrie had a growing suspicion that this was at least partly due to the efforts of the errand boy himself. His name was Tommy Williams, from Newlyn, and he always had an eye out for Dolly. Mr Tregorran had taken him on over the winter, while the fish was scarce, and Carrie half suspected him of choosing poor carrots on purpose to be sent back to Albert Villas with more.

'Right,' Carrie said. 'You put them by and I'll take them.' And when at last lunch was over, and the dishes washed, and the dining-room cleared and swept and she found herself finally free, she did take them.

She even screwed up the courage to speak to Mr Tregorran. 'Mrs Rowe has sent these back, so they aren't fit for the good houses. What about you let me have a few of them, cheap? My mother'll make something of them, I'm sure.' Father had his own, of course, stored in sand in a great sack in his shed, but a bit extra always came in handy. Especially now.

And Mr Tregorran – who was a relation to Captain Tregorran down the mine, and knew Father – weighed her out a pound of the wizened ones, and wouldn't even take her penny.

She walked home, humming to herself. She loved the walk, always had, even on a January day like today, when the wind tore at her skirts and the cold brought a glow to her cheeks and a stinging numbness to the fingers protruding from Miss Limmon's mitts. Home meant Mother and Father, and Bert Hoskins glowering over the fence at number twenty, and Katie's aunt next door thin and sour as a runner bean. It wasn't the same of course, with Katie in service up at the big house with her sister, and Father so pinched and ill. But home was home.

There was no figure waiting for her on the cliff-path, as she always half hoped there might be. She thought she had seen him, once or twice last summer. Always in the same place, by the wall in Crowdie's top field where she had hidden her bonnet, but always, when she got there, he had disappeared. It was a pity. She had looked forward to their meetings: he made her laugh, and he was easier to talk to than anyone she had ever met. But, although she had seen the boat in the harbour several times, she had not seen 'Mr Dinosaur'. He seemed to have become invisible.

Certainly there was no sign of him today. 'Too cold out, even for an invisible man,' she told herself, and hurried over the stile and down the path towards the house.

Seth was downstairs in the kitchen, fully dressed, when Carrie came in. It had cost him something, struggling from his bed, and by the time he reached the settle and lowered himself painfully onto it, he was gasping and giddy. But he was determined.

'I aren't finished yet, Cissie girl!' he said to his wife, and then wished he hadn't.

'Course you're not,' her lips said, but there was something in her eyes which gave him a different message. Drat the woman, she wasn't going to cry, was she? Bad enough these past few weeks without that, having to give up even his menial job at the mine and take to his bed like a baby.

But he need not have worried. He might be only a pale shadow of himself, but Cissie was the same Cissie still. She gave him a watery smile.

'Bit run down, that's all,' she said briskly. 'No wonder – up in that blacksmith's shop all weathers, in and out by that great fire, and with that cough on you, too. Got down on your chest, stands to reason. I wonder you let them keep you so long, Seth. Better off to have had a few days home before Christmas. Now it'll be weeks, shouldn't wonder.' She turned away, to set the kettle on the hearth.

She was quick, but not quick enough: Seth saw the water on her lashes. 'Let them keep him', indeed! It had been blind charity those last few weeks giving him a pay packet at all. A boy could have done twice the work – was doing it, by now. One of the young Goodenoughs had started the very day Seth left. Yes, Cissie was right. It would be weeks. Months even. But it was not the mine he would be going to then, but a colder, darker, lonelier place. Back underground, he thought to himself, where he belonged.

'And what are you smiling at, all secret-like, Seth Tremble?' Cissie was bustling about with cups and tea-plates, fresh bread, and home-made jam.

'Looking forward to a bit of that potato-cake and pickled beetroot you've got set by on the dresser,' he said, as lightly as he could. 'Comes to something when a man has to wait for his own daughter to come home before he can have a bit of a treat for his tea.'

'Don't you have too much to say, you great lummock, or you shan't have the bit of bacon I've kept back to fry with it!' Cissie said. But she was laughing, and the awkward moment had passed. 'Anyway,' she went on, 'you're a fine one to talk! Who is it insists on dressing up like Christmas every Thursday just because Carrie is coming home for a bit of supper?'

He laughed. 'Ah! She's a good girl. And settled down to that job something wonderful. I did wonder if she'd take to it. Got a quick tongue, our Carrie, and apt to speak before she's got her brain up to steam.'

Cissie thrust a cup of hot blackcurrant into his hands and busied herself with the frying pan. 'Yes, she's done well. And the Tuckers are pleased. Put her wages up and all, this year as well as last. Three shillings a week, it's fair money for a girl.'

She did not say what they both knew, that Carrie's half-crown was an important part of their own week's budget now. Seth had a few pence from the Miners' Friendly Club – thank goodness he had been persuaded to join it – and Miss Maythorne had come to the rescue again with a little cleaning job for 'Hoskins', so they would not have starved. But if it were not for Carrie there would be no bacon tonight, and very likely no pickles or jam. Certainly they would not have been eating *both*, although the preserves were all Cissie's own, made during the summer glut, and brought out to brighten winter from the store-cupboard under the stairs.

'Yes,' Seth said, 'Carrie is a good girl. Be glad to see her, any road.'

'Well!' said a cheerful voice. 'You can start now, then!'

It was Carrie herself, coming in without knocking, as she always did, her hands full of parcels, her cape slipping off her shoulders and her bonnet awry.

'My dear Carrie,' her mother said. 'Whatever are you like?'

Carrie grinned. 'Like Father Christmas,' she said, setting down her bundles. 'Don't know how he ever keeps his hood on! Brought you some carrots. And there's some rabbit's fur here, Mother. Mrs Rowe was going to throw it away, but I thought if we scraped it and nailed it up to cure, it would make a cushion for Father – or a pair of slippers even, if I can fetch home another one. Anyhow, it seemed a waste to throw it out, after I'd skinned the blessed thing. Here, let me poke up that fire for you – Dolly's taught me a good way with coals.'

She had taken off her cape and bonnet and was already kneeling at the hearth, poker in hand.

'My dear child, how you do run on!' Seth said. 'It wears me out to listen to you!'

But really he felt more alive than he had felt all day. He caught his wife's eye and they exchanged a smile. Somehow, the kitchen was already full of extra warmth, before Carrie ever touched the fire.

Emily Limmon was longing to be home. Not that the visit had not been agreeable – it always was. Adeline's house was pleasingly spacious and it was always satisfying to be driven about in a private carriage, however creaking and dusty, so that folk turned and stared, and children scattered out of your path. Besides, Adeline herself was amiable, the rooms were comfortable, and the food delicious – though not so comfortable and delicious that one was denied the satisfaction of knowing that things were often arranged just as well, and sometimes better, at Albert Villas.

So it was not that she was anxious to get away. No, her impatience was entirely on account of her news.

Miss Limmon had two pieces of news, and she was burning to be able to go home and tell Lorna. If only she could arrive home before Mr Tucker, and be the first with the information! The drive back seemed to take for ever, and though usually Miss Limmon enjoyed arriving at the door in state, this evening she could scarcely bear to wait while the coachman helped her down and got out the baggage.

Lorna was in the drawing room. 'Parlour' she called it, but Miss Limmon had visited with people like Miss Adeline, and knew better. She opened the drawing-room door and went in.

Her sister looked up from the letter she was writing. 'Emily!' she said mildly. 'You are back early. Oh drat!' She looked back at the paper. 'Now I've gone and crossed my nib and made a big blot! I can't get on with these steel pens.' She dabbed at the blob ineffectively with the blotting paper, and Emily saw with distaste that she had succeeded in getting ink all over her fingers.

'Well,' Lorna went on, taking up the paper and screwing it into the waste-paper basket. 'I was only writing to cousin Jennifer, and there was nothing to tell her in any case, so it doesn't signify. I should do better to write again, when I have heard all about your visit. How was Adeline? Did you drive out and see the sea? I'll ring for some tea and you can sit down and tell me all the news.'

Really it was perverse: all the way home her exciting intelligence had been burning holes in her tongue, but now that she had Lorna's attention she did not want to tell her. At least not yet. There was something extremely satisfying about knowing something that other people did not. Especially if the other person was Lorna. Lorna with her wispy hair and untidy ways, her brain as cluttered and confused as her writing desk; Lorna who had lacked steadiness, even as a girl, but who had managed to find a home and a husband for all that.

Emily sniffed. 'Oh, I daresay it would all seem very commonplace to you, you with your housekeeping and your artists to run!'

Lorna's 'artists' were a source of constant friction between them: or at least, they would have been, if friction had been a possible part of Lorna's personality. As it was, she simply smiled at Emily's strictures, and went on doing exactly as she pleased – in this case, going down to Newlyn to look at the work of half a dozen local artists. Strange bohemian folk who hung around the waterfront and had galleries on the upper floors of taverns. And Lorna went there! Once in a while she even bought a small canvas. Guineas and guineas for a dab of paint! And Edward Tucker didn't seem to mind! If only Papa had left *her* a little better off by the terms of his will, she would have known better how to look after her money. But Papa had not had a high opinion of women, and had left his estate in trust until marriage – which was why Lorna had money, and Emily had none, or none to speak of. And frittering it on foolishness!

Even now, Lorna was smiling vaguely, as though Emily's remark was the most natural thing in the world. 'Yes, I did go down to Newlyn yesterday. Forbes is doing some nice stuff. Quite a little "Newlyn school" developing. One young painter wanted a local woman to pose for a life class, but they persuaded him not to ask her. Husband would "throw 'un over cliff", Forbes said – and he probably wasn't far wrong. You should come with me some time, Emily. You used to be fond of exhibitions.'

Emily folded her lips. Lorna could be so difficult sometimes. It was true that, once, she had attended a lot of exhibitions and concerts, but that was when a certain gentleman had been paying her attentions. There had, almost, been an understanding between them. And then, just when she had let him know that she might look favourably on a proposal of marriage, he'd upped and gone to America with a bit of a thing half his age. After that she had naturally found that her interest in art had dwindled. It was bad enough, surely, to have been so publicly disappointed, without having her younger sister frequent the very same galleries, wearing her husband on her arm too, like a trophy.

'I've more to do with my time than hang around the waterfront with a gang of ne'er-do-wells,' she said sharply. 'And more concern for my reputation! And if by a "life class", you mean that he wanted to paint her in the altogether, I'm surprised that a respectable woman like you would even consent to talk about such a thing!'

She would have stalked out of the room, to show her displeasure, but she had not yet managed to convey her news. All this talk about art had deflected the conversation. She tried again.

'Adeline had a painting sent her at Christmas. One of her friends has a pretty hand at watercolours, and painted her own greetings as people used to do. So much nicer than these printed cards you see everywhere nowadays.'

Lorna said, 'Watercolours. A pretty hobby, but not art, do you think?'

Emily flushed. Lorna was dragging the conversation back to the galleries again. She said grimly, 'Adeline even had a Christmas message from overseas.'

'That's nice, dear. Now, do you suppose I ought to write Jennifer tonight, or wait until Edward comes home? Perhaps I could persuade him to add a note to thank her for the penwipers.' She laughed. 'Of course, if I had used them myself I shouldn't have spoiled the letter and have to write it again.'

Why couldn't Lorna listen? Emily said again, 'A message, from her cousin. From France, I told you. He's coming to Cornwall again.'

This time Lorna did say, 'Oh, the fisherman? Yes she was very taken with him, from what I gather. Helping her with plans for the estate, she said, though what a fisherman could advise about that, I'm sure I don't know. I thought he had been to see her several times.'

'Well, this is different. It's to be a proper house-party. In the spring,' Emily said, and added, as casually as she dared, 'Adeline says that she will invite me, too, to meet him. And he's not a fisherman, really. A proper gentleman, she tells me, with an estate of his own in France. Bereaved, poor fellow, and turned away from it to forget. Lonely, so Adeline says, and in want of a little society.' She could envisage it now. Adeline had told her all about him. The blue eyes, the tanned skin, the strong hands, the deep, accented voice. The foreignness of the man.

She had a hundred scenes in her imagination already. A drive out in Adeline's carriage. A walk along the Penzance promenade perhaps, while the band was playing. He was younger than she was, of course, but not by so many years; and he was mature, so Adeline said. A man who would enjoy the company of a sensible woman with respectable sensibilities.

Lorna cut across her thoughts. 'It's to be hoped he doesn't take it into his head to arrive just when Adeline's having her house spring-cleaned. She could hardly entertain him then, I should suppose. Ah! There's Edward in the hall! I can hear his voice.'

But Edward was not in the hall for long. They heard him taking the stairs two at a time, and as soon as he opened the door and Emily saw his flushed and flustered face, she knew that she had withheld her second piece of information for too long.

'My dear ladies,' he was saying, 'have you heard the news? I heard the crier calling it on my way up from the town. And the people on the down train from London are talking of nothing else. And to think we hadn't a single notion of it till this minute!'

'Why Edward,' Lorna said, getting up from the desk. 'What is it?'

He took her hands, and before Emily could get a word in he said, 'It's the Queen, Lorna. Poor lady. Taken ill on Thursday, and took to her bed all weekend. And this morning she was worse. They have had the best doctors, of course, but the news is very bad. The papers will be full of it in the morning. They don't think she'll live, Lorna. The poor dear Queen, God bless her, she's dying, so they say.'

CHAPTER TWO

The whole nation plunged into mourning. Newspapers carried a black band around their columns, church-bells chimed dolefully for hours together, and shops put up their shutters halfway or closed them altogether as a sign of respect. Women got up collections for mourning wreaths, and there were processions and special services at the churches.

It went on for weeks. Even Linny May rummaged in the camphor-box by her bed and brought out a huge old black cap edged with ribbons, which she had when her mother died. It eclipsed her, but she insisted on wearing it, and for weeks as she sat plucking chickens on the stool by the fire Ernie could see nothing of her but the great black mushroom on her head and the bony whiteness of her nose and chin peeping out from under the flounces.

Up at the clay-works, too, everything was in mourning. The company flag dangled forlornly at half-mast at the gate, while the clay-captains wore black bands on their shirt-sleeves, and draped black bunting around the portrait of the Queen which hung over the table in the counthouse.

Ernie was down on a clay-end all February, digging out. He was a streamer now, working at the bottom of the pit, while the hose-men above him kept the water coming in a constant stream to wash the clay down, and send the slurry into the settling tanks. Wet work. It was drizzling besides, and cold, and everything was soaking, even though he wore chest-leathers and oilers to keep the worst of the wet off. The damp clay seeped through to your very skin, and the water ran up the sleeves of your oilers and filled your wooden-soled boots. He looked at the man with him, white as chalk and wet from head to heel as though he had been rolled in white mud like a mummy, with only his eyes and mouth pink in his face.

'No good us wearing black down here, then,' he said gruffly. 'Ten minutes, and you'd never know the difference.' He dragged a muddy arm across his muddy face.

The man did not smile. 'Going to tell Vince Whittaker that, so he can make up a petition, are you?' He picked up his shovel and began to work again, lifting the heavy clay-spoil up and onto the waiting tram.

Ernie scowled. 'Vince is all right,' he said stoutly. 'Only got the miners' welfare at heart.'

The man spat, white spittle into white mud. 'Not what I hear,' he said. 'Always on about the exploitation of the workers. Have us all out of a job before you can say wink. Look what's happening out at Delabole.'

Ernie said nothing. He had heard about the trouble at the slate pit. The men there had been asked to take a cut in wages, and for longer hours too, in spite of a petition to the management.

'All the fault of they socialists,' the man grumbled. 'Should have left well enough alone, that's what!'

Ernie told Vince about it later, at the Tinner's Arms, over the pint of ale that he had learned to swallow without grimacing.

'Nothing is popular, first time about,' Vince said, with a knowing air. 'You listen to them, Ernie my handsome, and you'll still be down that pit with your oilers full of freezing water until the day you drop. Is that what you want to be looking forward to?'

Ernie put down his pint and looked at Vince in astonishment. Put like that, it didn't sound too attractive, but in fact, that was almost exactly what he *was* looking forward to. Clay-mining was a steady job, and barring accidents it would keep him until he could quarry clay no more. It was what most men did. He might make it to shift leader, of course, or even get a captaincy, but that was no easy job either – deciding which top to work, for what grade of clay, and when the drying pits were ready for clearing.

'Well?' Vince said impatiently. 'Is it?'

'No, I suppose not.' Ernie could feel that Vince was waiting for more, but he did not know what to say, so he said nothing. What did Vince expect – that he wanted to be Prime Minister or something?

'Do you know,' Vince went on, after a little pause, 'how many men were injured down British mines and pits last year?'

'No,' Ernie said again.

'Thousands,' Vince said, with the air of a conjuror producing live animals from his sleeve. 'Over a thousand killed. What do you think of that?'

'That's a lot,' Ernie said, dutifully. In fact, when you stopped to think about it, it was a wonder there weren't more. All those machines, and horses. And when it came to tin- or coal-mining, it was all underground, and if there were falls and slips, then people could get trapped and buried. Here at least, if a man was buried in a fall you could dig him out in a few minutes, and he'd be right as rain, supposing he hadn't swallowed too much clay, or drowned himself in the slurry. 'How many accidents in the clay?' he said, genuinely interested.

For a moment, Vince seemed irritated by the question. 'How would I know?' he said crossly. 'I don't carry an adding machine in my pocket.'

'I'm sorry,' Ernie said humbly. 'Only I thought you knew about troubles in the works, and that. Your dad was in the stoppages, wasn't he? The clay strikes a year or two back?'

Vince smiled. 'He was. You want to meet my Feyther. Doesn't work much now – too old for that, and those brutes of bosses won't have hair nor hide of you when you're no further use to them. Starve, for all they care. But his mind's as sharp as ever. Knows a lot of people in the Movement. You ever heard of Mr Morrison, down to Penzance?'

Ernie shook his head.

'Famous, he is,' Vince said. 'Writes for the papers and all. And speeches! On about how the working man is treated no better than a slave – working all hours, in dangerous places half the time, just to put a crust in his pocket, while all the time the bosses are making thousands of pounds of profit. Stir your heart to hear him, it would. You want to come down to Penzance one of these days, and hear him talk at a rally. Or come up and meet Feyther – Morrison thinks no end of him. Come up some evening, when we've been on early shift. Have a drop of tea and talk to him. He'll set you right. A social-thinker he was, years ago, though there wasn't such a word in those days. It's the coming thing, Ernie, you mark my words. Even the new King said it: "We are all socialists now." And we haven't heard the last of trouble in the clay pits, young Clarance. Not the last of it by any means.'

And he was sufficiently pleased with himself to buy Ernie another drink.

Carrie walked briskly down Causewayhead towards the market-house and the Greenmarket, looking out for Dolly as she went.

It wasn't often that the two girls found themselves in the town together, but it had happened today. It was Dolly's half-day and she was going to Tregorran's with the vegetable order on the way home – a task which she enjoyed, Carrie thought, because of the chance of meeting Tommy Williams. No sooner had she set off, though, than Mrs Rowe wanted paraffin for cleaning, and Carrie was sent off to fetch some. So she was looking eagerly down the road ahead, hoping to glimpse her friend.

'Hello!' a voice said, at her side. 'Where are you off to, in such a hurry?'

She wheeled round. It was a young man, a worker by his hands and boots, but in a tidy brown coat and waistcoat, with a coloured cravat at his throat. Been to the barber's by the smell of him, for his short hair was plastered down and reeked of macassar oil.

The boy was looking at her appraisingly up and down, smiling a little as if he liked what he saw. It wasn't altogether a pleasant feeling – she had never seen the fellow before, but there he was accosting her in the street, and running his eyes over her as though she were a carcass of meat, hung up for sale, and he was testing the quality.

'Had a good look, have you?' she said sharply. 'Well, it's no good ogling the merchandise, 'cause I ain't for sale.' She'd heard Bert Hoskins say that once, to a fellow he didn't like who was making eyes at his daughter, and it seemed to do the trick.

It did the trick now. The boy looked disconcerted, and shifted his gaze. Weasely eyes, Carrie thought. Pity; he would have been a good-looking boy else. 'No offence intended,' he said.

'None taken.'

'Only I thought you might have been someone I knew.' That was a lie, plain as your face. 'I've just come down to visit a friend of my Feyther's. I come from St Blurzey, up St Austell way.'

'Well, you'd better get back there – 'fore they miss you,' she said, and went to walk past him.

He blocked her path. 'Name's Whittaker,' he said. 'What's yours?'

She felt uneasy at this, from a total stranger in a busy street, but she planted herself squarely and forced herself to meet his eyes. 'That's for me to know, and you to find out. Now, I got work to do, and that's my friend down there I'm trying to meet up with . . .' because Dolly had just emerged from the butcher, carrying a great lump of suet to take home to her mother. 'So are you going to stand out of my way, or am I going to call a policeman?'

He stepped back, grumbling. 'I was only asking. Pretty girl like you.' But she was past him in an instant. If she had been a little younger she would have run down the street. As it was people turned to stare, and even Dolly looked up, saw her and waited.

'Whatever are you doing of, Carrie?'

Carrie explained. 'Proper pest. Didn't like the look of him at all.'

Dolly looked at the figure still loitering up the street. 'Shouldn't worry about him. Isn't from round here, any road. Never see him again, more than like. But you want to see something worth seeing, you come down here and have a look.' She led the way. 'There, what d'you think of that!'

Carrie gazed at the painting in the window. 'It never is!' she said with a giggle.

Dolly gave her a sharp little nudge. 'It is too. True as I'm here. That's Nellie standing with the fishbasket, and Maggie by the wall with the pilchards. He'd have painted my other cousin, too, only she's six months gone and she wouldn't have it.'

Carrie glanced around, embarrassed. Fancy Dolly talking like that, and in public! Supposing somebody should hear! But Dolly seemed oblivious.

'Queer folk altogether, those arty types,' she went on. 'Haven't got two pennies to rub together, most of them, to hear them talk; yet they'll spend a fortune on paints, and give good money to people just to stand still and be painted. You know, he wouldn't even let Nellie wear her good clothes? Wanted her just as she was, he said, with her old patched skirts and all. Ma wasn't a bit pleased when she heard. Folks'll think we've got no better, that's what she said. But he wouldn't have it.'

Carrie looked at the painting again. 'Good though, isn't he? I've seen them down landing the catch like that scores of times.'

Dolly let out a little snort of laughter. 'Call that art? What do they want to be painting things like that for, I'd like to know! Who wants to look at a lot of women sorting fish? Now, that's my idea of a picture!' She gestured to an oil-painting standing on an easel inside the shop. It was entitled 'Friends' and showed a solemn little boy in blue satin leaning against a tree with a black spaniel at his feet.

Carrie looked at the painting. 'It's pretty, I suppose,' she said grudgingly, 'but he looks like he's been stuffed to me – all stiff and puffy with glassy eyes, like that fox on Miss Limmon's table.'

Dolly giggled. 'Oh, Carrie, you are a one! But you know what I mean. It's a proper picture – not like those other ones. They're just . . . bits of normal life on canvas. There isn't a message or anything.'

'Perhaps that's what he wanted,' Carrie said slowly. 'Real life.'

Dolly looked up at her from under her lashes, and her eyes were dancing. 'Well, he'll be disappointed then,' she said, and her voice was bubbling with mirth. 'Come and have a look at this, and promise you won't tell!'

'What?' Carrie said, and Dolly pointed to another Newlyn painting, it showed a young 'jouster', a small woman in a ragged skirt and boots, complete with tartan cape and huge black hat, and a heavy creel slung on her back, full of silver, gaping fish.

'What d'you think of that then?' Dolly said, with such a meaningful air that Carrie leaned forward to get a better view.

The girl in the picture was bending forward, looking at the fish in her hand, so that her face was in shadow, but as Carrie looked more closely, she let out a great shout of surprise. 'My life!' She wheeled around, clapping her hand to her mouth, and blushing scarlet as passers-by stopped to stare in astonishment. 'Dolly, you never did!'

Dolly was crimson-faced too, laughing but defiant. 'I did, then! Three shillings he paid me to pose for that. A week's wages, for doing nothing.'

'But you're not a jouster, Dolly. Never have been.'

'Well, he didn't know that, did he? And that's jousters' clothes all right. Belonged to my Aunt Tillie, till she died. My mother was going to throw them out, or turn them to rags, 'cause they stank of fish, of course – everything does if you work down the fishmarket. I thought I might as well make a few bob out of them, before they went. Good thing I did. The boots fitted perfect, and Mother would have had them down the pawnbroker's quicker than lightning if I hadn't said my say. Besides, it isn't so far from the truth, is it? If it wasn't for the Tuckers, that's very likely where I would be – selling fish.' She glanced at Carrie shyly from under lowered lids. 'Might be yet, come to that.'

'How's that then?' Carrie said, but even as she asked she knew the answer.

'Well,' Dolly said, doubtfully, 'I shouldn't be telling you this, seeing he hasn't spoken to my Pa or anything, but it's that Tommy. We're walking out, you see, and thinking we might get married, if we can.'

'Married!' Carrie said, in genuine distress. 'But whatever will I do without you?'

Dolly laughed. 'Oh, won't be for ages yet – Christmas next year more than like. I'll be nearly seventeen by then. We got to get a bit set by first, and Tommy's got to get a place in a boat somewhere.'

Carrie nodded. Dolly had already told her how the fishermen worked 'shares' – each man giving his labour, and perhaps a share of the nets, in return for a proportion of the catch. The owner of the boat, of course, had the biggest share, but Tommy was not a rich man. He couldn't hope to own a boat, but a few nets, if he was careful – that he might manage.

'Besides, we've got our first three bob,' Dolly said, with a giggle. 'Out of that artist. And we're both putting by threepence a week. Mother will take it hard – she relies on my wages, especially in the winter, but it'll have to be done some time, and once I'm gone, there's one less to worry over.' She grinned. 'Now, don't stand there gawping like one of those herring, Carrie, we've got errands to run. Mrs Rowe will be in a panic as it is, with Miss Adeline coming.'

Carrie grinned. 'Be another shilling or two for your box, when she goes, with any luck!'

'Your turn next, Carrie girl. You'll be fifteen before so long. There'll be some lucky fellow chasing after you any minute. Look at that boy making eyes at you today. You'll have someone swooning over you, quicker'n wink. And a good thing too – give your poor father less to worry about if your future was settled. Now you go fetch that paraffin and I'll deliver this order to Tregorran's. And don't you go saying anything about Tommy up at Albert Villas. Miss Limmon would have me for pancakes if she found out. She's been madder'n a circus bear ever since she found you out skipping in the lane!'

Carrie made a face. That had been a week ago. She had gone out the back of Albert Villas in her dinner-hour and found two or three young girls with a piece of old rope tied to a gatepost. They were using it for skipping.

> 'Old Man Harry's down the mine
> Won't come back till dinner time
> How many pasties will he eat
> One . . . two . . . three . . . four . . .'

Counting a pasty for every skip.

They were hopeless skippers, those girls. Carrie could remember a time when she and Katie Warren could skip nearly a hundred. She felt sad, as though she had lost something. Suddenly, she could bear it no longer. She hitched her skirt up at the waist, tucked her petticoats into the tied legs of her knickers, and ran in to take her turn among the skippers. The girls giggled in delight.

'Forty-three, forty-four . . .' they chanted, clapping in time to her skips, and then their voices faltered and stopped.

The rope slowed, catching Carrie a stinging blow on the backs of her knitted stockings, and there was Miss Limmon standing with Mr Tucker at the end of the lane, and glowering like a gollywog.

'Carrie Tremble, come inside at once!' And then there had been no end of a lecture, with Miss Limmon puffing like a walrus, and even Mrs Tucker forbidding her to leave the house in her dinner-hour and stopping sixpence from her wages 'for creating a disturbance in the lane'. If it hadn't been for Mr Tucker, twinkling at her as though he was thinking of her skirts flying up over her knees and exposing her legs, it could have been far worse. Her skin prickled at the memory.

'You've gone all red,' Dolly said, bringing her back to the present. 'Wasn't that bad, was it?'

'You just want to hope Mrs Tucker doesn't see that painting,' Carrie said. 'She's always down round the galleries. Heaven knows what she'd say if she knew.'

'Not much she can say,' Dolly said. 'Anyway, she'd never see it was me. You didn't realise yourself at first, and you were looking. No-one ever recognises anybody from a painting.' And she was off.

Carrie lingered a little longer. 'Nobody ever recognises anybody?' Was that true, she wondered. It was tempting. Three shillings was a lot of money, just for standing still on your afternoon off. A bit of beef, or chicken, for Father to build up his strength. Oranges, even, though it wasn't Christmas by a long way.

She looked at the picture again. No, it was too risky – supposing Mrs Tucker heard of it! And then the artist would find out she wasn't a fishwoman and want his money back – and besides, she didn't have an Aunt Tillie to give her jousters' clothes in the first place.

'Mind where you're to, child. I've got work to do, if you haven't!' A stoutish man was trying to get past her, into the shop.

Carrie scuttled off to fetch the paraffin.

Miss Limmon was excited. No, she corrected herself. Not excited. That would be unbecoming. A little fluttered. That was better.

She looked at her reflection in the cheval mirror. Certainly she looked neat enough. Her new 'tailor-made' costume with its full sleeves and pointed waist looked fashionable, without being ridiculous. She had chosen heliotrope, a dull mauve, fitting after the Queen's death: one could not be garish, and grey made a woman look like a governess.

In fact, she had to admit to herself, she did look rather school-mistressy in any case. It was hard to know why. The white high-necked blouse with its deep purple trim was elegant. Her hair had been carefully piled in the latest fashion, and the straw hat with purple feathers (did she dare wear straw so early in the season?) was positively rakish. She had even dared to add a little carmine to her cheeks and lips.

Yet the figure which looked back at her from the mirror reminded her irresistibly of the unkindest cartoon drawings of Miss Buss and Miss Beale. Perhaps it was the result of the firm lines around her mouth and eyes. She leaned forward and practised a smile.

Yes, that was better. Definitely better. She picked up her gloves and held them nonchalantly. Yes. Perhaps a little tighter with the corsets would be better, but on the whole she was satisfied with what she saw. She gave herself another, elegant smile.

'Did you ring, Miss Limmon?' It was Carrie, the maid. Drat the girl. What right had she to come charging in here like a great gawky carthorse? Besides, she must have seen that preening in the mirror. You could tell by the way the girl was smirking to herself.

'You can take my luggage down, Carrie. And keep a sharp eye out for that carriage.'

'Yes, Miss Limmon.'

'And be careful with that millinery box. It's a new hat!'

What had she said that for? If she chose to buy herself a new costume and a new bonnet, then that was her own business. Though the whole household must have heard about it, from the fuss Lorna was making.

'But you never buy clothes without me, Emily! Look how upset you were when I bought those new corsets, and you couldn't find any to fit.' Lorna had said it all in front of the servants, too. 'Anyway, I am quite sure Adeline's Frenchman is not going to be swayed by a few ribbons and feathers. Either he will like you or he won't, and you won't help matters by flinging yourself at him, you know.'

Flinging herself! Because she had indulged in a new costume. Really, Lorna could be insupportable at times. If only the terms of Papa's will had left her a little more independent. Then she could have set up a small household of her own, and pleased herself. As it was, she thought grimly, one had to make the best of things.

In any case, she told herself, it was the merest coincidence that her new costume happened to coincide with the visit of Adeline's cousin. True, Adeline had talked about the man – Philippe, his name was – during her 'spring-cleaning visit' to Albert Villas, and certainly, the more she heard, the more attractive he sounded. A widower, poor man, and obviously in need of someone mature to look after him and take care of his needs.

Miss Limmon's reflection blushed. She was approaching forty, but she was prepared to undertake all the 'needs' a gentleman might have. The thought of it set her heart racing, and made her lips dry. But Lorna did it. She had often thought about it, lying alone in the dark, and wondering whether Mr Tucker had 'needs' very often: perhaps that very night.

She turned away, the cheeks in the mirror the same colour as her ribbons.

'Carriage is here, Miss Limmon.' That was Carrie at the door.

And Emily was so anxious to be gone that she even forgot to forget her gloves.

CHAPTER THREE

Philippe stood at the stone wall in the field above Penvarris and looked about him. Beautiful. The sweep of the cliffs, the shimmer of the sea. Primroses and violets softening the stone hedges and clustering under the stiles. And even out here, on the very edge of the rock, there were sea-pinks and daisies and the purple mist of the heather. Yet under it all, the solid heart of granite. An enchanted place. He had come to love this land.

All the same he was foolish to come here – to Penvarris. Supposing he did catch sight of her, as he had done once or twice last year? What then? Scuttle off like a sheepish schoolboy with her father's words ringing in his ears? Foolish to court the ghosts and memories which haunted this place.

The girl was growing up, his brief glimpses had taught him that. Still that glorious hair, and figure as slender as a reed: but the face was fuller now, and the coltishness had softened into grace. Though (he recalled with amusement) she was still apt to hitch her skirts to her ankles when she thought the cliffs were deserted, and scamper across the tussocky grass like a young racehorse. For the sheer joy of living. It made him feel young to watch her, though she would have blushed to know it. He had missed her company. Her freshness, her enthusiasm, her simple merriment. But he had been true to his promise. He had kept away.

Well, he could not stand here gazing all day long. He must think of his cousin, and the mission which brought him here, shorn and shaved and stuffed into a landsman's jacket with a white shirt and stiff collar. A house-party, to meet 'tenants and friends'.

Adeline spoke of planning a new kitchen garden too – the rhododendrons had been a great success – but he more than half suspected that there were other reasons for the invitation. This new-found interest in the grounds had given Adeline a fresh zest for life, and though she had never sought matrimony for herself, she showed an increasing interest in his own prospects. 'You are the last Trezayle,' she had teased him once, 'or you will be, if you are not quick about it!' He guessed that the 'friends' would include one or two eligible ladies. He was going to regret it, he could feel it in his bones.

But it had been irresistible. He loved to help her with her plans for the estate. It gave him satisfaction, not only because the land flourished, but because she blossomed with it, putting on a sunbonnet and white gloves and sallying out to dead-head the bushes, or cut flowers for the vases, until the fresh air brought a bloom to her own cheeks. Philippe had persuaded her to engage the lugubrious coachman's lugubrious grandson as a garden boy, and the youth had proved 'a treasure', transforming the ruined garden into well-tended beds with a kind of melancholic energy.

And there was something else in Adeline's letter, too, which drew him; it would have been dishonest to deny it. 'Mr Tavy,' she wrote, 'has busied himself for a twelvemonth and more, proving what you and I have known all along, that you are indeed a Trezayle. And, he says, there is another legacy – some secret which Uncle Will entrusted to the Tavys. So now you positively must come and put me out of my misery, or I shall die of curiosity, and Tavy will say you did it on purpose to inherit the house.'

He smiled at the recollection. Yes, certainly he must go, and arrive before the other guests, too, so that he and Tavy could spend a few moments investigating this 'secret'. Adeline would have sent the brougham for him, but he had chosen to walk – 'enjoying the air' as he told her, by which he meant loitering at Penvarris.

He was already later than he had meant, and he hurried on to St Just. Adeline was delighted to see him, delighted enough to make him glad that after all he had consented to come. He had called many times, when the *Plougastel* was in harbour. But a real 'visit' as Adeline understood it, with the boat tied up for a week or more, and his crew making free with the waterside bars while he played the visiting squire – that he had never submitted to. Until now.

'Well, cousin,' she said, looking him over from head to toe in that bird-like way of hers, 'you look every inch a Trezayle in that suit.' It was one of his uncle's, which she had looked out and sent down to the harbour for him, as though, he thought, he did not have a cupboard full of formal wear back at the *manoir*. Still, that was on the other side of the Channel, and the cabin of a fishing-boat was a poor way to transport fine cloth. He must see to it. Better to have a wardrobe waiting for him at St Just, if he was to become part-lubber when he visited Cornish shores.

'Not every inch,' he chided her, laughing. 'There is Breton blood in

86

these veins.' But he followed her into the drawing room, where Tavy was waiting with an envelope containing the famous 'secret'.

Even then, it was not a straightforward business. There was a long and tedious wait, while Tavy explained how he had proved that Philippe was, after all, legally a Trezayle; and so worked himself, by slow degrees, to the opening of the envelope.

'It entitles you,' Tavy said, 'to the possession of a cottage – it was left to your grandfather on the death of the tenant, William Polzeal. Some sort of arrangement he came to, in exchange for his part of the . . . er . . . catch, I understood.'

'The catch? The only thing Grandfather ever had in his fish-tanks were bottles of brandy.'

Tavy looked grave. 'Those are, however, the terms of the will. "Left in perpetuity to William Trezayle and his heirs." I should not like to raise your hopes, however – the cottage has been deserted for some while. There was, you see, no direct heir to be found.'

Philippe shook his head with a sort of sad disbelief, but Adeline said, 'I remember Willie Polzeal. Used to sail with your grandfather. He did live in a cottage over towards Pendeen – a real old recluse he turned to, in the end. But he's been dead and gone these thirty years.'

'There was, as I understand, some money,' Tavy said. 'But it was held in notes from that bank that failed. I imagine Mr Polzeal lost most of his fortune then.'

Adeline shot a look at him. 'Or spent it,' she said. 'You didn't know Willie Polzeal. Lived the life of Riley until the last ten years of his life. Had to come home then because they were looking for him in Plymouth. Had nothing left – couldn't have had, or he would have done something about the cottage before he died. It was falling down, even then. It's still there, what's left of it. Miles from anywhere, and nothing but rainwater to drink. There was a farmer used it for pigs, at one time, but it got too dangerous even for that, and it's gone to rack and ruin since. Didn't know he owned it, though. How did he manage that, James? Most cottages round that way are owned by the duchy, or one of the big estates.'

'It was part of the Penvarris estate,' Tavy said. 'All sold up when Lord Penvarris died. He had some land at Pendeen.'

'So,' Philippe said, 'I am a true Cornishman at last. A piece of Cornwall that is all my own.'

'Well, you'll have better by and by,' Adeline said. 'Nothing up there but gorse and rabbits – and not so many of those. But – is that a carriage? I think our other guests are arriving.'

She went to the window. 'Yes. The Curnows!' she said, and they went downstairs together.

He had met the Curnows before, pleasant, hard-working farmers from the estate who gazed at him curiously, as though perhaps he had three heads or an extra arm on account of his Breton ancestry.

Diavezour, he thought to himself. M. Dinosaur. The outsider. Well, he would be an outsider no more. This was his family home, where grandfather had lived as a boy – here in the best drawing room with its embroidered cushions, its harmonium with the discreet frills set around to hide its legs (lest, Philippe thought with an inward grin, a man's desires should be set aflame by the naked wood). He belonged here, and to prove it he set himself to discuss with Curnow the relative merits of cabbage and winter broccoli. He earned himself a grateful smile from Adeline, and the accolade of 'proper gennulman' from the farmer.

There was to be another guest this weekend, Adeline said, a dear friend, whom she had known for many years. 'She was badly treated, you see, very badly, by a gentleman in her youth and it has made her . . . well, a little less sweet-natured, you know. But she is easily hurt, all the same, and she has a tender heart behind it all.'

Philippe murmured wryly that the description hardly offered a recommendation of the lady. Adeline laughed. 'Be nice to her, Philippe, for my sake. Besides, you know, she has an interest in quite a large estate, which comes to her if she marries.'

'Why Adeline! I do believe you are matchmaking!' She coloured in delight. So he had been correct in his suspicions!

Matchmaking. It was absurd. But he could not be angry with Adeline. Rather, he was amused. It was the kind of thing, he conceded inwardly, that he might once have been tempted to do himself.

But first there were the Curnows, and he found himself telling them, as best he could, about the rose granite coast of Brittany, with its huge pink stones cast up and weathered into shapes smooth and sensuous as any sculpture ever made. 'Pink granite against green trees, and all against an azure sky,' he said. 'Or, in the winter, one thick grey haze!'

Adeline laughed, delighted. 'You could charm the birds off the trees, Philippe,' she murmured as they went into the drawing room. 'Mind you charm Emily when she comes.' He knew what that meant. He was to make conversation, escort the ladies on strolls on the cliffs and hand them in to dinner. Besides, he thought with a twinkle, Adeline was doubtless more than a little gratified to have an eligible man at her table, and if this Miss Limmon set her cap at him, she would be doubly delighted.

Well, it could do no harm to be pleasant to the woman. Adeline had been good to him, and if it amused her to play matchmaker he could indulge her by at least being civil. Perhaps this was the cure he needed – the balm that would soothe the aching place in his soul. Adeline thought so. Privately, he doubted it. His heart was with his crew, now, and his boat. He was saying as much, gently, to Adeline when the brougham was heard on the drive.

Adeline twinkled up at him. 'Well, you could do worse, Philippe. Emily has a substantial sum in trust – and she can't lay hands on a penny until she's wed. That would buy you a new boat, and turn her into a woman of property – though you have left it late. I believe half her fortune was with that same bank that Tavy was talking about, the one failed ten years or so back. Anyway, here she is.'

She went forward to meet her guest. 'My dear Emily!'

Emily was a stout, stern-looking woman, with shrewd eyes and a general air of being laced in and battened down. Hardly, Philippe thought, a woman to set a man's heart alight. But there was something in her smile and the glow in her cheeks which told him that she, at least, liked what she saw. When he pressed her hand she fluttered like a child, and he glimpsed for a moment the girl she once had been.

'*Enchanté!*' he murmured, and saw her catch her breath. Philippe Diavezour, he told himself firmly. Be charming if you must, but be careful. Be very, very careful.

But as far as Emily Limmon was concerned, it was already too late for that.

'Honestly! Old Button-eyes! She goes from bad to worse, I do declare.' Carrie set the candles and linseed oil down with a thump.

Dolly, who was shredding soap into a large pan of boiling water on the stove, turned to ask, 'Why? What's she been up to this time?'

'You must have heard,' Carrie said. 'She hasn't stopped since she came home. On and on about this Frenchman she met up at Miss Adeline's. Well, he isn't a even proper Frenchman, from what I can make out. He's called Trezayle. But you should hear her tell about it. Where they went, who they met, what he said to her, what she said to him. Went out for a walk on the cliffs to a ruined cottage, by all accounts. Think she'd have more sense at her age.'

'Romantic, I suppose?' Dolly asked.

Carrie cocked an eyebrow at her. 'Don't be daft. I know the place. Three walls and a mineshaft, and a wind that'd take the skin off you . . . But Miss Limmon's that taken with the idea, you wouldn't believe. You'd think she'd done something wonderful, not gone walking on the cliffs in a gale of wind to some draughty old ruin. On about it all the time. She's worse than you telling about Tommy Williams.'

'Shh!' Dolly said, glancing towards the yard, where Mrs Rowe was busy with a jelly in the outside safe. 'She'll hear you, and then there'll be some to-do. Here, we're ready for them candles now.'

She moved aside, still stirring, so that Carrie had room to break in the wax little by little, letting it melt in the hot soapy water. 'Well,' Carrie said, 'old Button-eyes doesn't care who hears! She was even telling *me* about it this morning when I went up to do the fires. "Have you ever met a Frenchman, Carrie? Such cultivated people. And a fisherman, too. But a gentleman. Most of our local seamen are so uncouth." '

'Oh, ta very much,' Dolly said.

'It wasn't me saying that, you goose! That was Miss Lemon-pips. So I told her, yes actually I did know a Frenchman, as it happened. And he was a sea-captain too, with his own boat. Used to walk me home to Penvarris one time, and had tea in our house. So she can put that in her pipe and smoke it.'

Dolly put her hand to her mouth to stifle a giggle. 'You didn't say that!'

'Well, it's true, as it happens. Here, you keep stirring that or we shall have it sticking! No, honestly, I did know a Frenchman once. With a proper French name – not Trezayle.'

'What did she say to that?'

It was Carrie's turn to giggle. She did her best impression of Miss Limmon, clasping her hands together at her chest and pulling her mouth down at the corners. ' "I find it hard to imagine under what circumstances you could meet such a person, Carrie." So I said, "Well as a matter of fact, Miss Limmon, he once bought a bonnet off me for a basket of fish." Well, you should have seen her face! Told me to stop my impudence, and threatened to speak to Mr Tucker. Don't think she will though. He'd only laugh.'

Dolly's eyes were round. 'My life, Carrie, I don't know how you have the nerve to make up these tales.'

'I didn't make it up, altogether. The bonnet was ruined anyhow, and he trod on it accidentally-on-purpose to save me getting into a row with my mother.'

'You'll be getting in a row from me, if you don't look sharp with that furniture polish,' Mrs Rowe said, coming in with the empty jelly-mould. 'Set it outside to cool now, and when it's good and cold you can mix in the linseed and turpentine. Mind you keep it covered, too, or it will spoil.'

Carrie and Dolly exchanged glances, and carried the heavy saucepan of boiling liquid between them to stand on the raised paving by the back steps.

'And while you're out there, Dolly,' Mrs Rowe said, as though she had just thought of it, 'that boy from Tregorran's is in the lane with the swedes and broccoli for dinner. I daresay I might turn a blind eye this once, if you wanted to go out and fetch them in.'

Dolly was off down the steps like a shot, and when she came back her cheeks were scarlet.

'What is it then?' Carrie asked, as soon as there was a private moment.

Dolly looked at her, her eyes shining. 'It's Tom, Carrie. He's got a place on a boat, starting tomorrow. James Marshall's boat. The boy Jenkins was drowned at the back end of last year, and they've been working short all winter, and been looking out for a man. They'll let him buy into the nets with his share of the catch. It's an old seiner, which isn't what Tommy wanted really. It's all drift-nets now – they catch anything. The seines were only really fit for pilchards – trap the whole shoal and bring them in alive. Still, pilchards are a good catch if you can get them, and Tommy's that pleased to have a share in a boat at all! He's been down to see Papa, Carrie, and it's all agreed. End of next year, I'm to be Dolly Williams.'

'Dolly!' Carrie said, and reached out to hug her friend. There might have been tears, but Carrie said lightly, 'You're just a copy-cat, that's what it is! Just because Miss Limmon's taken a fancy to a fisherman, you've got to have one too.'

Dolly flashed her a grateful smile. 'We'll have to find someone for you then! Seen that boy from St Austell again, have you?'

Carrie flushed. 'Weasel-eyes? He's a right pest he is. Turned up again last week – I had to send him away with a flea in his ear. Too big for his boots, that's his trouble. Thinks he's Christmas, and he's not even New Year's Day. Smiles at you as if he's doing you a favour. No, don't want him at any price, thank you very much.'

Dolly grinned. 'Well then, what about this Frenchman with the big feet?'

'He didn't have big feet,' Carrie protested, laughing. 'He was a nice-looking man, if you want to know. Quite struck on him, I was. Thought about him, many a time.'

'Perhaps it is the one Miss Limmon is so taken by. He'd take your breath away, by all accounts.'

'I told you,' Carrie said. 'He's called Dia . . . something. How could it be Mr Trezayle?'

'Well,' Dolly said, 'maybe Dia-whatsit is French for Trezayle. Bit of a coincidence, else.'

'Don't be so wet, Dolly. How many French fishermen do you think there are? Must be hundreds.'

'Well, they can't all be better-looking than all get out! Besides, if he was out Penvarris way, maybe he was going to St Just.'

It could be true, Carrie thought, with a little shiver. He had said he was looking for his family. But no, he could never be related to Miss Adeline. The Trezayles were gentry, good as. They wouldn't be sailing around in fishing boats. Or walking about on the cliffs when there was a perfectly good brougham in the coach-house. It was too absurd. All the same her heart was thumping uncomfortably, and her cheeks blazed.

'Well,' she said, turning the moment with a laugh, 'no good then, is it? Old Button-eyes has got her hooks into him already! No, you'll have to save me one of my own!'

Dolly's eyes danced. 'You hear what the man said when he went to the Salvation Army? "I hear you save fallen women. Well, save one for me." '

For a moment Carrie could not fathom what it meant, but when she did so she was genuinely shocked. 'Dolly!!'

Dolly chuckled. 'You wait till I find you this fisherman of yours. You won't look so prissy then.'

'Time enough for that,' Carrie said, and sounded in her own ears like Miss Limmon.

But as she lay in her bed, that night and many others, she puzzled over the problem. It couldn't be the same man. That face, that voice, that wicked wink. Imagine him with Miss Limmon. What a waste! It couldn't be him. Not possibly.

Could it?

Ernie cradled his ale-pot and sipped it gingerly. Vince had taken to buying a stronger brew lately, and it went to his head. 'My birthday, Saturday,' he said at last. 'Working on early shift, and Ma's making a figgy pudding, special. Sunday School treat's going up to Newquay, so we're going with them on the charabanc. Up there all the afternoon.'

'Is that good?' Vince had a way of asking the question which took all the fun out of the idea.

'Course it is,' Ernie said stoutly. 'Some looking forward to it, I am.'

Vince took a long, considered drink of ale. 'And what about you, Ernie lad? What are you going to do?'

Ernie frowned. 'I told you. Up to Newquay on the charabanc. There'll be running races, and cricket on the sand . . .'

Vince cut him off. 'No, I don't mean the birthday treat. I mean after. Here you are, sixteen on Saturday. What are you going to do? Scores of men are married at sixteen, stuck in the same job for a lifetime. Are you going to settle for that?'

Ernie felt embarrassed. He always did when Vince started talking like this, as if life was unsatisfactory, somehow.

'No,' he said, uncomfortably. 'Plenty of time for getting married. Anyway, I don't see you avoiding the girls.'

Vince laughed. 'Ah, I got three or four of them that wouldn't say no to me. But I aren't going to get saddled with a petticoat and prams, not for a good while yet. I'm going to make something of myself.'

'So am I too, then,' Ernie said.

'What you going to do?'

Ernie squirmed on his stool. 'I haven't made up my mind. Unless . . .'

'Unless what?'

'I did think about signing up, as a volunteer.' It was true. The idea of the bugle-boy had never ceased to thrill him, and now he was going to be sixteen. There was still a recruiting drive, he'd seen the posters.

'Sign up? For South Africa?'

'Of course.' What other war was there? 'I mean, scores of people have gone, from round here. Sort out the Boers and all that. Did you read about the reception they gave them when the first lot came home?' It was one of the things that stirred him – the hero's welcome give to the first volunteers returning after their year's service was up. 'Whole town turned out to meet them. Banners and bands and all sorts. Now that *would* be something, wouldn't it?' He could imagine it – people carrying flags and cheering, and all for him.

Vince was looking at him soberly. 'You can't mean it?'

'Yes I do,' Ernie said. 'I'm strong and healthy, and I'm sixteen, very near. And Linny May would be some proud. Why wouldn't I mean it?' The idea was getting hold of him even as he spoke.

For answer, Vince took him by the elbow and guided him to a recess in the corner. 'Because, my handsome,' he said, leaning closer, 'you're too valuable to be used as cannon-fodder, that's what. You heard of Spion Kop?'

Ernie nodded. 'Course I have,' he said. 'Terrible business. Bloody Boers.'

Vince shook his head. 'Bloody Boers, my eye!' he said, so fiercely that other drinkers turned and glowered in his direction. 'Bloody massacre, that's what. The British boys were badly prepared, badly equipped and badly led. And who took the brunt of it? The poor bloody infantry, that's who.'

'Here, mind your language!' Ernie said. It was one thing to talk about the 'Bloody Boers' – they were the enemy, after all – but it was quite another to pepper your language with the word as though it were an everyday expression.

'Language be damned!' Vince said, and downed his drink in a single gulp. It made Ernie's heart beat a little faster. Vince was like that. It made you feel quite manly to be seen about with him.

'No,' Vince went on. 'You remember the Vigo brothers? Volunteered from the pit the minute they started recruiting? You know what happened?'

'One of them was wounded, I heard that.'

'Half his shoulder shot away, and took a bullet in his face so he'll never talk again,' Vince said, slamming down his empty tankard. 'If you call that wounded. Not actually dead, I suppose. Might have been better off if he was. And you know what they invalided him out on? A pittance!'

Ernie took another sip of his bitter drink, uncomfortably. This wasn't the romantic picture he had painted for himself. 'What about the other one? Heard he got a medal.'

'So he did. For rounding up an enemy position. Group of Boers in a farmhouse suspected of mining troop-trains. And you know who he rounded up, Ernie? Three old men, a woman, and a boy. That's your precious army for you. Use you to feed the guns, or to do things you'd spit on a civilian for doing. And you would volunteer for that? No, Ernie. Rather you stay here and quarry clay. It's dirty work, but at least it's clean dirt!'

Ernie glanced around nervously. Suppose somebody should hear them? People had been tarred and feathered for less. He seized on the topic of the pit. 'Wouldn't be so bad,' he grumbled, 'if they'd put in that new pumping engine. Wish I was an engineer, I'd show them a thing or two.'

'Well, there you are then,' Vince said. 'You said it yourself. A mine engineer. Now there's a real ambition for you.'

Ernie gaped at him. 'An engineer? Me? But they're skilled men, look.'

Vince gave him a sour glance. 'And how do you think they got skilled, Ernie lad? Worked their way to it, that's how. And studied at night school besides. Didn't sit in taverns dreaming of playing soldiers.'

That was unfair. Left to himself Ernie would never have gone anywhere near the Tinner's Arms, and the thought of continuation classes filled him with dread, but he said meekly enough, 'What are you saying, Vince?'

'I'm saying you want to go to Dick Clarance and tell him, "I'm sixteen next week and I want to start as an engineer." And if he won't have it, tell him you'll go to another pit.'

'I couldn't do that.'

'You did it once before, and look what happened.' Vince got up, as though the conversation was over. 'No good thinking of being a soldier, if you're afraid of your own cousin.'

Ernie went home with his brains in a scramble. It was true what Vince had said. Confronting Dick Clarance had won him a proper job instead of being toolboy. And if he liked the work – well, the classes could come after.

He thought about it all night, and all the next morning, watching the water seep onto the floor of the end they were working, and ooze from the clay walls. A mine engineer. That was the job.

He couldn't eat his crowst at lunchtime, though Ma had sent him off with a good meat pasty. Instead he sat drinking his tea by the kiln, and when the others went back to their shift, or to the dry, he went into the office and found Dick Clarance.

His cousin was sitting in his shirtsleeves and bowler hat, sprawled in chair, a pile of papers on a table in front of him, and little row of clay samples waiting his attention.

'Well, young Ernie?' Dick's voice was not unkind.

Ernie had heard of 'quaking in your boots', but he was surprised to find that it was true. His knees seemed to be seized with trembling, and his calves actually quivered in the thick leather of his wooden-soled boots.

'What I want,' he managed to blurt out, 'is to start as a mine engineer. I'm sixteen next week, and I'd like to be a skilled man.'

There was a silence. Dick Clarance did not look at him, but picked up a sample of white dust and rolled it between a finger and thumb, testing the clay.

Ernie waited. Still his cousin did not speak. 'And if you won't have it,' he burst out, 'I'll go to another pit.'

Dick Clarance looked at him at last, raising his head slowly, and regarding him with cool grey eyes. 'Go to another pit?'

'Yes!' His heart was really thumping now.

'Well then, my handsome,' Dick said, 'you call at the count-house on your way out and draw what's owing. Because if that is what you feel, that is what you'd better do.'

CHAPTER FOUR

Ernie walked down the road away from the claypit like a mechanical man. Two miners, on their way to the late shift, called out 'Hello then, young Clarance!' but they seemed like creatures in a dream, their voices hollow and distant.

Whatever in the world had he gone and done now? His mind refused to take it in; it couldn't be true. But his fingers crisped over the money in his pocket and he knew that it was only too real. Out on the street and no job. What would Linny May say to that? Or Da, for that matter. Ernie shut his eyes against the picture of Da's face, and the hurt and worry he would read there.

Bloody! Bloody!! Bloody!!! But even Vince Whittaker's bit of swear did nothing to put stuffing in him. However much he cursed, and kicked the loose clay-stones to fragments, the world and his prospects remained depressingly unchanged. The future as Vince had painted it had seemed grey enough. Now it was a deep and impenetrable black.

He thought for a moment of going into the Tinner's Arms to see if a pint of strong ale would fortify him, but the thought of the seven and eleven in his pocket prevented him. Heaven alone knew where his next pay packet would come from, and he couldn't afford to squander this. Besides, the Tinner's Arms had been the beginning of all his problems. Whyever had he listened?

It was all Vince Whittaker's fault, he thought bitterly. The man on the clay-end had been right. After all, Vince was only a trammer himself. Didn't catch him going up to the management and demanding a change. Ernie was suddenly filled with a fierce, unreasoning fury. He had a good mind to go down and sort Vince Whittaker out, once and for all.

It wasn't a serious intention. Vince Whittaker was a lot bigger than he was, for one thing, and a skilled boxer to boot. Ernie had seen him at it, when they had set up a bout at the pit – farthing stakes and winner takes all, and Vince rarely went away without a pocket full of coins.

All the same he found himself walking down Bal Lane, towards the Whittakers' house. He knew where it was, of course, although he had never accepted Vince's urgings to 'Come home and speak to Feyther'.

He did not altogether know what he hoped to achieve, or whether he would have called, but the decision was taken for him. Vince himself was in the front garden, pulling cabbage by the look of it, and when he saw Ernie he straightened up with a smile.

'Ernie lad. Never saw the going of you this morning.'

His cheerful tone made Ernie madder than ever. 'No,' he said shortly. 'Nor likely to again, either. I spoke to Dick Clarance, like you said, and got turned out for my pains. Thanks to you!'

Vince's response surprised him. He had been expecting embarrassment, sympathy, apology even. What happened was that the other man came forward smiling and wrung him warmly by the hand. 'Ernie my son, you're a hero! You wait till my dad hears about this. A martyr to capitalist exploitation, that's what you are.'

Ernie did not feel much like a hero, much less a martyr. He felt a bit of a fool, if the truth were known. 'Sacrificed to the guns' as Vince had said. But Vince's delight made him feel a little better.

'Come in now,' Vince said, 'and talk to Feyther.' And he led the way into the house.

It was a clayman's cottage in the old-fashioned style, with a furze hearth and a crock of soup hung on the crook in the chimney. Vince's 'Feyther' was sitting on the bench behind the table, with a parcel of papers spread before him, reading by the light from the window and hurricane lamp – needed in the gloom of the kitchen even on a bright afternoon. Ernie was a little surprised. Not so many ex-clayers of Whittaker's age could read for pleasure, even if they could spare the time.

'Well, sit you down on the cricket!' Old Man Whittaker said, gesturing towards the three-legged stool beside the hearth. 'And who might you be, when you're home? No good waiting for that son of mine to introduce you, or we'll be here all day.'

'This is Ernie Clarance, Feyther,' Vince said. 'From up the Borglaise pit. Or he was till this afternoon. His cousin turned him off for asking to change his job.'

'That right?' Mr Whittaker raised his head to look at Ernie through the wire-rimmed spectacles balanced on his nose. 'That was a bold step, young feller.'

'Wasn't my idea,' Ernie said. 'It was Vince put me up to it.'

'That so?' The look through the spectacles again. 'Thought better of it since, have you?'

Ernie remembered what Vince had said about his father and the 'social-thinking', and he said sullenly, 'Well, it was right enough, I suppose. A man's got a right to ask, especially his own cousin. But it didn't turn out how I expected.' That was putting it mildly. Ernie was half afraid to go home.

Mr Whittaker leant forward on the table, sending his papers flying. 'Well, you've got a bit of spirit, I'll say that for you. More than you can say for that son of mine – all talk and no action, he is. Tell you what, young fellow, I've taken a liking to you. You stop here and Vince'll make you a cup of tea, and I'll put you in the way of something that might help you out a bit.'

Ernie was surprised to hear the old man talk about his son in this way. He had always thought of Vince as being an engine-house of action, getting up steam on his own account, and driving others. Old Man Whittaker made him sound like an empty whistle. Still, a cup of tea would not come amiss, and he watched while Vince raked over the embers and stood the kettle on the trivet over the burning turfs. Linny May used to have a turf fire, he had heard her say so many a time, but he had never seen one in use before. 'Old ways are best,' she used to say. 'Never get coal to bake like the old hearthplate. Brush back the ashes, and sprinkle a bit of flour on so it browns up proper, and then put on the baking iron and heap the embers round it. Best bread and cake you ever tasted!'

There was a baking iron beside the hearth here, too, obviously little used. Presumably Vince and his father, without a woman in the house, made do with soups and stews from the hanging crock, with a boiling of meat and taties in a net once in a way, and bought bread from Bugle. There was a bacon rack, though, with a half-eaten joint hanging from the planchion, and bunches of elderflower and wild angelica stuck up there to dry.

Old Whittaker was still looking at him intently as Vince lifted the hot kettle. 'What are you thinking of, Vince? We've got company. Use fresh tea-leaves, do.' Vince had been about to reuse the ones set on a saucer to dry on the windowsill, but at his father's words he got down the caddy from its place beside the salt box and the powder-flask on mantelpiece.

'Now then, young fellow,' Whittaker went on. 'If they got shot of you from up the big pit, and you are wanting employ, how about you go down to Little Roads?'

Ernie sighed. Little Roads was a much smaller, old-fashioned pit, two miles or more over Truro way.

'Owned by a cousin of old Borglaise,' Whittaker went on. 'And no love lost between them. You go down there and tell him you want to leave Borglaise's, he'll snap you up soon as look at you, you see if he doesn't.'

'Better than nothing,' Ernie said. He had visions, suddenly, of being back down a pit as the toolboy, sitting on a wet board trying to hold a boryer steady while two men were hitting it inches from his ear.

'Better than that,' Old Whittaker said. 'You tell him what you were earning, and say you are prepared to come over, if he pays you right.'

'But I got no choice,' Ernie said.

'Don't you tell him that, lad,' Whittaker said. 'You take your chance to put one over on the bosses. You want to go down there straight off, mind, while the iron's hot.'

Before Mr Joseph Borglaise heard anything different, that's what he meant. Ernie's heart was thumping louder than the steam-hammers when he got to Little Roads and asked for Mr Joseph.

It must have worked though, because when he walked into Buglers, with a jaunty air, and Linny May said, 'Haven't made you up to captain yet, then?' he was able to say, with a casualness he did not really feel, 'No. Left up the pit though. Gone to Little Roads. Starting tomorrow, mine engineer, two and threepence a day.'

The little gasp of surprise from under the flounced bonnet was music to his ears.

Father was worse. Carrie knew it from the moment she let herself in through the garden gate and in by the back door.

It was in the air. Not so much in the sound of the laboured breathing, wheeze and gasp, wheeze and gasp – she had grown used to that. Not even in the smell of camphor and goose-grease, or the warm damp of the steaming pot of herbs which Mother kept simmering in the front room, beside Father's bed, because the vapour was said to be good for breathing. No, it was something else. A stillness, a hush, as if the walls themselves were holding their breath and waiting. The tick of the mantel-clock and the rattle of a log settling on the fire seemed unnaturally loud and intrusive.

Mother came out of the front room, carrying a tray. There was a plate on it, laden with tiny treats: a morsel of jellied chicken, thin fingers of bread steeped in the yellow warmth of egg yolk, and a little pile of mashed potato, with flakes of white chopped into it, which might even have been haddock. The plate was untouched.

Carrie looked at the plate and then at her mother. 'Well?' It was all the greeting between them, but no other was needed.

Mother shook her head. 'Nothing. A few sips of broth, that's all. And that near choked him, poor man. You want to see him? He's sleeping now, but he'll be some glad to see you.' She stood back to let Carrie enter the room.

But Carrie was still looking at her mother's face. How tired she looked. How lined. How worn. Even the hands that held the tray had lost their vigour, and trembled a little under the strain.

'In a minute!' Carrie said firmly. She rather surprised herself. Mother had always been the rock, the anchor, and it was she who had obeyed. But now it was Carrie who took control, taking the tray and shepherding her mother into the kitchen.

'Now then,' Carrie said, before Mother had time to collect herself. 'You sit there on the settle for five minutes and have a cup of tea, before I have to start worrying over you as well. You look ready to drop.'

Her mother sank down thankfully on the wooden seat. 'Well, maybe I am a bit weary, at that. There's a lot to do, with my cleaning work, and looking after your father and all. I just don't seem to have a minute. And there's the garden, besides. This time of year, it gets away quick as wink: though I haven't been able to plant like your father did. How we'll do for potatoes this winter, I'm sure I don't know. I haven't put in half the crop he used to.' She gestured towards the tray. 'I tried to do a few things, see if I could tempt his appetite, but it didn't do a bit of good. Not even that lovely bit of chicken Mr Goodenough sent in. Some good, they've been, the neighbours.'

Her voice broke, and she began to weep. Carrie would have gone to her, but that would have been to stop the tears. Some instinct told her that this weeping, like the flood of words, was necessary somehow. It was important, though, not to start crying herself. She busied herself with the teapot, and with carrying milk and cups to the table.

'What did you eat yourself, Mother?'

Her mother looked surprised. 'I . . . I don't know. A piece of bread – something. Don't fuss, Carrie.'

But her daughter persevered. 'And when was this?'

'I don't know,' Mother said again. 'Breakfast, I suppose. But honestly, I'm not hungry. I haven't the stomach for it, with your father lying ill. It's him I'm concerned about.'

'Well, see you are!' Carrie said, aware that she sounded severe. 'Won't do him no good to have you working yourself to a shadow. If you don't eat and rest, it will be you sick next, and then where shall we be? Now!' she went on, setting the tray of dainties in front of Mother. 'You eat this, and I'll pour you some tea to go with it.'

'But this was your father's,' Cissie protested, her face so anguished that Carrie longed to hold her close and weep on her shoulder. But that would do no good.

'Well,' she said shortly, 'he didn't even touch it, did he? And you're not about to start wasting good food, I should hope. So, you get it down you, and let it do you a bit of good instead. The folk who gave it to you intended to help Father, and they'll do that best by bucking his nurse up a bit. Now, here's your cup of tea. You sit and drink that while I go and see Father. And have a bit of a rest while you're at it.'

Her mother took the plate and began to eat, mechanically, without appetite. It would have been all the same to her, Carrie felt, if she had been given workhouse gruel, instead of the tastiest morsels the Terrace had to offer. Still, the nourishment would reach Mother, even if the taste never did. She stood for a moment watching, and then slipped into the next room to see her Father.

As soon as she saw his face she was shocked by the change in him. It was only a week since her last visit, but the face had altered almost beyond recognition.

He was sleeping, if it could be called sleep, his eyes closed and his breath coming in great shuddering rasps. His head was propped on a pillow, and his skin had shrunk back against his skull – not white so much as yellowish and waxy, like an old tallow candle. His hands, too, were shrivelled to the bone – not thin, because of the broad bones beneath, but fleshless; and they clawed at the sheets as though each breath cost him dearly, unconscious as he was.

The room was heavy with steam and herbs and camphor, but there was something else more potent in the air. Already, he smelt of death.

Carrie leaned forward and pressed a kiss on the damp forehead. The breathing altered and the eyelids flickered open.

'Carrie!' His voice was already a ghost. It would haunt her for ever.

She brushed back the tears and managed a warm smile. 'Ssh,' she whispered, putting her finger on her lips. 'Silence is golden!'

The blue lips moved in the suspicion of a smile, and the cold fingers tightened around her own. Then the eyes closed again, and the terrible rasping began once more.

She sat for an hour, not moving, not even to wipe the tears from her face. She let them fall, heavy and warm on her bare arm, and when at last she rose to go, she disentangled her fingers from his so gently that she did not wake him.

In the kitchen, her mother too was sleeping, slumped uncomfortably against the settle, her head at an awkward angle. 'You'll be some stiff when you wake up, my lover,' Carrie murmured and, lifting her mother's head, attempted to slip a cushion beneath it. But it was too much. Mother stirred and woke.

'Whatever am I thinking of!' she said, struggling upright. Carrie saw the grimace of pain as the stiffness in her neck gripped her. 'Here it is, gone four, and the fire half out . . .'

'I'm seeing to it,' Carrie said. And she was – on her hands and knees, using Dolly's trick with the kindling to coax the flames into life. 'There! That's burning up nicely, so I'll put the kettle on, and we'll make you some supper before I go.' The plate on the tray was empty now, she noted with satisfaction.

'How's your father?' Mother said, ignoring the question of mealtimes.

'About the same. Knew me though. You're nearly out of camphor oil. I'll bring you some, next time I come – and anything else you're wanting.'

'Drop of fruit would be nice,' Mother said, and then added, in a rush, 'But it won't do a bit of good. Not even a doctor could save him now.'

Carrie said nothing. There was nothing to say. Only, on the way back to the Tuckers' she made a little detour to Penvarris chapel.

The door was unlatched, and she pushed it open. The chapel was empty. Only the dust danced in the shaft of evening sunlight over the wooden benches and the polished brass of the rails.

'Why, God?' she said aloud. But there was no reply. Only the golden dust-motes twirled like ballerinas – endlessly moving, endlessly still.

She walked home in something like a fury. Why should it be Father? Why him? Coughing his lungs out for the want of a doctor, while the medical men galloped to rich houses every day because some fine lady fancied she had taken a chill. Why?

But she already knew the answer. Doctors cost money. A guinea or more a visit, and even then there was often nothing they could do. A guinea – more than a month's wages. Unless . . .

By the time she reached Penzance, her plan was fully formed.

It was all very well, Ernie thought crossly, this earning 13/6d a week, but it didn't make you a millionaire, at that. Of course, there was a lot extra in his pocket now, even though he'd put Mother's share up to six shillings a week, but somehow there wasn't as much left over as a man might have hoped. It was largely on account of the tally-shop.

He knew, when he went to work at Little Roads, that it was an old-fashioned sort of a pit, but even so, he hadn't been prepared to find a full-scale tally-shop, where the goods you bought were set off against your week's wages, and often cost you more than at the market in Bugle, besides. He had tried to avoid it, at first, arguing that he was a single man, who didn't need flour and sugar or great clay bussas for storing, but the pit captain made it clear that something was expected, and he signed up for a new pair of canvas trousers for claying in.

' 'Tain't fair,' he muttered to Bob Sanders, one of the older engineers. 'I aren't going to see more than a shilling out of that lot, now.'

The man shook his head. 'Hard, they are, and that's a fact. When they pay you a pound, they want for you to spend fifteen bob of it at their blooming shop. Send round to your Ma they would, if they had to, and the man wouldn't go home till he'd got your order. Hard, that's what they are.'

The work was hard, too. No drying kilns and inclined shafts here – only the old settling pits, to dry the clay in wind and sun; and the digging was done 'flat' – lifting every shovelful up and over your own height to fill the kibble, which was then winched up and emptied into trams.

Mr Borglaise (Mr Joe, as Ernie had come to call him) was talking about putting in a new short-shaft pumping engine to replace the old one, but it was all talk, the men said.

'Believe that when you see it, my handsome,' Bob Sanders said. 'If it costs money to do, then there's no point holding your breath while you wait, neither.'

Ernie sincerely wished Mr Joe would think about a new pump. He had already spent several afternoons in company with the old one – fixed down a wet shaft, with a tallow candle for light, and that threatening to go out at any moment. After an hour your shoulders ached from the water falling on them, the sleeves of your oilies were full of freezing water, and the level rose under you, slow and steady, until the cold water came up to the seat of your canvas trousers.

'Pity he don't put in short shaft, then,' Bob Sanders said. 'A man could take that out and fix 'un in a nice dry shed, with a wandering lead to see by. But it won't come to it, you see, while he can put us down there – and the water that cold on your backside, you'd think something had bitten you!'

Ernie had a sneaking admiration for Sanders. He was the best engineer of them all – not only for machines, but for the real job: knowing the lie of the place. He knew the best angle to lay a button-hole launder, or how deep a digging could be before they lost the end and it had to be abandoned. He was from Launceston, and a lot of the men didn't care for him. 'An incomer,' they called him – but no one questioned his skill. Ernie liked him, but he took care never to be too pally when there was anyone to see.

Sanders had taken to him, too, it seemed. 'You got a feel for this, boy, at the practical end. You study your maths, my son, and you'll do.'

His maths! Try as he would, Ernie had not been able to avoid the continuation classes at the Institute. Twice a week he was down there, struggling with geometry or calculus, and twice a week he came home swearing that he'd sooner be down a wet end any day, and up to his knees in clay. He thought about giving it up, but Mr Joe kept asking, casual like, how he was getting on, so he gritted his teeth and struggled on.

Mr Whittaker helped him.

He was a frequent visitor to Bal Lane and the Whittaker house these days. Mr Whittaker had books, given to him by that Mr Morrison in Penzance, and he lent five or six to Ernie. Ernie didn't care for them much, except for the one entitled *Practical Geometry*, which explained things better than his instructor, and stayed calm, besides, if you didn't understand first time. The other books were mostly by people with foreign names, and went on about something called capital, and used lots of long words. Ernie used to keep them for a week or two and then hand them back and thank Mr Whittaker politely.

It seemed to make Mr Whittaker happy, and when Mr Whittaker was happy he taught Ernie how to use a slide rule. He was a much better teacher than the man down the Institute, and so was Bob Sanders – so when they came to slide rule calculations in class, Ernie found himself at the top of the group, and some of his other failures were forgiven. So it worked out very well.

Vince, however, did not seem so pleased. 'Who you come to see?' he said one night, when Ernie tapped at the door with a copy of *The Wealth of Nations* to return (unread). 'Me, or Feyther?'

'Well, both, I suppose,' Ernie said, aware of the need to say something of the kind. 'Couldn't fail to, could I, when it's down to you two that I got this job in the first place.'

Vince looked a little mollified.

'I couldn't do the slide rule without your feyther,' Ernie said, 'and without you I would never have stood up to Dick Clarance about being export . . . explore . . .'

'Exploited?' Vince said.

'That's the one,' Ernie said. 'So I wouldn't have moved, and then where would I be?'

'Tramming clay, like me,' Vince said, but he let him in with a smile.

Still, Ernie had been careful, ever since, to dwell on the hardships of the job. Vince liked that. He collected stories and took them down to Mr Morrison once a month. Morrison used them in his speeches, or his articles, Vince said – and paid the train-fare besides.

Well, there would be plenty of hardships today. Three weeks of fine weather had dried the settling pits, and there was a cry of 'Carre'en clay!'

Mining engineer or not, it made no difference today. Every man for himself down the cheeny yard; the men with long-handled shovels, the boys with a pair of boards. The cutter was already at work with his special cutting-tool, slicing the semi-dried clay into neat squares. The young men lifted their own lumps, the older ones lifted lumps out for the boys to carry to the stacks, sanded-side out, like lumps of solid milky jelly between their boards.

It was hard graft. The clay was heavy, and Ernie, as one of the younger men, was carrying his own clay to the stope. To and fro, to and fro, twenty pounds at a time on a long-handled spade, while the clay-dust got into your nose and throat, and the damp got everywhere. It made your arms ache and your back stiffen, and by the day's end the weight of dried clay on your legs would have dragged your trousers out from under your waist-belt, if it wasn't for the string tied under the knees to take some of the load.

Yes, this was something he could tell to Vince, later over a jug of ale.

But when he got home to Buglers he would say, proudly, 'Bonus today. Penny a square yard. Bob Sanders and I had the biggest stope by a mile.'

CHAPTER FIVE

It took Carrie the whole week to work herself up to it. She had warned Mother she might be late on her next afternoon off, but the thought of what she was proposing kept her awake nights.

In fact, she did not quite know what she *was* proposing. Dolly, who had posed as a model herself, laughed at her fears. 'Just standing still for an hour or two to have your picture painted. Where's the harm in that? No worse than a photograph, and people do that all the time! No, you just go down where I told you, and say Dolly Boas sent you. You'll have your three shillings before you know it. Go myself, I would, only I've been in one picture, and they won't be wanting me twice.'

'But I'm no jouster, Dolly. I got no clothes for it, not like you. An' besides, I don't know the first thing about fish!'

Dolly laughed again. 'Get off with you, you daft thing. Paint other things, they do, besides the fishwomen. People shopping, and knitting – all sorts. Just afraid of your life to go, that's all it is – but if you want those few shillings, it's easy money, Carrie girl. And they can't eat you, I suppose!'

Carrie wished she were altogether sure of that. Posing for a painting meant what Father called 'arty types', and the very words conjured up a world of goings-on which Carrie could only guess at.

Indeed, as she walked down to Newlyn the next Thursday, with her heart thumping so that she was sure the passers-by could hear it, and her cheeks already crimson with embarrassment, it was only the thought of that three shillings which stopped her from turning tail. She did not at all know what to expect. She had a confused impression that there would be 'sin' – girls in gypsy skirts above their ankles dancing dangerously to tambourines, and young men in flowing neckties and open shirts who sat up at night carousing with too much wine, and too much opium and tobacco. What on earth, an inner voice prompted quietly, would Father say?

'Were you looking for someone?'

The soft voice behind her made her literally jump, so that she whirled round in the doorway, gasping, her eyes wide and her hands clapped to her breast. There was a small, dark, balding man on the pavement at her elbow, blinking mildly behind thick, metal-rimmed spectacles.

Carrie gazed at him. He looked kindly – bewildered almost, with a luxuriant and rather lop-sided moustache. He was dressed rather oddly, in a rather old-fashioned, sober, cutaway jacket and mornington collar like Mr Tucker's, over a pair of startling broad-checked unmentionables. But he clutched a respectable-looking bowler hat in his hand, and when he said again, 'Were you looking for someone?' she found the courage to answer.

'I was looking for the painter, sir. I heard he lived here and was looking for models – and I need the money for my father,' she added hastily, dimly aware that her first words might have created a poor impression.

The man looked at her. 'Were you now? Well then, I suppose you had better come up.' And he led the way up the narrow staircase to the studio.

Carrie had never been in a studio before, and her first impression of it was the smell – a strong, chemical sort of smell that was somehow sweet, and with a hint of turpentine in it. And then, the mess. It was a room no bigger than her bedroom at the Tuckers', but every inch of it seemed covered in pictures – finished paintings stacked against the wall, half-finished and half-started paintings on the floor and table, and everywhere paint pots, palettes, brushes and splashes. The whole room seemed alive with colour.

'There is a sofa here somewhere,' the man said, moving a pile of sketches and a grubby cloth which might have been a painting smock. 'There, sit down, and let me take a look at you.'

Carrie sat down obediently. 'My friend Dolly Boas sent me,' she said after a moment.

'Shh!' the man said. 'Tip your head forward a little, so.'

Carrie did as she was told, the words dying on her lips. After a minute the man said, 'Well, I might use you I suppose – there's a nice line to your shoulders there, and I'm looking for a young woman to finish the group in that market scene.' He indicated a picture standing on an easel.

Carrie stared at it. It looked already finished to her.

'Well?' the man said, impatiently. 'Two shillings.'

'Two?' Carrie had been hoping for more, and her voice betrayed her.

'That's it. It's only a group – won't take more than an hour or so. What do you say?'

'Well,' Carrie said doubtfully, 'I suppose so.' Two shillings was a lot of money for an hour's work, and better than nothing, after all.

'Right!' The little man seemed suddenly exuberant, as if a great weight had been lifted from his mind. 'That's settled then. Will you come now? Or – no, I expect you would prefer to have some tea? My name is Rawlings, by the way. Mr Fred Rawlings – but call me Rawlings, everyone does. Now, tea. There is a pot here somewhere.'

Carrie glanced around the room. There was a grate, but it was empty, and there was no method she could see for preparing tea.

Rawlings moved a box of paints and picked up a teapot with a triumphant air. 'Eureka!' he said, and then, in an apologetic tone, 'Greek, you know. Now for the cup that cheers.'

Carrie half expected him to produce a coal-range from behind a paint-pot somewhere, but instead he disappeared out of the door with a cheery 'Wait a moment', and reappeared a few minutes later with a tea-tray laden with the full pot, cups, milk and some perfectly delicious-looking buns.

'The lady of the house,' Rawlings said, with a delighted grin. 'First-class rock cakes. See what you think!' He waved a hand towards the tray. 'I'll just make a sketch or two.' He picked up a pencil and began to draw.

It was clear to Carrie that if she waited for her host to pour the tea it would be cold before she tasted it, so, greatly daring, she took the teapot and poured out two cups. Rawlings didn't seem to mind at all. 'Ah,' he said, after five minutes or so. 'Tea! Capital!' He picked up one of the buns and bit into it. 'First-class rock cakes. Wouldn't you say?'

They remained for several minutes drinking tea, and eating the buns – which were good, Carrie thought, though not a patch on Mother's. She was wondering whether she dared to eat another, when Rawlings looked up.

'Well, now!' he said severely, as though the tea and rock-cakes had been all her idea from the outset. 'Mustn't sit here. Wasting the light. Come out into the yard – this is where I want you . . .'

The next hour was the longest Carrie had ever spent. He gave her a shawl to drape over her shoulders, and begged a deplorable old straw hat with a feather, and a basket, from the invisible baker of rock cakes. Carrie was to stand leaning on the railing.

It was purgatory. She had never in her life been one to stand still, and to be obliged to do so for minutes at a time proved to be more demanding than she could have imagined. There was an itch on her nose, her leg ached, and she had pins and needles in both arms by the time he said, 'Well, there we are – that's grand then.'

She glanced at the papers which he had pinned to his board. There were three Carries, each with a different tilt of the head, a different turn of the hand. And there were little patches of colour, too, touched onto the sketch – and even Carrie could see that he had caught in them the play of sun and shadow on the coarse material of her skirt and shawl.

'Two shillings,' he said, wiping his hands on a rag. He fished into a pocket and brought out a florin. 'There we are, young lady.'

'Is that all?' Carrie said, although only a moment since she had been wondering if she could hold the pose a moment longer.

Rawlings smiled. 'It is – unless you want to come by in a week or so and see the finished painting?'

'I don't know,' Carrie mumbled, but she knew that she would.

'What does your father want with that two shillings, anyway?' he said.

Carrie was surprised – he had hardly seemed to take in her remarks. 'I want it for a doctor,' she said.

He looked at her. 'You really want to make some money,' he said, 'you could come down and pose for the life-class. Ten shillings or more, they pay for that.'

'Life class?' Carrie said. Surely she was alive now?

'Without . . . all that,' Rawlings said, gesturing towards her.

She looked down in amazement. 'Without what . . . Oh!' She could feel the colour in her cheeks, and she clasped her hands across her chest as though the words themselves had removed her bodice and skirt and left her exposed in the afternoon sun.

'Well,' Rawlings said slowly. 'Depends of course, how much you want the money. But you'll come to no harm, I'll see to that. 'It's just . . . art. The human body is a beautiful object.'

Carrie was reassembling her own possessions, too scarlet-faced to speak.

'In any case,' Rawlings called after her, as she stumbled down the hall grasping her precious florin, 'come back and see the picture. And, as for the other thing – you think about it.'

She found her tongue. 'Oh, I couldn't do that! I couldn't even think about it!' she said.

But when she got to the Terrace, and saw that Father was no better, she found that she could do little else.

Vince was on about the Fair.

'You want to come,' he said, for the tenth time that afternoon. 'Look, you're on early shift – we can be away by two, get the train, and we'll be in Penzance by four. Hours at the fair we could have, before we'd need to catch the last train. I can even introduce you to Mr Morrison. Feyther's always saying you should meet him. Besides,' he cast Ernie a sideways glance over his pint-pot, 'there's a girl in Penzance I want to see.'

Ernie nodded. So that was what the fair invitation was about. That made sense. Somehow he couldn't see Vince devoting a whole afternoon just to the idea of visiting Corpus Christi Fair, however splendid it was cracked up to be. But to meet a girl, that was something else. And to see Mr Morrison. Vince and his Feyther were always talking about him.

'Proper gentleman, he is,' Mr Whittaker used to say, whenever Ernie went back to the cottage with his pile of unread books. 'University man, and very educated. Says there'll be a revolution in Parliament one of these days – the working man will rise up, and realise that in the dignity of his labour lies the real wealth and power of the nation.'

'Oh, yes,' Ernie said, striving to look interested. He thought about some of the clayers down at Little Roads, up to their armpits in sweat and slurry. If the wealth and power of the nation was the 'dignity of their labour', he thought, no wonder the country was going to the dogs! 'Yes,' he said aloud. 'Very interesting.'

He hoped that the visit to Mr Morrison was not going to be allowed to spoil the fun of a visit to the fair. Ernie had been to a fair only once, and even then it wasn't a big fair, like Corpus Christi at Penzance. He had loved it, the stalls and the noise and the sideshows and the fairings. He had even won a goldfish in a little glass bowl, though it had died a day or two after. He would even put up with meeting Mr Morrison if it meant a visit to the fair.

Ma and Da and Linny May were less than delighted.

'Lot of money, that is, and a long way to go just to see a few freak-shows,' Ma said.

'Wages burning a hole in his pocket, I'll be bound,' Linny May said scornfully. 'Don't know why the boy can't stay at home, and know when he's well off.'

Besides, there are plenty of freak-shows right here in Buglers, Ernie thought spitefully, but he only said, 'Well, I shall go, and that's flat. I'm working hard enough down Little Roads, goodness knows, and if I can't spend a few pence on my own pleasure, I don't know what the world is coming to. 'Tisn't as if I smoke, or anything.'

He hadn't meant anything about Da, who had just filled his clay pipe, with some difficulty, but his father put it down without lighting it.

Ernie was cursing himself for an idiot, but Linny May said, 'Spend enough of it down the Tinner's Arms, though, by what I hear. Boy your age, you ought to be putting a bit aside against your wedding, and keeping your eyes open for a nice girl. That's what your grandfather did when he was your age.'

'Pity he never found one then,' Ernie muttered, but too low for anyone to hear.

'That's enough, Mother,' Ma said. 'I suppose the boy can go to the fair, once in a way, if he's a mind to – though I'd sooner see him in better company. Here, I've got a toasted split for you! Where are your teeth?'

And the matter was settled.

After a moment or two, Da lit up his pipe.

'Aw, come on, Carrie!' Dolly said. 'You'd love it, you know you would. Here we are, with Miss Limmon gone off to St Just, the weather setting in fine, and Mrs Tucker saying she'll give us an hour to go up to the fair, Saturday – and what do you do? Sit here with a face like a poker and say you won't go. And your friend Katie Warren wanting to come with us, and all.'

Carrie's scowl deepened. It was true, she wanted to go to the fair. Half the town would be there, and Mrs Tucker was very good about letting them work extra, and giving them time off in lieu – she would never have done it if Old Button-eyes had been home.

Besides, there was Katie. Carrie hadn't seen her for weeks – Katie was working up at Trevarnon House with her sister; real gentry, the family was. Katie's half-day was Monday, so it was rare that she and Carrie could get together, but when they did it was like old times. Katie would chatter on about Mrs Trevarnon, with her headaches and her vapours, and Carrie would fold her hands and purse her lips and do an impersonation of Miss Limmon until Katie cried with laughter.

'Get on with you,' Katie would say, wiping the tears of mirth from her eyes. 'She's never as bad as that!'

'She is too,' Carrie declared stoutly. 'Worse! And you should see her these days before she goes off to St Just. Always half hoping that Miss Adeline's cousin will be in port and come to supper. My dear life, you never saw the like! Tries on every dress in her cupboard, and nothing suits! Stands in front of the mirror and puts them all on, in turn, with a face to match.' Carrie clasped her hands, raised her eyebrows and drew her mouth into a terrible simper. ' "How do I look, girl?" Only, of course, if I told her, I'd be halfway to Penvarris before you could say "knife".'

'Carrie!' Katie said, through her giggles. 'You are *wicked*! I daresay the poor woman is only hoping for a husband. Then she'd be married and gone – I should have thought that would have pleased you.'

'Well, it wouldn't then. Might be the Frenchman I used to know,'

Carrie said. She was fond of 'Mr Dinosaur', the thought of him gave her a warm feeling even now, and the idea of him marrying Miss Limmon made her heart give an unpleasant little thump. 'He's too nice for her, by a streak.'

'Oh, yes, your Frenchman. I'd forgotten him. Sweet on him, weren't you?'

'Don't be so daft!' Carrie said fiercely. 'Only you wouldn't wish Old Lemon-pips on Mr Kruger himself! You know, last time she went to Miss Adeline's I found her splashing attar of roses on her camisole before I packed it. At her age, too. And I'll swear she's planning to buy a bust-bodice. I saw the catalogues in her bedroom. It's unnatural, that's what it is.'

'Poor Miss Limmon,' Katie said.

'Poor Miss Limmon, my eye!' Carrie retorted. 'Poor Frenchman, more like. She's got her hooks out for him, more than he's setting out to catch mackerel.'

'Well, there's more to landing a fish than baiting the hook,' Katie said, and there the matter rested. But that was the thing about Katie, you could always talk to her. Carrie looked forward to their conversations.

'Well?' Dolly brought her back to the present. 'Don't just stand there looking like a thunderclap. What do you say? Are you coming to the fair, or not?'

Carrie sighed. 'You know how it is, Dolly. It seems wicked somehow, spending money on fairs, when I'm trying to save up for a doctor's fee for Father.'

Dolly nodded. 'Yes, I know, Carrie my handsome. Don't you take any notice of my fooling. Though I found sixpence on the street yesterday – pennies from heaven, Tommy says – so if you do want to come, you can have a penny or two, and welcome. Do you good, an hour at the fair. You're looking proper peaky, worrying about your father, and all.'

'Well, I'll see,' Carrie said, flashing her friend a grateful smile. 'I'm going home this afternoon, so I'll see how things are. Maybe a bit of an outing would do me good, at that.'

But when the afternoon came, she did not go straight to Penvarris. Instead, she found herself again in Newlyn, outside the little varnished door, hesitating.

This time, Rawlings did not appear. Not until she tapped on the door, and called softly, 'Mr Rawlings, are you there?'

He did come downstairs then, wearing the stained smock she had seen the week before. It was covered in smears of paint, and looked if anything, grubbier than ever. Oddly, though, the smock made him look suddenly like a proper artist, and she was overwhelmed with shyness.

'Well?' he said, peering at her over his spectacles. 'You called for me, I think?'

'I wanted to see the picture,' Carrie said, flushing. 'You said perhaps I should call back . . .'

'The picture?' He was looking at her as if she were a total stranger, and then suddenly he smiled. 'Ah yes – the picture. The street scene. That neck and shoulders – I remember. Come in, come in – don't stand there cluttering the street.' And he was away up the stairs and into the studio.

The picture was standing on an easel – like a school blackboard, Carrie thought. But what was in the picture took her breath away. There was the scene, as before, but now in the foreground there was a young woman leaning against a railing. There was a battered straw hat on her head, a tattered shawl over her shoulders, and a wicker basket on her arm. But what made Carrie catch her breath was the vision of herself – the slender arms and shoulders, the neat waist, the slight curve of the breasts, the long legs suggested under the clinging folds of the skirt. And the face, lively, intelligent, cheerful, yet with a suspicion of pain and worry about the dark eyes and the line of the mouth. You could see already, in the girl, the worn woman she might become. And yet . . .

'Beautiful,' Carrie said in wonder. The girl, she meant, though the painting was fine too.

Rawlings misconstrued her. 'Yes, I'm quite pleased with it. Light's good, in that corner. Though finding a buyer, that is a different thing. Now – tea, will you have?' He began scrabbling behind canvases and under furniture in a hunt, Carrie supposed, for his teapot.

'No, thank you,' she said hurriedly. 'I must get home. My father is ill.'

He looked at her for a moment, and then took off his spectacles and rubbed them thoughtfully, avoiding her eyes. 'Ah, yes. I recall. Well, about that other matter – the life class. If you did decide to think about it, I should like very much to paint you. You have good shoulders. I could go, perhaps, as high as a guinea?'

A guinea? That would pay for a doctor's call. She was trembling, but she faced him squarely. 'A guinea then, and I'll do it.'

'Splendid,' Rawlings said. 'I shall expect you then. Today week. Now, are you sure about that tea? The lady of the house makes the most splendid rock-cakes.'

Carrie made her escape. A whole guinea! And somehow, having seen that painting, she felt a little better about the prospect. She went into the town and spent her florin on some best beef and a bottle of iron tonic and strengthening medicine.

Mother was delighted, although she raised her eyebrows when she saw the packages. 'However did you . . . ?'

'I earned it,' Carrie said simply. 'I posed for an artist down Newlyn – a friend of Dolly's, he was.' That was stretching the truth a bit, but Mother looked relieved. 'Not a bit what you think,' Carrie went on, forcing the beef through a wire-sieve to make father's beef-tea. 'Tea and rock-cakes and a bowler hat. I'll take you down and show you the painting, if you like. Group of people, shopping. He's good, too, Mr Rawlings.'

And Mother said, 'Well, this tea'll do your father good and no mistake. And if I can get a drop of that strengthening medicine down him, perhaps we can build him up a bit. He seemed a bit better to me, this morning – moved himself on the pillow and ate a bit of mashed turnip.'

It seemed to Carrie, sitting beside the bed while her father drifted painfully between sleep and wakefulness, that she too could read the signs of hope. Perhaps, after all, she might go to the fair.

CHAPTER SIX

Saturday was fine, a bright cloudless June day. Ernie could hardly wait for the shift to finish, so that he could get up to the dry to wash and change. He had bought a new shirt and cap from the tally-shop, and very smart he felt as he made his way to the station.

Vince was late. So late that Ernie could hear the distant whistle of the train, and was beginning to think that he would have to go to the fair alone, before Vince finally came darting onto the platform.

He made no apology. Ernie was already put out, and the sight of what Vince had chosen to wear did nothing to improve his mood: a mustard waistcoat, a red silk neckerchief, and a jaunty pork pie hat with a feather. It put Ernie's new finery into the shade.

'Folks'll see you coming, and no mistake,' he grumbled as they crowded into the third-class compartment, and found an inch of wooden bench between a fat woman with a hen in a basket, and a thin, wooden, sour-faced man with a toothbrush moustache.

'Like it, do you? I put it on to impress Mr Morrison.' Vince wasn't at all apologetic. 'And there's that girl too. I'm near certain she'll be at the fair, 'cause I talked to the boy down the greengrocer's who's walking out with her friend. Seen her once or twice, I have, and I know she's got an eye for me – though she lets on that she hasn't. Not pretty, exactly, but there's something about her – all spark and spirit. Good figure too.'

Ernie scowled. He had seen Vince with his women before, and he didn't care for it – taking a back seat while Vince preened and leered. Though the girls seemed to like it, on the whole.

'Well, how you going to impress Morrison, then?' he said sourly. 'He isn't likely to turn up at the fair is he, gentleman like that?'

Vince looked triumphant. 'No,' he said, 'but he wrote Feyther to say he'd meet the train and give us tea before we went up to the fair. Heard about you, he has, and wants to meet you. Won't that be something?'

Ernie's scowl deepened. It was bad enough with Vince dressed up like a turkey-cock, without being obliged to spend a sunny afternoon on your best behaviour drinking tea with some fancy gentleman who thought he was doing you a favour.

But in fact, when it came to it, he quite enjoyed himself. Mr Morrison had hired a cab to meet them, and when they got off at Penzance, and heard the cry of 'Hansom waiting for Mr Whittaker and Mr Clarance!' Ernie felt his ears turn quite pink with pride. It was the first time he had ever ridden in a hansom cab – and the first time anyone had ever called him 'Mr Clarance' besides. Crowds of people were staring at them, as they climbed up, and he tried to sit up very straight and look as if it were an everyday occurrence. Even when Vince leaned over and whispered, 'Hansom is as hansom does!' he refused to be amused by his nonsense, and he arrived at Mr Morrison's residence in a sober and sensible frame of mind.

There was a small, fat man waiting to greet them, immaculate in a black suit and high collar. Ernie was ready to shake his hand and say how pleased he was to be there, but the man withered him with a glance and said, 'I am the butler, sir. If you wait here, I will tell Mr Morrison you are here.'

He disappeared, taking Ernie's new cap. 'Here,' Ernie said, 'cost me one and six, that cap. He'd better bring it back.'

'Don't be wet,' Vince said. 'What would Mr Morrison want with your old cap?'

' 'Tisn't old!' Ernie said sullenly, but when Mr Morrison came he saw what Vince meant. Mr Morrison was even smaller and fatter than the butler, and his little round pink face was creased into an enormous smile. But even to Ernie's untutored eye the cut and cloth of his afternoon suit spoke of bespoke shops and tailors and bills counted in guineas.

'Ah,' Mr Morrison said, as though he were genuinely glad to see them, 'you found us then. Capital! Capital! In here, I think.' He led the way into a room which seemed to Ernie to be full of every book that was ever printed in the whole history of mankind. They lined the walls and covered the leather-topped desk and stood in dusty piles on every windowsill and table. The room smelt of books, and of cigars.

'Make yourselves at home,' Mr Morrison said, gesturing vaguely to a pair of green buttoned-leather armchairs either side of the fireplace. 'Rogers – some tea for the gentlemen. Sandwiches, I rather think, and muffins too, perhaps.'

Muffins. A great plateful, toasted and buttered. Three kinds of sandwiches and a huge platter of plain cake besides. No wonder Mr Morrison was as round as a butter-tub, Ernie thought, if he ate tea on this scale every afternoon. Vince caught his eye, and winked, grinning like a magician who has just produced a rabbit from his waistcoat pocket.

But Mr Morrison wasn't eating. He had taken a muffin, but he was more interested in talking, or rather, in asking questions. He wanted to know everything about Ernie's new job, all about the claypit, the hours, the pay – even the safety of the place. Ernie was a little anxious about answering. It reminded him uncomfortably of a conversation he had once had with a policeman on the subject of knocking on doors in Bugle and then running away. Some of this seemingly innocent information, he thought, might easily be filed away and used against him in some completely unforeseen way.

But Vince seemed happy enough, prattling about the Borglaise pit. Though to hear him talk, Ernie thought, you'd hardly recognise the place. To hear Vince tell it, the whole thing was nothing but misery; all mud and dust, and standing up to your armpits in freezing water. He was sorely tempted to butt in. There was some pleasure in it, after all – they were a good bunch down at the Borglaise's (excepting Dick Clarance of course), and there was such a thing as pride in the job – knowing you'd done a good day's work, or that the clay from your pit was the finest in the district, and made the best china, too. A sight better than Little Roads, any rate.

' 'Tisn't that bad,' he said at last, when he could bear it no longer.

'I don't know how he can say that,' Vince declared. 'Turned off by his own cousin for asking for a rise, and him with a father lost an arm claying, too.'

'Did he, by Jove?' Mr Morrison said. He seemed to lose interest in Vince, then, and Ernie found himself the centre of a whole host of uncomfortable questions. Mr Morrison seemed to want to know everything about Da – as though he were one of the freak-shows up the fair, Ernie thought to himself.

'Well,' he said suddenly. 'That's enough about that. We ought to get to the fair, any road.'

It sounded awfully rude, even in his own ears, but Mr Morrison only said, 'Dear me, yes. Whatever am I thinking of? A working man's leisure is a precious thing. But you will, won't you, think of joining the Party? Or the Union, at least?'

'The Party?' Ernie was genuinely confused.

'The Independent Labour Party,' Mr Morrison said earnestly. 'It was founded last year. Only a small start, but there are good people in the movement. Get a candidate into Parliament, you see – represent the working man.'

'Into Parliament?'

'That's it!' Mr Morrison said. 'Universal suffrage – that's what this country needs.'

Ernie had never heard of 'suffrage' – it didn't sound very pleasant – but Vince said, 'Universal? You mean, women and everything?'

'We'll see it,' Mr Morrison said, with enthusiasm. 'You mark my words. Fifty years or so, they'll all have the vote. But now, I mustn't keep you gentlemen from your fairing. Tell your father I'll write him, Vincent – I've got some literature he should read. And as for you, Mr Clarance, I shan't forget your story in a hurry.' He wrung Ernie's hand. 'Uncommonly glad to meet you. Uncommonly glad!'

Ernie was uncommonly glad to be out of the house and walking up the hill towards the field where the fair was pitched. You could hear it a mile away; chatter, laughter, shouting, music and the showmen's cries.

'Come on then,' he said to Vince. 'Time's getting on.'

It was Vince's turn to glower. 'We'd have had a sight more time if you hadn't decided to witter on all afternoon about your da and his blessed accident. Don't know why you thought Mr Morrison wanted to hear all that!'

So Vince was jealous! Ernie knew enough to recognise the signs. He said, 'Had to keep talking, didn't I? Only way I could drag his eyes away from that waistcoat.'

That did the trick. Vince grinned. 'Reckon the girls will take a tumble to it, do you?'

'Soon know,' Ernie said. 'There are enough girls round here, for heaven's sake. There's enough of everything!'

There was too. Hurdy-gurdy men with monkeys in little Turkish hats and felt waistcoats, grinning on the ends of their strings and shaking their tin cups for pennies; booths where you could pay a penny to see the fattest lady in the world, or the bearded woman, or the amazing seven-legged cow; wrestling rings and coconut shies; bands and drummers; stilt-walkers and tumblers, jugglers, acrobats and elephant rides; and people everywhere crying their wares – flowers, fancy biscuits, pills, potions and lollipops.

'Grand, isn't it?' Ernie said in delight.

'She is, at any rate,' Vince said, nodding his head towards a group of girls huddled around the coconut shy. 'That's her. The one in the blue skirt, she's mine. A bit skinny, but a good-looker. You can have the curly-headed one. The little one's spoken for already.' He shouldered his way through the crowd to where the girls were standing.

Ernie followed reluctantly. You never knew what Vince would do in this mood.

'Hello, ladies,' Vince said, sweeping off his pork-pie with a flourish. 'Looking for someone to win you a coconut?' He put his hand, daring, on the girls' shoulders.

The curly-haired girl brushed it away in disgust. 'We don't even know you!' she said sharply.

She was pretty. And the other girl, too – a bit skinny, as Vince had said, but round in the right places, with a pair of flashing brown eyes.

'*I* know him,' the brown-eyed girl said. 'Or I've seen him, at least. Too often for my liking.'

'There you are,' Vince said, positioning himself so that the girls could not move past him. 'She does know me. I'm Vince Whittaker, from St Blurzey, and this is my friend, Ernie Clarance. Besides, I know Tommy, don't I, lad?'

A boy in a cloth cap, who was holding three wooden balls ready to throw at the coconuts, flushed and said, 'I suppose,' a little sheepishly.

The girl took a step back, defensive, and as she did so Ernie caught her glance. A little shock of recognition went through him. 'I know you too!' he blurted, before he had time to think. The girls, and Vince stared at him in surprise. 'At least, I met you – ran into you more like, one day in Newlyn fishmarket. Pouring with rain it was!'

The dark eyes flickered into the suspicion of a smile. 'So you did, too – not looking where you were going?'

'Course he was looking. Any man worth his salt would be glad to bump into you,' Vince said loudly.

Ernie ignored him. 'I'll make it up to you,' he said. He swallowed hard and said suddenly, 'I'll try and win you a coconut.'

She nodded, moving away from Vince and closer to his side. It gave him a real thrill of triumph, and he took his place in the queue. It cost him a sixpence, but at last the wooden ball dislodged the coconut from its stand and she claimed it triumphantly. Vince won a coconut second ball, but nobody paid any attention. It was Ernie from whom she took the coconut, with a smile. It was Ernie she asked a little later to help her over a muddy patch, and he offered her his arm proudly. Vince looked daggers, but when the muddy patch was over Ernie did not withdraw his arm, and she did not relinquish it. She was called Carrie, she explained, and this was her friend Katie, and the boy in the cap and his girl were Tommy and Dolly, who were going to be married.

And it was Ernie who walked her home when she decided that she must go over to Penvarris before it got too late: while Katie and Dolly threw hoops at the hoop-la, and Vince scowled and glowered and learned more about seine-fishing from Tommy Williams than he ever wanted to know.

'It's forward of me to let you walk me home, I know it is,' Carrie said, as they began to walk, 'and you with a train to catch and all. But I'd be glad of the company and no mistake – that friend of yours would be all over me if I let him, and my father's proper poorly, besides.'

He let her talk, sensing that his presence calmed her. It pleased and excited him, this walk in the late afternoon sun with a lively, lovely girl: and he felt proud, hoping that people noticed him. He was always awkward with girls, though he sometimes copied things that he heard Vince say – but this Carrie didn't care for Vince, that was clear, so he said nothing at all, just listened, and she seemed to like it.

When they got to the Terrace her mother was at the gate, watching for her arrival, and he was forced to introduce himself, blushing scarlet.

Mrs Tremble was kindly. 'It's good of you, to walk so far with Carrie. Have a cup of tea at least, before you go.' And he accepted, though the vision of Vince fuming at the station danced before his eyes. Well, Vince would have left him in an instant for a pretty girl, he told himself, and the tea tasted sweeter for the thought.

'Ernie can't stay long,' Carrie said. 'He walked me home because that Vince was pestering me. Won me this coconut off the shy. He's got to be back by eight, mind, to catch his train.'

The woman nodded at him. 'Some nice of you to come at all, all this way. Before you go, though, see can you open this here nut with an axe, I haven't got the strength these days, and Carrie'll want to go in to see her father. And you'll be some pleased with what you find, Carrie, I know.'

Carrie stopped, her hand on the door-knob. 'How's that then?'

Mrs Tremble smiled. 'He's some lot better this evening. Reckon it's that strengthening medicine you brought him. Managed to get a spoonful or two down him, and it's done him a power of good. You see for yourself.'

Carrie went, but she returned a moment later. 'Wants to see you, Ernie.' Her eyes were beseeching. 'I'm sorry to ask you, but it would mean a lot to him. He's that ill, you see, and since you've walked me home . . .' She tailed off.

Ernie nodded. He understood. Her father wanted to see the man she had brought home. Thought he was walking out with her, more than likely. It gave him a thrill of pleasure. Walking out with a girl – that would be something to tell them up at Little Roads, wouldn't it! 'Course I'll come,' he said gruffly.

How anyone could think the man in the bed was 'better' he couldn't imagine. The lips were blue, and the hands resting on the patchwork counterpane were purple-tipped, as though they were bruised with cold. The chest was puffed out like a pigeon's, and the rest of the body shrivelled to nothingness. But the man was awake, and there was a spot of colour on the waxen cheeks.

'This is Ernie, Father.'

The strained face gave a little nod in salute. 'Well Carrie, my handsome!' The voice was a whisper, flecked with blood. 'What you want to go and pick a clayer for?' The words were an effort, so that Ernie longed to breathe for him, but the eyes were laughing. 'Why not a tinner – proper job?' The man turned his head painfully towards Ernie. 'I'm sorry I aren't up to getting up to greet you today – got a bit of a chest.'

Ernie muttered, 'Some other time,' and then realised what he had said.

But Carrie didn't seem to mind. She looked at him gratefully, and said to her father, 'Yes, I'll have to bring him home again, shan't I, and let you look him over, see if he's fit?'

She probably meant it as a joke, but the sick man's hand sought hers and closed over it with unexpected strength. 'Yes. You do that, my handsome. I'd like that. I'll put on my clothes and meet him proper. You promise me now.'

The man would never wear his clothes again, even Ernie could see that, but Carrie nodded and said 'Promise' in a voice that was full of tears.

Ernie cleared his throat and made an excuse to go out to 'see after that coconut', and after a moment she followed him. 'He's asleep,' she said. 'Thank you for doing that.'

'Glad to,' he said, and stood dangling his cap. After a minute he plucked up courage to say, 'Can I really see you again?'

And she nodded. Nodded! All the way to Penzance, he was hugging the memory to himself. Taken home, and met the family. He was walking out, and with a real nice girl too.

Even Vince, fuming and fretting on the platform, could not spoil his joy. And when, walking home into St Blurzey in the moonlight, Vince said, 'Too much spirit for a woman, that one. Can't see what you see in her,' Ernie knew, with a wonderful certainty, that it had been the best day of his life.

Philippe looked after the retreating figures and frowned. Carrie and a young man. Well, it was his own fault. He didn't have to come here. Granted he was going to see Adeline, and that took him to St Just as it always did, but even then, there was no need at all to walk those miles; she would have sent the carriage and welcome.

But he had preferred to walk, and the long way too, over the cliff paths through Penvarris. He had to face the fact: he still did it in the secret hope of catching sight of Carrie. Never talked to her, of course, but looked out for her all the same. And now he had seen her. Well, it served him right.

Of course she would have young men flocking around her. It was natural. Why, then, did he feel so saddened, watching her go down the path, deep in conversation with that gangling young man with the foolish, amiable smile?

Philippe had let them, for once, walk right up to him. Ready to speak, this time – even her father could not object to his passing the time of day with Carrie when she was walking home with a young man. He had stood on a rock not ten feet from the path – and she had been so engrossed in talking that she had not even glanced at him.

Her father was right. A man is better in his own place. The lad was about her own age. Her own background, too, from the look of him. And they seemed happy enough together. The boy adored her – that was clear enough. And she had been smiling at him warmly, as though he were the Prince of Wales himself, instead of an awkward youth with patched boots and a shabby, ill-fitting suit. Philippe had thought of coming down and speaking to her, but it might have caused embarrassment. In his own smart jacket and cravat he was clearly a gentleman, and she might not have welcomed that.

But Carrie had not even noticed that there was a gentleman to see, she was so rapt in the company of that young, grinning fool – who was too young and too foolish to know the value of what he had. The same man who was handing her lightly over the stile at the bottom of the hill. Whistling, too. Pleased with himself, as well he might be.

Philippe gave himself a little shake. This was ridiculous. He was jealous. Jealous! Of a clumsy oaf in a cloth cap, for walking along the cliffs with Carrie. He could hardly expect the girl to live like a nun for the rest of her life, just so that he could stand at a distance and admire.

It was foolish. He would not come this way again. If he came to see Adeline he would take the carriage. Or hire a horse. Take the main road, not the path over the clifftops. He would not loiter as he was doing now.

He turned, and strode off purposefully towards St Just. It seemed, suddenly, a long, lonely way, and he was glad to arrive at Trezayle house and bury himself in plans for the estate, and the company at dinner. Even Miss Limmon, asking about his 'plans for his little cottage' in that exaggeratedly roguish way which had begun secretly to exasperate him, was preferable, tonight, to his own thoughts.

After dinner, he consented to stay a little later than usual, and play cards with the ladies. Adeline was delighted, and Miss Limmon was flattered. He did not care. He felt, in some obscure way, that it served Carrie right. After all she was a mere girl. It as nothing to him if she walked home with a young man. Nothing to him at all.

On Thursday evening Carrie took the other path to Penvarris. It was longer, steeper, a harder walk, but she could not bear that anyone should see her. Anybody looking at her, she thought, would guess at once.

She tried to put it out of her mind, to concentrate on the flowers, the sea-birds, the rise and fall of the waves, but it was no use. Her brain refused to focus. All she could see was that dreadful hour in the studio at Newlyn.

Fred Rawlings had been very nice to her. 'Over there, Carrie love, by the washstand. I've put it there in the light. Slip off your things when you're ready. I want you brushing your hair.' And he had turned away, to busy himself with brushes and palettes as though it were the most natural thing in the world to ask a girl to 'slip off her things'.

Her throat went dry and her fingers felt as big as sausages, fumbling at hooks and laces. She took off her blouse and bodice, and then, with trembling hands, her camisole.

Fred Rawlings raised his head and looked at her.

'No!' she cried, and leaned forward, pressing her hands to her chest. 'No! Not my skirt, no I can't.'

There was a long silence. Mr Rawlings said, 'That's all right, Carrie. That's very nice as it is. I've got your neck and shoulders, that's what I wanted. Now, can you come forward a bit, into the light, and pick up the brush, so.' He stepped forward and handed her the heavy antique hairbrush, so that she was obliged to stretch out one hand to take it, though she kept the other one pressed to her.

'Brush your hair,' he said, softly insistent.

Trembling, she lifted the brush, keeping the other hand across her, trying vainly to cover that intimate, shaming pink at the tip of her breasts. She could not look at him, but turned her head so that her hair came down between them, like a curtain, shading her face.

'Wonderful!' Rawlings said. 'That's just the mood. Innocent, yet provocative. Hold it. Don't move.'

And that was it. A whole, exposed, shaming and humiliating hour of it with a man gazing at her nakedness – yet he was detached, as though she were an object, a thing, without feeling or emotion. When it was over her eyes were red from silent weeping, and her flesh flinched as she drew on her camisole, as though her shame had been branded on her with hot irons.

Rawlings seemed unconcerned. 'Just the thing!' he said. 'Wonderful skin tones, just there as the sunlight struck it. Now then, did we have some tea?'

She could no more have drunk it than sipped hemlock, and as soon as he allowed her she slipped away, the guinea burning like a hot coal in her pocket. At least, she told herself fiercely, the guinea meant a doctor. And if a dose of strengthening medicine had done so much, what might not a doctor do?

At the Terrace the front door was open, and the house was full of the smell of fresh bread. The passage, too, had been scrubbed and polished. Father's door was shut, and she tiptoed past it, and out into the kitchen. There was a fresh loaf on the table and a kettle bobbed on the hearth. Her mother was in the garden, beating mats on the line.

She went out. 'Mother?'

The woman at the line turned, the carpet beater in her hand, but she did not stop. Instead she went on thumping the carpet, mechanical, her eyes unseeing, her face a blank.

In that one dreadful moment, Carrie understood.

'He's . . . gone, then?'

Her mother stood, not speaking, but the thumping ceased, and after a little a trembling began, until the carpet beater dropped to the ground and the woman stood shaking, with the tears coursing down her face.

Carrie sat down, suddenly, on the doorstep. Grief hit her like a cold wind. Her mother moved towards her and they clung together, Carrie with her arms around her mother's knees, Cissie with her hand stroking her daughter's hair. For a long time neither spoke.

Then Mother pulled away. 'He just . . . stopped,' she said, as if in wonder. 'This afternoon. I was there, just getting him a drink. He looked at me, and said, "She'll do!" and then, he just stopped. Like a clock. One minute he was there, and the next minute he wasn't. Just like that. I couldn't . . . I didn't know . . . I just kept going, doing things, until you got home.'

And Carrie, feeling the guinea burning into her soul, thought of what she had been doing while her mother polished and grieved. She held her mother tight, and said nothing, although she thought her heart would break.

Later, up in Penvarris Chapel the dust-motes danced in the silent sun, as though nothing at all had happened. Carrie went out of the chapel, and slammed the door.

PART THREE : 1902–5

CHAPTER ONE

Albert Villas was not the same without Dolly. She left, the first week in January 1902, to become Mrs Tommy Williams. Mrs Tucker would have kept her on and let her come in as a daily, but Dolly said no, they were going to move into his mother's back bedroom down in Newlyn until they could afford a place of their own, and she would be wanted to help with the fish.

The wedding was arranged for a Thursday – on purpose, because it was Carrie's half-day, and Mrs Tucker had agreed that she could take it as usual, though Miss Limmon pursed her lips and grumbled that girls took advantage, these days – leaving them all afternoon without proper help in the house, and the very day Dolly was leaving, too!

So, as soon as lunch was cleared away, Carrie went up to change. The room looked achingly bare and lonely – Tommy had come up early that morning with Mr Tregorran's fruit-barrow, and taken Dolly's things. Carrie opened her drawer and took out the bolster-case she had been secretly sewing. It wasn't a lot of present, but Dolly would understand.

The Tuckers had been good – Mr Tucker had sent the bride off with an extra week's pay in her pocket, and Mrs Tucker had looked out a good bonnet and gloves for the wedding outfit. Even Miss Limmon had presented her with a hand-made pot-holder, bought specially at a sale of work.

Dolly looked proud as punch at the service, though the spring bonnet and lace gloves assorted oddly with the January weather, and with her good serge Sunday suit, knitted stockings and black boots. Still, she was obviously pleased with herself and with her new husband, and was delighted to preside over the homely wedding breakfast of salt fish, new bread and hevva cake spread out in the Williams' best parlour. Dressed pilchards were an odd choice for a feast, Carrie thought, but the Williams lived so close to the fish-parlour that everything, even the hevva cake, had a finny taste to it, so perhaps it was wise, after all.

The odour of scales and sea-water hung over everything. In fact, when old Mrs Williams, a huge, hearty woman with a broad grin, and a clay pipe clamped continually in it, came over with her teapot and tried to talk to Carrie, she smelt so strongly of fish-oil that Carrie was obliged to plead a headache, and leave the celebrations early.

Poor Dolly, she thought, as she made her way to Penvarris. Mother's little house on the Terrace seemed so fresh and cheery by comparison, though even that was bleaker now. Even with the cleaning work which Miss Maythorne had organised for her it was always a struggle to pay the rent, and these days there was often furze rather than coals in the fire, the front room was left unused to save heating, and the gifts of pork, eggs and butter which Mother got for acting as midwife to women on the Terrace were an important part of the household economy.

If the rest of the winter was long and hard, Mother was in for a struggle. Perhaps Miss Maythorne would think of having 'Hoskins' back, as a lady's maid. The thought of Miss Maythorne reminded Carrie of the bonnet. Poor Dolly, trying to protect her finery from the rain, by putting her jacket over her bonnet to save the roses, and soaking her best blouse in the process. And to think that once she herself had left a good bonnet in the hedge for a French sailor-boy to play chuck-stones at. It made her blush to think of it. Or, something about the recollection brought the colour to her cheeks.

Supposing it did turn out to be her Frenchman who was Miss Adeline's cousin? What if Dolly was right about the name? No, couldn't be. Dino . . . whatever it was, didn't sound anything like 'Trezayle'. Anyway, Miss Adeline's cousin had a smuggler for a grandfather and had been to Cornwall no end of times, so Old Lemon-pips said, but Mr Dinosaur's family had a farm, and he had not been on the cliffs for ages.

He'd have made a good smuggler, though. The way he had dashed in to defend her over that bonnet. Such a shocking, clever thing to do. Ernie would never have thought of such a thing. Wouldn't have the gumption, she thought with a grin. Even now, she never had told Mother the truth of it.

'Carrie, my lover! What are you looking so pleased with yourself about?' It was Mother, halfway up the path to meet her, and Carrie had to tell her, in glowing detail, all the events of Dolly's wedding.

'Bless the girl,' Mother said, producing hevva cake which tasted, mercifully, of fruit and spices and flour. 'You'll miss her, though.'

And Carrie found that she did. There was a new maid, of course; Dolly's sister, sent up to take her place soon after. She was a small, timid girl, just thirteen, and to Carrie, who would be sixteen in the autumn, she seemed a mere baby. She was called Ellaline (after the actress, as she explained proudly) but everybody called her Ellie, except Miss Limmon, who just said 'Dolly' as though there had never been any change at all.

Ellie was sandy-haired and pale, so nervous that she lived in a perpetual fright, even of poor Mrs Tucker, who tried to be kind to her. As for Miss Limmon, the mere sight of her approaching was enough to make Ellie drop the sugar-bowl, or scatter the toast on the carpet, butter-side down. More than once, when Carrie went up to the attic bedroom, it was to find Ellie buried under the bedclothes, sobbing into the pillows. Carrie tried sympathy, but that made it worse, and she soon found that the only solution was to sit on her bed, purse her lips and do imitations of Old Button-eyes until even Ellie had to wipe her eyes and giggle. It won Carrie Ellie's undying devotion, but it was hard work. Yes, certainly, she missed Dolly.

They still met, of course. Not at Dolly's house, because it wasn't her own and there were already close on a dozen people living in it, but in the town sometimes, by arrangement. But even this was becoming less frequent. Dolly was wanted 'about the fish', and with one thing and another she was too busy to see Carrie often. Katie was busy too, up at Trevarnon, and their half-days rarely coincided, so they never seemed to meet either, these days. Carrie found herself more and more alone.

Perhaps that was why she began to look forward so much to seeing Ernie Clarance. He had taken to turning up in the lane, accidentally-on-purpose, on a Thursday afternoon once a month, when he could fix his shifts to suit. Mother liked him. Called him 'steady' – though no-one else on the Terrace thought much of a clayer – and always asked him to tea when Carrie allowed him to walk home to Penvarris with her.

He didn't have a lot to say, Ernie, but he was a good listener. He tutted sympathetically over Ellie, and Carrie's 'Miss-Lemon-pips' imitations made him laugh aloud, though he was (rather gratifyingly) a little shocked by them.

He was thoughtful, too. Good as gold in a thousand little ways. Didn't say a word about money being tight on the Terrace, but never came to see Mother without a little something to add to the tea-table: a few pickles, or a slice of bacon. He was earning good money of course – doing well as an engineer up at Little Roads – but even bacon-ends didn't grow on trees. And it must have cost him no end in train-fares, coming all that way. Meant a lot to her, his visits. And his letters. If he didn't come, he wrote:

not what you'd call love-letters, but better than that, in some ways. Real letters, full of news about his life, and all the things he had meant to say at their last meeting and forgot. She loved reading them, and answering them too, which she did shyly at first, but soon she was taking a wicked glee in describing Old Button-Eyes and her goings-on, knowing it would make him laugh.

Altogether, Carrie was beginning to find that Ernie was the brightest part of her life. But it was not until April, when Miss Adeline came to stay for her annual spring-cleaning holiday, that he started talking about marriage.

It was Vince who put him up to it. They had met, by accident, on the road outside Borglaise's – Vince on his way to the late shift, smart as all get-out in his waistcoat and breeches. It always amazed Ernie how Vince wore his good clothes to the pits: though he changed to his working-clothes in the 'dry' of course. Needed to, these days. Vince was working on the drying floors now, and Ernie knew what that meant. Floor hot enough to burn your feet through boots and all, if you didn't go out every now and then and stand in the water, and the rising heat turned your working clothes to rags in no time. Of course, Vince couldn't go home like that. But the dust on the road was enough to get into the cloth and ruin a good coat even by walking along it. Most men had a change of partly worn tidy clothes to walk to the pits in, but not Vince.

'Never know who might be looking,' he used to say, and Ernie always felt fair frumpy beside him.

This morning though, the contrast was worse than ever. Ernie was still in his mining clothes, caked from head to foot, and the wet clay seeping from between his soles and his uppers in little milky rivers. He had done no more than wash his face and hands before stumbling off homewards, unsteady and shaken. He was half ashamed to be seen.

Vince looked him up and down and gave a soft whistle of dismay. 'My dear Ernie, whatever on earth have you been about? Your face is whiter than your clay-boots. Look like you've seen a ghost.'

Ernie attempted a faint smile. 'Thought I was going to be one, a minute or two there,' he said, and heard his voice shake as he spoke. 'All ready to go out on the Bodmin Road, I was, and terrify the travellers.'

Everyone knew the story of the unknown man who occasionally appeared on the road to the moors. Appeared at the head of your horse, it was said, and seemed to be asking for water. But if you spoke it lifted its head, and there were only sightless sockets where the eyes should be, and seaweed in the beard. It was a tale to terrify naughty children, and Ernie himself felt a faint shudder at the thought of it.

But Vince didn't seem to notice. He only leaned forward intently in that way he had, which Ernie privately thought of as his 'union' look. He said, 'Ernie, my dear lad. What happened? Don't stand there looking as if you're about to fall over any minute, sit down on that stile and tell me all about it.'

So you can tell Mr Morrison, Ernie thought, but he needed to talk to someone. He sat down gratefully. 'Only goes to show,' he said, 'things aren't always what they're cracked up to be. Mr Joe, see – Bob Sanders's been on to him for years about having a new pump – short-shaft, and pump-head in the dry – and Mr Joe's been dead against it. Said the old one would see his time, and any road, tried ways were best. And then, before Christmas, he changed his tune. Found a short-shaft somewhere in a pit closing down, and here we were all of a sudden, nothing will do but we must have it installed and working before it's off the waggon, near enough.'

He looked at Vince, half-afraid of boring him, but Vince was nodding. 'And?'

Ernie warmed to his tale. 'Well, there I was, down this pit, see – clearing the shaft to fit the pump. Now, obvious, if we're putting in a pump, it's because there's water – and it's pouring in, near as fast as I can clear it; I'm sending up a kibble of muck, and then old Bob is letting down a barrel, and we take out the water before I can do no more. Inch or more every half-minute I should think – and that's just seepage down the bottom, let alone what's pouring in on you from on top and round the sides. So you can see we were working pretty sharpish – and further down we went, the worse it got, but we made twenty feet or more. There was only the two of us on it, me and Bob Sanders. He was up top, with the hoist and I was down the hole, see, ready to ride up in the kibble when we'd done – we didn't want it wider than we could help. Anyroad, I filled the kibble up with rubble and mud, and sent her up, and hollered out to Bob that we'd done it, near enough and when we'd cleared the next barrel of water, he could hoist me up. Anyhow, I sent up the kibble, and that was the end of it. No barrel, no bucket, nothing. Course, I hollered out, but nothing happened. No sign of Bob. Water up to my waist by this time and I didn't even have the bucket down to rattle the chain, nor nothing.'

While he told the story Ernie could feel the cold sweat breaking out again across his back and shoulders. Even Vince looked pale.

'Sides of the pit like glass, of course, and sheer as you like. Thought I was a goner there, for sure. Then somebody heard me and came over, and then of course they had me out in five minutes and I found out what happened.

Poor old Bob, lifting that last kibble, it was too much for his heart it seems. Dropped down right by the tram, he did – and of course, nobody saw him. And there I was up to my armpits and the water still rising.'

'Bob Sanders dropped down dead?' Vince was genuinely shocked.

'Dead as could be. Damn near took me with him,' Ernie said. 'Took me an hour to stop shaking. That's how Joe Borglaise came to let me off early.'

Vince grinned. 'Not all bad, then, is it? And I suppose you'll be made up a bit, now Bob Sanders's gone.'

Ernie hadn't considered that, but of course it was true. Mr Joe would be wanting an engineer. It was an alarming thought. Calculations on paper were one thing, making decisions about depths of shafts and angles of pumps in real life was quite another. Ernie had done only the simplest jobs so far, and even then he had relied heavily on Bob Sanders's expertise.

'My God,' he said aloud. 'Couldn't do it without him.'

Vince got up from the wall where he had been sitting. 'Course you could,' he said, brushing the dust from his good trousers. 'Mean a lot more pay, too, I'll be bound. You'll be able to go down to Penzance and see that skinny girl of yours every week if you want.'

Trust Vince. Never a good word to say for Carrie these days – you'd never guess it was him who had his eye on her first. But he was right! For the first time since that awful moment when he had seen his whole life flash before him, Ernie managed a grin. 'That would be one good thing,' he said, rising to his feet. 'Costs me a fortune in fares, she does. Keep meaning to bring her up to meet Ma and Linny May and all, but it's too far to ask her to come all on her own, and I can't afford two tickets.'

Vince went on brushing his trouser-legs. 'Don't know why you don't ask her to marry you, if you're that keen,' he said sourly. 'Might as well. She's tied you down good and proper as it is. Save you no end in train tickets, and you'll be earning enough with Bob Sanders gone. Room for the pair of you at home, isn't there, now your brothers have gone to Canada?'

Ernie sat down again, heavily. 'I could,' he said. The idea came to him like a bolt out of the blue. Somehow, although he had vaguely supposed that one day he might do something of the kind, it had never occurred to him as an actual physical reality. 'I could,' he said again. 'Couldn't I?'

Vince was staring at him, in a kind of exasperated perplexity. 'Well of course you *could*,' he said. 'But what would you want to do that for? Don't you want to get on, make something of yourself? I never meant you to take me serious. I was only saying – you're that wrapped up in her you might as well be wed. I'd have thought you wanted less to do with her, not more!'

Ernie began to feel rather foolish, but he said doggedly, 'I mean, if Mr Joe does make up my wages I could support a wife, couldn't I? Like a dignified man?' You could usually win Vince over, that way.

'Well,' Vince said, 'there's plenty of work at the pits. She could work at the linhay – same as your gran did, and your mother, too. If that's all you want for your wife.'

'She doesn't know anything about clay,' Ernie said. 'She's a tinner's daughter.'

'Well, she'll learn,' Vince said. 'There isn't that much to know. Scrape the rime off the blocks and stack them properly, doesn't take a university man to figure it out.' He managed to sound dismissive.

Ernie felt his ears turn red. 'Wouldn't take her long, anyhow,' he said stoutly. 'She's a clever girl, Carrie is. And if Linny May could do it, I'm darn sure she could. If she'd have me, of course. Think she would?'

Vince looked at him as though he still thought the whole idea was crazy. 'Well,' he said, 'there's only one way to find out. Perhaps you'd better talk it over with your folks, besides.'

He meant it as sarcasm, from his tone, but that is exactly what Ernie did, all the same. He told them next day, soon as ever Joe Borglaise had agreed to an extra shilling in wage-packet.

They were sitting in the kitchen, and Ma was stirring mushrooms into a bacon stew simmering on the fire. Da was talking about the state of the roads round Bugle way, and how the clay got in the muck so you couldn't get a good price even if you sold it to the farmers.

Ernie said suddenly, 'Thinking of getting wed. What you think of that, then?'

Ma stopped stirring, and Da sat still as stone, his half-filled pipe still wedged between his knees.

'That Carrie down to Penzance, is it?'

Ernie nodded.

'Well,' Da said, 'better bring her home here and let us look her over, hadn't you?'

Ma said, with a little laugh, 'And about time too. I was beginning to think we were never going to meet this girl of yours. I wanted to say something, but your da said wait, and you'd tell us in your own time. Well, you bring her home and welcome, lad. Hope she'll be good wife to you, that's all. When do you think to wed, then?'

Linny May gave a little snigger. 'Wed! Did you ever hear the like! Boy isn't old enough to wipe his own nose. Carried away by a pretty face, that's all he is, or a pretty ankle more like. Here he is, hardly two pennies to rub together, and already thinking about setting up a family. Be babies to feed before you can say "knife", you mark my words.'

'So there might,' Ma said, ladling soup with a faraway look in her eye. 'A girl. That'd be nice. Always wanted a girl.'

'Here, steady on,' Ernie said, feeling himself colour. 'I haven't even asked her yet, and here you are giving us a family! Wanted to talk to you about it first, of course. Anyway, she might not have me.'

'And why wouldn't she?' Linny May demanded, suddenly changing tack. 'Fine-looking boy like you. Good job, good prospects. Take after your grandfather, that's what. Real charmer with the ladies, he was.'

'Well, you let us know what she says. And bring her here to meet us, soon as you like,' Ma said. She gave Linny May some bread with her soup, and she had to put her teeth in, so no more was said.

'I'll ask her, then,' Ernie said, 'first chance I get.'

Carrie knew that something was up from the moment Ernie arrived. He looked peculiar, for one thing. Usually Ernie turned up in the lane on a Thursday in his good jacket and grey flannel trousers, but not today. He was sporting a flashy tweed coat and a mustard waistcoat, and he had abandoned his bowler for a little pork-pie hat with a feather. He looked like something off the music-halls.

'Whatever have you got on your head?' Carrie said. 'And that waistcoat? It's two sizes too big for you!'

Ernie flushed. 'Don't you like it then?' he said, and he sounded disappointed. 'Borrowed it specially.'

He sounded so miserable that Carrie regretted her words. 'It's all right, I suppose,' she said, choosing her words carefully. 'But you don't look like Ernie. I like you better how you are.'

He cheered up at this, and fell into step beside her, taking her basket. 'You're looking some pretty yourself, Carrie,' he said awkwardly.

She looked at him, surprised. He wasn't given to compliments, and her own dress was nothing special, just her old blue skirt turned and trimmed with new ribbons, and the same white blouse and shawl she always wore.

'No,' he said, catching the look, 'I mean it. Prettiest girl in Penzance you are – near enough, anyway. Here, you got much you want to do in the town this afternoon?'

There *was* something strange going on. Always when they met Carrie went down shopping – Thursday was market day, and most of the shops were closed, but there were good, cheap stalls, and some of the greengrocers, like Mr Tregorran, stayed open to sell fresh vegetables from their shopfronts.

'I was going to buy broken biscuits for Mother. Why, what's to do?'

Ernie squirmed and ran a finger around the inside of his collar. 'Only I thought we might go for a bit of a walk, instead of going straight home.'

She gazed at him. 'A bit of a walk? It's miles to Penvarris, how much walk do you want?'

He wouldn't meet her eyes, but gazed at the paving-stones. 'Thought we might go up through the woods – round Mount Misery and Creeping Lane. It's a nice day, look.'

Carrie glanced up at the sky. It was a uniform lowering grey, and a damp wind tugged at her skirts and bonnet as they walked. She laughed. 'Well, it's stopped raining, I'll say that!'

'Bluebells'll be out,' Ernie said.

Carrie stopped and gave him a long, sideways look. 'Well if you're so set on it, we'll go up the woods, then. Some sticky it'll be though, after this rain. But first I'll get these biscuits. Shouldn't take more than a minute or two.'

It took a little longer, in fact, because as they walked into the Greenmarket they met Dolly, laden with packages. She came bustling over to greet them. 'My life, Carrie it's good to see you. I've come up to get a few vegetables, and I was keeping an eye out for you. That's the trouble with fishing, plenty of food and oil, but nothing fresh without you buy it – and we can't grow much out the back of us, beyond a few potatoes, on account of the fish-parlour.'

The Williams' cottage was next door to the yard where they pressed and preserved the pilchards. It was an operation involving tons of salt, which leeched into the soil, and there was little room for gardens. The narrow street was a busy thoroughfare, with fishwomen lugging the fishbaskets in one door, and the carts waiting at the other for the finished product, hogsheads of pressed fish and barrels of fish-oil. In any case, Carrie thought, no self-respecting vegetable could grow in that stink. Already Dolly was beginning to carry it with her.

Dolly must have guessed her thoughts. 'Got muck on my boots from the pressing. Smells something chronic, doesn't it? Still, when you're in it, you don't notice so much. And the oil's some good for your skin. You look at my hands, soft as kid gloves, and all the women down the fish-yard says the same.'

What was the point, Carrie wondered, when the 'kid gloves' smelt of pilchards?

'Still,' Dolly went on, 'mustn't stand here gossiping. I've got work to do. And you two are going somewhere special – I can see! And, did I tell you, there's a house coming vacant just down the street from where we are? Tommy's on about getting it. It'll be a right struggle, but I'd be that pleased to have a place of my own. You come and see me some time, Carrie, and we'll put the kettle on. Mother would like to see you, too – you've been that good to Ellie. I don't know what she'd have done up Albert Villas without you, and she's some fond of you. Soon as we've moved, you come down and I'll show you round the fish-yard. Smells something awful, but it's interesting to see, *and* you'll get some fish to take home for your tea.'

'I'd be glad of some,' Carrie said, carefully avoiding any mention of the fish-parlour. A visit there held no attractions for her.

Dolly grinned. 'You can tell me all your news then!' she said, with a meaning look at Ernie's borrowed finery. She giggled. 'And I've got something to tell you, besides! Though perhaps you can guess – with us looking for a place of our own.'

'What did she mean by that?' Ernie said, when Dolly had gone.

'No idea,' Carrie said, although she had her suspicions. 'But she's been married a month or two, hasn't she?'

'Oh!' Ernie said, and turned scarlet. He lapsed into silence, and scarcely broke it until they had walked out to Newlyn and up the lane, through the wicket gate that led to the woods. It was an uncomfortable silence, although several times he looked at her and swallowed hard as though he wanted to say something.

At last he said it. They were under the canopy of the trees, and Carrie was trying to negotiate the path without getting her boots muddy. It was quite a game, trying to step from tree-root to tree-root without stepping in it, or getting your skirts in the mud. Ernie put out a hand to help her.

'I don't know what we're playing at, Ernie Clarance,' she grumbled, taking a long stride to the next dryish patch. 'Why couldn't we walk round the lanes like we belong to do, instead of coming in here in all this wet?'

Ernie caught her other hand. 'I thought . . .' he said, and fell silent again.

'Well?'

'I wondered if you might . . . well . . . I don't suppose you'd want to . . . ?'

'What, Ernie?' She was almost exasperated.

He looked up in surprise. 'Well, do like Dolly. You know, get wed.'

She was so astonished that she almost slipped into the puddle. 'Marry you?'

'Yes.'

'And that's why you borrowed that waistcoat and wanted to come walking in the woods?'

'Yes.'

She started to laugh. 'You silly thing! You could have asked me just as well wearing your ordinary clothes and walking a bit more comfortable.'

'So you will, then?' Now he had asked the question, he sounded more confident. 'I mean, we've been walking out for eighteen months. Stands to reason.'

That was true. She had in some part of her brain expected that one day he would ask her. Why then, did she suddenly feel the need to say, breathlessly, 'I don't know, Ernie. I don't know at all.'

He was looking hurt. 'You like me, don't you?'

She squeezed the hand which still held her own. 'Course I do – you know that! Wouldn't come walking with you if I didn't.'

'Well then!' he said. 'And I got a good job – getting a rise in wages too, so I can look after you proper. And we could still send a bit home to your mother, so you needn't worry about that.'

She pressed the hand again. 'It isn't that, Ernie – it's just, such a big step. And I haven't even met your family.'

'That's easy fixed,' he said. 'Next chance we get, you come up to St Austell, instead of me coming down here. They're dying to meet you.'

She hesitated. 'Well . . .' And then, seeing his face, 'Well, all right then, yes. I'll come and meet your ma and da.'

'And Linny May,' he said, making a face.

She laughed. 'And Linny May. I don't believe she's half so bad as you say. Yes, I'll come and meet them. But no promises, mind. I need time to think.'

But it was all he needed. 'You take all the time you need,' he said gruffly. 'Just so long as you come to the right answer in the end! And Carrie . . . ?'

'Yes?'

'While you're thinking, can I give you a kiss?'

Once again, she was unreasonably surprised. After all, he had just proposed marriage. She said, lightly, 'Suppose so. Give me something to think *about*, won't it?'

He put his arms around her then, and drew her to him. The kiss, when it came, was awkward, his lips dry and roughened against her cheek. He lifted a hand to her face, and she saw the white traceries of the clay, etched into his very skin, though his hands were clean and scrubbed. Strong, calloused, hard-working hands. She could do a lot worse.

Softened by tenderness, she turned her head to kiss the fingers, and he made to gather her in his arms again. She pushed him away, saying gently, 'Now! That's enough. Remember that I'm still only thinking. But you've said your say, and I've promised to come to St Burzey, so perhaps now we can walk home on the lanes like sensible people, before it comes on to rain.'

She was laughing, although she meant what she said. She needed to think. Ernie was a real nice boy. He loved her and she was genuinely fond of him – not in a romantic way, perhaps, but she was too much of a realist to expect fairy-tales. It would be a better marriage than many. But all the same, it was a big step. And once taken, there was no turning back.

She needed to think.

But Ernie's face as he capered back to the Terrace told her that he, at least, was already confident of her answer.

CHAPTER TWO

Philippe reined in the horse at the top of the rise and looked back down to the harbour. There she was, his new ship. His work with Adeline on the gardens and grounds had given him an interest in planning, and he had designed *Ploumenach* himself; the sleek and sinuous lines of her, the smell of her hull, the elegant tilt of her bow. *Ploumenach.* How beautiful she looked, breasting the slight swell, her paintwork and spars spanking new and sparkling in the April sunshine.

She had been completed swiftly, much faster than he had dared to hope. From the moment they had laid down the keel, she had built like a thing charmed. Each part had seemed to fit at once, exquisitely, planks to the ribs, deck to the hull. And from the moment the spars first took canvas, she went like a witch to the wind.

He was proud of her, proud of himself. He had become a man again, he thought, occupying himself with real things, new things, not dwelling on the past. Even at the *manoir* they had remarked on it, as he arranged the rebuilding of the dovecotes and the planting of artichokes for the Paris market instead of the usual 'brikoli', or cauliflower.

To prove it, now he had this ship: and had brought her to show Adeline, who, bless her, knew nothing of sea craft – but would be pleased and proud, because he was. And, true to his promise to himself, he was riding to see her on a rented horse, not loitering like a schoolboy on the cliffs of Penvarris. The cure, he told himself, was complete.

He turned the horse, and rode gently out onto the road towards St Just. There was little traffic, only a cart or two lumbering to market, and a pair of young gentlemen out for a leisurely canter. Otherwise, the road was quiet, and he drank in the spring afternoon, like a draught of good wine. He had come to love this land, so different from the country of his birth. A softness in the air, even the granite hedges blurred by the pastel muffler of bluebells and fern. The dust of the road was softened on his tongue by the scent of meadowsweet, and new-cut grass. Yes, life was good.

He leaned forward, trying to urge the horse to a canter. He was not a great horseman. He preferred the deep, insistent surges of the sea, not the unpredictable skittishness of a wayward animal; but he rode lightly, and the horse was obedient, acknowledging the authority of his hand on the reins. This was a sluggish animal, hired from a stable in town, a plodding, stolid creature with a will of its own, but even so, it picked up its gait at Philippe's urging, and shambled into a trot.

Philippe laughed, delighting in the motion, in the warmth of the horse's flesh under his thighs. A good ship, a fine day, and an easy ride along a pretty road with a good wine at the end of it – a man must be hard to please who could ask for more. And Adeline? He had brought the *Ploumenach* as soon as she could make passage, and there was little chance his letter would have arrived before him. He would surprise Adeline, with his presence, and with his ship. Would she be pleased to see him so, unannounced?

He turned up the drive that led to Adeline's house. It felt like a second home, now, this rugged granite building, and its new screen of rhododendrons, lit with a thousand pinkish blossoms, glowing with flower.

But the smile died on his lips. The picture he had so cheerfully painted for himself had vanished. The house lay open – every window bare and ajar, gaping like empty caves against the cliffs of the walls. And on the lawn, everywhere, huddled parcels of white, as if the last trump had sounded and the dead were assembling, heavy, lumpen and still.

A figure in white flickered in the doorway, and hesitated. 'Mr Philippe? Is that you?'

It was Maria, the maid, swathed in an enormous apron which covered her from head to foot. Even her head was engulfed in a huge, old fashioned mob-cap, and she carried the incongruous combination of a feather duster in one hand, and a pail of water in the other. Somehow, in all this, she looked older and frailer and more faded than ever.

Philippe slid down from the horse. 'My dear Maria. Is there something wrong?'

Her eyes followed his glance, took in the blank windows and the shrouded furniture scattering the lawn. She laughed, an unexpected high, brittle cackle of mirth.

'Wrong? I should say there is. Always is, this time of year. The woman has come about the distempering, and when she's here, there's nothing right about it. No matter what you do, you can't please her, and what we shall do with this here furniture if it comes to rain, the dear only knows!'

'Distemper?' He had some notion that he had heard of it. A disease was it, of dogs?

'Painting,' Maria said. 'Whitewash. Comes in here and takes the place over. Does a good job, mind. But, you'll be looking for Miss Adeline. She's not here. Goes away while Mrs Bluish does the whitewash. Always does. Staying with Miss Limmon and her sister, down to Penzance.'

'Gone away?' Philippe said, slowly, as though by savouring the words he could comprehend them better.

'Find her there, you would,' Maria said. 'Albert Villas, Victoria Road. You could come in here, but the place is that sticky with paint, there's nowhere to blow your nose.'

'Maria? Drat the girl, where's she to now?' A small, formidable woman in speckled black appeared from behind the house, wielding a paintbrush. 'Are you going to wash this hall down for me, or 'ave I to do it meself?' She scowled at Philippe, and he saw that the pattern of spots on her dress extended to her face and hands, and even to her hair, tied up in a headscarf. Mrs Bluish, evidently. ' 'Oo's this then?' she demanded.

Philippe was seized by the spirit of mischief, and even as Maria watched in astonishment, he took one of the paint-bedabbled hands and raised it to his lips. 'Philippe Diavezour, madame,' he said, bowing over it, like some foreign ambassador greeting a queen, and drawling his voice into a parody of his own accent. 'I salute your most excellent distemper.'

He swung himself up onto the horse. He would have liked to gallop away, but the animal consented only to a slow shamble. All the same, when he looked back he could see Mrs Bluish staring after him, still holding her hand in front of her, with an expression of bewilderment upon her face.

He was still laughing when he got to Penzance, turned into Victoria Road, and knocked lightly on the door of Albert Villas.

Emily was taking tea in the drawing room with her sister and Miss Adeline. Lorna was chattering on, as usual, about one of her galleries, and poor Adeline was doing her best to look interested. Really, Lorna could be a trial sometimes. Couldn't she get it into her head that not everyone was interested in Mr Rowlands, or Ratcliffe or whatever his name was?

'Really,' Lorna was saying, 'amazingly talented. Such a quality of light. I can't think why we haven't heard more of his work. We shall do, I'm quite sure. Anyway, he has a little exhibition this week, and I'm determined that Edward shall buy me a canvas or two. I wish I was a little bolder, there are one or two avant-garde pieces that I should love to own, but one can hardly hang them here, can one?'

Emily scowled. Why did Lorna do this? Talking about naked paintings in respectable company? Lorna thought it was 'arty', but it was just plain embarrassing for everyone else. Whatever would Miss Adeline think?

But Miss Adeline hadn't understood. She put her head on one side and said, in that birdlike way of hers, 'What sort of pieces, dear?'

Lorna gave one of her artless smiles. 'Oh, life studies. You know. Nudes.'

Emily could feel her own face blazing, and a small red spot appeared in each of Miss Adeline's cheeks. Even the maid Carrie, serving tea, stiffened visibly. Really, Emily thought, she would have to speak to Lorna about this – to Edward, if necessary. You couldn't have Lorna making an exhibition of herself in front of the servants.

But her sister was talking blithely on. 'There's one in particular, a girl brushing her hair. I'm sure Edward would like it. There's something about it . . .'

Crash! The girl had dropped the milk-jug on the floor, and was watching in horror as the liquid spread steadily between the broken pieces and soaked into the carpet.

'Carrie!' Lorna rarely raised her voice to the servants, but she spoke sharply now. 'This is unforgivable. We shall move into the breakfast room. Bring some more milk at once, and see that this is cleared up. Ellie shall serve us, if you are too clumsy. And the price of that jug shall come from your wages.'

Carrie, who was already on her hands and knees collecting the pieces, looked up scarlet-faced, and muttered, 'Yes ma'am.' She looked quite discomposed, Emily thought, and no wonder.

'Now, Lorna!' she said aloud. 'For once, I don't blame the child. All this talk about naked women – and how Edward would like it. I'm not surprised she was flustered. Transfer to the breakfast room by all means – and let Ellie serve the tea, if you suppose that any safer. But as for the price of that jug, I shall replace it myself if necessary.'

'Kind of you, my dear,' Adeline said.

Lorna had the grace to look discomfited, and as for the maid, she was so overcome with surprise and gratitude that she could hardly murmur her thanks. It was all extremely gratifying.

Her gratification was made even more complete by the appearance of Ellie. 'Gentleman at the door, ma'am,' Ellie said, blushing the colour of a beetroot. 'Says he's a cousin of Miss Adeline and could he intrude on your hospitality.'

Philippe? That was the only cousin of Adeline's that Emily knew of. But he was not expected now, surely? Thank goodness she was wearing her best green silk, in honour of Adeline's visit. She could feel her pulse race, and was glad of the embarrassment of the past few minutes to account for the colour in her cheeks.

'Philippe?' Adeline said, and suddenly he was in the room, filling it, so that the three of them, the maids, the cutlery, the spilt milk and all, seemed to dwindle in size and significance. 'Philippe, this is Lorna Tucker – and Emily Limmon you know.'

'Delighted! You must take tea,' Lorna said, before anyone else could speak. 'We were moving to the breakfast room. Carrie here had a little contretemps with the milk-jug. Bring us a fresh tray, Carrie, and Ellie, you clean up in here.' And she led the way into the next room with Adeline.

But Philippe did not follow her, as Emily expected. Instead he stood, staring at the servant girl, Carrie, as though his eyes deceived him. And she was staring at him, too, in a kind of horrified delight.

'You?' he said.

The girl clapped a hand to her mouth. 'It *was* you!' And then she said something that sounded like 'Dinosaur!'

Emily looked at her severely. '*What* did you say, Carrie?'

The girl flushed and stammered, 'I said, "Delighted, sir!" ' She dropped a flustered curtsy and hurried out.

And he was laughing delightedly, and staring after her, making no attempt to move. Emily gave a little cough. 'What an extraordinary girl. Come, Philippe. They will be waiting for us.'

He seemed to recollect himself. 'Of course,' he said, but he was still gazing at the door which Carrie had just gone through.

Emily could bear it no longer. 'What is it? You look as if you had seen a ghost.'

He had the grace to colour. 'I have. In a sense.'

She gave her little-girl laugh. 'That girl? I can't think where! Someone like her I expect. There are dozens of girls like that. She is a common type.' She darted him a look. 'Unless you are this French sea-captain she claims to have met, and sold a bonnet to, or some such nonsense.' There! That should settle it, once and for all.

But he did not share her incredulity, and laugh with her at the child's presumption. Instead, he smiled with delight. 'So, she has not forgotten me after all?' he said softly. 'Yes, I knew her well, at one time. She was a strange, gawky creature then. I have not spoken to her for a long time. How pretty she has become.' He turned to Emily. 'She used to talk about her job, at one time. And you, you must be . . .' He hesitated a moment

143

and then said, 'the lady who used to find her so clumsy at the breakfast table.'

Emily was not at all certain that it was what Philippe had first intended to say, but she forced her lips to smile. 'Still do, I'm afraid,' she said, as sweetly as she dared. 'She can be clumsy. When you came in, I was just agreeing to pay for that milk-jug she smashed on the floor.'

He rewarded her with a smile. A real, warm smile that lit his face. 'That was kind!' He held open the door of the breakfast room for her to pass in before him. The others looked up, interested at his words.

'I was telling him about the jug,' Emily explained, delighted that his praise should reach their ears.

Lorna grimaced. 'Emily is quite right. It was not really the girl's fault, I suppose. I forget how naive these country girls can be. I was talking about some paintings I saw in an exhibition. One or two were rather . . . daring, shall we say. But this Rawlings is awfully good.'

Drat Lorna. She had taken the opportunity to start on about her wretched galleries again. And the worst of it was, Philippe sounded genuinely interested. In fact, before the maid arrived with the tea-tray, it was all arranged. They were all three to go with him, and Edward, if he could be persuaded, and look at the exhibition that weekend.

'And you can come and see my boat,' Philippe said, smiling. 'Better than any picture.'

Well, that was something. She had always hankered to visit his ship. And if the price of that was a visit to Lorna's wretched exhibition, well, there was no help for it. She agreed graciously, and drank her tea in martyred silence. And all the time that dratted Carrie was coming and going, casting shy smiles at Philippe and looking at him with burning eyes.

When he left, Carrie brought his gloves. He stood with her in the hall and talked to her for minutes together. Like old friends, Emily thought. She strained her ears to listen, and heard him say, 'Did your mother enjoy the fish? And how is your father?'

The girl's father was dead, of course, so there was little Emily could object to, even when he took Carrie's hand and squeezed it. 'I'm truly sorry,' he murmured. And Carrie's eyes burned brighter than ever.

So Carrie was a pretty girl, was she? Is that what he thought? Well, she would see about that! 'Carrie! I shall want you upstairs when you have finished!' And she had the satisfaction of seeing the girl stammer and turn away. If Philippe came calling again, Emily thought to herself, Ellie should be sent to the door.

Carrie never knew how she managed to live through until Thursday. The idea of Mr Tucker buying that canvas was almost more than she could bear. It filled her mind from the moment she woke until the moment she slept, and even then her dreams were full of it. She could scarcely think of anything else – it was a wonder more crockery didn't go the way of the milk-jug.

More than anything else she longed for someone to talk to, but there was no Dolly to be found – she was out, working all the hours in the day to try to pay for the new house she and Tommy were renting. Carrie even went without her dinner and wasted her one free hour walking up to Trevarnon, to find Katie on her day off. But the news there plunged her in deeper gloom than ever. Katie's sister had got herself into some scrape up at the house, and they'd been turned off a day or two before, the pair of them – and disappeared, no-one knew where to. Carrie had never felt so bereft. She couldn't talk to Mother about this, and as for Ernie, whatever would he say if he knew she had been posing naked for pictures?

She wished, how she wished, that she could talk to Mr Dinosaur about it. He would have understood, she felt sure of it. But it was impossible. In any case, she thought sadly, he wasn't Mr Dinosaur, he was M. Philippe, a Trezayle from St Just, with money and land and all sorts. But he had been pleased to see her, you could tell that. And Miss Limmon hadn't liked it a bit, even Ellie had noticed. And there was nobody to tell about that, either.

Still, something had to be done about that picture. As soon as ever she was free on Thursday she made a bee-line for Newlyn and the galleries. She wasn't quite sure what she was hoping to achieve – the galleries might all be shut in any case, with it being Penzance market, and even if they weren't, she hadn't the slightest idea where to look for the painting. Besides, she had no clear plan about what she would do if she found it – beg Mr Rawlings to take it out of the exhibition, perhaps?

In fact, it was particularly easy to find. There was a huge hoarding advertising 'The Rawlings Collection – A Retrospective View', and a big hand with a pointing finger directing you. It was the same studio where she had posed for the life study in the first place, and her cheeks were blazing at the memory as she climbed the stairs into the attic room.

She would never have recognised it. The piles of paintings and half-finished canvases had vanished, and instead there was a series of neat screens with paintings hanging on them in rows. There were more on the walls, all tidily numbered, and Carrie could see that the neighbouring rooms had been arranged in a similar way. The whole place looked scrubbed and polished for the exhibition, 'cleaned up and prettified' as her father would have said. Mr Rawlings must have moved somewhere else to live. That hardly surprised her: it couldn't have been comfortable here, with the smell of paint over everything.

She looked for him among the people in the gallery, but couldn't see him. Perhaps he was keeping an eye on the pictures in the next room. There were a few people there already, pausing to look at a canvas here, or admire a drawing there. The work did look rather fine when you saw it displayed like this.

'Catalogue, miss?' A woman in black bombazine was at her elbow, offering a sheaf of papers.

Carrie shook her head.

'Threepence to view,' the woman said.

Carrie was appalled. It have never entered her head to think that there might be a charge for just looking at a few paintings. But there was no help for it, she had to find Mr Rawlings. She counted out her hard won pennies with a sigh.

The woman looked surprised. Obviously she had not expected Carrie to agree. 'Well, my dear,' she said, more kindly, 'you start here and work through the rooms in order. These are the earlier paintings, more recent ones are next door.' She had begun to say something about 'artistic development', but Carrie wasn't listening. Next door. That must be where the painting was.

She saw it at once. She could hardly fail to. There was a section entitled 'Life Studies', delicately screened off from the rest of the room, in case people might be offended. The picture was there. It hung on its own in the centre of the screen, as if it had been specially selected for display. 'Girl with a hairbrush.' Two gentlemen were looking at it.

Carrie felt herself turning violet. That was her body they were gazing at so unreservedly.

'Fine picture,' the older man was saying, taking his steel-rimmed spectacles off his nose, and folding them back into his fob-pocket. 'One of his best, in my opinion. Shouldn't mind buying that for my own collection. I've got one or two of Rawlings' sketches you know. Picked them up for a song a few months ago. Now he's dead, of course, prices will go up – they always do if a man has any talent.' And they moved on.

Carrie stood thunderstruck. Rawlings dead! That was why they were holding the exhibition, perhaps. But what could she do now? She couldn't ask him to withdraw the painting. He wasn't here.

The woman in bombazine was by her side again. 'You seem to know what you want,' she said. 'Straight over here like a homing pigeon. Lot of people seem to do that – can't say I'd fancy buying a picture like that, but there you are, no accounting for taste.'

A small, crazy hope flickered in Carrie's brain. Buying the picture. If she could do that, she could take it out of the exhibition. People had done that, you could see. One or two pictures had already gone, and there were notices saying 'picture sold' pinned across the space. She said, 'How much?'

The woman was looking at her in surprise. 'Well, you've an eye for art, I'll say that. Not many girls in your situation would even think of such a thing. Fourteen guineas, that is. Worth half as much again in a year or two.'

Carrie's heart turned cold. Fourteen guineas! More than a year and a half's wages. It was impossible. She would simply have to let Mrs Tucker and Miss Limmon come down here – and they would recognise her for sure. That would be the end of her job, more than like – and she'd wasted threepence into the bargain.

She turned away, tears brimming in her eyes. 'Rather like you, isn't she, that girl,' the woman said. 'That hair and everything.'

It was too much. The tears began in earnest, and Carrie began to walk blindly away. She did not look where she was going, and at the door she walked heavily into a man who was coming into the inner room.

'Now then, what is this?'

She looked up. It was him! M. Philippe, as she must learn to call him. Now she could not even hope that her secret was safe. Miss Limmon and Miss Adeline would be here in a moment, and everything would be revealed. She gave a little wail of anguish and made to rush past him.

He restrained her. 'What is it, little bonnet-hater?'

'It's that painting upset her,' the woman in bombazine said, appearing at her elbow. 'Or maybe it was me saying she looked like the woman in it.'

Carrie gave the woman a furious glance. Why couldn't she keep her mouth shut? Now he would be bound to look at that painting. Whatever would he think of her?

He did too. He walked over to it immediately. He was still holding her arm, and she was obliged to walk with him – anything else would have caused an even greater commotion.

He looked at the canvas. 'It is beautiful,' he said softly. 'It is you, isn't it?'

She felt herself trembling. She nodded. 'I did it for my father,' she said, when she trusted herself to speak. 'He needed a doctor, medicine – but it was too late. But I never expected *this*! And now Miss Limmon will come and see it, and she'll have me out of the place in no time.'

He said, still softly, 'She cannot see the face.'

'But you knew me,' she said, rounding on him bitterly. 'Even that woman said it was like me.'

'But you were here,' he said. 'Otherwise, who would think such a thing? Why did you come?'

He was so easy to talk to. She had always known it. She had felt it the other evening when he called so unexpectedly at Albert Villas. It would have been easy, then, to have confided in him, told him everything as she had done as a girl. She told him now. About Father, the mine, the illness, everything. How she had hoped to see Rawlings, and then how she asked the price.

He looked at her gravely. He had such nice eyes, grey-blue and deep, like the sea. 'Of course,' he said, 'such beauty deserves a high price.'

He was teasing her, as he had always used to do, but he was looking at her intently. She coloured, and dropped her eyes. 'So very lovely,' he said. 'A picture of innocence, and youth and beauty.'

She glanced up at him, but he was looking at her, not at the picture. She felt helplessly embarrassed, as though she was standing naked in front of him – as indeed she was, in a sense. She could think of nothing to say, except 'Whatever will Miss Limmon say? Mrs Tucker even wanted to buy the picture for her husband. He likes . . . things like that.'

He laughed. 'The man would have to be made of ice who did *not* like a picture like this,' he said. 'But Miss Limmon won't even notice, you'll see. You leave her to me.' He smiled down at her. 'Isn't it a good thing I came in to get a catalogue? Truly, you must not concern yourself.'

'Well . . .' Carrie said doubtfully. It was possible, perhaps. Monsieur Philippe might be able to persuade Mrs Tucker not to buy that canvas, at any rate. That would be something. And perhaps he was right – unless she was present, there was nothing to connect her with the painting. Not this one, at any rate. She hadn't seen the one of the street-scene. Somehow that one had paled into insignificance.

'I'll have to go. I got a train to catch,' she said. 'I got someone waiting for me at the station – going to go all the way to St Austell. Never been so far in all my life.'

'Someone important?' Why was he looking at her like that?

'Fellow from the clay-pits. Wants me to go up and meet his folks. Asked me to marry him, no less.'

'And will you?'

She looked at him. 'I aren't quite decided. Said I'd think about it. He's a nice boy, and I could do a lot worse. But it's a big thing, isn't it – marriage? Still you've got to marry someone, haven't you? Don't want to end up lonely in your old age.'

He turned away as if she had slapped him. Of course, she remembered, his own wife was dead. She could have swallowed her tongue – how could

148

she be so clumsy? 'Anyway,' she said hastily, trying to turn the moment with a laugh, 'who else would have me?' That was worse! Almost as if she was asking him to – as if he could, being a Trezayle and all! But the thought made her heart beat very fast and she felt her cheeks crimson. 'Anyway,' she said, all in a rush, 'like I said, I'll miss that train. And it's no end of a journey.'

'I must go too,' he said. He still seemed upset. 'Back to my boat. The tide will be turning, and I must see that Ramon puts out enough slack in the mooring. She'll ride lower than *Plougastel* when the tide is out.'

It meant little to Carrie. The words had a ring to them, like a magical incantation from a different world. She nodded.

'But trust me. I will deal with the painting. That much at least, I can do for you. Whatever Bert Hoskins thinks.'

Whatever did he mean by that? But he had already gone.

It wasn't until she reached the station that it struck her. To a man like him, accustomed to sail from one country to another, a trip to St Austell must seem like nothing at all.

CHAPTER THREE

St Blurzey was astonishing to Carrie. From the moment she got off the train it amazed her. Everything was so different from home.

No rolling green valleys, no granite hills, no straggling woods and whirling seagulls. Only a gaunt white landscape, unreal in its intensity – and everywhere, the chalky dust. Man-made mountains of it, outlined against the sky. Rivers and pools of it, so that the gutters ran milky. Every woman on the street carried a line of it, like an ugly seam of embroidery, around her hem. And the man who clattered past in a claycart wore a skin of it from head to toe, so that he looked more like the unpainted porcelain statuette on Mrs Tucker's dresser than a carrier. Even the settling-pits with their water of unhealthy blue seemed strange and cold – a world away from the homely reddish-brown streams of the tin-adits at Penvarris.

The welcome she got at Buglers was warm enough, however. Ernie had told her all about his family, so Mr Clarance's arm should not have been a surprise. She found though, that it was difficult not to stare at it, and while she was introduced she had to avert her gaze in embarrassment.

'Come on in,' Mr Clarance said heartily, wringing her hand with his own good one. 'Some pleased to meet you, we are. Ernie has told us a lot about you.'

'All good things, mind,' said Mrs Clarance, appearing behind him, wiping a pair of floury hands on her apron so as to shake hands in her turn. Carrie took to her at once, a little dimpled, apple-cheeked woman with a ready smile. She didn't seem to say much, but she radiated a cheerful kindliness, obviously adored her husband and son, and kept the peace with Linny May with a gentle firmness which Carrie quickly came to admire.

Linny May for her part was everything that Ernie had described. She sat on the cricket stool, busy with a bucket of beans, under a great white cap which reminded Carrie irresistibly of a lampshade. When Carrie came in she did no more than glance up under her flounces, wrinkle her lips over her toothless gums, and mutter, 'You've come, have you? Well, you'd better sit down and stop cluttering up the place.'

Ernie caught Carrie's eye and threw her a look of agonised pleading, as though he were begging her not to be offended. Carrie gave him a comforting grin – poor Linny May was not half as disagreeable as Miss Limmon could be, when she put her mind to it.

'And what are you smirking at, Miss?' Linny May demanded, as if she had heard the thought and determined to disprove it.

Carrie thought quickly. 'I was looking at the way you dealt with those beans. I wish you'd show me how – it would save me no end of time if I could do them so quick.'

There was a little silence, and then Linny May said, 'Well, you just bring that stool over here and I'll show you. There's a trick to it, see. It's all in the way you hold your knife. And Ernie, you get the poor girl a cup of tea – she'll be half-famished coming all that way on the train, and working all the morning too.'

And as Carrie moved the stool and submitted to a lesson on stringing beans, Ernie's da rewarded her with a smile and a wink.

It was not the most usual way for a girl to begin a visit to her young man's home, but it was quite a successful one, especially when Carrie exclaimed, 'That's much easier!' and began to string her own beans more quickly – though still she took care to do them a little more slowly than Linny May. Ernie and his parents were obviously grateful, too, and Carrie felt that she had accidentally passed some kind of test – though of an uncomfortable kind. It did make it easier though, when you had been stringing beans, to help Mrs Clarance with the plates, rather than sitting up straight in a chair on your best behaviour and waiting to be served.

Ernie's ma had gone to a lot of trouble, that was clear. It was quite a feast. There was cold pork and tomatoes, and seedy-cake and home-made bread and jam. Cream too, and that was obviously a treat – though it was a funny kind of bought cream, not clotted and golden straight from the farm, like Mother would have had at home. Carrie ate her fill. Ernie and Da tucked in as though food would go out of fashion, and even Linny May had hers cut up small and chumbled away with gusto. Only Mrs Clarance did not eat, moving a small piece of pork around her plate without touching it, and finding every opportunity to leave the table and serve the others. Once or twice, too, she put a hand to her side as though her stomach pained her.

Carrie glanced around the table, but none of the others seemed to have noticed. Ernie was talking to his da about the clay-yard, about someone 'hosing down the tips', whatever that meant, and Linny Ma was listening and nodding intently, unable to join in because of her teeth.

She spoke to Ernie about it later, as he walked her back in time for the last train. The moon was rising, and the claytips sparkled in the moonlight – like a Christmas card, Carrie thought, with the white dust tinselling the branches and the roofs of the cottages.

'Your ma all right, is she?' she ventured.

Ernie looked at her in surprise. 'Ma? Right as a trivet, far as I know. Whatever made you say that?'

Carrie was embarrassed. 'Dunno. Just, she looked to have a bit of a pain in the stomach, once or twice.'

Ernie grinned, relieved. 'Oh, that's nothing. Gets a bit of indigestion, sometimes, that's all. Took to you, though, you could see. And as for Linny May! Hear what she said as we left, did you? "You bring her back sharpish, and mind you don't lose her. Too good for you by half!" So, what do you think of that?'

Carrie laughed, but she was pleased, all the same.

'She's right about one thing,' Ernie said. 'Don't want to lose you.' He stopped and looked at her, his face white as the spoil-heaps in the moonlight. 'I believe I love you, Carrie girl.'

And he said it so sincerely that Carrie let him hold her hand all the way to the station. What would he say, though, if he found out about the picture? And supposing Mrs Tucker bought it, after all? What would Ernie and his family think of a girl turned away without a character?

M. Philippe had promised to arrange things, if he could. In the meantime, there was nothing to do, except hope, wait and pray.

Lorna positively insisted on everyone going to her confounded exhibition. Emily did her best to dissuade her. The weather was set fair, she argued, and they might have an agreeable walk to Madron, or take a jaunting-car to Marazion and have a boatman row them over to the Mount. It was a pity to devote a day of Adeline's visit to a stroll around a gallery.

Adeline, however, declared that she would be delighted to go, and thought of picking up a picture for the house at St Just. Of course, she could understand dear Emily's sensibilities; it would not be seemly for two respectable maiden ladies to be looking at naked portraits, especially in the company of gentlemen. 'But,' she went on, 'it is all perfectly proper, I understand. Philippe called by on Thursday to collect a catalogue, and the life studies are screened off quite discreetly, so there no need to see them, if you do not wish to. I am sure, my dear, that there will be enough paintings for you and I to feast our eyes on without the necessity of embarrassing ourselves. There are more than sixty other paintings, and some of them are very talented, so Philippe says.'

That removed the last reasonable objection, and Emily was obliged to agree to the plan, as she had promised. In fact it was not the prospect of the naked portraits which had made her so unwilling – it was simply the idea of visiting a gallery at all. It brought back too painfully the memory of a young, fair-haired man with a high collar and a waxed moustache, who had offered her his arm and taken her heart in exchange. True, she now had Philippe for company, but he was only half her escort, for he was bound to take notice of Adeline, who was his cousin, and no longer young, besides. Lorna, with Edward at her side, would never think of such things.

When she went up to her room to dress for the outing, Emily was by no means in the best of tempers. It promised to be an extremely dull and uncomfortable afternoon. Only the prospect of that visit to Philippe's boat comforted her a little.

That wretched serving girl seemed to be particularly clumsy and fidgety, too. She seemed to be all fingers and thumbs when she was asked to lace up the stays, and she put out the cambric petticoat when Emily had asked her, twice, for the moirette silk one, which rustled a little when you walked. But they got finished at last, and Emily looked at herself in the mirror. She hoped to create a little stir when she went down. The green figured costume was rather daringly based on the latest fashions from London, and not even Lorna had seen it yet. It looked well enough. This new pouter-pigeon look favoured her solidity of hips and bustline, but not even whalebone could reduce her waist to less than twenty-six inches, and even that made breathing difficult. It was to be hoped that Lorna and Edward would not take it into their heads to walk too quickly this afternoon. She took a last look, patted her hat with its long green feathers, picked up her reticule and went downstairs.

As the maid opened the door Emily stole a look at her. The fashionable ensemble must impress her, surely? But the girl seemed hardly to notice, just stared past her, as though she could see all kinds of imagined terrors lying in wait on the landing. She did not even respond when Emily asked for her green gloves, and had to be spoken to sharply.

'Pull yourself together, girl,' Emily said. 'Whatever has got into you?'

But she felt better when she went into the drawing room. Edward and Adeline were properly admiring, and Lorna, looking drab beside her, sulked in a highly satisfying manner. And when Philippe came a few minutes later, and kissed her hand, and made some remark about 'a little green pigeon' she began to feel that the afternoon was not altogether wasted, after all.

The gallery visit was, in any case, something of an anticlimax. For one thing, Adeline was quite right about the screens. There was no possibility of glimpsing the 'Life Studies' by accident. Emily was a little vexed by that. She could not have looked at them openly, of course, but the idea of having a discreet glance at them when no-one was looking had given her a delicious little secret tingle of wicked anticipation. But after all, it was not to be, and she and Adeline found themselves looking at the more respectable canvases in the company of Philippe, while her sister and brother-in-law went to look for the picture of the girl with the hairbrush. Lorna had quite set her heart on it, so it seemed. It was not at all fair, Emily thought crossly. Married ladies had so many advantages.

She turned her attention to the works in the outer room. She did not care for the style – depressing modern studies of fishing folk, who looked as disagreeable in the pictures as they did in real life, though there were one or two early landscapes which she quite admired. Adeline found a picture, a perfectly dreadful affair showing people in a market, but she seemed pleased with it and had it put on one side for the coachman to collect when spring-cleaning was over.

'I wonder you want that, Adeline,' Emily said. 'You wouldn't invite those people into your house if they were real.' But Adeline just laughed and said she had no need to, now – the picture made them look so life-like.

Lorna, though, never found her picture. She and Edward went behind the screens, but they were soon back. There were a lot of nice things, Edward said, but too shocking for public display. 'Anyway,' he went on, 'the one which Lorna particularly liked was gone already – there was only a big space on the screen, and a sticker across it, saying the picture was sold.'

'Perhaps it is just as well,' Emily could not resist saying. 'It wouldn't have been at all seemly.'

'Disappointing, though,' Edward put in, 'when we had walked down on purpose to see it.'

'Then you must all come for a walk down to the harbour,' Philippe said, 'and look at my new boat. I won't ask you aboard, it is no place for ladies, but you must see it at least, cousin. And it will have made your journey to Newlyn worth while. Prettier than any picture.'

And that was what they did. Philippe took Adeline's arm as they walked to the water-front, while the Tuckers and Emily followed, picking their way across nets and sinkers. Two fishermen, kippered by wind and salt, looked up from their rope-work as she passed. She caught the words distinctly.

'Look at that then. Trussed like a peacock. Lunnon lady, I'll be bound.'

A London lady! It made her cheeks glow with pleasure. Then Philippe came back and helped her to the harbour wall in her turn, and stood beside her to point out all the features of his ship.

How masculine he was, with all his talk of turning-winches and mooring-lines! She did not understand the half of it, but she listened intently, aware of the presence of his shoulder, only inches from her own, and the rise and fall of that delicious Gallic accent. No wonder they said that Frenchmen were so gallant and charming. It seemed no time at all before it was four o'clock, and time to go back home for tea and muffins.

All in all it was a surprisingly satisfactory afternoon, and she had hardly thought once about boater hats and handlebar moustaches.

Carrie came down the back steps on her half-day, wrapping her shawl around her. The afternoon was warm, but she was chilled – from the heart, it seemed to her.

She hadn't been warm since Saturday – not since the household had all gone to the gallery. Every time she was summoned little icicles broke out on her back. Nightmares danced before her eyes: Miss Limmon announcing at breakfast that Carrie was a wanton, with no right to work for respectable people. Or Mrs Tucker, saying that art was art, but girls who posed in the altogether were a different matter and would have to go. Or the worst nightmare of all – Mr Tucker, gazing at her with a knowing air when she went in with his bed-time milk and remarking that, if she hoped to keep her situation, more than her feet should be bare, next time.

None of it had happened. And somehow, the more it did not happen, the worse the waiting got. She felt as if she carried a private thundercloud over her head, and was waiting for it to burst. Ellie caught her mood, so there were two maids at Albert Villas with faces as long as fiddles.

Even Mrs Rowe had been exasperated. 'Oh, for goodness' sake, Carrie, whatever has got into you?'

It would have done Carrie good to explain, but there was no-one she could confide in. Not even M. Philippe. She had not contrived a single moment alone with him, even to hand him his gloves. Miss Limmon had seen to that.

How that Saturday passed she would never know. She went through the motions of dusting and sweeping, but her mind wasn't on it. Instead every inch of her body was listening for the returning footsteps, and when they came, she served tea in the best parlour with a heart that thumped so loudly they must all have heard it. Nobody said anything about pictures. M. Philippe came in a little later, and caught her eye when no-one was looking, but Miss Limmon sent Carrie off to the kitchen, so that was that.

On Sunday morning there was a dreadful moment – Miss Limmon sent for her. But it was only a question of dust on the windowsills. Carrie's mind had been so much on other things that she had neglected to get into the corners. She was so relieved that she submitted to her scolding meekly, and Miss Limmon – who had probably been expecting a sharp answer – even forgot to deduct anything from her wages. So that was all right.

Monday passed, and Tuesday, and no picture appeared. She was beginning to breathe again. Any canvas Mr Tucker had bought would surely have been sent up by this time. But then, on Wednesday evening, Miss Adeline dropped her bombshell.

'Well,' she said brightly, just as Carrie was serving the peas, 'I shall be back home tomorrow, I suppose.'

'It is to be hoped it has been well-aired,' Miss Limmon said.

'Oh, I've no doubt Maria will have seen to that. She hates the smell as much as I do. And then Philippe shall come to dinner – the poor man has been here quite a fortnight, and I have not had a moment to look at his plans for the house. He's talking of a conservatory, you know, where we might have a vine, and even melons, perhaps, as they do in France. I'm sure the poor fellow is loitering here on that account, though he swears he has business with the shipwrights. Still, he has two boats fishing now, so he can afford himself a day or two of idleness, I daresay.'

'We shall be sorry to lose you, Adeline.' Mr Tucker leaned back as Carrie handed the salver. Carrie pretended not to be listening.

'James will bring the carriage at one,' Miss Adeline said. 'He can go to the gallery before he takes me home, and pick up that canvas.'

Canvas! It was as well that the salver was nearly empty, or the table would have been inches deep in peas. Carrie's hand quivered, but she managed to steady herself, and Miss Limmon only said, 'Really Carrie! Can't you be more careful!' which was a mercy, really, because Carrie's trembling hands and burning cheeks seemed explained by the reprimand.

So the picture was coming, after all. The hands of the clock seemed to crawl round to one o'clock, and when the coachman came, and Miss Adeline sent Ellie off with the coachman to bring back the parcel for everyone to see, Carrie did not know where to put herself.

It was her half-day, and she should have gone. After lunch she was not required upstairs. She dawdled in the kitchen until Ellie came back, and then paced the floor, expecting the axe to fall at any minute. In the end Mrs Rowe dismissed her. 'Carrie, for goodness' sake! Leave those dishes and be away with you. And you, Ellie, get out the back and beat the rugs. I can't bear to see the pair of you drooping around my kitchen a moment longer, like a pair of wet weeks.'

There was nothing for it but to go. Besides, Ernie would be waiting for her down the lane – and if she didn't appear soon, he would come calling for her, and that would never do. She was in enough trouble as it was. So here she was clattering down the back steps. It was a relief to get out of the house, of course, but at the same time she couldn't bear to leave it.

And there, standing in the lane in front of her, was the Frenchman.

He had a big, flat, square-shaped package under his arm, wrapped up in brown-paper and sealing wax. It was the picture! The right size and shape!

But how had *he* got it? Surely Ellie had just carried it indoors? A wild hope rose in her. Had Monsieur Philippe been as good as his word, and somehow persuaded them not to have it, after all? Was that what he had come to tell her? Had he rescued her a second time?

'Monsieur Philippe!' She could scarcely breathe the words.

'Your picture, I think?' He grinned down at her, his eyes smiling.

She dropped her head and blushed. 'A picture of me, you mean.'

'No, little one,' he said, in that French lilt which delighted her so. 'I mean it. Just that. Your picture. For you.'

'For me?' She was startled.

He laughed, then. 'Of course for you! What should I do with such a picture? Take it to the ship and have that *laoz* Ramon smacking his lips for it? On a fishing boat there is nothing private – especially such a size as this. No, take it yourself.' He thrust it into her hands.

'Take it myself?' She looked down at it as if it would burn her fingers. 'And what shall I do with it? I can't take it home, a thing like this.'

He laughed again. 'Do with it what you wish. Burn it, if you must. Or, if you have a little of the sense I see in your eyes, take it to your – Saint Austell, is it? – and sell it there. It has some value, after all.'

Carrie's mind was racing. St Austell? That might be possible – to Truro, more likely. The train stopped there, in any case, and she was not known in Truro. And he was right. Fourteen guineas. It was a fortune.

'But . . . how did you get it?' He was a smuggler's grandson after all. If it was stolen, she thought wildly, there would be a hunt, policemen, prison. Better to face Miss Limmon and disgrace.

But he was gazing at her in surprise. 'Why, the same way as you hoped to do yourself. I bought it, had it wrapped, and took it away.'

'Bought it!' The enormity of what he had done struck her. 'Fourteen guineas, and you gave it to me?'

He looked at her, gently. 'There was a time,' he said softly, 'I used to look for you on the cliffs. There was . . . talk about you. Your father told me. It was thoughtless. I almost brought you to disgrace. So,' he smiled, 'this is a recompense. Besides – the fourteen guineas came from selling something of my grandfather's. So do not fret yourself. It would have pleased him, I think. A romantic gesture to save a pretty girl.'

She smiled at him, uncertainly. Put like that, it did seem romantic.

'Besides,' he said, 'I need to prove that I am not altogether a Dinosaur – not quite such a old, old useless creature as you used to think me!'

She laughed, her hesitation forgotten, and stood hugging the picture against her. A thought struck her. 'Who was talking about me, then? Oh . . . I know! Bert Hoskins!' She did not need Philippe's nod to tell her she had guessed correctly. 'Still, I wish my father hadn't said. Wasn't your fault, was it, there was nothing . . . I mean, you never . . . How could there be? You a gentleman, as it turned out, and me just a servant.' She was talking too much, remembering how she had blundered into talking about marriage at the gallery. Good as asked him to have her, if she hadn't said about Ernie. She had thought of it a dozen times, and blushed to remember.

'No,' he said. 'Of course there was nothing. Friends, that's all. And this,' he gestured towards the picture, 'is between friends.'

'But fourteen guineas!' she blurted out. 'How can I ever repay you?'

He looked at her for a moment, and the grey-blue eyes were as mischievous as ever. 'Why, how should any woman repay a scoundrel?' he replied lightly. 'With a kiss.'

Dear M. Dinosaur. He could have been reading her thoughts. She set down the picture against the wall, and ran to him.

He gathered her into his arms and kissed her, first lightly and then, to her amazement, passionately, a deep searching kiss that set her soul on fire and left her gasping.

And at that moment Ernie came around the corner, with his arms full of lilacs.

CHAPTER FOUR

When Ernie arrived at Penzance that afternoon, he was that anxious to see Carrie that he jumped off the train before it was fairly stopped, and took the platform running. The guard shouted after him, but Ernie didn't care. Today, she had promised, she would give him an answer.

He set off across the sea-front and up the hill so fast that people turned to stare. Whistling, too, enough to frighten the horses, and startle the telegraph boy off his bicycle. Ernie didn't care. Today was the day.

At the entrance to the lane, where he usually waited for her (followers weren't permitted to the house) there was a lilac tree in full bloom, drooping its fragrant blossoms over a granite wall. There was no-one about, and after a moment's hesitation he gathered a great armful. Carrie liked flowers, and he would give her these for a surprise.

He waited, champing like a tethered horse with impatience. Every minute seemed like ten. At last he heard the creak of the gate, and his heart began to thump as if he had run all the way from the station this minute.

Yes, no doubt of it. Carrie's voice in the lane. She would be here any moment. And another voice, foreign by the sound of it – must be that Frenchman of Miss Limmon's she was always on about. He could not hear what they were saying, but he could hear the voices perfectly. Come on, Carrie – this is no time to stand and gossip! He paced the entry, shifty with impatience. She was only around the corner. A dozen steps would bring her to him, and still she didn't come.

And then, her laugh. Ernie could bear it no longer. He strode up the lane, and turned the corner – and found . . .

Carrie! And in that Frenchman's arms! He gave a bellow of rage and pain and lunged forward, flinging those pathetic flowers in the air and clenching his fists for a fight. 'Here! Take your filthy foreign hands off her! She's mine, do you hear me, she's mine!'

He rushed blindly forward with some idea of knocking the fellow's block off, but the Frenchman simply raised one sunburned hand and fended him off as if he were a feather. It was humiliating. Ernie was no Samson, but he was strong – you couldn't lift shovelfuls of clay for hours at a time and be a weakling – yet this fellow, dressed up like a city gentleman, brushed him aside like a butterfly. Ernie picked himself and lunged forward again.

Everything happened at once. Carrie shouting, 'Ernie! Ernie! It isn't what you think!' The Frenchman, backing against the wall, continuing to fend Ernie off with one hand, and saying 'Listen! Listen! Calm down! Listen!' in a voice which rose to a roar. And then, suddenly, the creak of the back gate and a woman's voice so loud and unexpected that they all stopped, sheepish, and turned to face the speaker.

'What is the meaning of this?' Emily Limmon. It had to be. Just as Carrie had described her, her hands clutched underneath her chest and a face as pinched and disapproving as an old prune. 'This is intolerable! I will not stand for it.'

'Emily!' the Frenchman said. 'Miss Limmon! Whatever brings you here?'

'What brings me here? It is a wonder you haven't brought half the county running. I heard the commotion from the other side of the house.' She turned on Ernie. 'How dare you stand outside our gates and create such a perturbation? Who are you in any case, and what is your business here?'

He felt his ears grow pinker as he said, sullenly, 'Ernie Clarance, Miss. Come up for Carrie on her day off.'

The woman whirled around to confront Carrie, who was standing with her hand clapped to her mouth like a thief caught red-handed. 'So, not content with having followers up to the house, which you know is expressly forbidden, you bring one who bellows like a street-crier, and bids fair to have us all run in for a breach of the peace?'

Carrie flushed and muttered sulkily, 'Yes, Miss Limmon – I'm sorry, Miss Limmon. It shan't happen again.'

'No, it won't,' Emily said, 'or I shall cancel your half-day for good. Think yourself lucky, young lady. This is enough to have you dismissed.'

'Emily!' He had charm, that Frenchman, when he chose. He was choosing now. 'Of course you would never do anything so severe.' He stepped forward, smiling, and you could see Miss Limmon melting like butter before your eyes. 'I have not forgotten, you see, that affair with the milk-jug. And this, after all – was rather my doing than hers.'

Was it though! Carrie's employer might be won over by all this Gallic charm, but it wasn't going to butter any parsnips for Ernie. He was just about to say 'What do you mean by that, then?' when Miss Limmon said it for him. 'Your doing? How so?' Rather sourly, Ernie thought.

Philippe looked from him to Carrie, and back again. 'It seems,' he said slowly, 'that I have committed an indiscretion. Because I am French, perhaps. Ernie here is upset because he asked Carrie to marry him, last week – thought of himself as engaged, more or less – and I . . .'

But it was Carrie who went on, quicker than a flash. 'He gave me a present, didn't you, Monsieur? A wedding present. See, there it is beside the wall.' Ernie looked. There was a kind of package, wrapped in brown paper and sealed with wax on the string. He began to feel a little mollified. Perhaps that was true, at any rate. But that didn't explain . . .

'Why,' Miss Limmon was saying, as if she had read his thoughts, 'should you give the child a present? She is nothing to you.'

'Ah,' the Frenchman said, and the cloud seemed to have passed from his face. 'That is what Ernie, too, seemed unwilling to understand. But, as you know, I am Breton. For me, to give such a gift is normal.'

'I still don't see why,' Miss Limmon said crossly. 'And how did you know she was to be married, in any case?'

'She spoke to me last week,' Philippe said. 'She was intending to catch a train. To St Austell, I think she said. To meet his parents. Isn't that so, Carrie?'

Carrie said nothing. 'Well, girl?' Miss Limmon demanded. 'Can't you speak when you are spoken to?'

Ernie saw Carrie take a deep breath, then lift her head and look her employer firmly in the eye. 'Well, that's just it, Miss Limmon. I didn't know, you see – this Breton tradition. But I was in such a state, going to meet Ernie's family and all, that when I met him it just slipped out. And he talked to me so kindly, I just . . . told him all about it. And then, today, when he brought me the present, I was so surprised. I didn't know there was any tradition that in Brittany the first person you tell about a wedding has to bring a gift. So, when Ernie came I was just thanking M. Philippe for his present, and . . .'

It could be true, Ernie thought. Funny people, foreigners. Perhaps all this kissing business was just their way – and Carrie had known the man since she was a child. Like an uncle, perhaps. And the French did have this reputation for kissing – kissed each other, folks said, and in public too. 'Well,' Ernie said doubtfully. 'I might have got it wrong, and all.'

Miss Limmon rounded on him. 'Is this true?' she demanded. 'You asked Carrie to marry you? And she came to your house last week?'

'Yes.'

Carrie said, 'I'm some sorry, Ernie. But I didn't know about the present. Honestly I didn't.'

But something else had occurred to Ernie, something that was turning his mouth dry and his ears scarlet. 'Does that mean,' he said slowly, 'that you will marry me? That you decided yes?'

Carrie bit her lip. 'Yes,' she said. 'I suppose it does.'

Ernie's yelp of joy was louder than his cries of anger had been. 'That's wonderful! M. Philippe, allow me to shake your hand. I'm some sorry, sir, to have shouted at you like that, but you see how it is.' He let go of Philippe's hand, and turned back to the parcel. 'What's in the present, any road?'

'Yes,' Emily said. 'You should open it, Carrie, so you can thank M. Philippe properly.' She sounded a little curious. 'What could possibly be that shape? A tray, perhaps?'

But the Frenchman was smiling, and shaking his head. 'Oh no. That is another tradition. It is bad luck to break the seals before the wedding day. Unless you wish to sell it, of course.'

Ernie shook his head. 'Oh, no, sir. Couldn't do that. That's going to be like a symbol, that is. Our first wedding present. Remind me, too, not to doubt my wife, won't it, Carrie girl?' Suddenly, he wanted to be away from here. He snatched off his cap and said, as politely as he knew how, 'You will excuse us please, sir and madam, but Carrie and I have a lot of things to talk about. And here, Carrie girl,' he bent and began to gather up the lilac-blossoms from the dust, 'these are for you.'

'You'd best put this present inside,' M. Philippe said, and Carrie flashed him a smile and darted into the house with it. There was an awkward silence. Ernie busied himself with his blossoms.

'Well!' he heard Miss Limmon say in exasperation. 'What a way to comport oneself, and in public, too. I don't wonder, Philippe, that you found yourself in an embarrassing situation, with these people blurting out their business to strangers. Proposing in the street! It's all Lorna's fault of course; if she hadn't gone softhearted over that Dolly person and the greengrocer's boy, we wouldn't have this trouble now, I daresay.'

And the Frenchman, 'Now, Emily! Is it so very dreadful? A misunderstanding, that's all.'

'Oh, I daresay,' she said crossly. 'You are right, of course – a pair of silly children. Much more dignified to ignore it. But do you know, Philippe, that commotion brought me down through the back yard. The back yard! Me, in that horrible smelly place! It's full of nasty old mops.'

'Poor Emily!'

And then Carrie came back. Ernie had picked up the blossoms by this time, and he thrust them awkwardly into her arms and took her by the elbow. 'Come on, Carrie girl. We've got a lot to talk about.'

And Miss Limmon, behind him, turned to the Frenchman. 'Shall we go,' she enquired sweetly, in a voice which was designed for Ernie to hear, 'round to the front door, like *civilised* people, and Ellie shall fetch us some tea?'

Philippe watched Ernie and Carrie walk off down the lane. How engaging she looked, with her face flushed with consternation. How warm and vibrant she had been his arms. And there she was now, setting off for the afternoon with that oaf Ernie grinning like an idiot at her side. He wanted to run after her, to take her aside and urge her not to go ahead with that marriage. But he had trapped himself with Emily now, and there was nothing he could do.

After the events of the day he was more or less obliged to stay and drink tea with Lorna and Adeline. Emily was ready to tell them all about it, but he caught her eye and shook his head. She blushed like a child at being drawn into this private conspiracy with him. All the afternoon she smiled at him, little private smiles as though there were suddenly a new intimacy between them.

'Miss Limmon's friend,' Carrie had called him. Holy mother of God! A friend of Miss Limmon's, while that glory of beautiful youth allied herself to that fool in grimy grey flannel.

He had meant well, he told himself. When he had first met her at the gallery, and she had opened her heart to him, he had meant nothing but kindness. Buying the picture and having it wrapped to await collection had seemed a generous act. To save her from disgrace and anxiety. To do something gallant. For his own sake.

He had not meant, at first, to give her the picture. In fact, he hadn't known what to do with it. He took it back to the boat, intending to take it to France, perhaps, to the *manoir* – where no-one would recognise the portrait, and he could look at it as often as he liked. Because he would have liked. To dwell on her beauty. Her freshness, her charm, her artless confiding. But what was he thinking of?

It was unthinkable. Her father had said so. The girl herself had acknowledged it. Even Bert Hoskins knew it! There was a world between them. She was too young. She came from the wrong kind of family. She had no guile, no education. It was . . . unthinkable. He looked at the picture for a long time.

And then Ramon had come aboard. It was true, what he had said to Carrie: there were no secrets at sea. So he had wrapped it again, and he had brought it to her, hoping for gratitude. And, if he was honest, to see her again alone, knowing that the fires of delight would kindle in her eyes.

They had done that all right. He groaned, almost aloud. Done that, and what else besides?

He had not meant to kiss her. Or, if he did, it was to be a light, careless affair, suitable for a scoundrel. And what had he done? Lost himself in her youth, her sparkle. Listened to his blood and not his brain and kissed her as she deserved to be kissed; as he had kissed no-one, perhaps not even his wife, since he was a reckless boy.

It was partly because of the picture. He was honest enough to admit that. No man could hold that girl unmoved, while the vision of her body in that portrait sent gunpowder through his veins. But it was more than that. It was the feel, the scent, the vibrancy of her. He had acted like a fool – and a young fool at that.

And she had warmed to him. That was the worst of it. He had felt it, despite her. The arch of her back, the warmth and moistness of her lips. She had warmed to him.

And then that youth had come around the corner. Emily. There had almost been terrible trouble – Carrie dismissed, or some dreadful scandal. But Carrie had taken his lead, talking about presents and Breton traditions. How skilfully, only he knew. Not a single lie, and yet she had turned the truth aside – as he had done himself.

'I did not know there was a tradition,' she had said. Small wonder, since there was no tradition to know. They had become partners in their own conspiracy.

It was his fault. His. He had done it again. Sought her out in public, and drawn her into a situation where she might suffer. He had thought only of himself – of basking in her gratitude, of tempting her to a kiss. He had not thought of her, or of what other people might think. Bert Hoskins, he thought bitterly, would have had something to gossip of today.

And in the process she had agreed to marry Ernie. She had not consented before, she had told him so. And she did not love that boy. He was sure of it. Those lips against his lips did not belong to a woman who loved elsewhere. But to save them both from disgrace she had given her word. A life sentence. No-one knew that better than she did.

But it was not too late. If he could find her he could urge to change her mind. Later perhaps, when this incident was forgotten – there should be no shame in that. A woman was permitted to change her mind.

He must talk to her. Not on the cliffs, obviously – that young man would be with her still. But perhaps, when she returned to the house, he might waylay her then. He asked Ellie, discreetly, when she brought his gloves.

She looked at him, wide-eyed. 'Be back around seven, sir. They were going into town to meet Dolly this afternoon, instead of going to Penvarris. And Ernie's got to catch the train, half past six.'

Seven o'clock. It was a long time to wait, and he felt like a sneak-thief lingering in the lane. But at last he heard her step. He stepped out to meet her, and saw her face cloud in the evening sunshine.

'Carrie!'

She looked at him, anguished. 'What are you doing here, monsieur? You've been some good to me, I know, and I do thank you for it. But cost me my situation, it would, if anyone saw us here now.'

It was true, he could see it. He said desperately, 'But I had to talk to you. It isn't necessary, you know, to marry that young man. It was said today, but it doesn't have to be true.'

She looked at him steadily. 'What are you saying, sir?'

That 'sir' cut him to the heart. 'Why, nothing, except what I have already said. You need not be trapped into marriage with this . . . miner.'

He had not meant to say that. The word on his tongue had been harsher, savage even, but it would have been better by far. Her head went back and she said sharply, 'No shame in being a miner, where I come from. My father was a pitman all his life, while he could, and he liked Ernie besides. Some pleased when I brought him home. No, Ernie's a nice boy, and he loves me. I was thinking of saying yes anyhow. Thank you for thinking of me, monsieur, but now you must let me get off in, before there's the very devil to pay.'

'Carrie!'

She turned to face him. 'What? Why do you want to keep me here? Because I kissed you today and you kissed me? Well, so we did, and very nice it was too. But we can't be thinking of that, monsieur. 'Tisn't as though there ever could be anything between us – the likes of you and the likes of me. That's over and it's done, and there can't be any more of that. I'm Ernie's girl, now, and there's an end to it. And now, sir, if you have any kindness left towards me you'll let me go in, before Miss Limmon comes out and finds me, and I haven't got a job to go to.'

There were tears, almost, in her eyes. She was right. Damn it, she was right. That kiss, it had been for kindness and friendship past. And now, if he cared for her at all, he must let her go.

But not like this. 'Promise me,' he said, desperately, 'promise me you will not rush into this marriage.'

She turned her eyes to his, and there was weariness in them. 'Won't be before the spring, sir. Summer, more than like. Got to save a bit first.'

And then, at last, he stepped back to let her pass. Seven thirty. Too late, he thought bitterly. They had lost the tide. Too late to sail for Brittany tonight – they would have to be up betimes tomorrow. Like circumstance, he thought. No point in battling against it, better to ride out as it turned, and let the ebb carry you, just as later the rising tide under the keel would speed their journey back to St Pierre.

He would be glad to go. To set the *Ploumenach* against the wind – even in the teeth of a rising gale – would seem like honest toil. Simple, uncomplicated: a man and his ship against the elements.

He was better away from her. The curse of the Diavezours. He would leave a note for Adeline and go.

He could scarcely wait for the dawn, to shake the dust of England from his feet.

Vince was contemptuous when he heard. 'Tied to a pair of apron-strings, Ernie boy? Sooner you than me.'

They were sitting in the bar of the Tinner's Arms, on the way home from the pits. The shifts at Little Roads came out half-an-hour sooner, so Ernie had found himself waiting, as he did most afternoons – and he had already had a pint or two before Vince arrived.

They gave him courage, or he would never have retorted, 'Fine that is, coming from you! Always after the women, and still out there in Bal Lane eating bought bread, and setting your own tea.' He might have added 'and it was you suggested I asked her in the first place,' but even with the ale inside him, he knew better than that.

Vince looked taken aback. It wasn't often Ernie told him what for like that. But he soon recovered, and said with a long-suffering sigh, 'Ah, well, yes. But I could hardly leave Feyther, could I, at his age – and he wouldn't like it if I brought a bride home. I mean, a man is entitled to the fruits of his labour. He doesn't want to be handing it over in his old age to some bit of a girl he hardly knows.'

Ernie scowled at him. He had never thought of it like that. Maybe Ma and Da felt the same way – though they would never say so. They'd seemed pleased as Punch when he told them that Carrie had agreed to marry him.

Vince glanced at him and seemed to read his thoughts. 'I don't mean you, lad. Different for you, isn't it? I mean, your people are used to living cramped up like that. Houseful of boys and all that, until they went abroad. Most likely your ma misses the company. But me and Feyther, we haven't been used to it.'

'Some full of yourself tonight, aren't you?' Ernie said sullenly. 'Anyone would think you were like that fancy friend of yours down at Penzance – rattling round in a great big house, with servants, and going on about the plight of the common man.'

It was the first time he had ever dared to venture any criticism of Mr Morrison. Vince looked startled, but he took a more reasonable tone. 'Look here,' he said earnestly, 'Morrison is all right. We need people like him. Bit of money and education behind them. That's how they've kept the workers down for so long. Can't afford to strike, and can't argue well enough to make people see reason. Man like him now, that's different. Folks'll listen to him.'

'Oh, I daresay,' Ernie said. 'For what good it will do.'

'It's coming, Ernie, don't you make any mistake about that. I'm trying to persuade Morrison to come and talk to some of our men up at the pit. Starting up a branch of the Working Men's Union in Borglaise's Clay – a dozen or more members all paid up in the first fortnight, and they deserve a bit of something for their money. He'll put a bit of life in them.'

Ernie looked doubtful. 'Enough trouble in the world without you adding to it. What good did it ever do, all this striking? Only have the bosses down on you worse than ever, after.'

'That's where you're wrong,' Vince said. 'There's no end of educated people starting to talk about workers' rights. And not just here, either. You hear about what's happening in Russia? The students have gone on strike – and the professors are supporting them.'

Ernie scowled. 'What earthly good is that?' he retorted. 'Won't put bread in people's bellies just because a few students stop work. Can't call it work, any road – most of us would give our eye-teeth to have the chances they got. Ungrateful, I call it.'

'Ah, Ernie, you don't understand.' Vince's eyes were alight. 'This is just the beginning. It isn't just the universities. Last year when the students rioted, four factories went on strike and the workers helped to put up the barricades. They brought Moscow to a standstill.'

'Some victory that was! Half the town alight and the military brought in. You want to see that down Redruth and Truro?'

Vince shifted in his seat. 'Don't be daft, Ernie. But I'm saying – there's a movement. Even here. Look at the new split in the Liberal party. That young Asquith can do as he likes – but Lloyd George is going to start talking to the Labour boys. Everyone says so. And there's talk we'll have candidates for Parliament very soon. I wish you'd join the Party, Ernie.'

'Well,' Ernie said, pushing back his chair, 'I shall be a married man before so long, and I'll have other things to think of then, besides you and your politics. But all right, I'll come to one of your meetings. But only if you'll stop going on about it, and talk about something else.' It irritated him, the way Vince could turn a conversation. He wanted to talk about Carrie – and here they were talking about riots in Moscow.

Vince must have sensed his annoyance, because he got to his feet. 'No, no, sit you down, Ernie, and I'll buy you another pint. Drink to this wedding of yours. When is it to be?'

Drat Vince. That was a sore point, though he couldn't have known it. He put a brave face on it.

'Oh, next year,' he said airily. 'Give us a bit of time to save – and then we can move out into a place of our own after a while, and live a bit decent, not "all crowded up" like you say.'

Vince had the grace to blush. 'Well, you come up and see Feyther. He'll be glad to hear it. Wants to see you anyway. He's been looking out some books for you.'

Vince was right; Mr Whittaker was delighted by the news. 'Well, Ernie,' he said, while Vince was brewing the tea and putting the shop-biscuits onto a plate, 'your folks'll be some glad of this. Every parent's dream, it is, to have their sons married and the name carry on. I suppose Vince'll settle down, one of these days, but he shows no signs of it. Mind, you're doing well at the pits, so I hear. Easier for you to support a family on that.'

Ernie stole a look at Vince. He was pretending not to hear, but his ears and neck had gone very red. It was true, Ernie thought – poor Vince was only on the drying-floors, even now, and though there was skill in it, there was a lot more that was just brute strength and ignorance and being able to tolerate the heat.

'Ernie's coming to one of my meetings,' Vince said, to turn the subject.

'That so?' Mr Whittaker beamed. 'This calls for a celebration, all round. A bottle of the elderflower, Vince, from the under cupboard.' He turned to Ernie. 'Nice little wine. Home-made. Mr Morrison has it done, and sends a case up at Christmas.'

It was a good wine. A bit sour to taste, but after a sip or two you could feel your spirits lifting, and by the end of the bottle even Vince was in high spirits, the question of 'doing well' forgotten.

'I tell you what,' Mr Whittaker said. 'Down in that under cupboard,

Vince, there's a brass inkstand. Nice thing, with two proper glass inkbottles and all. You fetch that out and give it to Ernie here. Present for the new house, when you get it.'

The inkstand was a bit dusty, and heavy as all get out. Ernie was afraid that with all the elderflower wine he was going to drop it, but he muttered his thanks and staggered off with it to the gate. Vince came to see him off.

'Well, there you are then,' Vince said. 'First wedding present.'

'Not the first,' Ernie said.

'How's that, then?'

Ernie told him. Perhaps it was the wine, but Vince's answer startled him.

'Don't like the sound of that, then.'

'What do you mean?'

'Presents, from some French foreigner. Just because she's getting wed? Sounds fishy to me.'

'I don't see why. Your dad just give me something.' That was true and Ernie felt it rather reassuring himself.

'Well, you know your own business. But foreign, and a sailor? You know what they're like! Weren't you worried about it yourself?'

Ernie shook his head stoutly. If he did have doubts he wasn't going to admit them to Vince Whittaker. 'He isn't a sailor, he's a gentleman too. Property in France, and two boats he's got. Visits with the Tuckers, and has a cousin out to St Just. Used to call on Carrie's family one time – I've heard her mother say. Don't you be so quick to talk!'

And he walked off, irritated.

When he got home he showed them. They were delighted. Nothing would do, but he must put it up in the spare room 'ready'. No, he thought, looking around the room – Ma finding the brass polish for Da to clean the inkstand, Linny May fretting on about a new bonnet for the wedding – Vince was wrong. This marriage was nothing but a pleasure to the whole family.

And if Vince was wrong on that, he could be wrong on everything else. Perhaps not about the Union, but about how people thought and felt. Like Feyther, for instance, who would have liked a daughter-in-law of his own. Vince only saw what he wanted to see.

But all the same, doubts niggled at his brain all night. Foreign, and a sailor. Carrie was a pretty girl – and he hadn't told Vince about the kiss. Well, he would have to keep an eye on her, that was all.

And St Blurzey, after all, was a long, long way from the sea.

CHAPTER FIVE

Life at Albert Villas got back to normal, for a time, at least. Miss Limmon seemed sharper than ever, now that M. Philippe had gone. Carrie had been half afraid that he would come calling again, and disturb this painful peace, but there was no sign of him, and the household turned into a turmoil for the Coronation.

All sorts of things were planned. Balls and dinners and pageants for the family to attend, a luncheon at the house, and Mr Tucker wanted bunting hung from every window. There were clothes to worry about, too. Mrs Tucker had bought no end of things – all to be pressed and hung and folded away in tissue paper and mothballs until wanted. Even Carrie and Ellie were each promised a new apron and a cap.

And then, suddenly, it was all off. The new king was taken ill, and everything was postponed. One of those new-fangled diseases, 'appendicitis' they called it. Miss Maythorne told Mother that she knew someone who'd had it, and it was highly contagious, despite what it said in the papers.

Contagious or not, it put paid to the celebrations. One or two of the dinners went on as planned, but the organisers made them 'in aid of charity' and required a subscription to attend, so although Mr and Mrs Tucker went, Miss Limmon stayed home with a book, more often than not.

There was one caller who made Carrie a little hopeful, on Old Lemon-pip's behalf. An elderly gentleman, a good ten years older than she was, called half a dozen times. Kept a gentleman's outfitter's, so Ellie said, and was probably quite a catch. Carrie did a wicked impersonation of him, all creaking and arthritic, with hairs in his nose, until Mrs Rowe caught her at it, and gave her a good talking-to. 'Be a married woman, soon,' she said severely. 'Try and set a bit of an example.' So Carrie tried to mind her Ps and Qs, at least when Mrs Rowe was looking.

And then, one day, a visitor came to the Villas with distressing news. Miss Maythorne had been suddenly taken ill the day before, and went to her room. An hour later she was dead. A problem with her heart, the doctors said, but the woman knew better. Hadn't Miss Maythorne herself said that she knew someone with contagious appendicitis? It was terrible, naturally, but not altogether to be wondered at. People who had been to Miss Maythorne's 'mornings' should take particular care of themselves.

Miss Maythorne, dead? Carrie's first thought was for her mother. How would she do now, with the winter coming? There would not even be the parcel to look forward to at Christmas. And supposing it was contagious? She could hardly wait to get home on Thursday.

Mother knew. That was clear from the moment Carrie saw her. She was sitting in the kitchen, beside a fire which had died to an ember, tears in her eyes and a piece of paper clutched in her hand.

Carrie went over to her. 'Miss Maythorne?'

Mother nodded. 'Yes. And look at this. Oh, Carrie girl, whoever could have expected this?'

Carrie took the paper, fearing what she might find. But as she read, her mouth opened in astonishment, and when she finished the letter there were tears standing in her eyes, too.

'Forty pounds!' She stared at the words as though somehow they might change in front of her eyes. 'Forty pounds! And a life-tenancy in the gatehouse cottage. Mother, whatever shall you do with all that money?'

Mother lifted her head. 'Well, I shan't waste it, that's for certain. Keep me in comfort for a long time, that will. Eddie Goodenough says I ought to put it into a bank – or a society. They invest it for you, and sometimes you can end up with more money than you started.'

'Doesn't sound likely,' Carrie said. 'Money doesn't grow, like cabbages. But he's right about one thing. You ought to put it somewhere. Not safe, having it around the house.'

'You're right there,' Mother said. 'But I haven't got it yet, of course. I've got to go up and see this Mr Tavy. Sort out about this cottage too. Selling the rest of Miss Maythorne's property, apparently, but I can live in the gatehouse, long as I live.'

'Shall you go?' Carrie said. It seemed impossible to think of Mother living anywhere else – this little house was as much a part of her as breathing.

Mother sighed. 'Be best, wouldn't it? No rent to pay, and with that money I wouldn't be wanting for food or coals. See me my lifetime. And about the money – I'll go and ask Captain Tregorran, up the mine. He was fond of your father, and he'll know the best thing to do.'

Carrie got to her feet and began to coax the fire back to to life. 'I'm apt to be moving, too. Miss Limmon's talking of taking Miss Maythorne's maid, and handing me on to a doctor's family up Heamoor way.'

Mother looked startled. 'She never is?'

'It's all right,' Carrie said, finding some kindling to feed the tiny flame she had started. She didn't say what she secretly knew – that Miss Limmon had been wanting an excuse to see the back of her, ever since that day in the lane when she had come out and found her all but kissing M. Philippe. It still gave her nightmares, that memory. She put the thought away. 'Miss Limmon's got it all arranged. Nice people, they are. Came to tea, and spoke to me ever so civil. Not yet for a while, of course. The Tuckers can't take Myrtle or whatever her name is for a few weeks yet – with this appendicitis about you can't be too careful. But this family is going overseas, so their present girl is looking for a new place. I can go up there, and when they go abroad, I'll be getting wed. So it will work in beautifully.' She stood up. 'There now, that fire's drawing splendid. Where's the kettle? We'll do something about some tea.'

Mother got up too. 'Well, it sounds all right,' she said. 'Let's hope it works out for the best.'

And really it seemed to, for both of them. Mother didn't catch appendicitis. Her little gatehouse cottage was small, but snug and warm; and with Dick Turpin on the mantelpiece, and Mother's rugs and furniture, it looked more like home than Carrie would have believed possible. There was a little garden, with hollyhocks and a few winter broccoli already planted, and a porch with a wooden bench in it where Mother could sit and sew or knit, or drink tea with the folks from the Terrace who were passing on their way to Penzance. And it was nearer for Carrie.

Her own new position was as assistant cook, and although it was sometimes hard and tedious, it was interesting. She learned to sieve beef, and make sauces, whip up a cake and set blancmange. The senior cook, Mrs MacKenzie, was a dour, Scottish woman with a sharp tongue, but Carrie seemed to have lost much of her earlier clumsiness. 'Grown into herself,' Mother said, but Carrie thought it had more to do with being away from Miss Limmon's eagle eyes. Whatever the reason, Mrs MacKenzie seemed satisfied. Carrie worked wholly in the kitchen, and found that she rather enjoyed it. In any case, her mind was elsewhere, on the wedding that was to be.

Poor Ernie. Whatever would he have thought if he knew the truth about her? She tried to quell her conscience, but she could not altogether do it. First that dreadful picture. Kissing a man like that, and on the street too. And then telling a lie, as near as knife. And worst of all, she had enjoyed the kiss. More than she had ever enjoyed Ernie's caresses. There was a part of her which sang every time she remembered that kiss. Well, it was no good thinking about it. All she could do was try to be a good wife to Ernie when the time came.

She put the thought firmly out of her head, and rearranged her possessions in the little bedroom. It was small, poky almost, but it was warmer than Albert Villas, and the bed was less lumpy. She opened the bottom drawer of the lopsided chest, and looked in at the picture, still wrapped in its brown paper. Whatever was she going to do about that? Ernie had seen the parcel.

A thought struck her. She could replace it. Sell it, as M. Philippe had suggested, and buy another, the same size and shape. Cheaper perhaps, so there might be a little money besides. So long as it was wrapped in paper, in the same fashion, who was to know?

She rubbed the corner of the speckled looking-glass, and placed her treasures reverently in front of it. What would her father say, if he knew about all this? She looked at the box which he had made for her with such loving care, and lifted the ribbon to reveal the secret cavity. The three guineas Mother had given her for her wedding day were already nestled there, and Mr Rawlings' shameful guinea too.

She thought of Ernie and of M. Philippe's kiss. The 'markingtree' words of her box seemed to have a new and special meaning. 'Silence is golden.'

The whole of the autumn and winter seemed fairly to race past, and before you had time to turn around it was 1903, and the wedding getting closer and closer. The date had been set for the last week in April, at St Blurzey, though the banns had to be posted in Penzance as well.

Carrie had a slight twinge of regret that she wasn't to be wed at Penvarris, but it was a sight more sensible that way. She hadn't been to chapel – except for weddings and funerals – since the day of the dust-motes, so Carrie had no real claim to be wed there, though it would only have upset Mother to have said so. It was to be a quick ceremony down the registry, and then back to St Blurzey for a blessing. Easier all round, though it was a mercy her cousins had left the Terrace, and there was no-one left to see that it wasn't a 'proper' wedding, but only a legal affair. And what with no Katie, and Dolly expecting a baby any time, there really was nobody to ask except Mother – Miss Adeline would be at Albert Villas, so poor Ellie would never get an extra day off.

Ernie, on the other hand, had dozens of friends and relations, and even Dick Clarance came up trumps for the occasion and offered to pick Carrie's mother up from St Austell station in a waggon, to save her clothes on the muddy lanes.

Mother's clothes were worth saving too. Miss Maythorne, bless her heart, had left her 'Hoskins' most of her wardrobe, and household linen besides. Myrtle was fed up about it, so Dolly reported, and had regaled Ellie with long complaints about how unreasonable it was when all she got was three pairs of boots and a tablecloth. But there it was, she had left them all to 'Hoskins' and as Dolly said, Miss Maythorne's dresses wouldn't have gone anywhere near Myrtle, who had the figure of a young elephant.

It was Miss Maythorne's wardrobe, too, which provided Carrie's wedding outfit. A beautiful bit of beige cashmere, it had been a morning dress, but Mother soon had it apart and restitched into a costume, smart as paint, with a line of little daisies embroidered round the peplums, where the cloth had caught the sun. It looked a picture, with the bonnet and gloves which Miss Maythorne had to match – though Myrtle had got the boots, and Carrie had to make do with her old ones.

And it wasn't just the wedding clothes. Carrie went off on the train to St Blurzey with other things too. Undergarments – nainsook knickers with embroidery and baby ribbons! How Miss Maythorpe ever came to wear such things was hard to imagine, but it was, Mother said, perfectly respectable for a bride. And linen – pillow-slips and bolster cases, towels, drawsheets and antimacassars. Scarcely been used, half of them. True, it was hard to know what Carrie should do with a pair of tiny guest towels with the word 'welcome' picked out in openwork on the hem – especially up at St Blurzey, where any guest was apt to come with his hands sticky with clay – but it made her proud to have them all the same. She even parted with some of her precious savings to pay for a cab to the station, to carry all her things.

Mother refused to be thanked, though it was her legacy after all. 'I've got enough to last my time,' was all she would say, and indeed she had turned and altered half a dozen dresses for herself, to wear for best; and even the others weren't wasted. Carrie had got accustomed, in the last few months before her wedding, to arriving at Gatehouse Cottage to find Mother cooking or scrubbing, wearing an embroidered silk or figured taffeta with beading which would have been useless for wearing 'out'.

Ernie, for his part, was tricked out for the ceremony in his Sunday best, a pair of smart grey trousers and a shiny black coat with buttons. Linny May was there, bent almost double under her great bonnet, but refusing a stick. She crept along, the top half of her body almost at right angles to her legs, so that she only seemed to come up to your waist, at best, but the bonnet made up for it. A gigantic concoction of starched lace and flouces, with Linny May grinning toothless and triumphant in the midst of them.

Ma and Da were there too, and that awful boy Vince from the fair, and Ernie's cousins, and no end of people from the pit. Ernie was well liked, it seemed. And back at Buglers there was another nice man, who couldn't come to the service, who talked to her very pleasant, and turned out to be Vince's father, rather to her surprise.

She hardly tasted the wedding feast, though Ma had baked cakes and Mother had brought up pies and boiled a ham, specially. The men from the pits were friendly, but they kept on about 'tonight' till it made your cheeks burn, and never left off until Ernie said he would have to go, 'cause he was on the late shift, having taken the rest of the day to get married. And so they had drifted away, taking Mother with them back to the train, and Carrie was left to help with the dishes and preparing the supper, feeling awkward and in the way till Ernie came back.

And then, at last, they made their way upstairs.

'Nervous, are you?' Ernie said, and she was too embarrassed to say a word. But it came to it in the end. He reached out a hand and took down the parcel from the dressing-table where she had put it.

Her cheeks were fiery as he unwrapped it. He looked at it and grunted. 'What he want to give us a picture for?' he said. 'Meant to remind you of him, was it? All them boats?'

It was a watercolour showing the Mevagissey fleet at dusk. Carrie had been less concerned with the subject of the picture than with the size of it. It had been some game, finding something that would do, and then the shopkeeper in Truro had looked at her a bit old-fashioned, when she had insisted that it must be wrapped in brown paper, with sealing-wax on the string.

'Don't be daft, Ernie,' she said. 'He is a fisherman, what do you expect him to buy a picture of?'

He smiled at her. 'Yes, I suppose. Don't know what I expected. Don't think much of it, though, do you?'

'Well, we could always sell it,' she pointed out reasonably. 'He said we could if we didn't like it. It's worth a bit, I should think.' Seven guineas, to be precise. It was an extravagance, but the man in the shop had given her the full fourteen guineas for her portrait, even though it was second-hand goods, and no questions asked. Looked her up and down while he paid her, too, as though he knew perfectly well it was her body he was looking at in the painting. She had been glad to get out of the shop.

And then, to cap it all, she had run into someone she knew not fifty yards from the shop. In Truro, of all places. Fanny Warren, Katie's sister from next door down at the Terrace. But Fanny had troubles of her own. She and Katie were living in Truro now, she explained, and she was very anxious to get in touch with her beau from the Terrace. Could Carrie take a message? Carrie was glad to – the more Fanny talked the fewer questions she asked – though why Carrie should be in that part of Truro, if she was on her way to St Austell as she claimed, might have aroused anyone's curiosity.

It had been lovely though, to see Katie again; she had called once or twice, although Katie was too wrapped up in the affairs and tragedies of her own family to do more than send a message to the wedding: 'Wishing you all the happiness in the world.'

Carrie looked around, aware of the cramped conditions, the lack of privacy, the feeling of being a little in the way. This was her mother-in-law's house. Already she could hear the thump of Da's shoes as he took them off and dropped them beside the bed in the next room. No wonder Dolly and Tommy had fought so hard to find a place of their own.

'You know what, Ernie?' She was undoing her hair as she spoke, letting it fall in rivers across her face and shoulders. It reminded her of the picture, and her colour rose.

'What?' He was looking at her, hungrily, and she could see that the blood was rising in his cheeks too.

'I'll have to get a job.'

He looked surprised, but said cheerfully enough, 'Spoke to Mr Joe yesterday. Job up there at the linhay, any time you want.'

'So I'll be Linny Carrie.' She was finding a desperate need to talk, to fill the space between them with words, and prevent him from coming closer, if only for a moment. 'We'll need to save, mind. Get our own place.'

Ernie nodded. 'I got a pound or two, already.'

'I've got . . .' She was about to say 'eleven guineas' but some instinct prevented her. That would only lead to questions. She said instead, 'A bit put by.'

'Don't need money,' Ernie said, 'if I've got you.'

He put out the candle, and she could prevent it no longer. He pulled her to him, but he was clumsy and he hurt her in his eagerness. His caresses were as rough and dry as his kisses, and she lay awake long afterwards gazing into the darkness with hot tearless eyes, remembering Philippe's kiss, and the leap of her blood in answer.

There were some things, she thought, that it was better not to know. Then at least you didn't realise what you were missing.

★

Philippe took the helm himself and brought the boat gently to the harbour mouth. Jacques threw out the ropes to the gaggle of waiting men, and they warped her in and made fast.

The Philippe stood in the cockpit and surveyed the scene. It was encouragingly unchanged. The little ships in the harbour, their masts a cobweb of rigging, the blocks silhouetted like black birds against the sky. The town, a brood of granite houses nestling under the breast of the hill. All the bustle and business of the streets – horses, carts and carriages, boys on bicycles, men with handcarts, women with striped shawls and jousters' baskets slung across their shoulders loading the day's catch. Perhaps, after all, he would be in time. He should have come before.

The truth was, it had cost him a struggle at first, to decide to come at all. Battles with his conscience, with his sense of the 'unthinkable'. Adeline had been anxious, writing to ask his advice about a shrubbery she was planning, and urging him to come as soon as the weather was clement.

But in the end, he had known that he must come back. And as soon as he had made his mind up to it, he had been dogged by problems. They had delayed him, for months. Ramon, breaking his leg in a drunken fall. Repairs to *Ploumenach* when she broke her mooring and ploughed into a wall off Morlaix. The curse of the Diavezours.

But here he was at last, and he would do what he should have done in the first place: he would find Carrie and ask her to marry him. She was no longer a child, and if she was old enough to marry Ernie, she was old enough to marry him.

If only he was not too late. 'Shan't be married before the spring,' she'd said. 'Summer more like.' Well, it was early spring, and he had come as soon as he could. He was a fool. He had held her, had her in his arms, and he had let her go. Why had he done that? Why hadn't he confronted that young man and said there and then that he wanted her for himself?

Her father's words, perhaps. His own confounded pride. Well, he knew better now. He had woken a hundred times with the memory of that kiss on his lips and in his loins.

She might not have him. Why should she? She had filled his thoughts all winter long – but what of her? Had she ever thought of him? Well, he would ask her. There would be scandal, of course. Even Adeline would be horrified. A servant girl. But then, what was he? A jumped-up gentleman, rich on a smuggler's gains.

He should have come before. But *Plougastel* under her new skipper was fishing off Ireland. He had stayed behind with *Ploumenach*, intending to sail to Newlyn as soon as she was afloat again. Then Ramon had fallen – and, short-handed, he could only fish inshore. Fool!

'You do not like it here, *Maître?*' That was Loeiz. Tall now, striking in a flashy way, as his father would have been, once, before the rigours of wine and weather harrowed him.

Philippe smiled. He had been shaking his head again, almost unawares. 'I was thinking, Loeiz, of the folly of mankind.'

Loeiz spat, accurately, into the water, glittering with the glow of the late afternoon sun. 'Folly, eh? To contemplate, one must first experience, I think?'

Philippe laughed. 'Which means, you wish to go ashore, and come back in the small hours with a head like a furnace? Well, so it shall be. Ramon shall keep watch tonight, and you tomorrow.' The boy would come to less harm with Jacques than with his own father. 'For me, I am going ashore in search of my own folly.'

He did not go directly to Adeline. He went first to Penvarris, walking on the cliffs. It was Thursday, and he hoped to find Carrie, on her day off. But, as he approached the Terrace, he saw there was a stranger in the garden – a youngish, stout woman with toddlers at her heels, who looked at him curiously till he turned away.

He had not been prepared for that. He had expected to find Mrs Tremble, at least. He began to feel a strange emotion, almost a panic. What if he could not find her at all? It came to him that he had been nursing dreams – again – and that reality might be crueller that his imaginings. He might have lost her, truly and for ever.

Late as it was, he turned his steps swiftly to Albert Villas. The lilacs were out again, and he stopped, moved by a spirit of romance, to gather a few fragrant blossoms. He felt like a schoolboy again as he rang the bell.

Surely she would be there.

A stout, moon-faced lump of a maid opened it. 'Yes?'

He swallowed. Another stranger! 'I am in the right place? The Tuckers, Miss Limmon – they have not moved?'

His voice must have carried, because Emily was there, coming from the parlour with a haste that bordered on the unseemly. 'Monsieur Philippe! We were about to dine, but there is room for a fifth, I am certain.' She hustled him along the hall, and flung open the door, announcing, 'It is dear Philippe – he has come for supper. I have positively insisted. Send the order down, Lorna, do.' This because Myrtle was still loitering awkwardly in the doorway.

'Of course.' Edward Tucker was on his feet. 'Myrtle, run along and tell Mrs Rowe there will be an extra one for dinner. My dear fellow, we had no idea you were in town. You come most fortunately – Adeline is with us unexpectedly. She has been a little indisposed, and she has been here fully four weeks this year – I trust you did not have a fruitless journey all the way to St Just?'

That saved him some embarrassment, at least. That wretched Mrs Bluish and her distemper. He smiled, and shook his head.

'Myrtle shall tell her you are come,' Edward said, offering a chair by the fire. 'She will be delighted. Though it may be a moment or two – poor Myrtle is not the fastest messenger, and our other maid has the afternoon off.'

'Carrie?' He dared the word.

'Good lord,' Emily Limmon said roundly, 'I should think not. Carrie left us long ago. Went to a better-paid position, you know, and then went off somewhere to marry that boisterous young man of hers.'

She went on, talking about Adeline and the events of the New Year, but Philippe found himself staring at her without taking in the words. She had gone, of course she had gone, and he was five kinds of a fool to have imagined anything else. He felt absurd suddenly, old and foolish, standing there in the parlour with his arms full of blossoms.

'I brought these,' he said, proffering the flowers awkwardly. 'For . . . for Adeline. They smell so beautiful, isn't it so? I came to tell her only that I was in harbour – I did not wish to intrude upon your meal . . .'

'No intrusion at all,' Lorna said. 'And besides, Mrs Rowe will be making preparations by now.'

And then Adeline came down, looking a little frail but so delighted to see him that he was obliged to stay, while Emily gushed and smiled, and Mr and Mrs Tucker made small talk, until late in the evening.

'We must talk of the shrubbery when you next come,' Adeline said, when the meal was over. 'I have such plans for the house, but it needs your eye, Philippe. You saw my picture, didn't you? I bought it last year at that exhibition, but it really didn't suit the room. I brought it down out of the way of the distempering, and I've half a mind to give it to Lorna altogether. She did so admire Rawlings' works – though Emily doesn't care for it. And it looks so well there, don't you think?'

She gestured to a market scene, hanging over the mantelpiece, half hidden by his absurd flowers, which Myrtle had arranged a little in a vase. He went to it, glad of the opportunity to turn his head. The mention of Rawlings brought back too clearly that other portrait, and the woman in it. He bent over the picture and pretended to examine it.

And there she was. Carrie, a figure in the foreground. The turn of the shoulder, the lift of the head. They must have seen her, recognised her – but no, they seemed oblivious. Edward Tucker was talking knowledgeably about brush-strokes, and 'drawing from life'.

His heart thumped. 'It is a fine piece,' he said, keeping his voice level. 'If you ever consider selling it, Adeline, I know a collector who would be most interested.'

'A collector,' Edward sounded surprised. 'I thought I knew all the local men.'

'Well, in a small way. He bought one of the canvases last year, I believe, as well. He would offer a good price.'

Adeline laughed. 'Oh, nonsense. The picture looks perfect where it is. Take no notice of him, Lorna. You shall have it yourself if you have any mind to it.'

Lorna Tucker smiled. 'You shouldn't be so free with your investments, Adeline. It was a shrewd buy – if this gentleman of Philippe's wants it now, he'll be prepared to give twice as much for it in ten years' time.'

Privately, Philippe doubted it. He would have given a great deal to own that picture now. But there was nothing he could do.

He could not wait to say his goodnights and make his way back to the harbour. Perhaps, like Loeiz, he would try to forget himself in drink. He looked back towards the town. Everywhere lights twinkled, people were dining, dancing, working, sleeping. But for him, Penzance was empty.

Carrie wasn't there.

And without her, there was nothing to keep him there, either. Adeline would have to plan her shrubbery by letter. He strode into the taverns to find his men and, despite his promise to Loeiz, they sailed on the midnight tide.

CHAPTER SIX

Ernie was proud of the way Carrie fitted into the linhay. It didn't take more than a day or two before she had the hang of it, and although she wasn't as quick as some of the women who had been doing it for years, she didn't make a fool of herself, and break the clayblocks, or scream when the spiders and grammasows swarmed out from underneath, like some incomers did the first time they lifted dry blocks from the stack.

Even Mr Joe was impressed. 'Getting on all right, your missus,' he said, a week or two later, coming over to where Ernie was measuring up for sinking a launder. 'Saw her down there scraping blocks like a good 'un. Up to a ton a day already, and more before you can say wink.'

Ernie nodded, proudly. He tried not to look, himself, over to the linhay where the women worked scraping the sand (and the rime of moss and dirt which inevitably formed) from the blocks of clay which had been left to harden under the 'reeders' – the thatch which kept the rain off them. Joe had got a new linhay, too, further along the pit: where the clay was trammed in and dried in great pans in a heated shed, but that wasn't woman's work, at least at Little Roads, and you didn't need scrapers, neither. The clay came out bone dry and white as a dog's tooth. All be like that one day, and then where would the women be? He and Carrie would never get a place of their own without Carrie's wages. But she was up to a ton a day! Mr Joe paid piece-work, and that would be more than a shilling: good money for a woman.

Mr Joe seemed to read his thoughts. 'Yes, done well there, Ernie my son. Good little worker, she'll be. Though you'll have her in pod before you can say Jack Robinson, no doubt, and that'll be the last we see of her.'

Ernie blushed and muttered something. In fact, relations with Carrie in that department were not everything they might be. He was keen enough, and she wasn't unwilling exactly – but there was no joy in it for her.

He had plucked up courage to speak to Da about it once, though it had cost him a mumbling red-faced effort to do it. And Da had blushed like a girl and concentrated very hard on his pipe as he said, gruffly, 'Well, she's a woman, isn't she, lad? Not the same for them. Be different, maybe, when there's a child. In the meantime, you just be good to her.'

So Ernie had tried, but the way she lay there, soulless, when he was half bursting with it – it was enough to make any man lose his ardour. But he didn't say that to Mr Joe.

He didn't even say it to Vince Whittaker when they met that night on the road. Ernie had taken to going home straight from the dry as soon as he was changed, and Vince had missed him, it seemed.

'When are we going to see you down the Tinner's?' Vince said. 'Haven't set eyes on you in weeks.'

Ernie grinned. 'Married man, now, aren't I? Can't be out drinking every night.'

Vince looked at him sharply. 'And why not? Man's got a right to his own life, hasn't he? Work hard enough for it, when all's said and done. Can't let her keep you on a string like a pet lamb, Ernie my handsome.'

'No,' Ernie said. 'She wouldn't like it. We've only been married a few weeks.'

'All the more reason,' Vince said. 'You let her get into the habit of having you home, and you'll never see the end of it. Have you gardening and mending every hour God sends. Talk about the dignity of labour, Ernie lad, it doesn't mean you shouldn't have an hour or two of your own once in a way. Anyhow it doesn't do any good, living in each other's pockets. Look at any couple you know – happiest ones are where they know their place. She's got her concerns, and he's got his.'

That was true, Ernie thought. He'd heard Ma more than once tell his father to 'be out from under her feet while she got on a bit'. 'Well . . .' he said.

He shouldn't have weakened. Vince pounced on the hesitation like a hawk. 'Well, nothing. Come down now and have a pint. Do you good. What's a pint? Won't take you more than half an hour, and when you get home she won't even notice you weren't there.'

But it wasn't half an hour. It was nearer two. Carrie *had* noticed his absence, and his mother too, and his dinner was spoiled with waiting. But later, in the darkness of the bedroom, he found that with the drink inside him the coolness of her welcome disturbed him less.

'Come here, Carrie,' he said, aware that his voice would not altogether obey his brain, and that his fingers pulling at her nightdress were fumbling and clumsy.

She pulled away. 'Not now, Ernie. You've been drinking.'

'Yes, I have,' he said thickly. 'I'm sorry, Carrie girl, but I got to have this. I want you too bad.' The nightdress parted under his hands, and he fondled her breast. The touch of her skin sent the fire rising through him. The drink emboldened him, and he said, 'It's my *right*, Carrie.'

She said, 'Yes,' in a small voice, and let him, though she was stiller than a statue. He took her, ecstatically, because the ale in his veins dulled him to her stillness. Then he turned on his back and slept.

After that, he found himself at the Tinner's Arms more and more often. With a pint or two in him, he felt more of a man. In the end, even Carrie seemed to feel it, and submitted to him with a smile.

It wasn't how he'd planned it, he thought to himself, but it was getting better all the time.

Life became a kind of blur. Pit, pit and more pit. Carrie scraped clay-blocks, stacked and lifted them, until she could do it in her sleep. Even in her dreams she held the triangular scraper, and the dust got under her nails, in her nose and throat, and made her eyes dry and crusted. The summer sun beat down on her, making her skin dry and rough and reddened her nose, despite the 'gook' bonnet which was supposed to save your face from the worst of it.

And after the summer, the winter: and that was worse. Clay-slime that oozed into your boots, and the blocks so cold that your fingers ached with the chill of it. Carrie, who had only ever worked indoors before, suffered cruelly from chilblains and (though Linny May showed her how to boil up celery and use the water to wash her swollen fingers) she could have cried sometimes with the pain of it. And still she scraped. Week in, week out, with never a day's holiday unless the weather was too bad to work, and then it was twice as hard because Ernie would be off too, and there was 'nothing coming into the house but draughts and rain', as Linny May used to say. Besides, there was always more to do after.

But there was Ernie. More like her child than her husband, sometimes, but more and more the centre of her life. He was fond of her, and she warmed herself in that, like a hearth. No half-days now, out walking on the cliffs, but he still thought of her: and there were still times, when the weather was fine, when he'd say sudden-like, 'Need something down Bugle. You coming, Carrie?' And tired as she was, she'd go with him, and he'd take her hand and tell her about his wet-shafts, and his dry-shafts, and the line of the new lie. Just like old times.

Besides, Carrie was on piece-work, and by the time spring came round again she began to be skilled enough to do as the others did, fill her quota by working extra time for a week or two, and then have a free day once in a while, to go and see Mother. Mother had come up herself just after Christmas, and had a bit of goose with them, but she had caught a nasty cold and been really run-down after, despite Linny May's treacle, aniseed, and peppermint in her tea. So Carrie went down whenever she could. 'Worse than having you in Penzance,' Ernie teased, half-grumbling. 'Thought we'd done with buying train-tickets every five minutes.'

It was Ma who took her part. 'Let her be, Ernie. Her mother must miss her something dreadful, and besides, the poor woman must be nearly my age. Can't ask a woman of fifty to be catching trains like a youngster. Stands to reason. Anyway,' she gave Carrie a meaningful look, 'better to do it now, while she can. Time will come when Carrie won't be nifty herself.'

Carrie shifted on her seat with embarrassment. Ma was as good as gold, for the most part. They didn't see eye to eye on everything, of course. Weren't likely to, two women sharing a house. Three, if you counted Linny May. There were times when Carrie didn't scrub the saucepans to Ma's satisfaction, and days when Ma did things for Ernie that Carrie felt should have been her job, now. She got quite upset, one time, when Ma re-ironed his good shirt for him, but Da took her on one side.

'You got enough to do, down the linhay. Let her do it, if she's willing, and be grateful. Time will come when she won't be so able, any more.'

That was true enough. Ma was failing, you could see it. That pain of hers was getting worse, and the bloom had faded from her cheeks leaving her pale and waxy. Da likely said something to Ma too, because she began to come to Carrie and ask advice about recipes. 'Trained in a kitchen, Carrie, I thought you might have a tip or two.' So by and by they had come to rub along very well.

But this question of the babies was a different matter. Ma wouldn't let it alone. Forever asking if she 'felt all right' and 'wasn't sick in the mornings' until Carrie could have wept. For there was not a sign of a baby, despite all those evenings after the Tinner's.

'I suppose babies don't run in your family,' Ernie said once, and made Carrie laugh, though he couldn't see the absurdity of it.

But it was no laughing matter, this feeling of emptiness. For a time it had made her linger at every pram and cradle, and even stop sometimes on the way to the pit to watch the children playing in the street, filling jugs with the chalky water for 'milk' and playing mothers and fathers with their wooden dolls.

There were no dolls for Carrie. She was too old to pretend. And, as the months slipped past, she began to feel that there would be no babies either. She was almost eighteen. Most married women of her own age had a child long before – Katie was married, with a son, and Dolly had two babies with another on the way. Her latest letter was bursting with pride about their new place in Newlyn, and full of pressing invitations for Carrie to come and visit. But, somehow, while Ma fussed, and Dick Clarance's wife stopped her in the street to ask if there was any news yet, Carrie could not bear to face a houseful of children, and she made excuses not to go.

But she did go and see Mother. It was lovely to get away from the pit. Mother would have loved a grandchild, of course, but she didn't keep reminding you about it by boiling up syrup of arrach, and stealing sly glances at your waistline to see if the potion was working.

She did ask Carrie about it, once. Just said, ever so casual, 'Married life suiting you, is it?'

And Carrie had found it a relief to say, ' 'S all right. Grand, most of the time. Only, I aren't so keen on . . . all that. Wish I could be, for Ernie's sake.'

And Mother had come and sat beside her, close, with a cup of tea and said, 'Ah, you're unlucky there, Carrie. Pity, that is. Some are lucky, some aren't. Have to make the best of it, that's all. But don't you give up, my handsome. Might come right, in time. Your Ernie's some fond of you, I know that.'

'Oh, Ernie's as good as gold, most ways,' Carrie said. 'It's only . . . oh, I don't know. And he'd like to have a child, but we don't seem to, nohow.'

And then Mother did press her hand. 'Two things might go together, my lover. You can try too hard for these things. One of these days . . . you never know. You were late enough coming, when all's said.'

Yes, certainly, it was a comfort to talk to Mother. But there was another, more urgent reason why Carrie went to Gatehouse Cottage every month when she could. The picture. When she had sold it first it had seemed the solution to her worries – she had taken the money and left the dratted thing behind in a Truro shop, where it could not haunt her, or so she thought. But it was not as easy as that. The shop had sold it to a dealer – so they said – but it was still there, stacked against the wall with a pile of others, marked 'Awaiting collection'. Every time she went she could see the corner of the frame sticking out from under the others.

And she did go, almost every time she went to Penzance. The idea of the picture drew her, like a moth to a flame.

She would change trains in Truro, and walk the half-mile to the little shop where she had sold it. That was dangerous too – anyone might see her. Once she even glimpsed Vince Whittaker in the distance, and had to nip back into the shop out of the way until he had disappeared. But she still went.

Every time she approached it her heart would beat harder, and her throat felt dry: and when she peered through the doorway and saw the corner of the frame, even though the picture itself was not on display, she always felt a sudden rush of guilt and horror. Would the thing never go away? She had thought she'd got rid of it, and there it was lurking in the shadows like a phantom. The man in the shop always looked at her in that strange, leery sort of way, too, but even so she could not keep away, not while the fate of the picture was undecided.

And then, one day just before Christmas, it was gone.

'Oh, yes,' the leery shopkeeper told her, smacking his fat lips and looking her up and down, 'the dealer came in and collected it, for a client. Gone to Penzance, I believe he said. Could look it up for you – I might have the address upstairs, if you'd like to step inside for a minute?'

His eyes told her what that would mean, and she turned on her heel and fled. But instead of relief she felt a sort of panic. At least, while the picture was in the shop she knew where to find it. Now she had no idea. Penzance! It might find its way onto anyone's wall – back to Mr Tucker, anything.

The ghost of it haunted Christmas. It lurked under the potatoes, and leapt at her from Ma's figgy pudding. More than once she woke in the night in a cold sweat, and had to go down to the kitchen to wring out a cloth in water and press it to her forehead. And the worst of it was that Ma would wake and come down too, full of little secret smiles, until Carrie could bear it no longer and went back to bed, to toss and turn until night lightened into day and she could forget her worries in the daily tedium of the pit.

Even there, the fates seemed to be against her. The New Year started dismally, week after week of drenching rain, so that the clayblocks wouldn't dry. There was precious little for the women to do, and half the men were working short time or not at all. There wasn't the muck for Da to shift, either, in that weather: and there were motors now at the inns where they used to have horses, so there were thin times at Buglers. No chance to go gallivanting to Truro worrying after paintings, when Ma was at her wits' end how to feed them all. So the mystery of the picture loomed over her all January, like clay in an overhang, ready to fall.

Joe Borglaise was talking about putting in another drying floor – dry clay then, any weather, so he said – and there was quite a little ripple down at Little Roads. It would mean folk laid off, that was certain. Women mostly, which wasn't quite so bad, since the men earned so much more than they did: but still there were plenty of households where a woman in the linhay meant butter and jam instead of bread and scrape in good times, and the difference between some bread and none at all in lean times like these. Ernie and his Union pals were up in arms in about it. Wasn't fair, they said, being at the mercy of the weather like this. Wasn't like a coal-mine: you couldn't stream clay in a downpour. Ernie seemed to be off at some meeting most weeks now, and it irked Carrie. No money for her to go to see Mother, but enough for him to go to St Austell to listen to a lot of old speeches. And Vince Whittaker, it seemed, went all over. Paid for by some bigwig in Penzance, so Ernie said.

At last the weather eased and life at the pits went back to normal. But it had been a lean few weeks.

'Don't know what we'd have done, Ernie, if we hadn't had a few things in the garden, and I didn't have a bit put by.' Carrie had sacrificed one of her precious guineas to the family budget. 'Never get a place of our own at this rate.'

'Don't see much chance of it, any road,' Ernie said sorrowfully. 'Ma's fading, before our very eyes, and we can't leave her like this. Besides, Da and Linny May would never manage on their own.'

'Don't see how we'd manage ourselves,' Carrie said sharply, 'if we're going to be home twiddling our thumbs every time there's too much rain, or not enough.' Droughts were as bad as floods in old-fashioned pits like Little Roads.

'It's never so bad in summer. You can generally get work bringing in the hay, or something. Da and my brothers always did.'

Carrie looked at him. 'Got a good mind to write to Katie then, ask her if her husband could find a job for you, if things get hard. Builder and architect he is – they must need a pair of strong hands sometimes.'

'Don't be so daft,' Ernie said. 'They can't build houses in the wet, neither. And how would I get to Truro every day? And I'll not take charity if I can help it – so you can forget that idea.'

But Carrie did not forget it. She would ask Katie next chance she got. Go to see her maybe – yes, she would write and ask if she might call. And, she thought suddenly, perhaps she would get Katie to enquire about that picture. Supposing the man really did have an address? Katie was a lady now, and the leery shopkeeper wouldn't try his games on her. There was no need to tell Katie what the picture was *of*. Just 'a Rawlings painting', from the shop; that would be enough. Katie was too good a friend to ask questions, surely? And if she did ask, Carrie could explain that she didn't want Ernie or the Tuckers to know she had modelled for a picture. Could be any picture. No need to say more.

The prospect must have calmed her, for that night there were no nightmares and waking terrors. Only the other dream, which sometimes haunted her sleeping hours. A dream in which a Frenchman, with warm moist lips and laughing eyes, took her arm in his firm strong hands as they walked the sunlit cliffs together as they had done once, long ago.

And when Ernie came in, late, from the Tinner's and roused her from sleep – his breath heavy with beer and desire – she clutched the sheet in one hand tightly, as if she was clinging to the dream. And found the next few minutes sweeter than before.

'Ernie?'

Ernie looked up sharply at the sound of his name.

'What are you doing in Bugle, this time of the morning?' It was Vince Whittaker, hurrying down the street towards him, a brown paper parcel under his arm.

Ernie grinned. 'Could ask you the same thing,' he said. 'Doing the late shift, are you?'

Vince pulled a grimace. 'More's the pity. There's a girl down the public got a pair of eyes you'd kill for, but she's not free mornings. No, came in to send these books of Feyther's back to Mr Morrison in Penzance. But what about you? You don't belong to come to Bugle very often.'

'Came in see after some bolts for a launder,' Ernie said. 'Last lot we had were no more use 'n putty. And said I'd bring up a letter for Carrie while I was at it. Got her hands full, she has, with Ma under the weather.'

'Yes?' Vince was uninterested. 'Time to drop in the public, have you, and cast an eye on this girl I was telling you about? Just a quick pint, mind,' he added, as Ernie hesitated. 'Man's got a right to a bit of thirst, walking about for miles in this wind. Anyway, who's to know?'

And Ernie, like all who hesitate, was lost. 'All right, but only a quick pint, mind. I'll be missed back to Little Roads.'

It was good ale, and the barmaid was pretty, as Vince had said – but a bit common for Ernie's taste, with bold, dark eyes and a coarse tongue. She had spirit, though, Ernie thought. Be a handful that one, if you let her. He said as much to Vince.

'Two handfuls, with any luck,' Vince said, with a nudge.

'No, I mean it,' Ernie said. 'Have her own way, she would.'

'Suits me,' Vince said. 'Have her own way with me, any time. Anyway, you're a fine one to talk. Look at your Carrie. Got you up here, doing errands for her like a shop boy.'

'I was coming up anyway!' Ernie said. 'And 'tisn't errands, it's a letter.'

Vince sneered and drained his pint. 'That precious mother of hers, I suppose. Never saw such a girl for visiting her mother. Have you in the poorhouse before you can say wink.'

'Well, 'tisn't to her mother either,' Ernie said. 'It's to a friend of hers, down Truro.' He sipped the last of his ale, dimly furious at having to defend his wife.

But Vince just said, 'Oh, Truro!' with such a significant air that Ernie rounded on him.

'What do you mean by that?'

Vince turned away. 'Nothin'. I just said, "oh, Truro," that's all.'

'I know what you said. It's how you said it. What do you mean "oh, Truro"? What's wrong with Truro?'

'Nothing wrong with it,' Vince said. 'Leastways, I suppose there isn't. Only I've seen your Carrie there once or twice. In the street.'

Ernie let out a sigh of relief. 'That all, is it? Nothing in that. Been there many a time, going to Penzance.'

'Wasn't going to Penzance when I saw her,' Vince said. He motioned to the bold-eyed barmaid. 'Two more pints, Jeannie.'

'Well,' Ernie said, reluctant to think the worst, 'going to see this friend of hers she's writing to, I expect. Been friends ever since they were tiny. Come to be a lady now, she has.'

'Oh.' Vince took his drink. 'That what she told you, is it? Looked more to me as if she was going to see that fellow in the shop. Positively leering at her, he was.'

Ernie frowned. No, it wasn't what Carrie had told him. Carrie had told him nothing. 'What shop?'

Vince took a long sip before replying. 'Little shop in a side alley. Half a mile or more from the station. And no lady lives down there, I can tell you. Saw her go in there, twice, I did – and the fellow come out and watch her down the road, with his tongue half-hanging out his head, I'd say. Like you say, though, there's probably nothing in it. Only that I thought she'd seen me once, and she darted in the shop, quick, as if she didn't want to be spotted.'

Ernie felt as if the ground were opening under his feet. 'A shop? No! There'll be some simple explanation for it, you'll see. Anyway, this letter isn't to a shopkeeper, it's to this friend I was telling you about.'

'Supposing that *is* what it is,' Vince said.

'What, you mean there might be another letter inside?'

Vince shrugged. 'Shouldn't think so, for a minute.' He paused. 'One way to find out, though, isn't there?'.

Ernie stared at him. 'Open her letter? I couldn't do a thing like that!'

189

'Well then,' Vince said, 'it's to be hoped you're right about it, then, isn't it?' And he swallowed his pint and left.

Ernie sat for a long time, turning the envelope in his fingers. He couldn't. Carrie would never forgive him. It would be betraying her. He got up and walked resolutely to the post-box.

He was in the act of putting it in when something stopped him. Supposing Vince was right? Who was the betrayer then?

He went around the corner, into the shadows and inched the envelope open. He took out the paper with trembling fingers.

It *was* to Katie – full of newsy gossip about the pit, and Penvarris, and people they had known. Asking if she could visit 'to talk about a job for Ernie when the clay is slack'. That irritated him – he had said, plain as you like, that he didn't care to ask for charity. But there was worse to come. Much worse. There, in the postscript.

'I know it's asking a lot, Katie, but could you call in, or send maybe, to the art shop in Little Quay Street, and ask for the address that the shopkeeper promised me? Tell him it's about a Rawlings picture, and where it was to be delivered – he'll understand. If there is no address, don't worry about it, but if there is a message, perhaps you could let me know. Don't write it down though, tell me if I come to see about Ernie, like I said. I'll explain when I see you.'

He read and reread it several times, but the words refused to sink in. There was something. Vince was right. His first impulse was to rush home, confront her with it, wave the paper in front of her face and demand an explanation, but common sense prevented him. He should not have opened her letter, after all. And there might, just might, be a reasonable explanation for it. Art shop? She couldn't be buying pictures – there wasn't money to buy tea, sometimes. It must be a code for something.

But it couldn't be, not Carrie. A secret rendezvous? Well, there was a simple remedy. He would not send the letter. That way the message would never be passed, and there would be an end of it. If it was just a letter to Katie, there was little harm done. Carrie knew there might not be an answer, she had said so in the note. And if it was not just a simple letter, then it was better not sent at all.

He tore the letter into tiny shreds and, back at the pit, tossed it into the kiln-fire. He could not, though, quite control his fears, nor keep the trouble from his mood.

'What's got into you?' Carrie said. 'You're like a bear with a sore head this evening. Barking at poor Da like that.'

And he said, because he could contain it no longer, 'What's got into you, more like. Here's Vince tells me he's seen you hanging around Truro, in an art shop of all places. And never a word to me.' He was shocked almost, by the impact of his words. She sat down heavily, her face whiter than the sheet she was rolling. 'What is it, Carrie?' he said, more gently now. 'What's going on?'

She glanced at him, big helpless eyes, looked away and sighed. But it was a long time before she spoke. 'Well, yes, there is something. Perhaps I should have said something before, but it seems so silly. Remember I told you once that Rawlings did a picture of Dolly dressed up as a jouster? Well, there's one of me, too. It was in a shop, in Truro.'

'And you wanted to buy it?'

She coloured, a bright angry red. 'Don't be daft. Rawlings is worth . . . no end of money. Anyhow, I can't buy it now. It's gone. I did try to find out where to, but . . . there you are.'

'I don't understand,' he said. 'Why didn't you tell me? And how did you know about it in the first place? Why all this skulking in lanes? Vince Whittaker says you were off like a scalded cat when you saw him.'

She flushed again. 'Vince Whittaker! He would! I thought you wouldn't like it, Ernie. That's what. I just – happened to know it was there, and I thought you wouldn't like it. Now, can we let the matter drop, and let me get on with this bit of ironing?'

And she would say no more. But she was hiding something, he sensed it. He tried again, a few days later, and she flared up at him again.

'Whatever's the matter with you, Ernie? Nag, nag, nag like I don't know what. I wrote to Katie to ask for a job for you when the claying was scarce, among other things, if you must know. Not that it's done me the slightest good – I haven't had a skerrit of a reply.'

'Didn't like being asked favours, perhaps. Or her husband didn't.'

And Carrie turned that brick-red colour of dismay and said, 'Perhaps so. Or perhaps she'll write – later.'

There was a letter, in the end, and Carrie read it eagerly, but there was no mention of a job, or any invitation, of course. She wrote to Katie again, a long letter, and this time Ernie volunteered to post it.

He felt like a traitor, a rat, but he could not resist it. He ran his eyes feverishly over the letter. And there, at the end, was that postscript again. It was on a separate sheet this time, so it was an easy matter to remove the offending part and post the rest. That way, at least, Carrie would simply suppose there was no message and that would be that.

He read the last paragraph over, torturing himself, before he threw it into the fire. 'I hope you aren't mad at me for asking this, Katie. When you didn't say anything I thought perhaps you hadn't had my other letter, but if you don't answer this time I'll know for sure.'

Ernie had a prickle of conscience about that, especially when Carrie more or less stopped writing to Katie altogether, but he consoled himself. Whatever it was she was hiding (and there was something, he was absolutely sure of it now) he had put a stop to it.

But after that, nothing was ever quite the same again.

PART FOUR : 1911–1912

CHAPTER ONE

Ma Clarance died in the early hours of 20 October, 1911. Carrie was there at the end, as she had been so many nights this last year or two, sitting by the bed and rubbing the work-worn fingers in her own. Tonight though, there was no answering warmth, and Ma simply slipped away, out of the awful suffering which had so racked her stomach that death itself seemed a release.

Carrie looked down at the cold face on the pillow – peaceful now, and still kindly, though you would never have recognised the apple-cheeked, bustling woman whom Carrie had first known. Some sort of wasting sickness, it had been, with Ma getting thinner and thinner, and not all the iron tonics and malt extract in the world had done the slightest bit of good. Ma, like all St Blurzey folk, swore by china clay for stomachs, and over the past few years she must have swallowed enough to start a pottery, but it hadn't helped. Once, she even tried one of Linny May's old-fashioned receipts for a herbal remedy, an evil-smelling brew involving plantain and sow-thistle, but it had only made the pains worse, if anything, and in the end Ma had resigned herself with dignity. And now it had come to this.

Carrie stretched out a gentle hand and closed the eyes, then brought the bed-sheet up to cover the face, and went downstairs. The night was cold for October: she could see damp drifts of mist hanging vaguely outside the window, and the kitchen was chill despite the embers of fire in the stove. The air seemed to bite through Carrie's nightgown – the more so after the warmth of the sick-room, where a fire was always kept burning. She shivered, and turned her attention to the coals. Dolly's trick, she thought, as the dull red blazed into flame, and she lifted the scuttle to refuel the fire.

'I'll do that for 'ee, Carrie girl.' It was Ernie, tiptoeing into the room and startling her with his voice.

She turned, ready to tell him the news, but he said, quietly, 'She's gone then?' and she was spared the need to do more than nod silently.

'Ah, well,' Ernie said, and there were tears in his voice. 'Best thing for her, most like. Shame to watch her it has been, these last few months.'

She stood back and watched him, unprotesting, as he stoked the fire and set the kettle, but when he took up the teapot and the caddy she stepped forward to take it from him.

'Sit you down, Carrie!' he said, moving the pot from her grasp. 'You've done enough. If Vince Whittaker can brew a pot of tea, I can do it too, I should hope.' And he could too, even to swilling a little hot water around the pot before putting in the tea-leaves. Carrie watched him in silence, too dulled by the events of the night even to feel surprise.

Ernie poured the tea, hot and sweet, and they sat for a long time in the moonlight, sipping it and saying nothing. At last Ernie spoke. 'Linny May will take it hard. Sad thing, isn't it, to see your children buried before you? And as for Da, it will be the ruin of him. He's give up heart, anyroad, these last weeks.' He looked at her, cup in hand. 'Don't know what we would have done without you, Carrie girl. Better than a daughter to her, you've been. Ma always wanted a daughter. Or a grand-daughter – I've heard her say that many a time.'

Carrie pushed her cup away. 'I know. Well, there it is.' She hated it when Ernie went on this way. He must know how she longed for babies. Twenty-six. Almost too old to have a child now. There was Dolly with a houseful of children. Katie too, from her Christmas card. But not for her and Ernie. Nothing for them but clay, clay and more clay, till they turned to clay themselves. She put the thought aside.

'We'll have to go up and tell Da,' she said, getting to her feet and taking the cups to the scullery. 'You better do it, Ernie, I don't feel as how I can, tonight.'

'Da's here, my lover, and there's nothing to tell. I've been in and seen her.' And it was Da himself, stepping into the moonlight. His face glistened with tears, but his voice was steady. 'I'll have a bit of that tea, if there's any, and then I'll stop up and watch with her. She'd have wanted that.'

'I'll make some fresh,' Carrie said, and they drank it together. Ernie opened the fire-door on the stove, and they sat in the ring of light from the fire, as though the red glow was a physical link between them, quiet with their own thoughts.

It was only later, when she and Ernie went upstairs to their room and she sat on the bed, saying, 'We'll have to get her laid out, decent,' that the truth of it hit her. She thought suddenly of that still form in the bed next door, of the laughter that was forever stilled, and of her own father, and the tears began. Ernie came and sat beside her, awkwardly stroking her hair as she sobbed helplessly into the pillow.

'Come on now, my handsome, don't you cry,' he said. 'She loved you.' He did not often speak so, and his own voice was breaking,

She turned to him then, and wept onto his shoulder. He put his arms around her and kissed her, gentle in grief.

It must have been that night, she realised later – long, long after the funeral, and the aching, empty Christmas – that the baby was conceived.

Emily Limmon put down her china cup and stared at her friend in amazement.

'Whatever do you mean, Adeline, you won't be coming to Albert Villas this spring? You always come.' If Adeline didn't come, her mind calculated swiftly, there would little hope of seeing Monsieur Philippe when he came to Cornwall in the spring to advise Adeline on the estate.

Not, of course, that she was foolish enough to entertain any serious hopes in that direction. They had faded long ago. She had half expected him to marry – there had been some talk of a French widow-woman, who was probably after his *manoir*, but it had come to nothing.

She had had a suitor herself: the gentleman's outfitter with the hairy nose. He had called many times, escorted her to concerts once or twice and generally let it be known that he had intentions. Lorna, of course, was scornful. 'My dear Emily, the man is perfectly frightful. And such an age. He positively creaks at the hinges!'

And she had been stung to a retort. 'It is very well for you to say so, Lorna, but you have a husband and provider. It is very galling, you know, to be obliged to live on the charity of your brother-in-law, and be a mere nobody in society, simply because one cannot boast a marriage. Mr Matthews is a respectable man with an income, and a lady in my situation cannot afford to be too nice in her distinctions!' Mr Matthews though, was as slow to make decisions as he was to climb stairs, and it had taken him a long time to make a declaration. And then, in November – just when she thought that he was working himself up to it – he had caught a chill, and died of pneumonia. So here she was, un-spoken for again, and just when Philippe's liaison had come to nothing, too. Such a man, Philippe. So charming and courteous, and yet somehow foreign and dangerous. It would have been inhuman not to feel a little painful flutter at the thought. His presence always fanned a tiny, unextinguished spark in her. And now, it seemed Albert Villas would hardly catch a glimpse of him, even when he came.

'You must come to us during spring-cleaning, Adeline dear,' she said again. 'We are quite depending on it.' She took another sip of tea.

Adeline smiled. 'Another year, Emily, I shall be quite delighted. But this time, my dear, I have quite another enterprise in mind. You will never guess it. It was Philippe who suggested it, you know. I wrote at Christmas and chided him a little for neglecting me so, and said that life was dull here without him – and he wrote back to say there was a great deal to detain him at the *manoir*, and his boats are fishing off the Scillies and Ireland now – these new steam-drifters are catching so much, everyone else has to go further for their fish. But why didn't I visit him, he said.'

Emily put down her saucer with a clatter. 'And you are going? To France?' The very thought made her heart pound. Secretly she did a little mental calculation, and added slyly, 'Surely Adeline, you cannot be thinking of travelling all that way alone?'

It was daring, brazen almost – like asking outright if she could come as companion. But Adeline scarcely seemed to notice.

'No, dear, not quite that. Philippe is a dear boy, but I am not sure that at my age I can quite manage all those foreigners – the food and the language, you know?'

'Quite.' Emily was not sure if she was relieved or disappointed. Since that bank had failed and taken a lot of her inheritance with it, she had always had to be careful. She hadn't lost everything, of course, Father was too careful to have left 'all his eggs in one basket', as he called it, but enough. Enough to make a journey to France, even to see Philippe, seem an unwarrantable luxury. But it would not do to let Adeline know what she was thinking – it might seem like asking to be paid for. She said, to cover the silence, 'And one is never quite sure if one can drink the water. And travel can be so . . . exhausting, so I hear.' That was better – it made her sound quite a woman of the world.

'That's just what I thought,' Adeline said. 'But these new passenger liners are wonderful, so they say. Mr Tavy's cousin has just come back from a cruise all the way from New York – on the *Lusitania*, no less. Says it was magnificent – like a floating hotel. And of course, they speak English over there, and it makes such a difference. Although, if you want, I believe you can simply cruise there and back again, and only go ashore to visit.'

'New York?' Emily could hardly believe her ears. 'Why, that's such a long journey . . .'

Adeline's eyes sparkled like a child. 'Not so long, dear. Not now. The *Lusitania* can do it in less than five days. Think of that! Why, when I was young it could take five days to get to Scotland, and now there are young men with motor-bicycles driving from John o' Groats to Land's End in less than forty-eight hours. Besides, people are going to America all the time. You keep hearing of young men who do it – with wives and children, too.'

'But at your age, Adeline! Are you sure it is quite wise? It is so far!'

'My dear Emily,' her friend returned, rather sharply, 'I am not quite finished yet. Besides, I don't propose to swim! I intend to take a ship.'

It was a firm plan, then. Emily felt a sharp pang of regret. France, yes: possibly she might have scraped together enough for France, by being very careful. She might even have swallowed her pride and approached her brother-in-law for a small advance – he had recently inherited money from an uncle. But New York – that was impossible. She said, regretfully, 'It would be expensive, surely?' and instantly wished that she had not spoken the words aloud. It sounded rather disapproving. But in a way, she was. It was not like Adeline to squander money on fripperies.

Adeline seemed to read her thoughts. 'Well, yes, my dear, it would be expensive. But,' she leaned forward and continued in an altered tone, 'I fear my health is not as good as it used to be. My doctor has been urging for months that a long sea-voyage would do me good.'

'Scarcely a long voyage, if it is only five days.' Emily was aware that disappointment made her sound waspish. 'Still, I suppose you must do with your money as you choose.'

'As for that, there is only Philippe to think of,' Adeline said, 'and he is urging me to it. Besides there will be more than enough for him, even if I do make the cruise. And it would not be only five days, naturally. I should take a few days in New York, before coming back. There are cruises which visit Cherbourg and places on the way, so I could see France after all. And all without ever leaving the boat, except to see the sights.'

'I see,' Emily felt desolate. 'In that case, please give my regards to M. Philippe.'

'Oh, I shan't see Philippe, at least, not until my return,' Adeline said. 'The visit is to Cherbourg, not Brittany, and besides, he will no doubt be away fishing. Though you are quite right about one thing, Emily. It is a long way to travel alone. I suppose it would be out of the question for you to accompany me?'

There, it had come. And she would have to refuse the invitation. At least Adeline's last words had made it easier to bear. All the same, there was a long, terrible pause before the words came. 'I am afraid it would,' she said at last. 'That business with the bank – it has left me a little . . . stretched, you know.'

Adeline flushed, embarrassed at having caused embarrassment. 'Of course, Emily. Thoughtless of me. But Lorna now, and Edward? He has that inheritance, and Lorna did very well from those paintings. Do you suppose they might consider it?'

Emily felt the angry flush rise to her face. Lorna! Lorna of course had no money to lose in the bank collapse – she had spent hers patronising those dratted artists. Investment, she called it – and then when a dealer had called at the house he had offered a small fortune for the paintings. 'The best Rawlings collection outside London,' he had called them. In fact, a few canvases had made so much money that Edward was joking about selling up the tobacconist's and opening an art gallery. And there were many other paintings still to sell.

'Oh yes,' she said sourly. 'I'm sure Lorna would be delighted!' And then, ashamed of her churlishness, she added as sincerely as she could, 'Do ask them!'

'Well, I shall then,' Adeline said, nodding her head on its bird-like neck. 'If you won't be disappointed. I should hate you to feel excluded. April, I was thinking. When the weather is better.'

'Well, I hope you have a wonderful time,' Emily said, feeling more left out than ever. 'Supposing Lorna and Edward agree. They might not of course, and I don't think you ought to undertake it alone!'

But in spite of her best endeavours, they did agree, naturally.

When Ernie heard about the baby he was prouder than a turkey-cock, Carrie told him the news one evening, when he had come back from a late shift at the pit. Da was out, and Linny May had gone to bed, so there were just the two of them in the kitchen, and Carrie was serving his supper.

Ernie was telling about Joe Borglaise sending out for a jug of ale and treating the pit captains and the engineers to a sup of it. 'Never been known! Folks were wondering what was the catch. But it turned out to be on account of his wife had a son yesterday. Anyone would think she'd presented him with a dukedom, the way he was grinning and carrying on.' Ernie laughed. 'Watered the beer, mind. Wouldn't have been Joe Borglaise else.'

Carrie said, busying herself with the teapot, 'Well, it's to be hoped they don't expect you to do the same, then. We'll have enough to think of without buying ale for half the pit.'

He frowned. 'What you on about, Carrie?'

She turned away, not meeting his eye. 'When the baby comes.'

'The baby?' He put down his knife and fork and stared at her, beaming with delight. 'Our baby?'

She looked at him then, smiling, and her eyes were alight. She nodded.

'You sure, Carrie girl? This isn't a Fool's Day prank come early? I'm to be a father. You absolutely sure?' And when she told him, laughing, that she was as sure she could be, since it was only March, he slapped his knee and cried, 'Stap me!' in delight. He might have kissed her, then and there, only Linny May came down for a cup of tea, and Carrie winked at him, so he said nothing.

He couldn't wait to tell them down the Tinner's Arms. They pulled his leg something chronic, of course.

'Find out what it was for, did you then?' one of them said, but they bought him a pint, and another, and another. They knew, some of them more than others, how a man wanted children to put a seal on his manhood.

Only Vince seemed less than delighted. 'Well, it's very nice, of course, but you don't have to go on about it so. Happens all the time, you know.' Really, Vince could be a misery, sometimes.

'I don't know why you have to hang about with him, I really don't,' Carrie said, when Ernie told her the news. 'Down that wretched Tinner's night after night, and dragging you into this Union of his. If it isn't his blooming pamphlets, it's meetings over at St Austell! I don't know why you have to do with him. It will only lead to trouble. You'd be sight better off staying home with your wife – and your family!'

Ernie felt himself flush. The Union was a sore point. He had let Vince talk him into it, up to a point, but he had begun to enjoy it on his own account. He had discovered a little talent as a public speaker – he was better than Vince at it, in fact, because Vince always made you feel that he was preaching at you, but Ernie just talked – things that Mr Morrison and Feyther had told him – and people were starting to listen to him. They were even talking about making him a Union Organiser down at Little Roads.

Vince wasn't very pleased about that, but somebody had to do it, so when they voted for Ernie a week or two later, he agreed. There were getting on for twenty members out there now, and they needed a Branch of their own. He didn't say anything to Carrie. She had enough to worry about – carrying this baby was making her sick every morning, and what with going to the linhay most days and running the household into the bargain she had her hands full, because Linny May and Da couldn't do much.

'I don't know why you're down on the Union so,' he grumbled. 'Look at the coal-miners. Hadn't been out on strike three weeks, and they got their Minimum Wage Act on the statute books. Why shouldn't we clayers have a bit of the same?' Ernie had been to the big April meeting at St Austell only a few days before, and the speakers had quite fired him.

Carrie gave him a look that would have scorched iron. 'A bit of the same? Three hundred hunger marchers in Grimsby, there were, with their families starving for want of a bit of coal. And there was folks worrying that tin-mines might be turning men off, if there wasn't fuel for the pump-engines. What about them? Is that what it comes to, this "unity of the working man" you're always so keen on?'

'Well,' Ernie said sullenly, 'if your father hadn't joined the Miners' Friendly down to Penvarris, where would your mother have been when he died first?'

Carrie looked up from the sheet she was ironing. 'The Friendly is one thing. Getting up public meetings to complain about the clay-pits, that's quite another. And as for Mr Morrison and those articles of his – he'll say too much one of these days, you mark my words. I'm half-ashamed to go to the pits some days. And it's no good you scowling at me like that. You get yourself mixed up with this union speechifying, you'll get yourself turned off, and then where will we be? You want to think a bit more about your wife and family, and a bit less about Vince Whittaker, that's what.'

Ernie swallowed his soup. 'Listen to you a sight too much already,' he said, and stumped off to his meeting down at the Tinner's. When he came home, she turned away from him, and he did not press the point. If that was how she felt, let her! Wasn't as though there was anything to worry over – not like those letters. There was this baby too. Women were often a bit off at a time like this. He wouldn't worry about it.

He worried about it in other ways, though. Carrie was looking tired, and he said one evening, 'You oughtn't to be going down the linhay much longer, Carrie. Heavy work for a woman in ... well ... in your condition.'

Linny May, hideous in her black bonnet, gave a little snigger from the settle by the fire, which she had made her own since Ma had gone. 'Oh, stop your fussing, Ernie. You're more of an old woman than I am. Carrie's healthy enough. Bit of hard work won't do her any harm. Why, I remember when I was carrying my first . . .'

Ernie gritted his teeth, waiting for the story of martyrdom that was bound to follow, but Carrie, who seemed to have a way with Linny May, said, 'Yes, it must have been much more difficult then. I was thinking about stopping down at the linhay in a month or two, but you're right, Linny May, I'm strong as an ox. Can't go making an invalid of myself.'

Linny May put down the pillow-slip she was damping, and sniffed doubtfully. 'Well, I don't know,' she said. 'Can't be too careful. Not young, are you, to be having your first? And if anything should happen, what should we do without you? All the same, you young people. Only think about yourselves.' She picked up a bolster-case, sprinkled it with water, and rolled it, ready for ironing, while Ernie saw Da and Carrie exchange glances and smile, in perfect understanding.

He was unreasonably irritated, feeling excluded from their private conspiracy. He had never learned the art of getting Linny May to agree with him. He said sourly, 'Well, I'm off out of it. Got a meeting down the Tinner's to talk about these new conditions the Union is looking for. And if you are going to give up earning, Carrie, it's not a bit of good you complaining. We could do with a few things changing down the pit, if there's to be another mouth to feed.'

He jammed his cap on his head and set off for the public rooms. Vince was waiting for him with an air of supressed excitement. Ernie could see that he was particularly pleased with himself.

'Well,' Vince said, leading the way into the Workers Institute at the back of the Tinner's Arms, 'I've fixed it. Morrison's coming. To address the lot of us – all the men from the pits round about. What do you think of this, then?'

Ernie didn't think much of it. Looked just like school. Wooden seats had been drawn up in rows, and a table in front, draped with bunting, and topped by a glass of water and a jug. There was even a little wooden gavel on the table. 'Very nice,' he said, wishing it were going to be the usual sort of meeting; sitting in the snug at the Tinner's with a pint or two by the fire. He should have listened to Carrie and stayed at home.

But there was no getting out of it now, the men were beginning to file in. 'Sit down, do,' Ernie said to Vince, who was sporting a new waistcoat for the occasion, and hopping around the hall like a nesting sparrow – moving a chair here, and cloth there, and readjusting the water jug until Ernie would cheerfully have tipped it over him. 'Here's Morrison now.'

'Well, its a good turn-out for a little place,' Vince whispered, as though he were personally responsible for the presence of every man jack of them. 'We'll sit here at the front – I've got to make a speech of welcome.'

He did. Talked for ten minutes about nothing, and then sat down, puffed up with himself like a pouter pigeon. Then Morrison stood up.

You had to hand it to the fellow. When he began the men were doubtful – you could see it in the way they sat hunched like schoolboys in their chairs. But as he spoke, the mood altered. Men pulled off their caps, and listened, and when he had finished, stood up, clapping and cheering. Ernie found himself with them, stamping his feet and applauding until his hands stung. What Morrison said was right. Workers must stand together.

It was only reasonable. Coal sold for a lot less than clay did at the pit-head. Why should coal-miners have thirty shillings when the clayers were earning less than a pound a week? Why not fortnightly pay-packets too, and an eight-hour day? Ernie found himself on his feet and shouting with the rest. 'Bravo!' he shouted. 'Bravo!'

Vince muttered in his ear, 'Here, don't go wild, lad. Those demands weren't his idea – we've been saying the same since January.'

But Ernie's enthusiasm had drawn all eyes to him – Mr Morrison's too. And suddenly, to Ernie's embarrassment, the great man was holding up his hand for silence and saying, 'There's a young man here, a young man I've spoken to before. His story, and his father's story, is one of the most moving things I have ever heard – a tragic example of capitalist contempt for the working man. In the socialist world we fight for, this man's story could never have happened. I think you should all hear it. Friends, I give you – Mr Ernest Clarance.'

There was a little murmuring in the ranks. Ernie stood transfixed with horror, unable to believe his own ears. Most of these men knew him, and his father, and nobody had ever thought it was anything special before. Besides, whatever would Da think, having his story held up in front of people like a freak show? He could feel his cheeks blazing, and the cheers died in his throat.

But Morrison's hold on the crowd had not diminished. 'Ernie!' someone shouted. 'Er-nie! Er-nie!' It turned into a rhythmical chant, and soon the whole hall was joining in, stamping their feet and shouting, 'Er-nie!'

'I told you to shut up,' Vince whispered savagely, but there was no help for it. Half a dozen hands were pushing him forward, and he found himself willy-nilly at the front of the hall, with Morrison coming forward, beaming, to shake him by the hand.

There was a hush. They were waiting for him, hanging on every word. 'It's nothing,' Ernie said, wishing the ground would open and swallow him. 'It's only my Da . . .' and he told them the story in as few words as possible.

Everyone was staring at him, as if this tale, which they had known for years, was some sort of sudden truth. Looking at Ernie, too, as if they could not believe that this was the same man who had been so stammering and tongue-tied when he was younger. And then, to his cringing confusion, they were rising to their feet, cheering, and wouldn't sit down until Morrison led him off in triumph to the snug.

There, over a pint of ale, the enormity of it all engulfed him. What would Carrie say if she heard? And Da – Da would be livid! There was nothing he hated more than being made an exhibition of. And as for Linny May . . . He downed his pint in a single draught. Someone, clapping him on the back, bought him another. After a little, he began to feel better. Perhaps, after all, the story wouldn't reach Buglers. Dick Clarance wasn't at the meeting to tell tales, and after all, it was Morrison who was the star of the evening.

Somehow, he failed to notice the man at his elbow, saying softly, 'Mr Clarance, I'm from the *Graphic Messenger* . . .'

CHAPTER TWO

Ernie was down at Little Roads early every morning for the whole week following his impromptu speech. He had said nothing about it at home, and Carrie – who had some idea that any Union activity was somehow unbefitting a Christian – never asked.

Very little was said at the pit, either – the men were more concerned with Mr Morrison's speech, and the idea of a strike, which was growing in favour.

'Stands to reason,' one of them said. 'Look at the coal-miners' strike, and the way the government caved in on that. Public opinion, that was – and quite right too. It's only justice we're looking for, when all's said. It's the twentieth century – there's no call for folk to be sweating their guts out in all weathers, and paid a pittance for it. Morrison's right – good speech of yourn, too, young Clarance. Fair made my eyes smart, hearing you tell it.' And that was all.

Carrie apparently heard nothing about it. She was coming later to the linhay these mornings – after eight, sometimes, before she arrived, what with the extra work in the house and the sickness that seemed to take her after breakfast. Just as well, Ernie thought to himself. By the time she came in she was too busy scraping blocks to stand gossiping. Paid piece-work, of course, so it didn't matter, provided she stayed on and shifted her quota. She did, every time. Carrie was a good worker.

He saw her on Wednesday morning, sitting under the makeshift roof of reeders which protected the drying clay from the worst of the weather. She was sitting with two or three of the women – talking babies, by the look of it, for one of them was patting her own ample stomach, and laughing. Ernie turned away, embarrassed. Female talk! But at least they weren't on about Union meetings. He had been afraid that one of them would hear tell of it from her husband, and pass it on to Carrie, but it was almost a week since his speech – they were unlikely to talk about it now.

He went back to work with a lighter heart. It was a tricky task, and he was soon engrossed in it. They were driving in a new level to drain the claywater from the pit, and he needed all Mr Whittaker's teaching to determine the lie and angle of it. He was still calculating the flow-rates when the boy came for him.

'Hey Ernie, Mr Joe wants to see you. In his office. Straight away.'

Ernie was puzzled. Must be a problem with the level, he supposed vaguely as he knocked on the door and waited.

'Come in.'

Mr Joe was sitting behind his table. He didn't look like a pit-owner: more like a shift-captain, in his bowler hat and shirtsleeves, with his waistcoat buttoned tight around his burly frame. But he sounded every inch the part as he said, abruptly, 'What's all this I hear then, Ernie Clarance? Standing up at Union meetings and throwing your weight about?'

To say that Ernie's heart sank wouldn't tell the half of it. It seemed to dive down through his boots and halfway to the bottom of the clay levels, while his palms sweated and his breath came quickly. His mind had painted a thousand pictures, but he had never once imagined this. He took a deep breath and squared his shoulders. 'Never said nothing that wasn't true, Mr Joe – and never said a word against you or your pit.'

Joe Borglaise looked at him coolly. 'Just as well, Ernie lad. I aren't one to stand troublemakers at this pit. Telling about your da, were you?'

Ernie nodded. That wasn't so bad – Da's accident had been at the Borglaise pit, where Dick Clarance worked. There was no love lost between the two pit-owners, so Mr Joe wouldn't concern himself too much if folks were finding fault with the management and conditions at Borglaise Clay. Still, the subject of his speech seemed to be common knowledge after all. Ernie's ears burned uncomfortably at the thought of what they would say at Buglers when he got home. And Mr Joe would still have him down as a rabble-rouser. He tried to steel himself for the worst. Nothing though, could have prepared him for what happened next.

'Well,' Mr Joe was saying, 'might turn out to be a blessing yet. Got a fellow telephoned here this morning, from the papers. Heard you that Saturday and wants to come down and take some photographs.' Mr Joe glowered at Ernie. 'I told him straight your da was nothing to do with this pit, but the man said never mind. Make a good picture, he said – people working at the pits. Wanted you, first off – but I said "not likely". Told him he could have a few photographs of the place, but only if he showed the claying. Better than any woodcut poster, that would be – they did some postcards of the St Blurzey pit a year or two back, and they sold no end of extra clay, I hear. So maybe you've done me a favour after all, this once: but see you don't go making an exhibition of yourself another time.'

Ernie left the office in a daze. Newspapers. Photographs! It was all he could do to keep his mind on the job, and he dallied at the Tinner's Arms for a long time before going home, although Vince was nowhere to be found.

When he did get home, Carrie was waiting for him.

The news had reached the linhay late in the afternoon.

'You heard, have you?' said Winnie. She was a big, fat, buxom woman, with fourteen children to her name, and a thin apologetic husband who worked with the horses. She had taken to Carrie the moment she'd heard a whisper of the baby to come, and Carrie wasn't sorry for her company. 'Someone's coming tomorrow to take pictures of all us – though why anyone would want photographs of Little Roads is more than I can see. But Mr Joe is taking it serious. Had two kettleboys up the pit-head all afternoon sweeping down the paths around the clay-face. Sweeping the paths, indeed – there's a thankless task if ever there was one! Washing down the tramming carts, too, if you ever heard the like!'

The others laughed. 'Knew there was something afoot,' one of them said. 'There was a boy up here dinner time, scrubbing down the trestles. And he brought up a shrub in a barrel. I saw it when I went down – but it's too near they new kilns of Mr Joe's, and it's half wilted already in the heat.'

'Good job and all,' Winnie said sourly. 'Maybe Mr Joe will think twice about putting any more drying floors in. Clay comes out of them dry enough to ship – clean as a whistle besides, and where's the job for us girls then? All these machines, it'll go too far, you mark my words. Your da'll tell you that, Carrie – won't be a drop of horse-muck for him to sell if these motors keep on taking over the roads.'

Carrie nodded. Da had said about it. Several local inns had taken to running motor-charabancs instead of horse-carriages: and last week there had been seven cars through Bugle, all in one day. When there were fewer horses, there was less muck and, what with the oil on the roads, even that was nothing like the quality. Muck-collecting didn't pay like it used to.

But one of the younger women broke in. 'Oh, talk sense, Winnie! How could motor-cars ever take over from the horses? Always be carts. Stands to reason. And bal-maidens too.' The women at the pit sometimes called referred to themselves that way, though to Carrie, raised in a tin-village where women once worked breaking ore-stones, the idea of clay-scrapers being bal-girls was always ridiculous. 'In any case,' the woman went on, 'if this man's coming to take photographs, I'm going home tonight to look out my best apron and bonnet. Good mind to starch the flounces.'

Carrie looked around the group. Their big 'gook' bonnets would look a sight better starched, she thought: but a few minutes scraping clay would have them dusty and drooping again in no time.

'Never saw such a fuss,' Carrie said. 'You'd think we were expecting the King for dinner.'

'Don't want to be in the paper looking like something the cat brought in,' Winnie said. She gave Carrie an appraising look. 'You want to borrow my second bonnet, my handsome? Everyone's making a bit of an effort – look at this trestle, so clean it's a shame to spread clay on it, and dirty it up.'

Carrie laughed and fetched two of the clay-blocks from the stack under the reeders. The blocks were heavy, although they had long since dried, and they were rimed with dirt, mould and moss. She set them down on the trestle, picked up the scraper and began to shave the whiskers off them. 'Well,' she said, 'I've come to work, not to have me picture took. What's it all about, any road? What they want to come up here for?'

'All on account of that Union meeting Saturday, by all I hear,' Winnie said. 'You know. The one where your Ernie did so well.'

Carrie felt the pit of her stomach lurch. 'Ernie? What has Ernie got to do with it?'

The woman's face turned scarlet. 'Ernie never told you? Shouldn't have said nothing, most like. But you'd have heard any road, in the finish. Gave a speech he did – some speaker, too, by all accounts. About his da and the accident and all. The man from the *Graphic Messenger* was there . . .'

Carrie could feel the blood drain from her face. 'Ernie gave a speech? Down the Union? And Joe Borglaise knows about that?'

'Bound to,' Winnie said. 'On account of the photographs.'

'Well, he won't get no photograph of me,' Carrie said.

'Can't see how you'll avoid it, my handsome, if Mr Borglaise says so,' Winnie said. 'Anyhow, where's the harm? Lot to be said for the Union, seems to me. Stop the machines taking over, with any luck – and get some decent wages for the folk into the bargain.'

But Carrie wasn't listening. 'That Ernie!' she muttered to herself. 'Hasn't got the brains he was born with. Getting mixed up with the agitators – and a time like this too, with another mouth to feed before so long. You wait till he comes home! I'll tell him what for!'

And that evening she did tell him. Not in the kitchen, where Linny May might have listened, but upstairs in the stuffy intimacy of their bedroom. Before ever she gave him a drop of tea, he had a piece of her mind.

She was not often angry, but tonight the words poured from her in a cold, furious torrent. 'You are a tomfool, Ernie Clarance!' she finished. 'How you haven't got more sense I can't imagine. And your poor da, held up like a spectacle! And with this photographer coming everyone is talking about it. Do you know, some man in a motor stopped him this very day and gave him a shilling! A shilling! As though Da was a beggar. Heard about his "troubles", so he said. Da's that upset he's gone out – haven't seen him since supper! Near in tears he was. That's what you've done, Ernie Clarance. You and your Union!'

'It's only the truth, Carrie! He lost an arm in the pit and no-one cared a farthing.'

She rounded on him. 'So what good have you done him, holding him up like that? All he had was a bit of self-respect, and you've taken that from him. Feeling bad enough, he was, with Ma gone, without you making him into a peep-show. And for what? So you and Vince Whittaker can make a song and dance about "clayers' minima", and get yourselves in the paper! Is that it?'

Ernie looked put out. 'Well, of course it isn't. I never knew the man was coming from the papers. Never heard of it until Joe Borglaise told me about it this afternoon.'

'Told you special, did he? So he's got you down as a trouble-maker already. Fine thing that'll be, if this strike happens, won't it? First sign of trouble, who do you think he'll get rid of? And once you *are* out, that'll be the end of it. Never work again, more than like. Never thought of that when you were leaping up making speeches, did you?'

Ernie put on his plaintive face. 'Well, hold on, Carrie – I never meant to make a speech at all, it was that Morrison dragged me to it. Recognised me on account of I went to his house with Vince . . .'

She interrupted him. 'Vince! I might have known he'd be at the back of all this. Where will Vince be when you're out on your ear? You with a family to support?'

'On strike, that's where, Carrie girl. If Joe gets rid of me you'll be glad of the Union. Strike pay, there'd be – and other men would down tools too, if I was put off on account of it.'

'Don't talk daft!' Carrie retorted. 'Strike pay! How long do you think that would last us? Look what happened to the coal-miners! And if they did down tools – what good does that do? Only more men to have strike pay out of the same kitty, seems to me. And who paid for it in the first place?'

'We can put pressure on the pit-owners,' Ernie said stubbornly. 'We withdraw our labour, they'll soon change their tune!'

Carrie snorted. 'Who taught you that? Vince Whittaker? Withdrawing labour, eh? Well, we'll soon see about that. You men aren't the only ones can go on strike. I'm your wife, Ernie Clarance, more's the pity – and I'll run the household, same as I've always done, and cook your tea, seeing as how I'm doing it in any case. But I'm going to get a bed moved downstairs into the front room, and I'll sleep there from now on. And you can brush your own clothes and clean your own boots besides!'

She glared at him, defiant. He stiffened and clenched his fists, and she was half afraid that he would strike her, but after a moment he turned away, sullenly. 'Have it your own way, then!' he said. 'I'm off down the Tinner's.' And he went out, slamming the door.

'Where are they all off to?' Linny May said, when Carrie went back to the kitchen. 'No proper dinner, either of them.'

'No,' Carrie said. 'We'll eat it, shall we, you and me?'

But she had no appetite for it, and although she struggled downstairs with the mattress and wore herself out, she did not sleep until much later, after she had heard the door shut twice, as first Ernie and then his da came home.

When the day for the great cruise came, Emily found it quite difficult to say goodbye. It was her own fault, she told herself – Adeline had asked her first, and she had declined – but all the same it was hard to keep a civil smile on her face as Lorna was helped into the hansom cab which would take them to the station, and Edward hovered on the pavement, overseeing the stacking of a dozen parcels, packages and packing-cases which were being bestowed by the driver.

'Careful with that one,' he was saying urgently. 'It is my wife's hats. She will need them on the cruise.'

'Think of it!' Lorna kept saying. 'A cruise. A proper cruise. Like gentry, we shall be – and on that beautiful ship, too. Do you know there is a ballroom, and restaurants and everything?' Lorna seemed to be intent on rubbing salt into the wound by dwelling on the delights that her sister would be missing. She could be awfully thoughtless when she chose.

'Very nice, Lorna, I'm sure,' Emily said sourly. 'Though if you want a luxury hotel and a restaurant, you don't have to go bobbing about on the Atlantic to find them. You could have the same thing in London for a fraction of the price.'

'But we shan't be in London,' Lorna said. 'We sail from Southampton, and then it's New York – and we shall see ever so many places before we come home. Adeline has arranged it wonderfully. It's rather extravagant, of course – but it will be rather exciting, don't you think, to be a proper lady once in a while?'

'Well you won't be that, will you, dear? I mean, you aren't travelling first class, or anything like it. Still, I'm sure it will be quite delightful – though what Father would have said about squandering money in this way, I really can't think.'

Lorna laughed. 'Poor Father. He never did trust us with anything, did he? And now here's Edward, even more mad-keen for this cruise than I am, now it comes to it. Do you know he has ordered new luggage – a whole set of it, and no expense spared. We shall only do this once, he said, and we might as well enjoy it. Edward can surprise you sometimes.' She settled herself into the cab and gave her husband a radiant smile.

Emily thought irritably that nothing Edward could do would ever surprise *her*. She had half hoped, until the last, that he might have suggested paying for her ticket too, but nothing of the sort was ever hinted at. Perhaps, she thought ruefully, she should not have rejected his patronage so scornfully in the past. Well she regretted it now.

All the same, he could have offered – but what could you expect of a man who let his wife consort with artists? It was the money from those Rawlings paintings that was paying for this – and everyone knew what sort of an artist *he* was. She was much better off as she was, having nothing to do with it.

She sighed. She would never have guessed how much she longed to be going with them. The sights they would see! The places they would visit. It was in vain that she told herself that she was happier and safer at home in Penzance – secretly she had to own that 'being a real lady for once in a while' would have had charms for her too. But Lorna would never think of that.

Edward, at least, seemed to realise something of it. He left her with quite a little sum 'for housekeeping', as the last of the parcels was bundled up behind the driver. 'Just apply to Mr Tavy if you need anything,' he said, and then he squeezed in beside Lorna and a pile of leather hat-boxes, and the cab clattered off in the direction of the station.

Emily watched them go, and even waved goodbye with the semblance of good grace, but when she went back into the house, and its echoing emptiness closed round her, she almost gave way to hot, bitter tears of disappointment. If it weren't for Ellie, coming in with the dinner tray (Emily could not bear to dine alone at that great table), she might have come to it.

As it was, she contained her feelings. She ate her dinner, and retired to her room with a book. But her heart was not really with *John Halifax, Gentleman* – it was rattling through the night on a train, bound for Southampton, and a proud new ship berthed at the port. She had seen and heard so much from Lorna and Adeline that she could almost see it, with its four funnels and gleaming paint. The RMS *Titanic*.

It was four more days before she heard the news.

CHAPTER THREE

The disaster drove every other story from the news pages. The *Graphic Messenger*, lacking the photographs on which it had based its reputation, featured woodcuts of the tragedy, showing wide-eyed women in nightshirts clinging to weeping children, and brave bandsmen playing on the sloping deck while the water lapped around their feet. There were accounts too, a little later, from people who had survived – nightmare stories of frenzy, confusion, heroism and watery death in a freezing hell of darkness and fear. It made Carrie's blood run cold to read them.

She did not often see a newspaper. The narrow budget of Buglers did not normally run to such luxuries, but since the visit of the photographer from the *Graphic Messenger* she had been anxious to see the results, and she had found the requisite pennies from somewhere. After a few weeks, however, it was clear that her worries were in vain. Stories about one-armed clayers and local discontent had paled into insignificance alongside the terrors of the sea. It was clear that no picture was ever going to appear.

Winnie and one or two others were disappointed, after starching their bonnets and all, and so, rather surprisingly, was Joe Borglaise.

'Here we were, with a chance for a bit of a free puff,' he said to Ernie one day in Carrie's hearing, 'and this ruddy liner goes and ruins it. Your da will never make the papers now.'

They thought so at Buglers, too. Ernie was relieved: Da, who hadn't spoken a word to him since the incident of the shilling, finally gave him grudging 'G'night', and the ice was broken. Even Linny May, cowed into silence for weeks by the chilly atmosphere in the house, found her tongue.

'Course they didn't publish no photograph,' she said one evening, when Carrie was turning over the pages of an old *Graphic Messenger* and tearing them into spills for the fire. 'What makes you think they'd want to look at your face, Ernie Clarance? Vainglorious, that's what you are. Don't know where you get it from. Not from my side of the family – they never had such a high opinion of theirselves.'

'Humble and proud of it,' Ernie muttered under his breath, and in spite of herself, it made Carrie laugh. Life at Buglers was returning to something like normal. She thought for a moment of suggesting casually that she might go back to sleep upstairs, but decided against it. Ernie might take it as an invitation. Time enough for that after the child was born. Mother, in her letters, was full of injunctions 'not to go overdoing it': as long as she stayed downstairs, Carrie reckoned, she had a decent excuse not to be 'doing it' at all.

She turned back to the paper, tearing it along the column lines, and twisting it carefully. Then stopped.

'Oh my lor'!' she said, very softly. 'Great God in Heaven!'

Linny May put down the pillow she was stuffing and looked up sharply. 'Whatever is it? Better be something, language like that. Lose your salvation you will, with that tongue!'

And Da, putting down his pipe with his good hand, and touching her lightly on the shoulder, 'Here, steady on, girl. No need to go all trembling and shivery. Published something, have they, after all?'

Carrie shook her head, not trusting her tongue to make words. She thrust the paper towards him.

Ernie seized it at once. 'Why, it's nothing at all about us,' he said in a puzzled tone. 'It's only a list of . . . oh! Tucker! It's never them, Carrie, surely to Heaven. What would they be doing in a boat?'

'Albert Villas, Penzance,' Carrie said, finding her voice from some-where. 'Says so, and all. And Miss Adeline with them.' Her mind was filled with a hundred pictures. Soft-boiled-eggs and third Thursdays. Mrs Tucker and her wispy ways. Mr Tucker and his milk, and the blush-making pictures on his wall. Two shillings to see your feet. Vanished for ever, swallowed up by icy-cold water, halfway to America. It couldn't be. 'Yes,' she said aloud. 'It's them.'

Ernie was searching the column. 'Not that Miss Limmon, though. Wasn't with them, it looks like – more's the pity.'

She rounded on him. 'Don't you speak ill of the dead, Ernie Clarance.'

'She isn't dead,' Ernie said. 'That's what I'm telling you.'

But she was in no mood for his fooling. 'The Tuckers were good to me, and Miss Adeline too – Monsieur Philippe's cousin, that was. Many's the time she's given me sixpence.' What demon drove her to mention Philippe's name, and set her own heart beating fast, even at a time like this? She smoothed out the paper again. 'Says here there's a memorial service

'. . . oh, no, that's over and past. Couldn't have gone anyway, Mr Joe would never have let me.' She had not even dared, these past few months, to take a day off to go and see Mother – they would be short enough of money as it was, when she stopped working, without her taking days off and not getting paid at all.

'Can't see,' Ernie said slowly, 'as how he could rightly stop you. You are on piece-work, when all is said and done. If you don't earn for the day, you don't earn, and there's an end of it. Not as if there was a minimum, like the Union is always asking for.'

Carrie looked at him sharply. She didn't hold with his Union talk, and he knew it, but, do him justice, what he said was true sometimes. 'You think?' she said.

Ernie pressed his advantage. 'You don't want to worry about how Mr Joe will manage. Plenty of people to work, if you don't, and even if there wasn't, I'm sure the lack of your quota wouldn't put him in the workhouse. Turn you off soon enough, he would, if it suited him, I daresay.'

'That's enough . . . !' she began, but Da interrupted.

'Well, you'd be stopping up the pits in a week or two any road, Carrie girl. If you've got a mind to go to Penzance, pay your respects, I can't see how it would do no harm. See your mother too, while you're about it. Nice for you, time like this – a girl needs her mother, and you know she's not fit to come up here no more.'

Carrie nodded. Mother in her little cottage was content, but frail as a pressed flower. She hardly went out without a stick, and she hadn't ventured the long train-journey to Buglers for years. It was tempting, and she still had a few guineas hidden in her box, though some of it had gone on little treats for Ma over the years, or bits and pieces for Mother's Christmas. But now there was the baby to think of. She shook her head. 'Lot of money,' she said.

To her amazement it was Linny May who spoke. 'My dear child, don't sit there with a face as long as a fiddle. If you want to go, go. All us here know the respect due to the dead, I should hope – and an old employer of yours, too. Mr Joe would be glad enough to think you'd make the effort for his funeral. Course you should go. Besides, if you don't go now, it'll be two to worry over the next time, and there's no joy walking miles with a stone of child on your arm, I can tell you.'

'We'll manage here, for a day or two,' Da said, while Ernie nodded. 'You think about it, Carrie.'

And she did think about it. It was an attractive idea. She could see Mother, for one thing, and maybe now, with the baby coming, she could visit Dolly at last. And she would call on Miss Limmon. Poor Mrs Tucker. And Miss Adeline. She wondered how M. Philippe was taking her death . . . She put the thought aside. She must not think about that.

But she would go to Penzance.

Everything had been attended to decently. Emily had seen to that. The black wreaths on the front door, the knocker muffled in its black 'glove', the drapes at the windows decently drawn, and straw in the street to muffle the horses. Mourning outfits for herself and the servants, and special cards with their black edges. Everything had been done.

Why then, did she feel so horribly guilty?

Perhaps it was because there had never been a funeral. There had been a service, of course, but there couldn't be a real funeral, without the bodies. She would have liked to do it properly, a pair of black horses with feathers and a proper hearse with coffin-bearers and curtains. And a place where you go and mourn. But that wasn't possible without the bodies – and the bodies had never been recovered.

It haunted her dreams, that idea. Lorna, silly, wilful, insubstantial Lorna, refusing to get into the lifeboats without her husband, knowing that she would die. 'We'll go together,' that's what she said, by all accounts. Emily felt the lump in her throat, and the crawling caterpillar of horror began again at the base of her spine. 'We'll go together,' while the boat sank.

How could Lorna be so foolhardy, so out-of-character determined, so . . . brave? But Lorna had died only once. Emily was condemned to live it again, night after night, watching behind black eyelids as the icy waters swirled and closed.

Adeline had been found. Clinging to a piece of wreckage, but dead. Quite dead. And buried decently at sea. 'A long sea journey. For my health.' Emily could weep for her. Tears of grief and rage.

And guilt. She too should have been there, battling the freezing waves, fighting for a place in the boat – and she would have fought, she knew. Tooth and nail, treading on people in her terror. Not her sister's dignity. 'We'll go together.' Over and over, like a reproach.

She had envied them. Actual envy. Watched them go with bitterness in her heart, her smiles insincere. She had wished them 'Godspeed' to their deaths, and raged that they had the means to go where she had not. And now everything had come to her. Every last penny that the Tuckers owned.

They did not understand, the people who called. Tavy was good, arranging matters without fuss, and telling her what to do and whom to write to – keeping her busy, so she did not think. But the others, the people she had called friends, were an added burden. Ghouls. Vultures, wheeling about the dead.

The minister, for instance, who had come to see her this very day: whey-faced and solemn, with his consoling handshake and his funereal features. She ordered tea and thanked him for his kindness, but inwardly she was raging: 'Go away, you stupid man. It should have been me, can't you see? It should have been me!'

'So kind of you, Reverend,' she said, passing the potted meat sandwiches which Ellie had brought up on a tray.

'These things, my dear lady, have some higher purpose which we cannot see. Dark strands in the great tapestry. Always think of that.'

Would he be so smug, tucking into his second slice of cake, if it had been his own family out there, dying in the ocean?

'And you will, of course, have quite a little nest-egg.' She stared at him – what an ill-bred thing to say, and at such a time! She would have told him, firmly, to mind his own business, but his next words made it clear why he had raised that indelicate topic. 'I'm sure you would wish to endow some little memorial. A stained glass window, say, or a nice brass tablet for the church?'

Emily managed to mutter that she would think about it, but the presumptuousness of it roused her to a cold fury. As good as asking her for money, now she had some. She might have endowed a memorial, if she had thought of it for herself, but being asked so pointedly! 'I will discuss it with my solicitor,' she said, rising to her feet more promptly, and much more pointedly, than politeness would allow. 'And now, if you will excuse me, I have letters to write.'

She did have letters to write, at Mr Tavy's prompting, though writing was not easy. Letters to Cousin Jenny, who would never send penwipers to Lorna again, letters to bankers, letters of thanks. And last, and most difficult of all, a letter to Philippe.

Courtesy demanded it, but how should she begin? She tried it several times. 'Dear M. Diavezour.' Too formal, surely. 'My dear Philippe.' Not formal enough. She had just begun to write 'My dear Monsieur Philippe . . .' when Ellie came into the room.

Emily sighed. She did not want interruptions now. 'Well, girl?'

'Excuse me, Miss, there's someone come calling at the front door.'

Emily frowned. Where else would anyone come calling? 'Well, who is it?' She dreaded it, this courtesy calling. People she hardly knew, avoiding her eyes and speaking platitudes, avoiding the names of Lorna and Edward as though their deaths were not, after all, the reason for their coming.

'That's just it, Miss.' Ellie *would* call her that, as though she were a schoolmistress. 'It's Carrie.'

For a moment the words made no sense at all. Then enlightenment dawned. 'Carrie, the maid? That Carrie?' The girl with the mimicry and the loud young man with lilac blossoms. The girl with Philippe.

'Yes, Miss. Come to pay her respects. Read about it in the paper, she says. Should I show her up? Only I didn't know.'

Emily thought for a moment. 'Very well.' She could understand now why Ellie had hesitated. It was difficult. How did one receive a person who had been a servant? – and yet she could scarcely turn her away. Standing, she decided, by the mantelpiece. And there was no need to offer tea.

When Carrie came in it was clear that she, too, felt constrained. Emily made no move to greet her, only smiled – a little, not too much – and said, 'Carrie?' You would be forgiven, she thought, for not recognising the girl. She had become a woman, neat in a run-down sort of way, in her worn coat and much-mended boots, but filled-out, rounded. She had lost that gawky coltishness, and had really become . . . what was it Philippe had said? Pretty. Beautiful almost.

'Carrie?' she said again.

'Oh, Miss Limmon, I came to say . . .' The speech, obviously well-rehearsed, broke down and the girl burst out, 'Oh, I'm that sorry. Poor Mrs Tucker. And Mr Tucker too. And Miss Adeline took with them. Awful, that's what it is. I don't know what to say.' There were real tears in the girl's eyes, and Emily, to her chagrin, felt a hot stinging in her own.

This would never do; she could not show that sort of weakness before servants. She took a step backwards, and gave a stiff, awkward nod. 'I see.'

There was a silence. The girl stood there, twisting the corner of her shawl, as if she were waiting for something. The silence seemed to yawn between them like a pit.

'Was there something else?' Emily said. Drat her voice, it would insist on quavering in an unladylike fashion. But the girl did not seem to have noticed. Instead she thrust her hand into a pocket and drew out a battered bunch of violets.

'Here,' she said, 'I brought you these. Isn't much, I know, but they're for you. Miss Adeline and Mrs Tucker liked these, I know.'

It was almost too much. Emily buried her face in the flowers, as though she were merely smelling their scent. Then she blew her nose discreetly. There was a pause, and then she cleared her throat and managed to say, 'Very nice.' She did not trust herself to say more.

The girl was still fidgeting, moving from one foot to the other, as if she felt uncomfortable. 'Well,' she said at last, 'I can't stand here chatting . . . I just thought I'd come and say how sorry I was, that's all . . . I'm sorry if I came out of turn.'

Emily shook her head. 'No, no. Thank you for the thought.' It was inadequate. It sounded false. She had an impulse to put out her hands to Carrie, but she checked herself fiercely. 'Thank you.'

The girl looked at her for a moment with hurt in her eyes. Then she turned away. 'I can see myself out.' But Ellie was already at the door.

When Carrie had gone, Emily buried her face in the violets once again. The bruised petals gave off a sweet, strong fragrance, and the tears stood on them like dew. She remained there motionless for a long time, before Ellie came back into the room.

'Excuse me, Miss. There's a man come up from Mister Philippe. Asked me to give you a message. He sends his respects and hopes to visit later today if that's convenient, offer his "gondolans" or some such. Some funny foreign man – hardly understand a word he's saying. Wanted to be off, but I said wait, because you might want to invite M. Philippe for dinner.'

Philippe. In Penzance. Now. Coming here. Emily took a grip on herself.

'You did right, Ellie.' She turned to the window; it would never do to let Ellie see that she had been crying. She tried to collect her thoughts. What would be appropriate? 'Not dinner, I think, but send word that I should be pleased if M. Philippe would join me for tea. About four, perhaps. My lawyer is calling around then.' Half past four, that should give her time for a long tête-à-tête, without scandalising the neighbours. She held out the violets behind her, without turning round. 'Oh, and put these in water for me. In my bedroom, I think. And I shall need washing water sent up. Something has made my eyes water.'

But as she splashed her face she was thinking about Philippe. They would advise her, those two, as they had advised Adeline. Not on the personal things at first, perhaps, that would be ill-bred, but the practical problems – who to contact, what to sign, what to do with the tobacconist's shop. And even as she thought of it, she felt strangely eased, as though she had already handed over a physical burden.

Perhaps, later she could ask Philippe's personal advice about the real problems. What to do about Lorna's things. And that dreadful private collection of Edward's – all those nude paintings. Edward had meant to sell them, but she could not expose herself to that. And she could hardly show them to Tavy. Philippe, on the other hand, was a man of the world. Perhaps, some time, she would pluck up courage to ask him about those.

She decided, though, not to mention Carrie's visit. Philippe had always seemed to have a particular soft spot for that girl. But that was a long time ago. If the name wasn't mentioned, the girl would probably never even cross his mind.

He had come as soon as he heard the news. Tavy, for whom he had come to have a grudging respect over the years, had written, and he had come at once, but it was still too late for the public memorial services.

It was always dreadful, coming back. Everything about the place reminded him too sharply of the past. That awful day when he had sailed into harbour, so confident of his plans, so patronisingly ready to forget the gulf between them and ask Carrie to marry him. Every stone in the harbour wall was etched into his soul like an engraving.

There was the cliff on which he had seen her pass. The stream where he had trodden on the bonnet. The house and village where she had lived. Even the ruin of old Willie's cottage at Pendeen brought her back to him – her shining eyes as he handed her the Rawlings painting, and talked of Grandfather's 'ill-gotten gains'. And then she had kissed him.

He had returned to St Just every year for Adeline's sake, to discuss plans for the gardens and the house. But he had never willingly come to Penzance. Now, though, he had been obliged to. He had matters to attend to with Tavy. Adeline had been as good as her word and left everything to him; he would have to deal with the estate. And, he supposed, he would have to visit Emily Limmon, to offer his condolences. The poor woman must be distraught. He had already sent Loeiz with a message to Albert Villas.

But first there was the estate to think of. Poor Adeline and her plans! He had seen it like this before. The same gutted look, the same shrouded furniture on the lawn. Except that this time there was no Mrs Bluish, no smell of distemper. Only Tavy, and a valuer from the auction-rooms, in pinstripe and high collar, and, following him everywhere like a spaniel, a foreman in a brown dustcoat with a pencil stuck behind his ear.

'You are quite sure, now, Mr . . . er . . . ?' the valuer said to him. 'All of it? You want all of it to go into the sale? There is some valuable stuff here – unfashionable of course, a bit heavy for modern taste, but good wood. This Georgian furniture will be worth something one day.'

Tavy gave a discreet cough. 'I rather think,' he said, bending his long neck and fixing Philippe with a beady eye, like a cadaverous sea-bird, 'that you would be wise to postpone any final decisions about selling. I've seen it too often – people who sell up a family home when there is a bereavement, and live to regret it later.' He said it with such feeling that Philippe looked at him thoughtfully. Yes, he recalled, Adeline had mentioned in one of her letters that Tavy had lost his own wife recently.

'We could put it in store for you, Mr . . . um,' the valuer said.

Philippe sighed. He had tried several times to get the man to pronounce his name properly, but he despaired of it. He despaired still more of attempting to make decisions about this furniture. He turned back a corner of a dustsheet. Adeline's mahogany writing desk gleamed back at him. Poor Adeline. Since that wretched business over Carrie he had neglected her – pleading business at the *manoir*, fishing off-shore out of Brittany, and avoiding coming to Cornwall more than once a year. He had even tried to escape from that, by persuading her to go on that terrible trip!

It had been selfish, of course – wanting her to be happy without an effort on his part, without having to come here and remind himself of what he had lost. And thanks to that selfishness, now he had lost Adeline as well, and poor Mr and Mrs Tucker with her.

Death by water. He could imagine, more that most, what that might mean. Poor, poor Adeline. The Curse of the Diavezours. Not fair that it should fall on her. He left fall the corner of the dustsheet.

'Yes,' he said heavily. 'Perhaps you are right. I shall sell it in the end, I think. Perhaps not straight away. I don't know. It is no use to me.'

The man in the wing collar and pin-stripe inclined his head slightly. 'If you do want to sell, Mr . . . ah . . . Sir, I think you should consider sending some of this to London. There isn't the market for things of this quality locally, not in this quantity all at once. We would lose quite heavily . . . at least, you would, sir . . .'

Philippe looked at him without interest. It was all the encouragement the fellow needed. 'We could take it off your hands, sir, the house too, if you wanted. We need time to inform the papers, circulate interested parties . . . a house of this quality.'

It was a solution, Philippe thought. If he sold the house, he need never come here again. He could start his life afresh, as Grandfather had done.

But Tavy intervened. 'I think M. Trezayle should consider carefully. He might sell some of the ornaments, the art-work perhaps.'

The pinstripe looked perplexed. 'Trezayle? I understood . . . .'

Philippe said testily, 'It's a long story. But I will be guided by Mr Tavy. Yes, very well. Organise it as you please. But you will keep me informed, no? You have my address in France?'

The pinstripe was bobbing delightedly. 'Splendid, splendid. We might do very well with the art-work. We have a specialist art auction twice a year. There are one or two pieces. . . .'

Philippe looked at him, suddenly alert. '*Laoz!*' he said, startled into patois. 'So there are. Where are the paintings?'

'In the stables, they are,' the foreman said. 'Ninety-seven pictures, two samplers and an etching.' He pronounced it 'itching'.

'*Bennoz Doue!*' Philippe muttered in Breton, and almost grinned at their incomprehension. 'I want a particular painting – if it is still here. Adeline threatened to give it away, at one time. Can you find it? A market scene.'

'The Rawlings?' the valuer said. 'You have a good eye, sir.'

'I'll find it,' the foreman said, and set off with his list. Tavy went with him. With the lawyer looking into his affairs, Philippe thought, he would never be cheated, at least.

When the lawyer was gone, the wing-collar craned forward confidentially. 'If I may suggest, Mr Trezayle, I wouldn't withdraw that – it's the crown of the collection. Unless you want it for your own use.'

Philippe looked at him, his heart suddenly unreasonably light. 'Yes, I wish to withdraw that picture, for my own use.' Strange word, that. How did one 'use' a picture? To gaze at? In that case, yes, for his own use, certainly. 'I am a particular admirer,' he said unnecessarily, 'of that . . . oeuvre.'

The man looked at him shrewdly. 'Well, now. That being so, you might be interested. I think I know where I can lay my hands on one or two others. Fellow in Penzance had quite a collection. Dead now, poor man, but we may be able to persuade his heirs to sell. I understand Tavy is acting for them . . .'

'I don't suppose,' Philippe said suddenly, 'there is a particular painting – a girl with a hairbrush?'

The man looked knowing. 'Couldn't say, sir. There was a picture on the market, a year or two back. From Truro, I believe it was. Collector from London wanted it. But we were outbid. May have been this chap in Penzance. His sort of taste. We do have some others, if you are interested in that style of painting, sir. Tukes, mainly – the naked boys on the beach . . . ? Women in the bath. Or is it only girls, sir?'

Suddenly, in spite of the dreadful business which had brought him here, Philippe had a desire to laugh. The fellow thought he wanted erotica. 'No,' he said, 'just Rawlings. But if you can lay your hands on that particular picture, I'd be glad if you would sell as much of this furniture and silver as is necessary, and buy it for me. Whatever the price.'

'Leave it to me, Mr Trezayle,' the man said, laying his hand on Philippe's sleeve with a little nod and wink as the foreman and the lawyer came back across the yard.

' 'Ere you are, sir. Market scene,' the foreman said, ostentatiously scratching the name from his inventory, and showing it to Tavy to sign. 'Sealed and delivered.'

Philippe took the picture away under his arm, though they offered to send it. When he was safely out of sight he stopped and gazed at it. Yes, there she was. Carrie. His Carrie. He would never let the picture go again.

Now, he felt, he was fortified enough to make his courtesy call at Albert Villas.

CHAPTER FOUR

Carrie walked down the steps of Albert Villas, her cheeks blazing. Old Lemon-pips, then, was as sour as ever! Standing there like a stone statue, with hardly a civil word to say, and Carrie come all the way from St Blurzey to pay her respects.

Still, she wasn't sorry. She had come for the sake of Mr and Mrs Tucker, she reminded herself. And the day was not wasted. She would go down and see Dolly.

She had spoken to Ellie about it, when the girl had opened the door to her.

'Think your Dolly would mind if I went down to say hello?' She had been talking in a whisper, as if she were still a housemaid herself, and Miss Limmon might suddenly come down on her like a ton of bricks for chattering in the hall.

And Ellie had whispered back, 'No, she'd be thrilled to see you. Always saying how she'd asked you, and you never came. Thought maybe you didn't like to, with it being down the fishmarket and all. 'Tisn't everybody's cup of tea, down there – even my family have given up and moved, now my mother's gone. Only Dolly down there now, out of all us sisters and cousins.'

Carrie felt a little ashamed. Dolly had thought she was looking down on her. 'No,' she said, 'wasn't that at all. Only I thought she'd be busy, with the babies and all.' That was almost the truth. 'Love to see her, I would.'

'Know where she is, do you?' Ellie said. 'Fairmaids Lane it is, down by the fish-parlour. Only a door or two from where his family used to live. Or if she's not there she'll be down the pressing-floors, or up the fishmarket. Won't be far. She'd be thrilled to see you – not like some I could mention.'

This last with a glance towards the ceiling, and Miss Limmon in the room above.

Carrie smiled. 'I might just go and call,' she said. 'There's just time before I go to Mother. And it's on the way, more or less.'

She found the house without difficulty. The spit of the Williams' old place on Fairmaids Lane, tall and narrow with a big room over for a sail-loft, and a front courtyard rutted to wasteland by the drays and carts coming to the fish-palace. The same tangle of ropes and nets and lobster-pots piled against the wall, and the same all-pervading stink of fish. The front door was open, and an urchin boy of eight or nine, in patched trousers and a man's jersey, far too big for him, was lolling against the door-jamb. When Carrie approached he stood up and scowled at her ferociously.

'What you want, then?'

'You know where Dolly Williams is?'

The boy looked at her with mistrust. 'Who's asking?'

'I'm Carrie Clarance,' she said. Was there some problem, that the boy was so mysterious? 'I used to work with Dolly . . . Anyway,' she went on, suddenly changing tack, 'shouldn't you be at school?'

'Oh,' the scowl lifted, and the boy smiled, revealing a huge gap where his front teeth had once been. 'No shoes this week, so I'm home helping me da. Going to steep his mackerel-lines for him, I am.' He gestured through the open door toward the kitchen, where something was giving off clouds of evil-smelling steam. 'Boiling up a bit of oak-bark cutch – nothing like it for toughening the lines.'

'Dolly's not in, then?' Carrie said.

'Down the fish-cellar, Ma is. Got in a few fish and they're salting them today.'

'Ma?' Carrie said. 'Dolly Williams is your ma?' It wasn't possible. She had always imagined Dolly with babies, small smiling creatures in bibs and shawls. This child was half-grown, almost to her shoulder, and he had the tough, knowing eyes of a street-urchin. This couldn't be Dolly's son. But yes, a quick calculation of the sums convinced her that it could. 'What's your name, then?' she added quickly.

'Andrew Peter,' the boy said. 'Like in the Bible. Fishermen, see. But round here they call me Drew. You want to see me ma?'

Carrie was half-tempted to say no. She couldn't imagine a Dolly who was the mother of this child – they would be strangers to each other now. But she nodded.

'I'll show you,' Drew offered. 'Jimmy, Bill, Jonah – you keep an eye on them nets till I get back, you hear?' Three figures, each a little smaller and

226

more ragged than the last, appeared from the steam-filled kitchen in answer to his summons. 'I'm going down the fish-house to find Ma.'

And he led the way.

Carrie had never been in a fish-palace before, and she was not at all sure what she was expecting, but certainly not this. The centre was open, and cobbled like a courtyard, set about with cast-iron pillars which held up a rough roof high overhead. The floor was slippery with fish, the more so became it was not flat, but sloped down to a sort of shallow stone gutter. It was littered with pilchards, and as Carrie watched two men tipped out hundreds more from a heavy, open two-handled box.

There were barrels too, mostly empty, though one or two already groaned under heavy pressing wooden screws and the weight of the granite pressing-stones. Along the far wall was a modern concrete tank, like an outsize laundry sink. Most of the room however, was taken up by a dozen or so women, who seemed to be building a great white block of salt. It took a moment for Carrie to realise that the block was made of fish – thousands of them, laid expertly in a line, nose to tail, tail to nose, each layer coated with generous handfuls of coarse salt from a bucket, so that only the very tips of the fish were visible. Everything – cobbles, barrels, tank, women, the heavy weighing hook suspended from a corner beam – was covered in blood, brine and scales, and the gutter ran with a stinking trickle of fish-oil from the pressed barrels. The smell was indescribable.

Carrie was ready to beat a retreat, but Dolly had seen her. Already she was straightening up, and rubbing her hands vigorously on her sacking apron, while another woman bent to take her place at the back-breaking job of building the wall of fish and salt. The takeover was so smooth that the rhythm of the work scarcely faltered.

'My dear Carrie! Knew you at once. Some surprise, this is. Whatever brings you here?' Recognisably Dolly – the same twinkling eyes, the same smile, though the figure had grown wider with child-bearing, and the face was weather-beaten and lined. The odour of fish hung around her like a shawl.

'I went to Albert Villas about Mrs Tucker,' Carrie said. 'Ellie said to come down.'

'Dreadful business, isn't it?' Dolly said. 'Thought of calling up there myself, but I can't really, smelling of fish like this. Still, I'm some glad to see you. Just hang on a minute till I finish this, and then we'll have a good talk. I'm dying to hear all your news.'

'But your work!' Carrie said.

'I'm only helping out, and they've near done now – the rest of those pilchards will go in the brine-tank, and they don't need the hands then.

Only, a great shoal came in, too many for the tanks, so we've got the old presses going. Lovely it is, to see a great load like that come in – you hardly see a pilchard these days. Mostly we're just pickling herring. It's these newfangled drift-boats. Won't be a fish left in the sea in a hundred years, you mark my words.'

'Glad to,' Carrie said, 'if I'm around by then.'

Dolly looked at her for a moment and then burst out laughing. 'You haven't changed, have you, Carrie? Still sharp enough to cut yourself. Here, wait a moment till I set another pressing stone on that hogshead, and I'll come back to the house and make a bite of tea for us. Worst of it's done here now, and I'd best be away home to see after the boys.'

'Growing away, aren't they?' Carrie said.

'Seen them, have you?' Dolly beamed with pride. 'Good boys they are, and a proper help to me and Tommy when they can – but tell you the truth, Carrie, there's times I wonder how I'm going to see the six of us fed and clothed, especially in the winter with the fishing so bad. Tommy's working handlines and lobster creels now, and trying to get a share in a drift-boat, for all he complains about them. Needs to. This is the first time the seine's been out in a twelve-month.' She arranged a sling around one of the heavy granite weights, to hoist it into a position, where it would press down on the waiting barrel and send the precious train-oil seeping out.

'Here,' Carrie said. 'I'll help you.' She tried to roll the pressing-stone onto the sling, but it was too heavy, and for a moment she felt as if she were being torn in two. 'My life! Some weight in that,' she said, as she straightened up, panting.

'Bound to be, to press the oil. But they roll of their own accord when there are pilchards coming,' Dolly said soberly. 'Never believed it, till now, but Jonah, my youngest, woke up in the night and said he could hear the stones moving – and this morning, first light, there were the pilchards. Shan't ever laugh at those tales again.' She broke off. 'Hey, Carrie my lover. You all right?'

'It's nothing,' Carrie said. 'Give myself a bit of a wrench, that was all. Cup of tea, and I'll be right as rain.'

But she was not as right as rain. Halfway to Mother's the pains got worse, and closer together, and by the time she reached the cottage she could scarcely place one foot before the other before a new spasm took her, and wrung her bodily like an old pillowslip twisted in a pair of merciless hands, forcing the sweat from her forehead.

Ever afterwards, she could not remember how she got there, but she found herself in bed, lying on an old sheet, as Mother sat tearing a bolster-case into strips and the kettle bobbed and sang, while the pain took her and tore her, a red rage of agony, over and over and over again.

Philippe sat on the edge of his chair and chafed inwardly. He hated all this. It was bad enough coming to Albert Villas in the first place – the house was full of Carrie's absence, and she was there, in his memory, at every turn of the stairs, standing with a tray in every doorway.

It was foolish. Carrie had been long gone from this place, and there had been women, too, in his own life. A smiling dumpling of a farmer's daughter who would have sworn black was white if it pleased him – and believed it, too – but he had stopped short of proposing marriage, knowing that the cow-like gentleness of those eyes would irk him, in the end. And then his widow-woman, a small, smart, efficient *boulangère*. He had been in danger there, for a little, but he had seen, in time, that although her flesh was as soft and white as the bread she baked, her heart was given to her business, and that her sharp, crisp exterior would soon grow stale and hard – like her bread again. And his own heart? That had never been threatened.

He looked around the room again. Emily simpering at him, and at poor Tavy, who didn't seem to mind it. The conventions of taking tea at Albert Villas irritated him, as always. The whisper-thin sandwiches, the ladylike slices of madeira, the delicate china cups which seemed to hold no more than a teaspoon of tea, and which he was obliged to hold awkwardly between a finger and thumb. It was enough to make a man yearn for an honest brew in an enamel mug, and a man-sized hunk of bread and cheese.

But it was churlish to feel that way. It was obvious that Emily appreciated his call. She wanted his advice, too, and far from the smalltalk or the funereal platitudes he had feared, he was able to sit down with Tavy and discuss some down-to-earth information on taxes and duties. He learned a lot himself, that would help him to deal with Adeline's estate, and Emily seemed genuinely grateful to have him there. She was turning to him simply as a friend, he told himself. If there was a sparkle in her eyes and extra points of colour in the sallow cheeks, then surely it was for Tavy, who was putting himself out to be particularly charming to her – or as charming as it was possible for a cadaverous old skeleton ever to be.

Then the vicar came, with some scheme about a memorial tablet in the church. Tavy excused himself and left. Philippe made to do the same, but Emily got up and walked with him to the passage-door. 'There is one thing,' she confided, her voice low. 'Edward had some pictures – I should value your advice. They are not . . . how shall I put it . . . the sort of pictures that I would care to be associated with, and I seem to remember that you know something about art. You were interested in buying one once, for a friend who collected, I think you said.'

He thought of the market-scene, now hanging incongruously in his dry-locker, and smiled. 'Ah yes,' he said. 'I should be delighted to help you, though I cannot do it now. I must sail tomorrow, but I shall be back in a week or two, to deal with some matters relating to Adeline's estate. I will call again then.'

She rewarded him with a smile so warm he wondered for a moment if it was wise to have agreed. But the maid, Ellie, was waiting to see him out. He slipped her a sixpence, remembering that Adeline had always done so.

She flashed him a smile of gratitude. 'Thank you, sir. And I'm sorry sore about Miss Adeline, if you don't mind me saying. Miss her something awful I will. I was saying so to Carrie only this morning.'

Carrie! The word stopped him in his tracks. He felt the colour drain from his face. 'Carrie? You've seen her? I thought she had moved up the country.'

'Oh, yes, sir. She has. But she came up to see Miss Limmon, she did, say how she was sorry for the Tuckers and all that.'

'How is she?'

He said it so urgently that the girl looked surprised. 'Looking blooming, sir. Being married suits her. Think she's gone down Newlyn to see Dolly, so you might just catch her if you're going down there to your ship.'

'Thank you,' he said. 'Thank you.'

He did go to Newlyn, too, but his heart was no longer in it. The words rang in his ears all the way down to the harbour. 'Being married suits her.' She was happy. He should be pleased.

'*Laoz!*' he cursed softly.

He walked the streets for an hour, but he caught no glimpse of her.

Ernie was on his way home from a Union meeting at the Tinner's Arms. He was feeling pleased with himself. His speech had won him a good deal of applause, and more than one free pint. It was a good speech – all about the Sidney Street siege, and how the strikers that had been shot dead last year had 'written their names in blood on the pages of history'. The men had liked it, too, and cheered him till the barman came in and threatened to have the law on them for disturbing the peace. He was only joking, mind.

Vince wasn't laughing. The better Ernie spoke the less Vince seemed to like it – though it was him who asked Ernie to speak in the first place, and it was his meeting, when all was said and done. Tonight, though, he seemed to be looking for something to find fault about.

'You should have said something about the suffragettes,' he said, 'and about this divorce-law reform. Supposed to be standing together with them on this, we are. Still, I suppose you wouldn't want to see that, would you? Married man like you?'

Ernie sighed. Vince was always going on like this – jawing on about women and how to handle them, though he still didn't have a woman of his own, Ernie noticed.

'Look at Carrie, now,' Vince said. 'Off down to Penzance without you, isn't she? Wouldn't let her do that if she was mine, Ernie lad.'

Ernie scowled. 'Well she isn't yours, is she?' And then he added, daringly, 'Though there was a time you wouldn't have minded, if I remember right.'

Vince said sulkily, 'Never would have met her if it wasn't for me, so just you think of that, another time. Any road, there's plenty of girls would have me if I asked them.'

'Like who?' Ernie was put out by all this talk about Carrie, or he would never have said that. But Vince didn't seem to mind.

'Well, there's Jeannie, for one,' he said – a bit too eagerly, Ernie thought. 'You remember – barmaid over at Bugle once. Gone to Redruth now, but she gave me her address and asked me to write and all.'

'Hardly an engagement yet then, is it?' Ernie said, but Vince looked so put out that he added more gently, 'When you going to bring her home, then, this girl of yours?'

Vince looked uncomfortable. 'Well, I don't know. I aren't in any hurry, and there's plenty of other fish in the sea. Don't want to be tied to a pair of apron-strings like you are – afraid to stay down the Tinner's and have a pint with your friends when you've a mind to. Anyway, don't think that Feyther would think much of her.'

'Whyever not?' Ernie said. It was hard to think what Vince's easy-going Feyther would possibly take objection to, unless she supported the Tories and believed in suppressing the Union. 'She hasn't got two heads, I suppose.'

He wished afterwards he hadn't said it. The girl must have moved on for some reason – she could have had an accident or anything. But Vince mumbled, 'No, course not. It's just . . . she's got a child, and that.'

'Oh,' Ernie said. And then after a minute, 'Married, was she?'

Vince looked abashed and stared at his feet in the moonlight. 'Fellow let her down,' he said at last. 'Wasn't her fault.'

'Oh,' Ernie said again, and there was a silence. A woman with a child! No wonder Vince was ashamed to bring her home. The Whittakers would never hold their heads up again. 'Still, like you say, there's other fish in the sea.'

231

'Wasn't her fault,' Vince said again. 'Morrison says so.'

'Must be true then, mustn't it?'

Vince threw him a venomous look. 'You're in some poor temper tonight. On account of that Carrie of yours being away, is that it?'

'She'll be home by this,' Ernie said. 'Never you fret.'

But she wasn't. He walked in, doffing his cap, and looked around the kitchen in dismay. There was bread and cheese on the table, but that was all. No welcoming hiss of kettle, no smell of cooking supper. No Carrie.

'Where's she to, then?' he demanded. 'Should have been home that last train.'

Linny May huddled herself to the fire. 'Well she isn't, is she?'

'Where's me tea?'

'On the table.' Linny May gave her toothless grin. 'Bread and cheese. Best eat it before it gets cold. Your da and me had a drop of stew she left, but you weren't here to have it, and I aren't cooking twice, at my age.'

Ernie frowned. 'Where's she to?' he said again.

'Up and left you, I should think. Wouldn't blame her if she did, you coming home full of ale, and cavorting with that Vince Whittaker every night until all hours.'

'I'm not cavorting,' Ernie said. 'It's politics, that is. Talking about calling a strike they are, again, like the stevedores are doing.'

'That's what I said. Cavorting,' Linny May said. 'Any road, I don't know where she is, no more than you do, so it isn't a bit of good you going on at me. Now, are you going to eat that cheese, or will I put it aside for your da when he comes home?'

'He's out and all?'

'Gone up the station,' Linny May said. 'Bit of a walk, he said.'

Ernie said no more. He knew the signs. Da and Linny May were as anxious as he was. He ate his tea, but the cold fare seemed bleaker than ever. He was still chewing the last of it when Da came in.

'No sign,' Da said. 'Must have missed the train, that's all. Or found her Mother ill and decided to stop the night.'

'Well,' Linny May said. 'No way to find out, is there? We'll just have to wait till morning.'

Da put his hand on her shoulders. 'Don't you fret, Linny May. Anything awful, there would be a telegram, or the police. Know soon enough then, we would.'

But the next morning there *was* a telegram. The people next door came out on the street to watch the boy deliver it on his bicycle.

Ernie tore it open, almost afraid to look, but then, to the amazement of his neighbours, he flung the paper in the air and almost danced with joy.

'A daughter! I'm a father. I got a little girl. And Carrie's OK. Linny May, you hear that? I'm a father. A father! Think of that now!' And he was everywhere at once, wringing Da's good hand till he winced, and even planting a kiss on Linny May's wizened cheek.

'Get off, you soft thing!' Linny May growled, but she was grinning with all her gums at once.

It took Da to hit a sober note. ' 'Tisn't over yet, Ernie lad. Some small baby, that'll be. Good thing it's a girl – they're hardier as a rule.' He smiled. 'Still. A grand-daughter. Quite something, that is. If only your ma was here to see it. Where's that wine Mr Whittaker gave you, Christmas, Ernie? This calls for a drink.'

CHAPTER FIVE

It *was* a small baby. So small that Mother had made a bed for it in a shoebox, and was feeding it warm milk and water with an eye-dropper.

Mother had been wonderful. Knew what she was about, of course – for years, down at the Terrace, Cissie Tremble had seen every new baby into the world, and there were some who said that things weren't half so easy, or well-ordered, now she'd gone – even the ones who'd paid for a doctor or a midwife to come and all.

Carrie had been thankful, in those long, tortured hours, for Mother and her skills. Telling her when to push and when to stop, and fixing up a leather thong for her to strain on, and another to bite on when the pain was bad, to stop her screaming or putting her teeth through her tongue.

And when it was born, at last, it was Mother who washed and warmed the tiny thing, and kept it stirring into life. Impossible to imagine that such a small creature could cause such agony. It was a girl, of course, but Carrie couldn't think of the child as 'she'. It was so small and wizened, all head and eyes, with fingers like spider's legs, it scarcely seemed a human thing. And so feeble. Impossible that it should survive.

But against all the odds, the baby did survive. Again it was Mother's doing. Mother, whose own health was failing, but who got up a dozen times a night to heat milk and feed the child. Mother, who seemed to have found a new lease of life. Carrie herself could never have done it. She had lost a lot of blood, and for a time it was touch and go for her as well, lying listless on the pillow, her face whiter than a clayman's boots.

The neighbours were good, sending in broth and jellies for Carrie, and always willing to lend a hand filling the kettles and coalscuttles that kept the bedroom full of warm steam.

'Best thing out for an early baby,' Mother said, and it seemed to work, because after a week the child was taking sweetened milk and water from a dampened twist of cloth, although it was still too weak to suck, and feebly stirring its arms and legs. 'The minister's wife was round this morning with some dolls' clothes of her daughter's – though why *she* came I don't know, for I've been chapel all my life. Didn't say no, though. Fit the child a treat – and you can put them on her, Carrie. Time you were taking an interest.'

But what Carrie felt was closer to alarm, as her mother passed her the tiny shrivelled thing, transparent as a tea-cup. Could this scrap of humanity possibly have caused her all those hours of anguish? She looked at the child, wondering at the smallness of the limbs, the face no bigger than a large watch-case, the miniature blue veins in the closed eyelids; and with an experimental finger she gently prised open the tiny clenched hand. Four thread-like fingers closed upon her own, and in that instant Carrie felt a rush of tenderness such as she had never known. This was her child. Her own daughter.

'Hello my blossom,' she murmured, and the child turned towards her, mouth questing. 'Knows my voice,' Carrie went on, in wonderment.

'Of course she does,' her mother said stoutly. 'Stands to reason. Been listening to it long enough while it was in your belly. And you were always one with enough to say! Now, you get on and wrap that child warm. Do her no good at all being out of the covers like that.'

Carrie fastened on the tiny dress, bonnet and jacket – made for a doll, but on that little form they seemed gigantic. The baby though, looked immediately more lifelike, as though it had donned a personality at the same time.

'Grand then,' Mother said, taking the baby and placing her tenderly back in the cradle which had 'come in' from one of the neighbours. 'Turned the corner at last, I think. Thought what you're going to call her yet, have you, Carrie love? Ernie will be coming in a day or two, and he'll want to know.'

'I called her Blossom,' Carrie said, 'but that isn't rightly a name, is it? Sounds more like a cow.'

'You could choose a kind of blossom,' Mother said. 'Plenty of them. Cherry now – you heard of folks called Cherry when I was young: or Holly, that's a nice name.'

'Or May,' Carrie put in, 'like the princess. And you were christened Mabel, too. She can be called for you. And for Miss Maythorne. Maybelle Anne. May for short.'

'That's very nice,' Mother said, 'but a bit fancy. See what Ernie says.'

But Ernie, when he arrived, was so thrilled with his daughter, he wouldn't have minded if they called her after the Mahdi of Khartoum, as

Carrie said afterwards. He just kept saying 'perfect, perfect' over and over, and counting the baby's arms and legs every time he passed as if he expected her to have sprouted an extra limb or two while he wasn't looking.

'You stay here and rest, long as you need,' he said to Carrie before he went back to his train. 'We miss you something terrible, but we're managing. Linny May's doing a bit of cooking, though it's not what you'd call fancy, exactly, and Mr Whittaker's been as good as gold. Sent Vince down with half a pressed tongue, and brought a bottle of elderflower wine he had off Mr Morrison. Hit it off with Da he did, something handsome.'

'Vince?' Carrie had never heard Da say a good word for Vince.

'No!' Ernie laughed. 'His pa. Mr Whittaker. Brought down the wine, and stood there jawing on the doorstep an hour or more, till Linny May lost patience and asked him in. On and on about old times – but he knows his clay-pits does Mr Whittaker, and Da was impressed, you could tell. Never thought I'd see the day.'

'Well, you thank him if you see him,' Carrie said. 'Half a crown for the baby, that's very generous.'

'Working-class solidarity,' Ernie said, but Carrie wasn't going to be drawn. There was a long silence, and Ernie said, 'So you just get better and come home. Maybelle Anne, it's going to be, is it? Mr Whittaker will be pleased to know.'

But, as Carrie found out later, it was Linny May who was most pleased of all. 'Gave the baby my name,' she told everyone she met in the village, even poor Mr Lobb who had lost a relation in the *Titanic*. 'We'll have to find something else to call her when they come home, or we shan't know which is which.'

But she need not have worried. The child was baptised Maybelle Anne, but no-one ever called her anything but Blossom.

Dolly heard about Blossom's arrival on what Tommy always called the 'local telegraph' – she had it from one of the cooks who bought their fish, who had it from the vegetable shop, who had it from Crowdie, who had been talking to Cissie Tremble on his way to town. And no sooner had Dolly heard it than she was collecting things up – old cardigans, socks, knitted jackets and shoes that Jonah had grown out of – and piling them into the creaking old perambulator.

'If she had this child up to her mother's,' she said to Tommy, as he sat lacing hooks onto his newly cutched hand-lines, 'she won't have a single thing handy. And we aren't needing these, this minute.'

'Might do again though,' Tommy said, reaching out a hand to pinch her as she passed. 'Don't you be so quick to give things away.'

' 'Tisn't a give, it's a lend,' Dolly said. 'Just till she gets up home and has her own. Good pal to me, Carrie was, and kind to our Ellie. Mother always said so, rest her soul.'

'Well, you be good to who you like, so long as you save the best for me,' Tommy said. 'Only we've to be a bit careful with our pennies, Doll – don't have to tell you that, I know.' He grinned, that wicked lopsided grin that always melted her. 'Good job the best things in life are free!'

'Like Drew and Jimmie and Bill and Jonah?' she said, laughing. 'Tie a knot in it, that's what you want!' But they both knew that tonight, like every night when Tommy was home, there would be the risk of another child: so that for weeks Dolly would be counting the days and holding her breath for fear she had 'fallen' again, and the family budget would have to stretch a little tighter still.

All the same she was up early the next morning, and once Drew and Jimmy were off to school (for the pilchards had meant 'new' boots from the pawnshop for the whole family) she packed up her perambulator and set off to visit Carrie.

It was the first time she had been to Mrs Tremble's, and it was a longish walk pushing, even after she had put some of the train-oil from the fish-cellar on the squeaking wheel. But she found the house easily enough, though people turned to stare, and sniff, as she passed.

Carrie and her mother were pleased to see her, you could tell, though Dolly could see that the smell of fish troubled them. Carrie wouldn't take the clothes, either, though a moment's glance at the baby showed her why. That child could have gone swimming in the smallest garments that her chunky boys had ever worn. The lend of the pram, though, was accepted gratefully.

'Be glad of it,' Carrie said. 'Get all the stuff to the train, though how I'll get it back to you I can't see.'

'I'll send one of the boys down to fetch it from the station,' Dolly said. 'You let me know. Won't be for a week or two yet. How's Ernie managing?'

Carrie pulled a face. 'Surviving. Doing like Vince Whittaker, I think, shop bread and butter and a big stockpot on the stove. Have to be – shouldn't think he and Da could boil an egg between them, and Linny May can't do much beyond mashed potato and fried eggs. Easy to chew, I suppose, so I don't know if it's can't or won't. But they're managing all right.'

'He must miss you,' Dolly said, thinking of Tommy, and how he would feel if she was away for weeks together. 'I wonder he doesn't come down here and find a job for a bit. There's a couple of claypits out St Just way.'

Carrie shook her head. 'No call to do that. I'll be home in a brace of shakes – and anyway, it's not so easy, with Linny May and his da to think of. Besides, it's a poor job, claying round Penvarris – half clay-stone it is, and it's all to be blasted out and ground down before it's a mortal bit of use. Ernie's not used to that. They're laying men off, too, not taking them on. This weather's not a bit of good for claying, either. Don't know what weather *is*. Too wet and you can't dig it, too dry and you can't stream it. Worse than farming, it is, for the weather.'

Dolly looked at her friend thoughtfully. Carrie had given so many reasons why it was impossible, that you would think she didn't *want* her husband to join her. She changed the subject to babies, and the next half-hour passed in a trice.

Mrs Tremble came in with a cup of tea. 'Drink up then, and it's time you got up out of bed for an hour, Carrie my lover. Want to start building your strength. And Dolly – don't take this wrong, but there's hot water on the stove; I didn't know if you wanted to wash your hair or anything.'

Get the fish-stink out of it, she meant, but Dolly didn't care. It was near impossible at home to do anything to shift it – the smell of fish would be in the bucket the minute you drew water. 'I'd love to,' she said sincerely, 'but I haven't got time, today. Got to be back to help with the fish directly. I wouldn't mind though, to soak my face and hands a bit – see if I can get the stink off them.'

Mrs Tremble bought a washbowl and jug and some home-made soap, and Dolly steeped her hands in the sweet water until they wrinkled. 'There,' she said at last. 'A sight better, that is. And now I'll be off, my handsome, and let you dress. But anything you want – any time – you just let me know. Pleased to help, me and Tommy. And look after that dear wee soul. Let me know about the pram.'

She took back the clothes, any of which would have gone round Blossom twice, and carried them home in a pillow-case, slung over her shoulder like a sack of coal. It wasn't elegant, but it was comfy. She was embarrassed therefore, as she turned into Fairmaids Lane, to come face to face with a gentleman she recognised.

'Monsieur Philippe!' The words were out before she thought, and he was looking at her, perplexed. 'You don't know me,' she said, 'but I know who you are. I used to work for the Tuckers. I was a maid there . . . me and Carrie Tremble. She's pointed you out to me in the harbour many a time. Talked about you no end.'

He was smiling, suddenly. It was a wonderful smile, making his face radiant and joyful, but there was something devilish and delightful about him too. No wonder Old Lemon-pips had fallen for him. And Carrie as well, she recalled.

'You knew Carrie?' The voice was a treat into the bargain – rich and deep with just a touch of foreignness. Just as well I'm an old married woman, Tommy Williams, she thought, or I'd be after him myself.

'Just been to see her, matter of fact,' Dolly said, finding her tongue. 'Took her some stuff for her new baby, but it was small-born, and my lads were whoppers.'

'Baby?' Was she imagining it or was there pain in the blue eyes? Yes, of course, she remembered Carrie saying. The man had lost a child of his own. She rattled on quickly. 'Dear little girl. Ever so tiny. Wasn't due for months yet – but Carrie's thrilled to death of course. And her husband. Fit to burst with it, from what Carrie says. Proud as punch she is, sitting there, with this tiny mite in her arms, smiling like a witnick. Pretty as a picture.'

Why did that make him turn away as though she'd slapped him, and then take his leave in a hurry? She hadn't said anything, had she? Pretty as a picture. Nothing wrong with that.

When she got home her hands smelt of fish from handling the baby-clothes.

Philippe strode down the harbour towards his ship. Automatically, his eyes checked the rigging, the sheets, the mooring ropes. But she was riding perfectly to her lines; Loeiz and Jacques had paid out the slack as the tide dropped, as well as if he had been aboard himself. Ramon, presumably, was trying to drown himself in whisky in one of the harbour bars.

For the captain had not been with his boat all afternoon. He had come back to Cornwall to see Tavy, and had spent four gruelling hours signing papers and affidavits. There was English and French law to think of.

Tavy had been urging him to make a will of his own. He had never thought of such a thing. And there was nobody, nobody at all, to whom he could leave anything. The boat perhaps, to the crew. But who else? This was how Adeline had felt when he had come first to St Just. But there were no cousins left in Brittany to arrive on his doorstep. With him the Trezayles died, and the Diavezours too. While Carrie bore the child of that clayer with the large, pink ears. It make his heart sink.

'You must do something,' Tavy had urged. 'You can't put it all in a sea-chest and hide it, like your grandfather! You see what troubles that led to! And what will you do with that cottage at Pendeen, by the bye?'

'I don't know,' Philippe answered shortly. 'What is there to do with it?

There's nothing but a ruin. Any more than I know what to do with this estate. Let me think about it.' And that was how the matter had been left.

But what *was* he to do about it? There was a part of him that longed to sell it and sail away once and for all. But there was Cornwall in his blood, he had known it from the first time he had set foot here. There would come a day when his back would stiffen, and his limbs ache, and there would be no fishing for him then. The *manoir* in France was haunted by memories of Eved, and he had learned to live with those. But the cliffs of Penvarris were walked by another ghost. Which will you choose, *maître*, when you are old?

And what about that cottage? He had dreamed once, of rebuilding it – some fine house growing from the ruins – of marrying Carrie and taking her there: of leaving it, perhaps, to his sons. And now? There was nothing there but ruins. Ruined cottage and ruined dreams. Drat Tavy. He had all but forgotten about it. Why did the fellow have to bring the whole wretched business up again?

Emily Limmon and her paintings. He had promised to help over those, – would have to visit as he had promised, though she spoke of the paintings as though the topic burned her tongue. What were they, he wondered? He had seen paintings, photographs even, in some of the seamen's bars, which would have made Emily Limmon burst out of her buttons with rage and indignation. (What a picture that would make, he thought irreverently, and could not suppress a smile.) But it was not likely that Edward Tucker had collected pictures like those.

Yet there was something. Probably it would be best simply to recommend that she get them crated up and sent off to auction. That way she needn't ever handle them herself: they would simply be part of Edward's estate. That should satisfy her. But it was odd. He would have loved to have a look at those paintings. Another piece of unfinished business.

Carrie. His mind went back to it like a tongue seeking a sore tooth. Carrie. 'Being married suits her.' 'With a baby girl.' 'Pretty as a picture.'

A picture? *Loaz!* Why had he not thought of it before? If Edward had a collection of pictures, why not *Girl with a Hairbrush*? Was that what brought a blush to Emily's cheeks? Tucker, feasting his eyes on a half-naked servant girl?

The thought brought a sour taste to his own tongue. Damn Penzance. It was a cursed place.

He put a hand on a stanchion and swung himself aboard. 'Loeiz? Jacques? Man those lines,' he called in Breton. 'We'll warp her out.'

'But *Maître*,' Loeiz said, 'my father . . .'

'Can drink himself to the devil for all I care,' Philippe growled, and then, more gently, 'We'll just lie off and fish for an hour, and then bring her back. I'm weary of land-life.'

Jacques leaned over the rail and spat expertly into the water. 'You'll catch nothing,' he said sourly. 'Wind's wrong, and rising. And you'll have to look sharp for the tide.' But he was already loosening the warps.

'I know it, old friend,' Philippe said, using the patois affectionately. 'There is a storm coming, and we cannot go far. But I need the wind in my hair.'

The old man looked at him squarely for a moment. 'You'll sail out, and for an hour you will forget the land. But it will solve nothing. Some time you must come back.'

'The ropes!' Philippe said stonily.

They came back at dusk, a weary haul against wind and tide. Ramon was there, drunk, tearful and repentant, and ready to hawk the fish single-handed round the hotels as a recompense. But there was little to sell. They had caught almost nothing. Jacques had been right.

On both counts.

CHAPTER SIX

May lengthened into June, and June to July, and still Carrie found reasons
not to return to Buglers. It had been taken for granted at first – the child
was too weak to withstand a long train journey, and Carrie herself had a
lingering fever which left her listless – but by midsummer these excuses
were getting hard to sustain.

Mother, of course, was glad to have them. 'Like old times, it is,' she said
more than once, 'having you back in the house, and a baby to see after.
Does my old heart good, that it does. There's been times, these last few
years, when I've felt useless, as though I wasn't good for anything any
more. Better than a tonic, having you here.' And she would busy herself
with knitting, or sewing, and going off to Penzance to spend precious
shillings from her little legacy, though the pile of sovereigns must have
been getting mighty thin by now. Still, she wouldn't be denied. Mother
was thoroughly enjoying having somebody to fuss over once again.

Ernie, though, was getting fed up with it. To start with he was
concerned for the child and hadn't minded. But by midsummer he was
voicing his discontent. Blossom, although still tiny, was 'blossoming' as
Mother put it, and Carrie was back on her feet and able to get out and
about pretty much as ever.

But there always seemed to be something which prevented her from
going home. First it was the trains. The workers in the Port of London had
gone on strike and called for support 'from all transport workers
nationally'.

'Don't know when we shall get home if this carries on,' Carrie said to
Ernie on one of his fortnightly visits. 'Hope to bring everything to a
standstill, they do. Might do it too – the miners' strike almost stopped the
trains, along with the mines and factories. Nobody can work without coal.

Nobody can work without transport, either. Where would Joe Borglaise be without someone to take his precious clay to the ports and potteries? No, can't say when we'll be home.'

'Well, I seemed to get here all right today,' Ernie said reasonably.

'Well, we weren't going to come today, were we? Blossom isn't strong enough yet by a long way. Ask me in a fortnight, when you come again.'

But two weeks later, when the transport strike had collapsed, it was a question of the weather. It had been dreadful, storms which battered ships against the rocks or drove them into Mount's Bay, and then when the wind dropped, day after day of drenching drizzle. The farmers despaired of their crops, and the women shook their heads and muttered that it was only to be expected, with these new flying machines disturbing the atmosphere.

One of Mother's neighbours came in with some lettuce and cucumber for Carrie 'to cool the system', though the fever had long since subsided. 'Stands to reason,' she said, as she sat in Mother's kitchen to drink a cup of tea and admire the baby. 'Rain is up there in the clouds, we know that, and these young men driving their machines right through it – bound to knock it down. Unnatural, that's what it is. If God had meant us to fly he'd have given us wings! That fellow now, flying into Truro last week – crowds of people went to see it, but look what has happened. Raining fit for Noah, and cold enough to freeze the toes off you.'

Carrie had to smile, but it was no laughing matter. The rain was beginning to affect the pits again, Ernie said. 'Isn't like a tin-mine, you see, Mrs Tremble – you can't rightly dig out clay when it's pouring rain. Turns the bottom of the clay-level to sheet ice besides.' He drained his cup of tea and turned to Carrie. 'Joe Borglaise is beginning to talk about turning men off, and then where should we be, with only Da's money coming it?'

Carrie threw him a look. 'Can't your precious Union do something about it?' she said. 'Should have thought if enough of you signed a petition you might have got the rain called off!'

Ernie was not amused. ' 'Tisn't a joking matter, Carrie. It's been bad a month or two, and there'll be real trouble if it goes on much longer. Men working piece-time are feeling the pinch, and it'll be a sight worse come the winter.'

Carrie laughed. 'Can't see you'd notice the difference. Cold and stormy enough for winter now, seems to me. But I can't bring the child home in this, Ernie – we'd get drenched, the both of us, and catch a chill – and where would you be then? Ask me again in two weeks.'

And so it went on. In the end even Mother noticed it. She came in one evening when Carrie was bathing Blossom in the big earthernware bowl by the fire.

'Doing fine, now, isn't she? You'll have to start thinking about taking her home soon. Her father's getting anxious.'

Carrie lifted the big towel that was warming on the clothes-horse and patted the baby dry. 'Well, he'll have to *get* anxious, that's all.'

Mother gave her one of her old-fashioned looks. 'You'll have to go some time, my lover. I love to have you here, you know that, but your place is there, with your husband.'

Carrie was about to protest, but for once, Mother was unsympathetic. 'I know it isn't always a bed of roses for you, Carrie, but he's your husband, and that's that. You said yourself it might be different if you had a child – well, now you have, and you'll just have to put your mind to it. In any case, it isn't fair on Da and Linny May, leaving them there all this time with no-one to see after them. I aren't throwing you out, my lover, no-one could be happier to have you – but it's your happiness I'm thinking of.'

So in the end even Carrie could delay it no longer, and 20 August was set as the date for Blossom to come home. Even then there was a last-minute panic – Carrie had read of an outbreak of food poisoning in St Austell, and almost refused to come – but at last everything was arranged. Dolly herself came to meet Carrie on the road and accompany her to the station, to take back the perambulator which carried Blossom and her belongings to the train.

Blossom herself was wrapped warm, for the day was still chilly though the rain had ceased. She was a healthy enough baby now, but at four months she still looked like a child of only a few days old. Her little face was pink and puckered, and her eyes were wide and unfocused under the knitted hat which Mother had made for her. Carrie too had been busy with her needles, and the two brown paper bags tucked into the bottom of the pram were stuffed with little dresses and jackets which she had made, or which had been given by neighbours.

'I'd like to have given you something myself, my lover,' Dolly said as they pushed the squeaking pram up the hill and down into Penzance, 'only I haven't got anything half-decent, and she still isn't as big as any of mine were, new-born. Still, I'm glad you've used the pram.'

'Couldn't have done without it,' Carrie said with feeling. 'Doesn't matter if it's a bit old, it does the job. I've had Blossom in it every afternoon this last month, if ever the weather looked something like, and she's slept in it under the front porch every day, come rain or shine. With the hood up and a warm cover over, she's had a bit of fresh air every day – and never mind the weather. Been a real boon, it has.'

Dolly smiled. 'Glad we could let you have it. You timed it nicely, Carrie girl – another few months and we'd have been needing it ourselves, it looks like.'

Carrie glanced at her under her eyelids. 'Another one on the way?'

Dolly smiled, but it was a tired smile. 'Looks like it.'

'Want a girl this time, I suppose?'

'Well, yes and no,' Dolly said. 'Love a girl, I would, but a girl means a whole new set of clothes, and goodness knows what. At least with the boys I can buy new for one, and then hand down to the others. The fishing has been that dreadful this summer, Carrie, you wouldn't believe. That one haul of pilchards the day you were in to the cellar, and since then there's been nothing to speak of. And if this new National Insurance Act comes in next year we shall be ruined for sure – sevenpence a week they want for share-fishermen, just because they own part of the boat, and there's many a time Tommy doesn't bring home more than a shilling or two, especially in winter.'

'Isn't it supposed to pay you something if you're unemployed?' Carrie said. 'I remember Ernie going on about it.'

'Make you unemployed, more like,' Dolly said. 'No, well, that would be fine enough. And going to a doctor if you're sick, too, without wondering will you be able to eat next week. But it's finding the money to pay, week on week – that's what worries me. Fish or no fish, we still have to eat. And with they heathen up to Plymouth fishing on Sundays, it isn't easy. Tommy swears he'll never do that, but it will come to it one of these days, see if it doesn't. Was a time it was only the French went fishing on a Sabbath.' She stole a glance at Carrie's face. 'By the bye, I saw a Frenchman the other day – well, weeks ago, I suppose it was now. Your Monsieur Philippe.'

Carrie felt her cheeks turn to scarlet. She said, evenly enough, 'Poor man, lost his cousin in that dreadful *Titanic* accident. How is he?' She wished she had suggested taking the long route to the station, via the harbour, but it was too late now.

'Asking after you,' Dolly said. 'Mind, it is a while ago, and I haven't seen him since. First time I've spoke to him. Nice-looking fellow, isn't he? No wonder Old Lemon-pips was smitten. Well, here we are then, will you be able to manage all those bundles on a train?'

'I expect so,' Carrie said. 'If not, I'll leave some of it at St Austell, and Ernie can come down and pick it up later.'

'Pity you won't have the pram that end,' Dolly said. 'Perhaps Ernie will buy you one.'

'Shouldn't think so,' Carrie said. 'It's a big expense.'

'You never know,' Dolly said, with a knowing smile. 'It might come in handy again.'

Carrie thought of the hours of searing agony that the birth of Blossom had cost her. She couldn't endure all that again. She thought of Ernie and those nights after the Tinner's, and felt a flush of panic. Her bed, she presumed, was still downstairs, or if it wasn't she could soon make it so. And no one would be surprised, with the child so wakeful. And later? She put the thought away. She turned to Dolly. 'Come in useful? Oh no, I shouldn't think so,' she said. 'I shouldn't think so at all!'

Ernie was delighted to have them back at Buglers. The sight of his daughter filled him with unreasoning pride. He would have taken Blossom down to Little Roads and shown her to every man jack in the pit personally, if Carrie had let him. As it was he went straight to the crib first thing when he came home, and held out his stubby fingers for the baby to grab hold of, to make her gurgle and smile.

'Leave the child alone,' Carrie said. 'I've just put her down, and here you are waking her up again.'

'Well, you didn't ought to put her down till I've come,' he protested. 'Chap wants to see his daughter a minute once in a way.'

'Don't be soft, Ernie. How am I supposed to make your bit of tea with the child in my arms? Besides, I never saw such a man for babies. Great girl, you are.'

But the next evening it would happen all over again.

It wasn't like Carrie. Carrie belonged to be good-tempered and accommodating on the whole; though she could be a proper fire-eater when she'd a mind to. But this was different. It wasn't so much temper – he could have dealt with that – it was more as if she had withdrawn from him altogether, as if only the shell had come back to Buglers and the real Carrie had been left behind.

It was only when she was with the baby, or sometimes with Da and Linny May, that he saw glimpses of the old Carrie. And she wouldn't shift back upstairs. He asked her two or three times, and she kept finding reasons, until one night they had a real row about it, and Ernie left off in the end for fear of losing her altogether.

'Don't fret, Ernie lad,' Da said unexpectedly, the following day when Carrie was out getting water from the stand-pipe. 'I remember your ma was a bit peculiar when our first was born. Wouldn't eat nothing but carrots for weeks after – and then one day she was over it, and that was that. Be the same with your Carrie, shouldn't be surprised.'

'Nothing the matter with her!' Linny May said, from her perch on the settle. 'Always find something to find fault with, you do, Ernie Clarance. Bit worried about the child's health, that's all, and not surprising. If a fisherman caught a fish that small, they'd make him throw it back.' But Linny May was just as devoted to Blossom as Ernie was, and if you came into the room a bit unexpected, you could often find her singing to the baby; 'If you want to know the time ask a policeman,' or some other music-hall song, in her toothless cracked voice.

But there was something wrong with Carrie. Not physically – she was looking rosy-cheeked again, and prettier than ever. The fellows at the pit nudged each other every time they saw her, and made remarks about how he'd wear himself out before his time, having a wife like that. And he laughed too, and said he was only just getting into practice, but secretly he knew that it wasn't wearing out which was the problem. Rusting, more like it.

For the trouble with Carrie was in her attitude. It wasn't the housework, like it was with some of the women – she kept it neat, and as clean as it was possible to do when you had clay-carts rumbling past the door and filling the air with dust. And it wasn't the cooking – he would have been pleased to have her home on that account alone. Linny May's thin soup and cold potatoes had given way to Carrie's stews and hotpots, raw fry, pasties and home-baked bread.

No, the trouble was something else. The way she flinched aside when he put a hand on her waist. She would offer a cheek to be kissed, and he would find it colder than clay. She was cheerful enough, on the whole, busy and active, but when she smiled at him, it was her lips alone which smiled, while her eyes seemed elsewhere, wistful, distant and alone. He could not reach her, and every day the gulf between them seemed deeper and wider.

They did not argue, except about two things: about her sharing a bed, and about his involvement with the Union. In vain he tried to make her see his point of view, but she was always adamant, and in the end he gave up.

He went to the Tinner's with Vince and tried to forget the whole sorry business. There, at least, he seemed to be of some importance.

'Listen,' Vince said, buying him the sixth pint of the evening. 'On the fifth of September the West of England boys are going to present a petition to the clay-owners. Don't you think we ought to be doing the same? Workers standing together – isn't that what we say?'

'A petition for what?' Ale did not speed Ernie's thought-process.

'For higher wages, boy, what else would it be? You know if we got another shilling a week, we'd still be worse off than the men were in 1896?'

'How d'you make that out then?' Ernie was disbelieving. 'I get no end more than my da used to get, he's always saying.'

'Yes, but what could you buy with it, that's the thing,' Vince said. 'Your pa and mine were talking about that last week, and they worked out you couldn't afford to eat half so well these days – and that's without this National Insurance money they're talking about taking off the wages.'

'Thought you were all for National Insurance?' Ernie said.

'Well, I am,' Vince said. 'I'm only saying. So, what about this petition then? Can you get one sorted out at Little Roads? Get everyone to sign it, and then hand it to Joe Borglaise. A rise in wages, or a strike, tell him.'

Ernie looked at him. 'Not much point, is there? You know what he'll say. All this rain, and he hasn't turned more than a handful of workers off, so it's been a poor month for the pit. Can't afford it, that's what he'll say.'

'Then you'll strike.' Vince put down his pint-pot with a clatter.

'If we do that he'll turn the lot of us off.'

'Well, then he won't be digging out any clay, will he? And then he loses money. And he won't find men to take your place. That's the strength of the Union, Ernie lad. Hit him where it hurts – in his trouser pocket. And there'll be a demonstration, a parade with bands and all, down to Nanpean on the Saturday following, in support of the petition. We clayers are on our way, Ernie lad. They'll have to take notice of us now.'

Well, Ernie thought, and about time too. Nobody took any notice of him, even in his own home – and he the wage-earner too. Well, he would organise a petition, and go on the demonstration as well. And he would say nothing to Carrie, unless she asked.

She didn't ask. She never asked, these days, where he had been or what he was doing. Perhaps it was just as well. He managed only a hundred signatures to his petition, but he presented it to Mr Joe all the same.

Some of the workers in other places achieved a rise of two shillings a week, but Joe Borglaise said he could only afford sixpence. He put the petition in his drawer and made a list of the men who signed it. Ernie did not like that. His own name was at the top of the list. Still, sixpence was better than nothing. He mentioned it casually at tea-time; an extra two shillings at the end of the month.

But still Carrie said nothing about it at all. He went to the demonstration, and had far too much to drink.

August had been a bad month for fishing. The storms of the last few months seemed to have cleared the sea, and Tommy was glad to bring home a few gunny fish, or a basket of mackerel, or bass if they'd been fishing deep. He had a small share in a drifter now, but no sooner had he found his place than someone started in Mount's Bay with a steam-drifter – not only covered more water, Tommy said, but frightened the fish away.

Altogether it was thin pickings – though there was a little excitement when sharks were reported off St Michael's Mount. Tommy went out to see them, but all he brought home were a few ray-fish, wings outstretched, dangling like fishy seagulls from the handlines.

'I've a good mind,' Dolly said one evening, as they were sitting by the fire, with the boys tucked up head-to-tail in the big bed upstairs, 'to take a bit of this out to Cissie Tremble. Saw her when I went out to see Carrie, and she said then she'd be glad to swap a bit of produce, eggs and that, for a drop of fresh fish any time. And I'm that sick of ray-fish. Few eggs and potatoes would go down a treat.'

'Got time, have you? And it's not too far?' Tommy said, looking up from the piece of rope he was splicing. It was like Tommy, always worried about her overdoing it, when she was expecting a child.

She pushed back a strand of hair with a fishy hand, and went back to her filleting. 'Time? I should think so! Hardly an hour's work down the fish cellars, now – everything's going in the brine, and any fool can do that. We haven't had the presses on since those pilchards came in. Talking about setting up a smoke-room, they are, and smoking the mackerel and herring. There isn't the call for the pickled stuff, like there used to be.'

'Close it down altogether, I shouldn't wonder,' Tommy said. 'Most folks prefer their fish fresh in any case – and with modern ice, and the trains, you can have the morning's catch on the table in London by next day, and not even get out of breath.'

'Well,' Dolly said, 'there'll be no fresh fish tomorrow, with your boat not even out tonight . . .'

'Too much wind,' Tommy put in. 'Won't be a thing to catch out there, except your death of cold. Better tomorrow – might even be tunny brought in on the swell.'

'All the same, you won't want me out with the handcart tomorrow,' Dolly said. 'I can sell this bit of filleted to the shop, like I always do, but after that there won't be much beyond mending Jimmy's trousers, and trying to get a few of these clothes dried off – might manage it, if there's no rain in the wind. If I put Jonah in the perambulator, I can take him with me – bit of air will do him good. And I'll ask Mrs Green next door to keep an eye on the others in case I'm late.'

'Sounds all right,' Tommy said, and after a moment, 'What you going to do with those eggs?'

'Might scramble them up,' Dolly said, 'or make a few pancakes, stretch it out a bit further . . .' They spent a happy half-hour thinking of rival ways to make the most of their treat.

Visions of pancakes and griddle cakes were still floating before her eyes the next afternoon, when Dolly set out on the traipse to Cissie Tremble's house. She had Jonah in the pram, with a parcel of filleted ray-fish at his feet, wrapped in newspaper to keep it clean, though the smell of fish brought the seagulls. They kept swooping over the pram until Dolly beat them off with a stick.

When she got to Gatehouse Cottage the door was open, and a smell of fresh baking filled the air. Always a good cook, Cissie Tremble. Dolly tapped at the door nervously. There was no reply.

She tapped again. Silence. 'Cissie? Mrs Tremble?' No sound but the ticking of the hall-clock.

Dolly put the brake on the pram and ventured into the hall, still calling, and when she came to the kitchen she stopped and smiled. Cissie was there, propped into the corner of the settle, her eyes closed, her baby-knitting still on her knee, and the kettle hissing where she had been steaming the wool to reuse it.

'Cissie,' Dolly said, coming to shake the woman from sleep, though it seemed a pity to rouse her. 'Cissie. I've come for those eggs. Brought you a nice piece of ray-fish . . .'

But even as she touched the arm she knew the truth. Cissie Tremble would never be eating ray-fish ever again.

PART FIVE : 1912–1913

CHAPTER ONE

Carrie took the loss of her mother very hard – worse, even, than she had been when his own ma had died. But she didn't turn to him, this time, as she had done then.

He had rather hoped she might – though he felt a little ashamed of himself for even thinking of it, at a time like this. But he had hoped, and she didn't do it. Instead she seemed further away from him than ever. She divided her time between the baby and the funeral arrangements, and though she was pleasant enough if you spoke to her, it seemed to Ernie that grief and loss had driven her into herself, and he could not reach her.

She busied herself doing things for the funeral. 'A lot to see to,' she said, but he couldn't see that there was all that much left for her to do. The funeral costs were covered – Carrie's father had paid in regular to the Funeral Club, and that meant that the Miners' Friendly would see to all the arrangements. Captain Tregorran wrote, particular, since Carrie was living away. A decent funeral up at Penvarris, with a cast-iron cart and a pine coffin, and four mourners in top hats with crepe ribbons – all paid for out of the Funeral Fund. And there was a plot already, where Seth was buried.

Mother had even chosen her own hymns – did it long ago, when her husband was buried – so there was not even that for Carrie to worry about.

There was the food, of course. Carrie was expecting quite a crowd. Her mother had neighbours down at Gatehouse Cottage, as well as the folk from the Terrace. Dolly Williams wrote to say she would give her a hand with the funeral feast, but Carrie went down the day before, all the same, taking Blossom with her. It was as if she couldn't wait to get out of the house.

Ernie took the day off, and went down with Da for the funeral. Linny

May had to be left behind, though she put on her mourning bonnet and her best black frock, in honour of the occasion.

Carrie was right about the crowds. The little chapel was full to bursting – not just Mother's friends, but men from the mine who remembered Seth. Dolly Williams was there, and no end of flowers. There were even the Trevarnons from the big house near Penzance. Ernie was rather embarrassed to see them. He had never thought Katie would turn up: she and Carrie had rather lost contact after he failed to post that letter, and they only exchanged Christmas greetings now. But she had been fond of Mrs Tremble and had come to pay her respects. Seemed a nice woman too, Ernie thought. Not a bit of side about her. Told him all about herself – what a struggle she'd had when her architect husband died, and how she'd come back to Trevarnon, where she had once been a housemaid, to marry the son of the house whom she'd been fond of all along. Told Ernie to call her Katie, and sang along in the hymns like a good one. Made him feel bad about the letters, but there it was. What they didn't know couldn't hurt.

'As well we did a bit of extra,' Carrie said, as they went back to the house after. 'Though there's nothing special to offer the Trevarnons. Don't know whatever they'll think. Used to the best, now, Katie is.'

'You've done us handsome,' Ernie said, looking at the plates of sandwiches, the tongue and ham and tomatoes and saffron cake, and the gallons of tea. But it was no good saying – he knew Carrie of old. She was fussing about the food as a way of keeping busy, so she did not have time to feel and to think. Well, let her fuss. If she was worrying about the sandwiches she wasn't fretting over Katie not answering her letters.

He spent the whole afternoon on tenterhooks in case something was said, but he needn't have worried. Carrie seemed positively anxious to avoid too much conversation with her old friend. Katie seemed a bit hurt, Ernie thought, but she probably put it down to Carrie being upset about her mother. The whole day passed off without incident, and people said it had been a real nice funeral.

Then there were Mrs Tremble's affairs to set in order. Not much, in fact. The money Miss Maythorne left had been put into an annuity, on Captain Tregorran's advice, and that had died with Cissie. Gatehouse Cottage, too, was only a life tenancy, so there were only a few bits of furniture and clothes to see to. Just as well, Ernie thought. If it hadn't been for the Estate Office wanting possession of the cottage, Carrie would have made it an excuse to spend still more days away from Buglers.

As it was, they simply piled everything into two packing cases and took it all back to St Blurzey. Carrie took everything into her room and spent hours 'sorting' it, as she said. He looked in once or twice and offered to help, but she was doing nothing, just sitting on the bed surrounded by little piles and staring into space, or shifting things aimlessly from one side to the other. She would emerge with her face blotched and streaked with crying, but if he attempted to comfort her she shook him off and denied that anything was the matter.

He worried about all this, but it *was* her mother, after all, and he did his best to be understanding. He even stayed away from Vince and Union meetings down at the Tinner's, though they were having special meetings and rallies every week now. Carrie didn't like him going there, never had – and besides, there was that list of names in Joe Borglaise's desk which made it a little easier to stop at home.

But a week or two before Christmas his resolution snapped. It was Linny May who did it really. It was one evening, after a hard day at the pit. He was bouncing Blossom on his knee and Carrie was telling him not to as usual, because the child had just been fed, when suddenly Linny May piped up from her corner.

'Going to order a goose this Christmas, Ernie? Or can't we run to it this time?' She sniggered. 'Won't signify, any road. Already got one goose in this family, seems to me, even if we can't eat him!'

Ernie could feel his ears turning a dull pink. He put Blossom down and stood up slowly. Da and Carrie stopped what they were doing and watched him from the corner of their eyes – he could sense their gaze upon him. There was a terrible silence.

'Talking to me, are you, Linny May?' His voice seemed to fill the room.

The old woman was taken aback, he could see it. Usually he did no more than sit and glower at her jawing. She shifted on her seat, and her gaze faltered, but she said boldly enough, 'I didn't name no names, Ernie Clarance, but if the cap fits, wear it.' She nodded at him defiantly, the flounced bonnet flapping. 'Might as well wear a cap, and all. Never did wear the trousers, that's one thing certain!'

Perhaps it was the mention of the cap that did it, or perhaps it was simply the stress with Carrie, or just that he was suddenly tired of her niggling. Something within him snapped. He strode forward and seized her bonnet – that foolish thing of ribbon and black-edged flounces – and taking it in both hands, pulled it firmly forwards over her nose and face. He did not harm her at all, but it made her look ridiculous.

'Goose I may be, but I'm the wage-earner in this house, and don't you forget it. You live here because I choose to keep you – sitting by the fire all day, and if you're not eating or sleeping you're finding fault! Just you take care that my patience doesn't run out, or you'll find yourself up the workhouse, and they won't stand for your nonsense. And neither will I, no more, so just you mind your manners in future.'

Linny May made no attempt to move the bonnet but sat completely still. She looked somehow crushed, sitting there with her bonnet over her eyes. Da and Carrie were motionless too. Only Blossom in her crib gurgled and cooed. Ernie felt a sudden rush of power, as if he had discovered a new authority.

'I'm off out,' he said, settling his cap on his head. 'I don't know when I shall be back, so don't expect me.'

The Union men, down at the Tinner's, gave him a hero's welcome. They were talking about more demands to the pit-owners in the New Year, and when they put his name up for the protest committee, instead of Vince, he accepted without demur.

They did have a goose for Christmas, a scrawny one from the Tribute Shop up the pit, stopped out of Ernie's wages. Carrie stuffed it with a few breadcrumbs and onions and a bit of pork, and made it stretch to a meal for them all. There was a pudding too, which Carrie made, and she contrived presents for everyone from a pair of good linen sheets which Mother had had from Miss Maythorne. It took her hours, and even then the seams were lumpy: Carrie never had been a needlewoman. But there they were on Christmas morning – a new shirt for Ernie and Da, a linen cap for Linny May, and a dress for Blossom using the embroidered ends.

Ernie had brought in a bough of evergreen and Da made a hoop to hang in the kitchen with an orange for everybody tied among the branches. But for all the treats it was a bleak Christmas. Da had caught cold, and was wheezing and coughing so that he couldn't even taste his pipe. Linny May had never been the same since that episode of the bonnet – it was as if Ernie had extinguished her with it, like the Spirit of Christmas in Mr Dickens' story that Carrie had learned in school. And she and Ernie were like strangers to each other, more like lodgers in the same house than husband and wife. Carrie often thought about her own mother and father, and the unspoken warmth and understanding which there had been between them. You could almost warm your hands at it, like a fire, but in this house there seemed to be nothing but the cold grey of ashes.

Only Blossom was a simple joy. She was still a frail child – never would be strong, more than likely – and she was a bit slower than most babies when it came to learning things. Winnie from up the pit had a baby born in July, two months later than Blossom, but he was already sitting up and rolling over and trying to crawl. Blossom was still content just to lie there and gaze, though she had a tooth now, and could hold a toy if you put it in her hand.

'Stands to reason,' Winnie said, calling by with a slice of hot figgy pudding for them all for a bit of a treat Christmas night. 'Early born, late learning. Wonder she made it at all, little scrap like that. Be a bit behindhand all her life, most likely, but she's a pretty little thing, and there's nothing the matter with her brain. Look at her smiling at me now, and reaching for my beads.' Winnie had put on her best 'pearls' from the pedlar in honour of Christmas. 'Like a little snowdrop, she is, with those veins showing through and her skin white as petals. Not like our Lennie, look, round as a barrel, and pinker 'n a pig.' And she held up her fat, wriggling baby for Carrie to admire.

'Anyway,' she went on, 'getting big enough to leave, he is now. Me sister will have him in the day, if there's a place for me down the linhay. She'll have to bring him down to the gates for me to feed him, of course, but I've done that with all the others. I'm going to ask Mr Joe for a place, soon as there's one vacant.' She hesitated. 'My sister now, she'd have Blossom too, if you wanted, Carrie. Few pence extra a week would help her out, and likely you could do with your bit of earnings, with the baby and all. Mr Joe'd find a place for you, quicker 'n light – he's always been good like that. There's some pits won't have a woman back once she's married, let alone with children. Worse than a shop, some of them.'

Ernie looked up from the settle, where he was sitting with a book which Mr Whittaker had sent him. He wasn't really reading it, Carrie knew. Ernie never was much of a one for reading, but it was Christmas, and he could afford to be idle for an hour, turning over the pages and sitting up stiff as a peacock, half-strangled in his new shirt.

'Well Joe Borglaise isn't doing you any favours,' Ernie said. 'Doing himself one, more like. Easier for him to take on someone a bit handy, and not a bit of a girl who'll have to be trained up all over. Don't matter a bit to him who scrapes his clay-blocks – it's all labour to him. Never mind if the children are running wild and their mothers not home to feed them from dawn to dusk, so long as his precious clay is up for shipping.'

Winnie drew her breath sharply. 'Here!' she said. 'My children aren't running wild – never have been, and I'll thank you not to say so, neither.'

Ernie shook his head. 'I aren't saying that,' he said. 'It's Mr Joe I'm on about. It's like it says here.' He tapped the book in front of him. 'If it wasn't for the law, he'd have children up the pit six and seven years old, like they belonged to do years ago, and be proud to do it. Cost him less, that's what he'd say, and never mind if they drowned in the slurry.'

Carrie took a deep breath. She hated it when Ernie started in on his

Union talk. But Linny May broke in. She took out her teeth, which she had been using to chew the figgy pudding, and said, 'I remember that. Started down the linhay soon as ever I was old enough to lift the blocks. Never did learn my letters. No school in them days, just work, work, work, in the pit and out of it.'

'There you see!' Ernie said triumphantly. It wasn't often Linny May agreed with him.

She seemed to feel it, because she added, in a wavering voice quite different from her stout declaration of a moment before, 'And for what? So I could end up a feeble old woman, living on charity and made to feel it too.'

Winnie looked at her and said, in her forthright way, 'Yes, it's a shame really you're so old as you are, or you could have looked after Blossom yourself.' There was no malice in Winnie, and she meant well enough, but Linny May looked furious, and Carrie was hard put not to laugh. 'But my sister would do it, Carrie, and be glad of the few coppers. So you think about it, my handsome. I'd be some glad to have you back there.'

'We can manage without,' Ernie said stoutly.

'Old, indeed!' Linnie May snorted indignantly, 'I was looking after children before you were born!'

This time Carrie did laugh aloud. 'It's a thought, though, Winnie,' she said. 'We can manage, but a bit extra would be handy. I'll think about it, when Blossom is stronger.'

If anything happened with this protest committee, she thought to herself, and Ernie found himself without a job, a few extra shillings could make all the difference. She still had eight of her eleven guineas, two hidden in her box, and the rest in a tin up the chimney. Somehow she had never told Ernie about that. But the time might come when even that would not be enough. Ernie could say what he liked about strike pay, but the railway strike had cost the unions thousands and thousands of pounds. The clayers' union wouldn't have that sort of money. Yes, definitely she would think about going back to the clayworks. Or cleaning. Or something.

Christmas was frosty, and then in the New Year the rains all but stopped them working clay at the pit. Da came home grumbling that the horses seemed to have stopped production too, with all the motor-traffic on the roads. And when payday came, even Ernie began to see that there was something to be said for the idea of Carrie going back to work.

Dolly had a wonderful Christmas. The new baby was born just a week before – a girl, to Tommy's delight. It was a hard birth, the worst Dolly had known, but the child was healthy and within a few days Dolly was on her feet again, and active for the feast.

'Going to be a picnic though,' she said, looking at the child sleeping peacefully in the crib. 'All very well having boys, but what we going to do with this one when she gets a bit older? Haven't got but the two bedrooms in the place.'

Tommy laughed. 'Put her up the net-loft with the creels,' he said. 'Plenty of room up there.'

Dolly wrinkled her nose at him.

'No,' he said, 'plenty of people do. I've seen my father sleep up with the nets plenty of times when I was small. Anyhow, we shan't have to worry about that for a year or two. She's all right where she is for now – in the cradle by our bed. Unless we got another one, of course,' he added slyly.

Dolly flapped a hand at him. 'You! Get off with you. One-track mind, you have.'

She went to chapel Christmas Eve and came back saying the child was to be called Ellaline Joy. Tommy said it was a daft name, Ellaline was all right, after Ellie, but who ever heard of a child called Joy?

Dolly, though, was adamant. It was in the sermon, she said. The night is long and full of weeping, but Joy cometh in the morning.

'That's just how it was,' she said. Tommy couldn't argue with the preacher, so there it was. Ellaline Joy, 'Little Ell' for short.

'More of a little 'ell than a Joy,' Tommy said, when the baby woke him in the night, but he was good really. He never did complain about the babies, when they cried or wailed or got under his feet, not like some men. And he was that proud of his daughter.

There was a proper Christmas feast, and all. Tommy had been out with the handlines and brought home a couple of eels – this time of year! They had them, jellied and savoury with plenty of potatoes and swede turnip too, and there were some apples which Ellie had brought in – they were going poor and Mrs Rowe up at Albert Villas was throwing them out, but with a handful of flour and a few currants they made a handsome apple cake for after. They all of them ate till they could eat no more.

'King George himself couldn't have supped better,' Tommy said, as they sat around the kitchen fire, and loosened their buttons.

'And Queen Mary never made jellied eels like our ma,' Drew said, and they laughed till the tears ran at the idea of Queen Mary in her crown standing in the kitchen skinning eels.

'There's plum jam for tea, too,' Dolly said. 'Katie Trevarnon sent it down, special. Some good she's been, since that funeral. Put in an order for fresh fish every week we've got 'un, and if I go up with it, she comes down to the door herself and if there's a penny or two in it she'll never take the change. Some different from that Miss Limmon. Send the fish back, she will, if she don't like the look on its face!'

Tommy laughed. 'Taking it serious, I suppose, now she's running the household. Never had it to do, before, poor old soul.'

'Poor old soul! Keeping Ellie up there all day, and Christmas too! Just so she can sit in state and eat her bit of roast beef all alone.'

'Well,' Tommy said. 'Can't be much fun for her, nobody in the house. Must miss her sister something awful.'

'Yes,' Dolly agreed doubtfully. 'At least she's got the legal things sorted out now. Quite a to-do, Ellie says, with no end of lawyers coming and going. Question of whether Mr Edward died first, and left things to Mrs Tucker, or whether he didn't. But it's all sorted out now, and it's all come to Miss Limmon in the end. She's even been able to get those pictures sent off for the auction. Had them crated up for I don't know how long.'

'Pictures?'

'Some paintings he had. Bit saucy, from what I hear – he had a few on the walls of his bedroom when I was up there, but there were a whole lot more, it seems. Ellie never was allowed to see them. Never will, now, I suppose. Supposed to be worth hundreds of pounds, they are. Anyway, it seems that M. Philippe was a bit interested in the pictures too. You men – you're all alike.'

'What you mean, saucy?' Drew said. He had got three walnuts and a penny in his Christmas sock, and had spent the afternoon trying to crack them with a hammer.

'Like you! Ask too many questions,' Dolly said. 'Now, you coming to help me set the crocks on the table for our tea? I want to eat a bit early, and get Little Ell down so I can write a note to Carrie. Nice letter she sent, asking after the baby.'

After tea she did write, a long letter, telling Carrie all the news, about Little Ell, and Drew's new front teeth, and the jellied eels. And, knowing that Carrie would be interested, she added a long paragraph – everything Ellie had told her about Monsieur Philippe and the pictures.

CHAPTER TWO

The auction of Edward's paintings was scheduled for March. Philippe was still in England, dealing with the tenancies on Adeline's estate. It was a process which seemed to Philippe to be taking an unconscionably long time, but Tavy assured him that legal matters were always slow, and evidently Emily, too, was finding them so. By the time Edward's affairs were settled and the tobacconist's shop sold it was already the New Year, and the auctioneers had apparently advised her that she would get a better price for the pictures in spring, when more buyers were in London.

Emily was reluctant to have him go to the auction. She offered a thousand reasons, but her real motives were obvious. She was mortified by the prospect of Philippe being present when Edward's collection was made public. All the same, he determined to do it: until he saw the catalogue.

She had shown it to him with reluctance. Not shown him, even. Gestured towards it, her face scarlet with embarrassment, as he was leaving Albert Villas after a conference with Tavy. 'The catalogue you wanted. For the auction.' And then, as he made to turn the pages, 'No, please, do not open it here. Not in front of the servants.' She handed it to him, gingerly, as though the list of titles – *Nymph Bathing*, *The Temptation of Pan*, *The Bath* – would scorch her hands, as they had burned her cheeks. 'Only, I suppose you must have it, if you are to advise me.'

He did not tell her that he wanted the catalogue for reasons of his own. *Girl with a Hairbrush*. Why had he not thought of it before? It was obvious. It could only be Edward, surely, who had bought the painting?

Everything pointed to it. Lorna with her preference for local artists. She had particularly admired Rawlings -- singled out that very canvas at the exhibition, and would certainly have bought it if Philippe himself had not forestalled her. If the picture had come up for sale, Edward would have wanted it. The more he thought of it, the more certain he became. Someone in Penzance with 'a certain taste' had wanted the picture, so the auctioneer had said. There were certainly nudes in Edward Tucker's collection. Emily's blushes had been testimony to that.

He could hardly wait to get back to Trezayle to leaf through the catalogue. He had already given his instructions to the auctioneers: *Girl with a Hairbrush* for M. Philippe, whatever the cost. Up to a hundred guineas. And to think that he had owned it once for fourteen! More than that, if he had not been such a fool – such a stubborn, blind fool – he might have had more than the picture. He might have had the girl herself.

Marriage suits her. And she has a child.

He turned the pages of the catalogue with fingers that trembled. The picture was not there.

Disappointment hit him like the slap of cold spray. He read the list again. No. There were some remarkable titles – no wonder Emily had been covered in confusion – but *Girl with a Hairbrush* was not among them. There was nothing, even, which might have been the same canvas under a different name.

He put down the catalogue with a sigh, amazed at the strength of his own feeling. He would not go to London. If 'his' picture was not in the auction, there was no point in it. Tavy might go, as Emily's representative – and that would spare her blushes, too. As the Tuckers' solicitor Tavy could be seen as representing Edward, rather than his sister-in-law, and there would be a sort of distance, a formality in the arrangement. He wrote a brief note to Albert Villas, suggesting it. Emily, when he saw her next, was quite embarrassingly grateful.

Tavy too, seemed to be delighted by the request. That rather surprised Philippe. A visit to London seemed to offer little attraction for a cadaverous old solicitor from Cornwall. Philippe himself had been to the capital twice on Adeline's account, and he could imagine how it would be. A long and tiring journey, and then, when you arrived – what a hurly-burly! The crowds. And the roads! Motor-buses, all roar and smoke and screeching brakes. Motor-cars, scores of them, growling and grinding. Bicycle bells. Hawkers. Horses. Carriages. Sandwich-men demanding Home Rule for Ireland. Electric light. People jostling in the huge stores for the latest fashions, and newsmen crying their wares. 'Pankhurst Trial – pictures!' 'Death of Captain Scott – latest! Read all about it!' Nothing but noise and hustle.

And then the need to take a taxi-cab, or the new underground train, merely to arrive at your destination – everything was far too distant to walk, and the streets too confusing to follow. Little there to draw an elderly man – but Tavy seemed positively to relish the commission. Indeed, as Philippe was going to Exeter in search of a chandler's man, Tavy suggested that they take the same train and make part of the journey together. He was quite insistent on the matter. There was something, Philippe thought, that Tavy wanted to say.

At first it seemed he was mistaken. The solicitor settled himself in his seat, and after a few cordialities, busied himself with looking out of the window. Philippe followed suit, watching Marazion and the Mount flash by, the railway banks already creamy with primroses and the first shy daffodils of spring.

They were almost at Truro before Tavy, sitting opposite, coughed a little, craned his bird-neck confidentially and said, 'You may tell me this is none of my business, my dear fellow, but you had at one time, I think, a personal interest in these pictures of Emi . . . of Miss Limmon's?' Philippe's face must have shown his astonishment, because Tavy went on, 'I understand from the auctioneer that you gave . . . special instructions.'

Drat the fellow – did he suppose that Philippe shared Edward's interests in erotic painting? He shook his head. 'Not paintings,' he said, 'painting. Just one. It was sold locally, and I believed Edward may have bought it. But it seems not, after all.'

Tavy said, 'Ah!' and leant back in his seat. 'Of particular value, was it?'

'It's a Rawlings,' Philippe said shortly. 'I believe all his work has some value, these days.'

Tavy was looking at him quizzically. 'I wonder,' he said at last, 'that you did not mention this to Miss Limmon. She would have accommodated you, I am sure, if the picture was in the collection.'

Philippe felt himself flush. What business was it of Tavy's? But the man was looking at him shrewdly. Perhaps, Philippe thought with a sudden rush of hope, he knew the whereabouts of the painting. Tavy represented a lot of people, after all. There was one way to find out. 'Since you are my solicitor,' Philippe said carefully, 'perhaps I should tell you, in confidence.' There, that should ensure that the man said nothing to Emily. Professional discretion ran in Tavy's veins. 'It does have a particular value to me. *Girl with a Hairbrush*. The subject of the painting is . . . well, someone I know. Someone I wanted to marry . . . still would marry, if I could. Naturally, I did not want Miss Limmon to discover this.'

Tavy nodded. 'I see.' He gave a little cough. 'Then I take it . . . ah . . . that you and . . . ah . . . that Emily . . . Miss Limmon is . . .'

A bright spot of colour was burning in each of Tavy's cheeks. I am being asked about my intentions, Philippe realised with surprise. The cheek of the fellow!

'Emily Limmon is a family friend, nothing more.'

Tavy said, 'Ah!' again, and the carmine spots on his cheekbones deepened. The man was blushing. It wasn't *his* intentions they were discussing, Philippe realised, suddenly. Tavy had intentions of his own. That was why this tête-à-tête had been arranged. 'I understood,' the solicitor went on, 'that you and she . . .'

Philippe shook his head. 'Nothing of the kind, my dear fellow,' he said warmly. 'I have been her adviser, nothing more. Not so much of an adviser as you, perhaps. I know that Emily thinks most highly of you, and your opinion.' He wanted, suddenly, to offer Tavy some encouragement. 'Thinks most highly of you indeed,' he said again, with unaccustomed warmth.

Tavy said, 'Ah!' for a third time, and for a long time lapsed into silence. Then, suddenly: 'You know her, Mr Trezayle, better than I do. Would she, do you think, feel it a presumption on my part? I am not, after all, a landowner like yourself.'

And Philippe, who had been thinking of someone else, had to drag his attention back to the present. A landowner. Yes, he was. Well, he looked it now. English too, in his double-breasted suit and his turn-down collar and tie. No more of Uncle James's hand-me-downs from Adeline's cupboards, but made for him brand-new by a tailor in the town. With a hat and gloves, and even a pair of stout shoes instead of polished boots. A Cornish gentleman.

'What do you say, Mr Trezayle? Would you . . . could you . . . speak to her? See how the land lies?' Tavy, his bird neck bobbing. 'I should hate, you know, to endanger our professional arrangements. But I am a widower now, and . . . Miss Limmon is a fine woman.'

And a wealthy one, Philippe thought with amusement. There was not only Edward's estate, there was the money which her father had left her in trust until marriage. Tavy, as her solicitor, must know about that. But yes, he was a pleasant enough fellow, and Emily wanted a husband. She and Tavy – that might work out very well. 'I will speak to her, of course,' he said, and they lapsed back into silence, like old friends.

It was Tavy who spoke first. 'If I can be of help to you, of course, my dear fellow, you have only to ask. Should you intend to sell Trezayle House, for example?'

'I haven't decided,' Philippe said. It was true. He had asked himself the same thing a thousand times and come no nearer to an answer. He did not think that he would live there, beyond a week or two a year. There was the house and farm in Brittany, for one thing. And there was still the fishing – both boats in commission now – the old *Plougastel* with a smart young skipper and crew, and himself just the owner, taking a third of the profit. Even the *Ploumenach* didn't need him any longer – Loeiz was grown to a man long ago, and with him aboard Jacques and Ramon could handle ship and nets without the *maître*. Out fishing off the Scillies at this moment, no doubt – and for a moment he yearned to be with them, sweating at the ropes in honest sea-boots and sou'wester, instead of sitting like a landsman in the train, squirming in his collar.

But there was something about Cornwall which drew him, like an old iron nail to a magnet. Now that he had found the house, he could not bear to sell it. Though it would die with him, he thought wryly. The last of the Trezayles.

Being married suits her. And she has a child.

'And a will,' Tavy said, as Philippe collected his hat and prepared to get out of the train at Exeter. 'You should think of that. Settling your own estate. And that old cottage at Pendeen. Something must be done with it.'

That was true, too. He could hardly leave it to go to rack and ruin with neglect. But somehow, he had avoided visiting the place. Dreamed once of building there, with Carrie as his bride. Well, it was no good. He could not simply ignore the matter, as he had done so far. One more trip out to Willie Polzeal's cottage on the cliffs, and then he would lay the matter to rest. Sell the place and have done.

He went the next day, saying nothing to anyone. It was an unpleasant day, 'mizzling' with rain, Grandfather would have said, and one glance at the cottage told him it was hopeless. The place was even more ruinous than the last time he had come here. Now only the walls and chimney remained, with empty spaces like blank eyes where the windows and doors had been. It was roofless, with grass and lichen sprouting from the crevices, and the flagstones of the floor long since lifted up and taken away for use elsewhere. No Carrie now, to build a home for. No romantic dream to cherish of a great house on the cliffs rising from the ruins of the old.

Besides, as he realised with a wry grin, the story of the bequest had got around in the district. There never had been a well, but the remains of the garden had been dug over deep by local children, looking for smuggler's treasure, and the ground was furrowed with little trenches. Like graves, he thought, but they too were empty.

Well, it was better this way. Sell the land, if he could find someone to buy it. Put it all behind him. He turned away, back to the harbour, feeling as old and lonely and empty as the cottage on the cliff.

★

Despite what Winnie had said, Mr Joe had no room for them down at the linhay. He had put in another drying floor at the back end of last year, which dried the clay quicker 'n wink, so it didn't have time to grow green whiskers, and there now wasn't the same work for the women. There were some jobs still, of course – he hadn't closed the old settling tanks altogether, and there were the blocks already in store which had to be scraped, but Mr Joe was looking to turn his women off, not to take them on. Even Winnie had to find a job cleaning, and she'd worked down the claypit from a girl.

Ernie wasn't altogether sorry. The extra money would have been welcome, no mistake, and he'd have agreed to anything which might lift Carrie from this glum mood that was on her; but he was secretly glad all the same. Carrie was a married woman, and her place was home, especially with the child being delicate. Blossom was coming up to a year old, but still sickly.

They wouldn't have wanted Carrie's money if the pit-owners would only pay a decent wage for a decent day's work. Even Mr Joe's extra sixpence, which he had agreed to after the petition, had proved to be given with one hand and taken back with the other: if you hit poor rock or bad weather and had to work over to finish the job it made not a farthing of difference, you had your fixed wages, and that was that. The men were tired of it, and no wonder. The coalmen had a minimum now after that strike, and so did the railways; why shouldn't the clayers have an eight-hour day and a fair wage? Especially with this new National Insurance wanting fourpence a week from a man's wage before he'd seen a halfpenny of it.

He tried to make Carrie see it. He had hopes of persuading her, now. There was a Methodist preacher was speaking out in support of the unions, and writing in the papers too. Carrie had always thought there was something about Unionism unfitting to a Christian. 'The rich man at his table, the poor man at his gate' – he had heard her sing it scores of times, whenever he came in from a meeting of his committee. But with a preacher taking their side, and Methodist too, maybe she'd change her tune.

She wouldn't listen.

'You know what I think, Ernie – I've told you till I'm blue in the face. This strike nonsense – it's all very well in theory. But theories don't put food on the table. All these open-air rallies! You "come out on strike" as you call it, and what do we eat then? Thin air sandwiches? It'll end in trouble, you see if it doesn't.' And she turned away.

Da wouldn't have it, either. He still really blamed the Union for 'holding him up like a sideshow' as he said, and that shilling still rankled. His friendship with Mr Whittaker had altered his mind a little, enough to come to an open-air rally one time in St Austell and hear what the speakers had to say. But he wasn't persuaded.

'Striking – that gets you nowhere,' he said. 'Trouble is,' he added as if he had thought of it for himself, 'men like Mr Joe, they don't really understand clay. Just put up the money and pay the wages; wouldn't know a clay seam if they fell in it, half of them. And the same other way on. You and me, we don't know his worries – getting it to the ships and potteries, and finding out new uses like talcum powder and paper and that. Want to talk to each other, that's what, like Ralph Whittaker says.'

' 'Tisn't talk we want now, it's action,' Ernie said, but Da never would come to another rally. There was one most weeks, now, somewhere or another. Falmouth, or Nanpean, St Austell, Bugle – all over. After Easter, as the weather got better, more and more men were turning up to them. 'Coming out like bluebells,' as Ernie said. Word would go round the pit, and men gathered in the open air to listen to the speakers – or to heckle them, often as not.

And more and more often, the speaker was Ernie.

It wasn't easy, mind. Some men were dead against what the Union stood for. Striking was all very well for the coal-miners, but it wasn't the clayers' way, they said. They had a job and glad to have it. And there were some who took heed of the paragraphs in the newspapers entitled 'Socialism or Christ?' as though the two things were naturally opposite.

But still, when Ernie had finished speaking, there were often a score of people signed up for the Union.

Once or twice, the mood got ugly. 'All very well, we signing up,' one burly man in a vest shouted at a meeting at St Blurzey. 'What are 'ee going to *do*, that's the question?'

There was a murmur of agreement. It was a warm evening in late May, and some of the men had slaked their thirst a bit before the meeting started.

'You tell 'un,' another man chimed in. 'Knock a few heads together, that's what wants doing.'

Ernie held up his hand for silence. 'Well, we shall do something and all,' he said. 'The committee has decided. Tenth of next month, we're going to petition the pit-owners.'

There was a murmur of discontent. 'Petitioned 'un last year, and where did it get us?'

'Well this time,' Ernie said, 'it's different. Twenty-five shillings a week basic, or we go on strike. And this time, by Heaven, we'll do it and all!'

Carrie knew that something was afoot. Ernie kept coming home with that air of suppressed excitement, like a steam engine without a safety valve. He was too full of it even to eat his tea, most nights, and he was off straight after to one of his dratted meetings.

'Talking about a strike, they are,' Winnie said, coming in one night after scrubbing the Workers' Institute.

Carrie nodded. Ernie hadn't said so, but she wasn't surprised. She and Ernie didn't talk much, these days, unless it was about Blossom, or the pain in Linny May's arm, which seemed to be getting worse by the week. Certainly they never talked about the Union. Her fault, more than likely – when he had wanted to tell about it she hadn't wanted to hear. And it had been meeting after meeting these last few nights. Ernie was hardly home at all, and when he was, there was some man come to see him, and whispered conferences in the passage. No, it wasn't a surprise.

All the same, she would sooner have heard it from Ernie. Winnie must have guessed she didn't know for certain. Still, there was no point in confirming people's suspicions. She nodded again.

'Thought it would come to it,' she said, trying to sound as if she'd known all along, and pummelling the bread-dough as though it were Ernie or Mr Joe himself. 'Get the bit between their teeth, these men, and there's no stopping them.'

Winnie made a little face. 'Might be a good thing, and all,' she said. 'Give the pit-owners something to think about. Some of the shift captains are saying they'd back the men, too, if it came to it, and that would give Joe Borglaise something to put in his pipe! He thought the captains would stand firm behind him and turn the men off if they went Union, but they aren't going to, seemingly.'

Carrie changed the subject. 'How's the little one, then?'

Winnie laughed. 'Little? Lennie? Bigger 'n a badger that one, and into more things than a ferret. Your Blossom asleep, is she?'

'Is now,' Carrie said. 'Tired herself out, most like. Pulls herself to her feet, these days – and crawling everywhere. Fair wears me out to watch her.' She couldn't keep the pride out of her voice. 'All behind I am. Should have made this bread first thing.'

'You wait till she starts walking,' Winnie said, with the knowing air of a woman whose children walked long before they were fifteen months. 'Have your hands full then, and no mistake. Only wish mine would go down as quiet as this of a morning. You sure you won't think of joining me in a bit of cleaning work, Carrie, while you still got a bit of peace in the house? There's work for two, up the Institute.'

Carrie was about to say no: the thought of spending her time away from

Blossom was hateful to her, and besides, now that Linny May had this pain, she was more needed at Buglers than ever. But if the men were coming out . . . 'I'll think about it,' she promised. 'Now, wait while I put this bread to prove, and I'll make a drop of tea. Take some up to Linny May as well. She's resting in her bed.'

And when they had finished their tea, and the bread was in the bread-oven baking, Blossom woke, and Linny May came down, so it was time for lunch. Ernie was on early shift and would be home at three, so she put some by for him as well.

But when he came in, he didn't eat it. He just stood in the doorway, his eyes bright as fires.

'It's started,' he said. 'Gave them the demands last week, we did, and they've been shilly-shallying for days. Twopence here, and threepence there – no good to us. We've had meeting after meeting and we've waited long enough. So we've done it. It's started. Thirty-five men at Carne Shents are out. It's happening, Carrie. The strike's begun.'

CHAPTER THREE

There had been mutters of discontent in the claypits for a long time, but like Dick Clarance's cocoa, once you took the lid off it seemed to have become stronger for the brewing. Once the first step had been taken, everything seemed to happen at once.

Ernie came out on the Thursday, and took five Union members at Little Roads with him. They went up, orderly, to the site office, and told the pit captain. They would have told Mr Joe direct if they could, but he hadn't come in to the pit since the troubles started.

The captain listened to them politely, his thumbs tucked in his waistcoat. 'Well,' he said, when Ernie had had his say, 'you see how it is. I've got a job to do, same as the next man. And my job is to see the clay gets shifted. Now you are good workers, especially you, Ernie, and I'd be some sorry to see you go. You go back to your work, quiet-like, and I'll put in a word to Mr Joe when he comes in, in support of your wage-demand, and no names named. But you walk out now, I can't take you back after. Choice is yours.'

For a moment Ernie wavered. No job after – what would Carrie say to that?

But Bill Gibbs, one of the Union men, broke in. 'Can't take us back, you say? Won't frighten us that way, boy. See what happened to the railmen. Won their wages and a bill in parliament to say no-one would be sacked for supporting the strike. Same with us, isn't it lads? Cornish motto that is – "One for all and all for one" – and shame on you for not coming out with us. Up the Union, eh Ernie?'

And Ernie, seeing all their eyes upon him, said, 'Up the Union!' and the deed was done.

He didn't go home straight away. He might have gone up to the

270

Tinner's, but it was early yet, and anyway he saw Dick Clarance in the street haranguing the men from the other pit and urging them to go in to work. He would have to, of course, being a captain, and Ernie couldn't hold it against him, but he had no appetite for a family quarrel. He turned his steps out of St Blurzey, and found himself in Bal Lane outside the Whittakers', without altogether meaning to.

Old Ralph Whittaker was in the garden, sitting on a wooden chair from the kitchen, picking raspberries into a chipped bowl. He got up when he saw Ernie, slow and stiff with his arthritis.

'Hello, Ernie lad. What you doing here, this hour?'

Ernie looked at him. 'Out on strike,' he said. It was the first time he had uttered the words, and it gave him an odd sort of pleasure, proud but embarrassed.

Mr Whittaker nodded. 'Good for you, then, Ernie. Dignified protest, that's what wanted. Time for a pot of tea, have you then? If you don't mind setting the kettle for yourself.'

It was what Ernie had half hoped for, and he led the way into the low kitchen and soon had the kettle hopping on the fire.

'What's your da have to say about this, then?' Mr Whittaker said, as Ernie poured the brew.

Ernie felt himself colour. 'Won't be too pleased, I shouldn't wonder. Doesn't hold with strikes.'

Mr Whittaker laughed. 'No, always puts duty first, as he sees it. "Ours not to reason why" – that's your da.' Ernie must have looked as blank as he felt, because the old man added, 'Poetry, that is. Didn't they teach you that at school? "Ours not to reason why, ours but to do and die." Soldiers, they were, in the Crimea. Stupid bloody marvellous heroism. Obeyed orders, even though it killed them.'

'Different though, isn't it?' Ernie said. 'Soldiers. I mean – soldiers!'

Mr Whittaker looked at him sharply. 'You think so, lad? There's plenty wouldn't agree with you there, either. Still, that's another question. But your da now, he'd do the same, soldier or not. Duty first. One of the best, mind, your da – salt of the earth. Lot of time for him, I have. And he may not like strikes, but he'll not stand in your way if he thinks your heart is in it. If you think it's your duty to the men.'

That was a different way of looking at it. Ernie could see how Da would understand that. 'Yes,' he said. 'Thanks.' Mr Whittaker had a way of giving advice without making you feel stupid. 'More tea?'

'I won't, but here's Vince coming. He'll be glad of a drop, I'll be bound.'

But Vince was not interested in tea. He came in, striding. 'We're out,' he said triumphantly. 'Thirty men at least, and more to follow.'

271

'Me too,' Ernie said.

Vince threw him a quick glance and a nod. 'Well, you want to come with us? We're having a rally, a demonstration, starting down St Blurzey High Street in twenty minutes.'

'You're not going to Redruth instead then?' Ernie enquired sourly. It was a sore point between them. A dozen times or more lately Vince had absented himself from a Union meeting where Ernie was speaking because he had 'business in Redruth'. Ernie remembered Jeannie, the self-willed Bugle barmaid with the child who had given Vince her address, and privately thought that he knew what kind of 'business' it was, too.

Vince frowned and shook his head, glancing at Mr Whittaker. Feyther didn't know about the girl even now, Ernie thought.

'No,' Vince said, as though Ernie had never spoken. 'Men in the band have gone home for their instruments, and we're going to march into St Austell.'

Despite himself, Ernie was carried along. 'What for?' he said, but he was already getting to his feet.

'To rally support. Show the men who are still working how strong we are in the Union. Here.' He picked up a stout stick from the pile in the hearth. 'You take this. I've got a pickaxe handle.'

'What for?' Ernie said again. 'When we said "strike", we didn't mean it that way!'

But Vince didn't smile. He shook his head impatiently. 'It's not *for* anything. It's like the band. Make a bit of a show. Make you feel you're really marching. Like soldiers.'

'Ours not to reason why,' Mr Whittaker said softly.

But Ernie wasn't listening. He took up the stick and weighed it in his palm. It felt solid and real. 'Right,' he said. 'Let's go.'

'Here,' Vince said, as they hurried down Bal Lane towards the procession, 'you want to mind what you say in front of Feyther.'

'So it was that girl?'

Vince frowned. 'Well, so it might have been. But it's over now, and I shan't be going down there again. So let's hear no more about it. Anyhow, I'll have more to think about than women, with this strike. Listen to that band tuning up now, something handsome it'll be.'

They joined the straggling line. It was a bit hard to know what to do with the stick, as they marched along, but the band struck up a rousing hymn and the men joined in lustily, and then Ernie got the hang of it. And really, as they marched through the streets, it did feel like an army – marching towards a better future, and ready to take on anyone who threatened to take it from them.

★

Carrie was worried. At first she had been angry, but there was no time for anger now – only worry. The Union, after a week or so of getting its affairs in order, was giving strike pay. It wasn't much, only ten shillings a week, and then Ernie insisted on giving back a shilling to the strike fund. All the men were doing it, he said, to help out those who weren't paid up in the Union, but who had come out in support. And there were plenty of those, if you believed what people said. Thousands of men out.

But that left only nine shillings a week, instead of a pound and more that Ernie had been bringing home. It was something, certainly: without it they would have been desperate, but Da's few shillings became precious, and after a week of scrimping and saving and cutting down on meals she spoke to Ernie again about the idea of going scrubbing with Winnie.

'If I'm going to do it,' she said, 'I'll have to look lively. There's more than us struggling with this strike, and if I don't take the work there's plenty will. And it would be three mornings – that's half a crown a week, more than a quarter more than we're getting now. So you'd better make up your mind to it.'

And Ernie, who had sat down to a supper of turnip soup for the second night running, grumbled and fretted, but in the end he saw the sense of it.

She tried to leave Blossom with him. He didn't like it. 'Me, mind the baby? I thought Winnie's sister would have her.'

Carrie folded her arms and confronted him. 'And wants a shilling a week for doing it. Bit of scraping, and I can feed the five of us for that, and then some. If you were working, Ernie, it's one thing. But I can't have her up the Institute, Da's out working all the hours there are, and Linny May's not fit to do it. And you're stood there idle. It's your baby too, Ernie Clarance, so you can sit and mind it for an hour or two. I only leave her with you when she's asleep.'

'But I've got a rally!' Ernie protested. There was a rally every morning, these days. It was as if the men needed to be meeting, just to give themselves something to do.

'Well, take her with you,' Carrie said, but it was no use. You couldn't parade Blossom about for miles in the dust and heat, or have her stood out in her pram at the Fair Ground meetings for hours at a time. It might be August but there were still showers, and some days were damp and windy. And Ernie was right – it would have made him a laughing-stock. In the end she went to her chimney-box and took out one of her precious guineas. It was worth it, to leave Blossom in safe hands.

It worried her though. The strike was only a fortnight old, and already they had broken a guinea. If the stoppage lasted much longer, it would be all her little hoard disappearing.

Ernie never asked where she got the money, and she didn't tell him. He seemed to suppose that his food appeared on the table by magic: and indeed, sometimes she did seem to work miracles, boiling up turnip tops for greens, nettles into nourishing soup, and adding flour, scrubbed potato-peel and onion to the bacon rinds and lard to make warming savoury patties. Linny May, strangely, came into her own, and remembered recipes of her mother's involving cow's-heel, ox-cheek or giblets, so they managed meat once a week. There were things in the garden too, beans and apples and damsons, with it being August: and it was Carrie's boast that all through the strike they never once went hungry, though they came perilously near it once or twice.

Matters down in the village went from bad to worse. She stopped the man from the tribute shop, one time, to ask for some soap, flour and candles, but when he heard her name he struck off the order, saying that Ernie wasn't at the pit no more, and she couldn't be provided. It was a blow. Up till the strike the man had come to the door every week, demanding orders. The tribute shop was dearer, but they gave you credit. Now everything had to be cash, though as the weeks went by the shopkeepers often did let you have a little on the slate, and even rationed the staple foods, so the black-legs still working couldn't come and buy up the lot.

She was beginning to think of 'black-legs' and 'scab labour' herself. Everyone was talking of it, and although she hadn't wanted the strike, things had gone so far now that it would be a pity to see all the effort go for nothing. She was even tolerant of Ernie and his endless meetings – the men spent their time now listening to 'turns', singers and comedians, down at the Worker's Educational, or writing parodies of songs to keep their spirits up. Once they even marched all the way to Indian Queens, and took a train home! Carrie was wild when she heard that! The fare would have bought milk and arrowroot for Blossom.

And then the Glamorgans arrived.

The Chief Constable had warned several times that there would be extra police brought in. There were men roaming the street, and often 'armed', as the papers called it. Mostly it was just sticks and boryers and old dubbers and shovels, and the men just carried them as they marched. Some of them even tied handkerchiefs to the tops and waved them like banners. But once or twice it had been ugly. Men going in to work were met by the strikers, and there was name-calling and swearing, and scuffles. All the same, there was not much clay being shifted, and most of the pits were shut.

Non-strikers started to get their windows broken – not while they were in, mind you, and nobody was hurt, but they would come home and find a stone through the glass. Nobody knew who threw them. Carrie asked Ernie once, but he shrugged his shoulders and looked helpless. 'Doesn't do us no good. Dignified protest, that's what we want.' She decided that he really didn't know who did it.

And then there was that business down at Nanpean, and things really began to turn nasty. There was an explosion on the windowsill of a non-striker's house in the middle of the night. Blew in all the windows and frightened the family half to death. Dynamite, from one of the clay-pits: being engineers, a lot of men knew how to use it, and they had not walked out of the pits empty-handed.

It was after that the police arrived. A hundred of them from Glamorgan, and reinforcements from Devon and Bristol as well. Looking for troublemakers, people said.

Carrie was really worried now. There had been strikers shot for rioting in Wales only months before, and it was these same Glamorgans who were on the streets then.

'You haven't got explosives hidden, have you?' she begged Ernie, the day after, but he only shook his head and told her not to be daft.

With the extra police, though, the mood was shifting. A lot of people who weren't in the Union were talking about giving in and going back to work before there was trouble. They'd been out a month, and there was no sign of the owners agreeing terms: and the men who weren't paid-up members weren't getting strike pay, either, though there were payouts, and lots of people were sending donations: not only money, but food and clothes. Mr Morrison sent £20 to the Union, and a box of coals to Ernie and Mr Whittaker besides. Carrie was glad of it. The nights were starting to draw in, and there would soon be a frost in the air. Blossom, at least, needed warmth in the evenings.

By the end of August Ernie was looking pale and drawn. 'We're picketing tomorrow,' he said, wolfing down the broth which Carrie had made from a few turnips and by boiling up the knucklebones for the second time. 'Men at the gates of every pit. Show them we're serious, or we'll have people cracking and going back in. Vince and me are going up Bugle. Don't know when I'll be back. And you'd better start looking out a few things we can pawn, Carrie. This strike could be a long business.'

'Well, Philippe?' Emily was sitting at the big table in the dining room facing him, her hands clasped together and pressed down hard on the table-top. 'You have something to say to me.'

Drat Tavy! This was all his doing. They had met, the three of them, to discuss the possibility of auctioning some of Laura's watercolours, since the March sale had been such a success. They had just agreed to go ahead, and Emily was serving tea when Tavy suddenly stood up and and made his excuses. 'I will leave you to it. I am sure you have a great deal to discuss,' he said, casting a meaningful glance in Philippe's direction. 'That matter we were talking of in the train.'

Philippe wasn't altogether surprised. Tavy had alluded to it once or twice, in the past few weeks, but somehow he had never found a convenient moment. But now Tavy had forced it on him. He was to 'see how the land lay'. Perhaps it would not be as difficult as he thought. Emily was half expecting something of the kind – that much was obvious. The glowing look of gratitude she had bestowed on Tavy as he left made Philippe suppose that she had a fairly clear idea of what it was that Tavy wanted him to say.

All the same, it was difficult to know where to begin. He said so. 'I really don't know where to begin.'

She coloured, the flush beginning behind her ears and washing over her face, but she sat serenely. 'I cannot help you,' she said archly, 'if I do not know what matter we are to discuss.'

Philippe shifted uncomfortably. 'I wished to talk to you on a . . . personal matter.' He saw the flicker in her eyes, caught the little intake of breath, and added quickly, 'Not for myself, you understand. I am speaking for . . . a friend.' He allowed his eyes to flicker in the direction of the door.

Her glance followed his. 'I understand.' She smiled: a secret, knowing smile.

Philippe felt a swift rush of relief. This was going to be easier than he had thought. Of course, she was probably half expecting this. Tavy had been assiduous in his attentions.

He smiled in return. 'I thought you would. I take it then that if he . . . if a certain gentleman who has lost his wife . . . were to hope that his friendship with you could some day be more than professional, then you would not object to that?' Damn it all, this was appallingly difficult. He was beginning to sound like an affidavit himself. Next time, he thought sourly, Tavy could do his own asking.

Emily was the colour of the red velvet curtains. 'You may tell . . . your friend . . . that I should be more than honoured.' She stretched out and caught his hand. 'Honoured.'

He patted her fingers. 'He will be delighted, I am sure. Though, it may be a little soon . . .' Tavy's wife had been dead for little more than a year.

She smiled again. 'Of course. I understand perfectly. And please tell your friend that he is welcome to call, at any time . . .'

He got to his feet, embarrassed at playing matchmaker. 'And now, Miss Limmon . . . Emily . . . I must go. *Plougastel* will be coming in and I am already late.' He was suddenly anxious to be gone, and she watched him go, still smiling.

Ellie saw him out. He could not resist the impulse to linger on the doorstep and ask, 'And how is your sister? And Carrie?'

'Dolly's doing grand, sir, but I aren't so sure about poor Carrie. No end of trouble up there at the claypits.'

'Trouble?' His voice was sharp with concern.

But Emily was calling. 'Ellie? Are you there, girl? I want you upstairs directly.' And he was obliged to let her go.

He went down to the harbour and watched for the *Plougastel*. *Ploumenach* was in already, warped in and moored up since morning, the catch long since unloaded and sold to the waiting fish-women and carts. But *Plougastel* had been in deeper waters, and she was due back at sundown.

He roved restlessly among the piled ropes and rusty anchors, conspicuous in his landsman's suit. Trouble at the claypits. What could that mean? He felt helpless, useless. Once he offered to catch a mooring line, thrown from a little trawler that was berthing, but the Cornishman at the helm only shook his head and called, 'Mind out, sir, got to know what you are doing with these things!' The crewman tossed it to a lad in a fisherman's jersey and sea-boots.

Philippe scowled for a moment, but then the irony of it struck him, and he smiled wryly. The trawlerman had stepped ashore by now and was making fast. Philippe looked at him squarely. 'I might have managed to moor you up, all the same. I've been at sea once or twice,' he said, and taking the stern-line he cleated it in expertly. 'Was the fishing good?'

The man looked from him to the cleat and then grinned and shook his head. 'Nothing out there. These steam drifters break up the shoals. No money in fishing these days. Still – better out there than up the claypits at St Austell.'

Philippe caught his breath. 'I heard there was trouble,' he said. 'What's happening, exactly?'

'Men are on strike,' the fisherman said. 'Been out for weeks. But that's not the half of it. Brought in Welsh police from the coal strikes and baton charged them yesterday. People with their heads laid open. Scores of people hurt. They had to set up a cottage as an emergency hospital, they were that many wounded. Women and all.'

'Women?' Philippe felt as cold as if he had been suddenly immersed in the North Sea. 'How, women?'

'You want to talk to the harbour-master,' the fisherman said. 'He's got a brother works on the trains. He'll know fitter'n me. Bound to be more news, by this time. Whole town was hopping, from what I hear. I'm Tom Williams, by the way. Say I sent you.' He offered a sunburned hand, and Philippe clasped it in his own.

'Philippe Trezayle,' he said, briefly. 'They call me Diavezour, in the harbour here.' He wanted to find the harbour-master and hear the news.

But the man did not release his hand. 'Monsieur Philippe? The one that Emily Limmon set her cap at? Well, I'll be blowed. Small world, isn't it? I'm Tommy – married the maid up at Albert Villas. You remember Dolly? She's often spoken about you. Knew you were a fisherman, o' course, but never would have known you, togged up like a city gent. No wonder you could tie a cleat.'

Philippe smiled, but he was anxious to be off. He withdrew his hand. 'I will find this harbour-master.'

'We'll do better than that, boy! There's been fellows from the Union trying to get up a subscription to help the striking families. Down the Harbour Tavern they'll be, this time of night, trying to catch the men when they come in. You come on with me, and we'll have the proper tale. Drew!' He turned to the boy in the outsize jumper. 'You give a hand with these mackerel for me. And tell your mother I'll be late for me tea.' And as the boy clambered back on board to help with unloading the catch, he turned on his heel and led the way to the harbourside bar.

Philippe was not a bar-dweller, he left that to his men. Ramon was here now, one arm round a buxom woman, the other clutching a pint tankard, while he sang, loudly and not very tunefully, a coarse folk-song in Breton. One or two people were watching him, trying to join in the chorus, and Philippe was slightly anxious. With Ramon, the line between raucous singing and a drunken brawl was sometimes a fine one.

But most of the customers were ignoring the sideshow. They were clustered around a table in the window, and there was a buzz, an almost physical burr of excitement, like a wasp in a bottle. A man in shirt-sleeves and a waistcoat was sitting at the trestle, telling a story with an intense passion. Philippe could see it in the way he moved, and the way the crowd swayed with him, although from this distance he could not hear a word. He tried to elbow his way through the crowd to hear more clearly.

'. . . more than two dozen women in the crowd, there were – a pram even, and they police just charged at them, like they were animals.'

There was a murmur of protest. 'Got no business bringing foreign police down here, any road!' somebody said, and got a round of applause.

'Only come to support the men, they women had,' the clay-man went on. 'But the police charged down the lane laying about them in all directions. You never saw anything like it – narrow lane it is, and there were people running and jostling, and whenever the police found somebody they set about them – batons, truncheons, the lot. I saw one fellow, his head that covered with blood you couldn't see the face on him. And of course there were bicycles and all sorts, tipped over in the lane, and people trying to run over them, and tripping up, and then the police would be on them – and did they ever let them have it when they caught them! Here!' He rolled up his left sleeve with a dramatic gesture. 'You have a look at that!'

His forearm was swollen, the skin red, yellow and black with bruising. A dozen hands reached forward to replenish his drink.

'Let them have it, did you, boy?' someone shouted. 'Give them good as you got?'

The crowd fell silent. Assaulting a policeman, that was a serious offence.

The man seemed to sense the mood. 'Had a few sticks and stones, stands to reason,' he said. 'You would have and all, with they charging at you like heathens. Pushed one of the women, too – gave her a great shove and down she went. Well, that made us see red, I can tell you. Proper set-to, it was. Wasn't needed either. Last week we had the St Austell police turn us back, civil like, and we went home quiet as lambs. Singin' hymns we were. But start laying about us with batons – and up-country policemen too. Weren't standing for that, boy!'

'What happened in the end?'

The man downed one of the new pints. 'Drove us off, didn't they? But it isn't over yet, you mark my words. More ways than one to catch an oyster, and clayers don't forget easy. Some of them policemen want to be a bit careful, walking out on their own, nights!'

'Shameful, that's what it is!' a woman said. She was sitting by the curtains drinking a thick brown liquid from a heavy glass. 'Surprised the tradesmen don't refuse to serve them.'

The man laughed. 'Can't refuse, exactly, can they – them being police and all? But it's amazing how often the shops run short of things, just the minute the Glamorgans want them. Haven't had more than a bit of bread and cheese since they've been there, some of them. Amazing thing – the shops were full of all sorts until just a minute before!'

There was a general chuckle.

'And when they wanted ale sent up – nothing could be found to shift it except the old dung-cart. Converted now, of course, but we know what it was! Laugh! Thought I should have died.'

'Serve them right too,' the woman said. 'Why should they have the fat of the land, and the strikers' families starving? Here's threepence for your subscription, and welcome to it. Buy a few eggs, and either give them to a striker's wife, or if you can't find one, throw them at something blue in a helmet!'

There was more laughter, and the money began pouring in. Coppers, mostly, a few pence here and a few there, but after a few minutes there was more than four pounds on the table.

'I'll get back,' the man said, when he had thanked them sincerely. 'Picketing tonight. We've got two men on duty outside all the works, every night of the week. I'll take your good wishes. It'll give power to our arms. We won't forget this – and we'll win in the end, boy.' He dropped his voice. 'Explosives, some of the men have got. And a pistol. They think we're finished, they've got another think coming!' He finished up his pint, and made for the door.

'Do you know Mr Clarance?' Philippe had been searching his memory for the name, and when it came he stepped forward and challenged the clayer.

'Ernie? Course I know Ernie. Grand speaker he is. What about him?'

'Was he hurt? Or his wife?' The picture of that pram, caught in a baton charge, swum before his eyes.

'Ernie? No, wasn't there till after – there was a big rally up the Fair Ground, and he was addressing them up there. Made a great speech, though, afterwards. Bee-stings. That's what he called for. Bee-stings. Never win by fighting them in the streets, he said – they'll only bring the army in like they did at Llanelli, and there's no arguing with bullets. March decent like and have your protests, and no violence. But fight them in little ways, make their life a blooming misery – flat tyres, missing tunics, glue on their boots . . . and nobody to know who done it. Bee-stings, he says. Not enough to make a court-case out of, but enough bee-stings'll kill a man, sure as strangling. And we'll give it to them, too, good and proper. And who . . . ?'

But the question was never asked. There was a roar and a thump, and a chair swirled through the air and crashed down on a table. The whole tavern turned to look.

It was Ramon, drunk and dishevelled, lurching towards a bearded fisherman brandishing a chair-leg in one huge red hand. '*Gwregel di' porcel!*' he shouted, and you didn't have to speak Breton to know that it was no compliment.

'Ramon!' Philippe called, but it was already too late. Ramon had entangled his feet in a bar-stool, and was lying full-length and unconscious on the tavern floor. And the man standing at the tavern door in helmet and cape, and taking a lively interest in the scene, was evidently a policeman.

CHAPTER FOUR

'Right!' Ernie said. 'This'll do.' He put his dark-lantern down carefully and settled himself slightly against the cold granite of the wall. The night air was chilly, even through his jumper and jacket, and as he sat he could feel the prickly dampness of the grass against his trousers.

There was a crack and a rustle in the bushes behind him and a dark shadow emerged. Vince sat down awkwardly. 'Turned my blooming ankle in the dark,' he said. 'Why can't there be a bit of moon when you want it?'

'Ssh!' Ernie hissed. 'Keep your voice down. Whole road is living with policemen. Got everything, have you?'

For answer, Vince tapped the stout stick he was carrying. 'Picked up a few rocks, too,' he said. 'Never know.'

'Won't come to that,' Ernie murmured. 'Bee-stings, that's what this is about. Get into the shed and put that motor-charabanc of theirs out of action.'

'How?' Vince had his boot off and was rubbing his ankle in the light of the lantern.

Ernie had been thinking about that. 'Take a wheel off. That's simplest. And there's a pile of bikes somewhere, too. Take off the saddles and chains and stick them down the well. That'll slow them down a bit. All we've got to do is get across the lane.'

Vince began lacing his boot on again, keeping his head and voice low. 'I know where Bill Giles put that dynamite to,' he said. 'I can get it, easy. Do more than slow them down, that would.' Ernie shook his head in the darkness, but Vince went on, 'I can't see the difference. Damaging police property either way.'

'Supposing we're caught?' Ernie's voice was a whisper.

'Yes,' Vince answered, in the same low tone. 'Supposing we are? Aren't going to tell us we're naughty boys and stand us in the corner, are they? You got something, in case?'

Ernie fingered the round stones in his own pocket and said nothing. His throat was dry and his heart was thumping louder than the pump engine at Little Roads, but there was a tingle of excitement too. This was it. Real action.

There was a noise beyond the wall. Lights on the road. 'They're coming. Get down.' He reached out and pressed Vince bodily downwards, so that they were both flattened into the grass. On the other side of the hedge they could hear footsteps, the creak of a wheel, the murmur of voices. The light of a bull's-eye lantern flickered over the stones, hesitated, moved on.

There was a long, agonising wait.

'Now!' They wriggled forward out of their hiding place, and flitted like shadows across the roadway and over the wall to the shed. The door was padlocked.

'Have to take it off its hinges,' Vince whispered. 'Told you we should have brought that dynamite. But there's a bike here, all right, just leaning on the wall. We can have that, easy.'

They knelt beside it in the darkness. Ernie held the light while Vince busied himself with the saddle-bolts. 'There!' he said triumphantly, giving it a final twist. The bike fell to the ground with a clatter.

They froze. From somewhere far down the lane a Welsh voice. 'What was that?'

'Quick!' Dousing the lantern and back in the darkness to crouch behind the wall. A long, long silence. Then movement.

Ernie edged himself upwards. Two policemen, one wheeling a bicycle. He could see their capes and helmets, and the flash of metal at the belt. They stopped. So close. Only yards away – he could almost hear their breathing, smell the polish on their leather boots. The thinner policeman leaned on his bicycle. He was young, almost a boy.

'No!' he said, and Ernie could hear the Welsh lilt in the voice. 'Nothing out here. Silent as the grave.'

The other man was older, burly, with thick-set shoulders and a determined air. 'I tell you, I heard something. By the shed.'

Ernie dug his fingers into the wall, holding his breath. They could hear his heart, surely? There was a silence.

'No. A rabbit, perhaps.' He said 'rah-bit'. The words hung in the air like smoke.

Vince moved. Suddenly. A darting run, out into the open of the field. A shout. 'Up the Union!'

Ernie froze. 'What the . . . ?' The bull's-eye flashed up, and the field was full of light. Vince, trailing a bootlace. He looked up. Bent. Threw.

The rock skimmed past Ernie's ear, and suddenly he too was on the move. The older policeman was scrabbling up and over the wall: Ernie heard the thud of his boots as he landed. The bike his mate had been wheeling fell with a crash and a second form appeared, briefly outlined against the sky.

Ernie was running. Helter-skelter down the field. A dip at the bottom. Stepping-stones. The stream.

Vince was already across. He followed, feet slithering on the wet stones, the blood singing in his ears.

'Come back! Stop! Police!'

But he kept running, up the hill and over the fence, into the shelter of the trees. Vince was beside him, panting. The two dark forms were in the hollow, hesitating. The lantern flickered.

'Can't find the crossing!' Vince gasped, between gulping breaths. 'Well, I'll give them something to look for! Put that lantern out at least.'

He held back in the shadows, but his aim was good. They heard the thud of it as it hit, and as the lantern fell, saw the policeman clasp his hand to his arm. They were a good way away but the stone had stung. Vince threw another. And another. Ernie tossed one of his. It fell in the stream with a splash, and the tall policeman staggered backwards, shaking the water from his hands and face. His helmet fell off.

Vince threw another stone into the stream. Deliberate, this time. The burly policeman got a shower. Ernie laughed. It seemed in slow-motion somehow, and even his laugh came out slowly – 'Ha! ha! ha!' Then the burly policeman seized the light and waded into the stream, and they were running again. Through the trees, round the corner, in the gate and into the front passage at Buglers.

Ernie made to shut the door but the shouts and lights were following them. Better to leave it ajar, the house dark and sleeping like the others in the row. The small hedge and the patch of garden was between them and the road.

They stood there, backs to the wall, flattening against it, their chests heaving. The hall was empty, except for a box of things Carrie had put by for the pawnshop. He could see the boat picture sticking out of it. Time stood still.

Voices in the lane. 'In one of the houses, that's what. Never find them now without waking the neighbourhood.' The lantern danced. 'Mind, there's a door open here.' The figure came to the gate, leaning and peering.

'Here!' Vince swooped towards the box and picked something out of it. Ernie's fingers curled around something heavy and glass, and then he too was hurling it with all his force towards the form that was walking, slowly and menacingly, towards the path.

There was a soft, horrible, splintering thud. The policeman keeled over, falling without a sound. Vince stood a moment, his face a portrait of horror.

'You've done it now, boy!' he said, and stepped forward to slam the door. Outside there were lights, shouts, whistles. But they were out through the back door, and running. Running.

Carrie awoke to a thundering at the door.

'Police! Open up!'

She swung her feet out of her 'bed' on the front-room settee, and wrapped a shawl around her shoulders. Blossom had woken too, and was crying fitfully. She took up the nightlight, scooped the baby up into her arms and went to the door, still blinking with sleep.

There was a policeman there, a big burly man with a moustache. His face might have been kindly: it was not kindly now. In one hand he held a lantern, in the other a truncheon. Carrie took a step back.

'What is it? What do you want?'

She looked past him into the road. All the way down the street people were opening windows, holding up candles. A woman's voice called, 'What's all the row? Children here are trying to sleep.' At the gate two men with lanterns were bending over someone lying on the ground. They straightened up, and Carrie saw the glint of their polished buttons. Policemen.

She dragged her eyes back to the man on the doorstep.

'Where's your husband, missus?'

She frowned. 'Out the pits,' she said. 'He's a picket. They're all out tonight.' She looked back at the figure on the road. It was stirring, being helped to its feet. In the moonlight she could see an ugly dark stain on the side of the white forehead, a stain which trickled as she watched. The figure slumped, and was caught by the two men beside him. A sudden wild fear gripped her. 'That's not . . . ?' She looked at the man's face.

His eyes were as cold as ever but his voice was kindlier as he said, 'No, missus. That's one of our lads. Knocked out cold by something – two men stone-throwing. From this house, it looked like. Wonder it didn't kill him. So, I'm asking you again. Where's your husband?'

She shook her head. 'I told you. Out the pit somewhere, picketing. He's not here. Leastways, I never heard him – and I generally do. Comes in around dawn and makes himself a cup of tea. Enough to wake the dead.' But even as she spoke she was aware of the back door, standing open behind her. And she had heard a door close, surely, in her sleep? Someone had been here.

She shivered. 'You better come in,' she said, though it wasn't the cold which chattered her teeth. 'Night air is bad for the child.'

The man nodded. 'I'm going in,' he called to the gate. 'How is Evan?'

A voice answered from the darkness. 'Needs patching up, but he'll do. Wants a stretcher really.'

'There's a ladder,' Carrie said, and could have bitten her tongue out. 'Out the back.' Out the back where Ernie was probably hiding, waiting to be discovered.

The policeman smiled. 'I'll get it then, and just have a look around.' She stood back to let him pass her in the doorway. 'Who else is in the house?'

'We are!' A voice from the stairs. Linny May was standing there, in a monstrous flounced nightgown and nightcap, looking like a miniature ship in full sail. Behind her, Da: his coat pulled over his shoulders, showing his stump, his legs thin and white in the moonlight.

'They're looking for Ernie,' Carrie said. 'Someone's been hurt.'

'Well, they'll look a long time,' Linny May said, baring her toothless gums in a hideous smile. ' 'Cause he isn't here. But they're welcome to look. And put that child in bed out of the cold, Carrie Clarance, or there'll be more'n one wanting a stretcher.' She came down, stiff and slow, but suddenly it was Linny May they were all watching. 'I'll set the kettle, since we're not to have any sleep tonight. And as for you' – she turned to the policeman – 'if you want that ladder, you'd best fetch it, before your friend gets better of his own accord.'

Carrie darted into the front room and tucked Blossom back under the blankets. The child cowered down into the warm nest and looked at her mother with wide wondering eyes. 'You go to sleep,' Carrie murmured, planting a kiss on her forehead. 'Mummy won't be long.'

She went out into the kitchen. The policeman was standing by the back door, the ladder in his hand. No Ernie. She breathed a sigh of relief.

Linny May picked up the kettle. 'You want some warm water out there?' she said, nodding towards the front door.

The man shook his head. 'We'll take him back on this. Don't you worry. I'll take this out, and then I'll have to look around. Sorry to disturb you, but we have to be sure.'

He sounded more friendly now. He went out with the ladder, and

Carrie started to speak, but Linny May shook her head. 'Hold your hush,' she said. 'We aren't out of it yet.'

Carrie threw a glance at Da, but he was hunched up by the fire with his pipe, saying nothing.

The policeman came back. No-one had moved.

'Get on with it then,' Linny May said, folding her lips. 'Get it over, and then perhaps decent folks can get back to their beds.'

The policeman flushed. 'You stay here then,' he said.

'Where did you think we were going?' Linny May demanded. 'And mind you don't wake that baby.'

They heard him moving about upstairs, opening cupboards, moving furniture. In a few moments the lantern appeared on the stairs. Carrie went out into the passage and the man poked his head around the front-room door, holding the lantern high. He didn't go in. Ernie could have been under the settee, Carrie thought, and never be found.

The policeman came back into the kitchen. 'He isn't here.'

'She told you that,' Linny May said, with a little leer. 'Went down the pits, picketing. Done it every night for a week. Well, you've been down the garden, is that the lot? Or are you going to go out looking for whoever *did* throw that stone?'

He flushed. 'Here,' he said suddenly. 'That back door was open. You don't tell me you leave that door open all night. Somebody went out.'

Carrie's heart stopped. In all the commotion she had hoped the open door might just be overlooked.

But Linny May looked him squarely in the eye. 'Of course they did,' she said stoutly. 'I don't know where they keep the privy in your house! I went out myself, and if you're any kind of a gentleman you'll say no more about it. Tried to get upstairs when I heard the door – never expected to have gentlemen coming in here and me in my nightdress, at my time of life!'

It wasn't true. Carrie knew it wasn't true. Linny May had never been out to the privy at night in all the years Carrie had been at Buglers. She had her chamberpot like anybody else – and the man had been up looking under the beds, too.

The policeman seemed to be thinking hard. 'Well . . .' he said.

'Don't be so soft,' Linny May said. 'Think the girl would have sent you out the back for a ladder if her husband was out there hiding? Have a bit of common sense!' She frowned. 'Mind, I did think I might have heard somebody in the front garden when I was coming down to the privy. Some of those hooligan lads from St Austell, more than like.'

The man's face cleared. 'Yes,' he said. 'Might be it at that. Always a few who'll take advantage of an upset, to create their own bit of bedlam. Still, we'll catch up with them, whoever it was – should have stuck to throwing stones. They'd found this when I went out with the ladder. That's what did the damage, by the look of it. And we should be able to find out who this belongs to – somebody's bound to have seen it.' He produced something from a leather pouch at his waist. 'Well, goodnight. We will have to come back and speak to your husband, but I'm sorry to have disturbed you, ladies. And you, sir. Goodnight.'

Carrie saw him to the door. That is, she walked down the passage and opened the door while he walked through it. But she saw nothing. The only image in her mind was the thing which 'did the damage'. It came from the writing-set which Mr Whittaker had given them, and which she had reluctantly put aside in the box to pawn. A heavy cut-glass inkbottle – so heavy that it had not broken. Not even when it had hit the policeman, and laid him flat.

Ernie was guilty. She could have no further doubt of that.

Ernie came home at six. He and Vince had made it back to the Whittaker house, and huddled in the kitchen, too scared to sleep. Five o'clock, when the first men should have been going off to work, if the pits were open, Mr Whittaker came down.

Ernie told him everything. It was a relief, in fact, to get it off his chest – though Vince interrupted and contradicted at every turn's end.

'Well,' Vince said, when Ernie was telling about the stream, 'I never really hit him. You did – but I just gave him a good dousing. You shouldn't have ever suggested we took stones in the first place.'

Ernie stared. 'But it was you . . .' It was no good, he realised. Vince would stick to his version of things, and who would ever doubt him? It was Ernie who had been the big noise at Union meetings, Ernie who had urged the men to 'bee-stings' and action, Ernie who made the speeches and got the applause.

'What we going to do?' he said helplessly.

'Give yourselves up,' Mr Whittaker said. He was cutting bread and jam, and hoisting the kettle onto the trivet with difficulty. 'Behave with a bit of dignity. It should never have come to this. Protest, you want – not violence. Won't do the cause any good. You start attacking policemen, and people will start turning away. There's a lot of good men in the Union, and they don't want truck with this kind of nonsense.'

'Policemen laid us out, up at Bugle the other day,' Vince said. 'Good and proper. Baton charges, and all that – and charging at women too.'

'That's just it,' Mr Whittaker said. 'Had the whole county behind you then, near enough. You stand up like a man, and you might still see it. Something might come of it yet.'

'Yes,' Ernie said gloomily, drinking his tea without really noticing. 'Six years' hard labour, that's what.'

Vince looked at his father. 'You going to turn us in then?' It was a sneer, almost.

Mr Whittaker took a piece of bread and butter. 'If they ask me questions, I shall tell the truth. But I'm not going making trouble. You got to make your own mind up. You do the right thing, and I'll help you any way I can.'

'Well, I know what I'm doing,' Vince said. 'I'm off out of it. They don't know it was us – not for certain sure. And there's no end of men leaving the district. Looking for jobs, half of them. If I had the money, I'd go to America. They wouldn't find me there.' He looked at his father, as if Mr Whittaker might magically offer the fare.

The old man got up heavily. 'You're grown men, and you have to make your own minds up. But if you're talking plans, I'm going upstairs. What I don't hear, I can't tell them.'

Vince watched him go. 'There,' he said. 'Even Feyther won't argue with the sense of it. Get out, Ernie, while the going's good. It'll all blow over in a week or two, and that'll be that. They'll have more than us to worry about.'

Ernie said doubtfully, 'I could do that, I suppose. Get somewhere else and try and find a job. Not claying. But I don't know any other trade.'

'You got hands,' Vince said. 'Plenty of farmers need men, this time of year, with the harvest to get in. Men've always done it, if times are bad.'

'What about Da and Carrie and Linny May? Can't just leave them behind.'

'Take Carrie with you,' Vince said. 'She's handy, Carrie is – and she's done a power of things in her time. And for the others – you had your Union money this week?'

Ernie nodded.

'There you are then. You pay the rent for the quarter, and they'll be all right. Your da still brings in a shilling or two – and once you've got a place, you can send for them.'

'Send for them?' Ernie had never in his life thought of leaving Buglers.

Vince was impatient. 'Well, there's nothing for you round here, boy. Mr Joe will never have you back, you said yourself – and after this you'll be blacklisted everywhere. No, you clear off and start afresh. That's what I'm going to do, and do it now.' He stood up and began taking his waistcoat and hat down off the peg.

'Where will you go, Vince?'

'I dunno,' Vince said, though it was clear he'd made up his mind to something. 'London maybe. Or Plymouth. Jeannie's gone up there. She's got a bit of money put by. Maybe I'll get her to marry me and go to Australia.'

'Thought you'd stopped seeing her, all of a sudden.' Vince had said as much, only a week or two earlier. That was when he had started throwing himself heart and soul back into the Union. Like tonight.

'Couldn't go up Plymouth after her, could I?' Vince sounded furious. 'On strike pay and all. What would Feyther have said? But she'll be glad enough to have me, I know.'

'What about your Feyther? How will he manage?'

'Oh, Morrison'll see after him. Always does.' He glanced at Ernie's face. 'And if I get sorted out, I'll send money back. Might work my way to America. There's plenty who do. But you want to make your mind up smartish, Ernie Clarance. Pa says he'll tell the police what he knows if they come looking – he means it too. So you want to do something, you'd better do it, while the iron's hot.' He was walking around the room stuffing things into an old sack – boots, socks from the drying line. He meant it, Ernie saw. He would pack the sack and go, then and there.

Ernie got to his feet. He felt rather foolish. He held out a hand. 'Well, this is goodbye, then.'

'I suppose it is. Yes.' Vince moved the sack into his left hand to give Ernie's fingers an absent-minded squeeze. 'I best be moving. Want to catch the early train, before they start looking.'

Ernie went to the door. Vince did not look up. He called 'Goodbye' to Mr Whittaker, but there was no answer. He went out into the cool autumn air.

By the time he got home he had made up his mind. He would go – this very morning, him and Carrie. Back to that farmer at Penvarris she used to talk about, see if they could get a job bringing in the harvest. Pay the rent, buy a ticket, and go.

Bill Giles passed him on the road, red-eyed from picketing all night. 'All right then, Ernie?'

Ernie stopped. 'Not really, Bill lad. Had a bit of bad news – going to take Carrie back down where she came from. Might not be back for a week or two. Try and get a bit of work, farming, perhaps.'

Bill nodded, sympathetic. 'There's plenty has – though what we shall do if we're still out when the winter comes, Lord knows. Quiet night?'

Ernie nodded. 'Quiet as the tomb.'

But his heart was beating like a traction engine all the way home. To his surprise, Carrie didn't argue, tell him what a fool he'd been. He would have felt better if she had. Instead she seemed trampled and subdued. The police had been round in the night, looking for him, and the whole house was in a state of suppressed panic.

'You clear off,' Linny May said fiercely – she had been amazing, Carrie said, standing up to the policeman like a suffragette – 'we'll manage. But there might be trouble if you stop here – a lot of folks will take it bad, wounding a policeman. You get that baby somewhere safe. But Da and me, we'll be all right. Never been strikers and they know it. Leave the money, Da'll see to the rent.'

Da said very little, and nor did Carrie. Ernie tried to put his arms around her – 'I'm sorry, Carrie – I never even knew I hit him, I was aiming at the lantern' – but she brushed him aside.

Blossom was wailing, 'Mar . . . mee. Mar . . . mee.' The child was too young to understand, but she knew that there was trouble in the house.

Carrie picked her up. 'Never you mind, Blossom, at least we'll be going home.' Then she turned to Ernie, her eyes full of hurt and resignation. 'Well, we'd better go if we're going.'

So she and Blossom would come with him. He felt absurdly hopeful, grateful for that small mercy. They packed a few things, and by ten o'clock they were all three of them on the train to Penzance.

CHAPTER FIVE

Altogether it was a grim journey. Carrie felt like a pulley-line, stretched taut, ready to break. Blossom seemed to sense that something was wrong and cried fretfully all the time. Carrie hadn't slept, and the child's noise made her wearier than ever. By her side, Ernie was white-faced and nervy, jumping like a scalded cat every time he saw a uniform.

'For heaven's sake, Ernie – that's a railway porter!' Carrie said, as they walked down the station in Penzance. 'Well, we're here. What do you want us to do now?' Now that the tensions of the journey were over she felt suddenly stubborn and angry. Ernie had got them into this. He could get them out.

But he turned to her with such a face of despair that her resolution melted. 'We got to eat, Carrie. And find a roof over our heads. Thought we might go out and ask that farmer friend of yours could he use a pair of gleaners. You know, the fellow used to give us eggs for your mother when we walked to Penvarris, courting.'

Carrie adjusted Blossom's weight on her shoulder. Crowdie. He might help them if anyone would, and certainly there would be work, supposing there weren't a dozen others already paid to do it. She sighed.

'We'll have to walk then,' she said with a kind of dull resignation. 'We've already used half my savings to pay the train.' In fact, her little hoard from the chimney was not entirely exhausted. She had dipped into it only twice before – once to come to Mother's funeral, and once when Ernie's strike-money had not gone far enough to buy good nourishment for the child. This morning she had produced a guinea – enough to pay the fares and keep them a day or two if it was needed, and tied another into the tail of her petticoat. Ernie had been able to give Da the whole of his ten shillings strike pay.

But there was more. Money that Ernie never guessed at – five guineas hidden in her basket, in the little box her father gave her. She hadn't told Ernie about that. Not yet. That was her last desperate insurance. Blossom, at least, would not starve.

The walk to Penvarris seemed longer than it used to be, with Blossom growing heavier at every step, but they got there at last. It was strange, looking down at the Terrace and knowing that those familiar houses were no longer home. Strangers living there now – people she didn't know to speak to, and children who watched her coming with bold, curious eyes.

'You ask him,' Ernie said, when they came to the corner of the lane leading to Crowdie's farmhouse. 'He knows you.'

'Thought you were the one for the speeches,' Carrie grumbled, but she went all the same, and tapped at the door.

Crowdie answered it himself. He was surprised to see her, but he listened sympathetically. 'Carrie my handsome, you know I'd help if I could, but there's nothing doing to speak of.' He must have seen her face, known that she was seeing that long, weary walk back to the town. He said quickly, 'I can give you a bit of work for a week or two – just clearing the last of the fields and bringing in a bit of fruit, but I can't do more.'

For a moment she couldn't speak, her eyes misting with thanks.

'Only be six shillings a week, mind,' Crowdie said. 'And ten for your husband. That's what I pay the others, and if I treat you different there'll be trouble. But you can sleep in the barn – it's warm enough there, and we'll look you out a blanket for the child.'

Carrie shook her head. 'Won't come to that, I'm hoping. Bert Hoskins still on the Terrace, is he?'

Crowdie nodded, understanding her thoughts. 'Yes, he was cousin to your mother, wasn't he? She was some good to him, I remember. He might give you a room at that – Bert's a miserable old mortal and mean as sin, but he wouldn't like folks to say of him that he let his own kith and kin sleep in a barn when he had a room to give them, at least without a reason. But you want to find yourself something proper, Carrie, soon as you can. Old Bert's as mean as Croesus.' He looked concerned. 'But, whatever brings you here like this? You in some kind of trouble, my lover?'

Carrie closed her eyes and shook her head. 'It's this strike,' she said, not answering him directly. 'Ernie's been in the Union. Talked too much as usual and the owner says he'll not have him back. And it's getting ugly, the mood. Police have used batons, more than once, and people started getting hurt. Policeman knocked out right outside our door last night. We couldn't stand no more of it, not with the baby.' It was all true, she thought frantically. It was only what she *hadn't* said that deceived him.

293

Crowdie looked thoughtful. 'Yes, we heard it had been bad. Well, I'll do what I can for you, my handsome. But you want to go up and see Katie Trevarnon, Katie Warren that was. She's the one. Do something for you and be glad to.'

Katie! She had wondered about it, standing on the platform in Penzance. But she couldn't turn to Katie for help. Not after last time. What *had* happened to make Katie refuse even to answer her letters? She had asked herself the same question a thousand times. Went to the shop perhaps, and had that leery shopkeeper breathing all over her? Or saw the picture and wanted nothing more to with Carrie? Katie had strong ideas about morals. Or just didn't like being asked to find a place for Ernie, like he said. Must have been something, because Katie had never mentioned those letters from that day to this. Took weeks before she wrote back at all, and then not a word about Carrie's problems. Carrie had not known how to reply, and the friendship had dwindled to the briefest of greetings at Christmas. And if Katie had felt that then, when she was only an architect's wife, how would she feel now, when she was the mistress of Trevarnon House? No, she could hardly apply to Katie again.

Something of her thoughts must have been evident on her face, because Crowdie said, 'Still, that'll do another day. You get yourself down the barn for now, and I'll be down to see you directly. Have a bit of a rest and you can start this afternoon – and glad of it, by the look of you. Bit of bread and fresh milk suit you, would it? You look half perished.'

It was magical, the old warm neighbourliness of the Terrace. It cheered her, even in these bleak moments, as she sat on the warm straw eating the bread which Crowdie had promised, and the cheese and apples he had brought down besides. She thought of it later that afternoon, as she bent her back to the stubble, along with the other women, and Blossom sat on an old blanket under the hedge and watched.

She thought of it even that night, tucked up in the narrow bed in Bert Hoskins' cheerless cottage. Crowdie had been right. Old Bert valued the opinion of his neighbours too much to turn them away, and get himself talked about for a skinflint. He had submitted to letting them the tiny back bedroom with grumbling bad grace.

Even so, it was going to be some game, managing here with Blossom. Not a drop of water in the room, nor a crumb of coal for the fire, and the chimney not swept in a twelvemonth. And Bert wanting a shilling a week for the privilege. Cousin he may be, but he wasn't a charitable home, he told her.

Still, it was better than sleeping in the barn like a pair of tramps. She would manage somehow, and, she told herself, desperate times called for desperate measures. First time it rained and there was no work gleaning, she *would* go up to Trevarnon and speak to Katie Warren. After all, it could do no harm, and it might do a bit of good. And at least, for now, they had food in their stomachs and a roof over their heads; and if the mattress was lumpy and damp, at least there was Ernie, pitifully grateful to have her and Blossom in bed beside him.

She consented to let him put his arms around her, to keep warm. That much, and no more. But he went to sleep, all the same, with a smile on his face.

Despite her resolutions, it was several weeks before Carrie plucked up courage to go to Trevarnon, and when she did, Katie wasn't there. She might have guessed – the house looked empty, even as she walked up the great drive under the avenue of trees. Windows shuttered and closed, and the great front door shut and forbidding. But she thought she detected movement at one of the upper windows, and, greatly daring, she climbed the steps and rang the little iron bell.

There was a long pause, and then a girl in uniform came to the door. For some reason it took Carrie by surprise. She had known, of course, that Katie had married money – she had said so to Ernie hundreds of times. But coming face to face with it like this, somehow that was different. Imagine Katie Warren from the Terrace having servants!

And such a house too! Carrie caught a glimpse of it through the open door. Like a palace. The hall was twice the size of the biggest room at Buglers, and there was a great thick red carpet up a wide staircase at the end of it, with more paintings and statues and stuffed foxes than a museum. And that was only the passage!

'Yes, madam?' the maid said again, looking from Carrie to the baby in her arms. Carrie looked down at herself, aware of the tattered state of her skirt and blouse after three weeks in the fields, and the red rawness of her hands. She flushed.

'I came to see Katie – that is, I came to see Mrs Trevarnon. I used to know her once, years ago, and I . . . well, I wanted to ask her advice.'

The girl smiled, a professional sort of smile for dealing with unwelcome callers. 'I'm afraid Mrs Trevarnon's not here.' She must have seen Carrie's lip tremble, because she added more kindly, 'Gone up to Plymouth for a month or two with Mr George and the children. They often do, in the summer. And they're going on to London for a week or so afterwards. But I'll tell her you called. What was it about, exactly?'

It was impossible to tell her, of course. Carrie forced a smile. 'Oh, it's nothing. Just, I was hoping to speak to her. But you can tell her I came. Carrie Clarance my name is. Carrie Tremble that was.'

The girl nodded. 'Oh yes. I remember the name. Well, certainly I'll tell her. Mrs Trevarnon will be sorry to have missed you. Can I say where she can find you, when she does come home?'

Carrie thought about that for a moment, but then shook her head. 'We're on a farm at present, but we're moving on,' she said. It sounded dignified, at least. 'I'll come back in a month or two, and hope to find her then.' If we are not all in the workhouse before then, she thought bitterly.

'Do that,' the girl said. 'I'll tell her.' And there was nothing for it but to turn away, leaving the maid looking down the path after her, with a look of puzzled curiosity on her face.

We must look a sight, Carrie thought. Blossom had been sucking bread and her little face was streaked with crumbs. Who would have us, looking like this? She felt suddenly desperate. Somewhere, deep down, she had been relying on getting help from Katie. There was no more work at the farm – whatever were they to do now? Three pounds fourteen and six, she still had that, and a shilling or so to come from Crowdie. They could manage, if only she could find work.

She hesitated a long time before going to Albert Villas. Only desperation would have driven her. Ellie let her in, and Carrie tried to tidy herself in the hallstand mirror.

Miss Limmon received her upstairs. She looked less buttoned-up than she used to, Carrie thought, and there was more of an air about the place. Flowers in vases, and pot plants in glass cases. Even Miss Limmon's dress was a little more generous in cut and fashionable in style than once it had been.

At the sight of Blossom, however, Miss Limmon's face looked more like a sucked lemon than ever, as though Carrie had brought a wild animal into the house. All the same, she listened patiently and didn't send them off with a scolding as Carrie had half expected. Instead she seemed almost to consider the idea.

'Of course it would be quite impossible to offer you anything like a maid's post,' she said, looking at Blossom. 'That would need someone to live in – but, I just might be able to find you something. It's only a possibility, of course. I can't promise. I must speak to Mrs Rowe about it. We do entertain a little more than formerly, so with Christmas coming you might come in as a daily and help out in the kitchen. Only until you find something else, naturally. Something more suitable for a woman with a child. You would not expect, of course, to bring it to the house. And if I can't manage to take you myself, I'll ask around.'

It was a good deal more than Carrie had hoped. It wasn't altogether the answer to a prayer. The place would offer, at best, only a few shillings a week. But she would get her dinner, and she could always take a bit of it home, as Dolly used to do.

Dolly! A sudden thought struck her. Dolly! Perhaps she would look after Blossom – she'd be even gladder of a shilling than Winnie's sister would have been. There would be precious little left of Miss Limmon's wages, of course, by the time they found a room somewhere – but she still had her seventy-four shillings. They might manage a month or two. And by that time, Katie would be back.

'Only until you find something else,' Miss Limmon said again, as though she was thinking better of it already. 'And only if Mrs Rowe agrees. But I must make it clear, Carrie, that there is no question whatever of you working above stairs this time.'

'No, Miss Limmon,' Carrie said dutifully. 'And thank you very much. You've been kind.' It *was* kind. Anyone with half an eye could see that Miss Limmon didn't really need any extra help at all.

'Well, come back and see me at the end of the week, and we'll see. And Carrie . . .'

'Yes, Miss Limmon?'

'Thank you . . . for the violets. It was . . . appreciated.'

Carrie went out of the room in a whirl. Thank you for the violets. So that was it. Poor Old Button-eyes had appreciated them after all.

She told Ellie about it, in a hushed whisper as they went downstairs.

'It only goes to show,' Ellie said. 'It's true what they say, good deeds come back to you. "Cast your bread upon the waters and it shall return unto you . . ." '

' "After many days",' Carrie finished. 'I know.' And she was feeling so lighthearted after her visit that she added, with a spark of her old spirit, 'Though who would want soggy bread anyway, I'd like to know?'

Ellie laughed doubtfully, but she was sure that Dolly would have the baby, and welcome. 'Glad of the money,' she said.

Carrie treated herself to a horse-bus home, and for the first time since they left Buglers she felt almost hopeful. Things were working out, after all.

Ernie didn't go with her to Trevarnon. Mrs Trevarnon was Carrie's friend, after all, he said – he'd only met her that once, at the funeral. If it came out that the letters hadn't arrived, he thought, better for it to look like an accident, and not have him standing there turning pink to the tips of his ears and giving the game away.

And for another thing, Crowdie had found a job for him that afternoon. Clearing stones. That would mean a few more shillings in the kitty, and it was a job he could do even in the driving drizzle. They had been lucky. There had been steady work so far. Three weeks of late summer sunshine had seen the last of the corn brought in, stocked, ricked and covered for winter. They had finished only the night before. The men had worked into the darkness roping the rick before the rain, but it had been done in time.

But the extra hands were being turned off. Crowdie had been paying them off, one or two at a time, for the past week. If it wasn't for Carrie being an old friend, they would have earned nothing for days. Ernie knew it, and though he was grateful, it shamed him. A man should be looking out for his wife, not have her supporting him.

Perhaps that was another reason why he had not urged her to go to Trevarnon sooner. He had tried to find work round about. Even went down to the tin-mine one evening late, but the mine was struggling to pay its own men, let alone take on a clayer who knew 'less about tin than a Red Indian'. So in the end she had gone: 'first wet day,' as she always said. She took a letter with her to post to Da.

He had written to Da, previous – or at least Carrie had. Just to tell him that they were safe and well. And Da had written back – a curt note, saying not to worry, he and Linny May had made their own arrangements and were moving out of Buglers after Michaelmas. Going in with Mr Whittaker, since he was on his own. Vince, it seemed, had never been home again since that morning, but had written to say he was up in Plymouth with some woman, hoping to marry her and take a boat for somewhere abroad. So that Jeannie *had* taken him back after all. Trust Vince to fall on his feet and find someone to look after him.

Ernie sighed. He could see the sense of Da's plan. They could share the rent, and Da and Linny Ma could do a bit around the place which Mr Whittaker could never do for himself. Get that old hearth-oven going again, perhaps, though Linny May was not so sprightly as she used to be.

Still, Da wouldn't like it. See it as charity, like as not. He must have really taken to Mr Whittaker to agree to go at all, though there wasn't a lot of choice, really, without he went on the parish and took poor relief. And he would have liked that even less. Poor Da. Ernie sighed again. What had he brought them all to, one way and another?

He bent his back to the stones again. It pleased him, this job. He could lose himself in it, forget about the stupid events which had brought him to this pass, and take pleasure in physical labour in spite of the rain. He didn't mind rain. A clayer gets used to working in a bit of wet. And he was good at this work, at least as strong and skilled as anyone else. Not like handling that stupid corn, slithering and sliding off the pitchforks, and leaving him looking like a fool while the other men moved twice the volume in half the time with swift, deft flicks of the wrist.

If only the wretched strike would finish, perhaps he could look for a job again down at the claypits at St Just. Couldn't do it now, of course, with the works out everywhere – and even then, his name might be blacked everywhere in the industry, just from leading the Union. Never mind what they'd say if they knew about that policeman.

But they couldn't know it was him. Not for sure. Carrie had said that a dozen times. Come to the house and he was nowhere to be seen. And that glass bottle, nothing had come of that either. Still looking for the man who did it, Da said, but not him in particular. Just as well he'd said what he did to Bill Giles! And now there was a story that someone had shot a policeman in the leg, up at Halviggan at a Union protest, and there was no end of a hue and cry about that instead.

But he couldn't convince himself. He still shook like a leaf every time he saw a uniform, and imagined policeman everywhere. He expected at any moment to feel a heavy hand on his shoulder.

At least, that was how he felt. But when it happened – when, suddenly, standing there in the rain outside Crowdie's barn, there was a crunch of feet behind him and a hand did fall on his shoulder – he found he wasn't prepared for it in the least.

He whirled around, still half hoping it would be Crowdie, or Bert Hoskins grumbling about Blossom's clothes drying in the bedroom. But it was the stuff of his nightmares. A policeman, muffled up against the rain, still holding his shoulder in a fierce grip and saying softly, 'Mr Ernie Clarance?'

Ernie gave the man a push and ran for it, but they caught up with him at the gate. They were two of them, and they looked as if they meant business. He sighed.

'All right then,' he said, and made a clean breast of it.

When Carrie got back to the Terrace Bert Hoskins was waiting for her, with all her possessions packed in a bolster-case. 'Aren't having jailbirds under my roof,' he said. 'So don't you go thinking it.' He went in and slammed the door, and that was all he would say.

She got the story from Crowdie. Ernie had been arrested. Taken to Penzance police station and committed for a hearing at the police court. Could be the Assizes if they found him guilty. Crowdie didn't know what the charge was exactly. 'Endangering the safety of a policeman', at the very least.

It was ironic really. If he hadn't been scared to death of his own shadow they might never have caught him at all. The two policemen at Crowdie's were there on quite different business, as it turned out.

Crowdie told her about it, sitting her down at the kitchen table in the big farmhouse and pressing a glass of hot milk and brandy into her hand. She had been shaken enough to hear about Ernie, but when Crowdie produced the alcohol she knew at once that there was even worse to come. Crowdie was chapel, like her father, and never drank in his life except 'medicinal'.

'Policemen were here about your husband's da,' Crowdie said, 'and his grandmother. Moving house they were, with all their furniture and belongings on a cart. Going to a Mr Whittaker, it appears. You knew about that?'

Carrie nodded.

'Well, that was it, you see. Went up past one of the claypits and there was a demonstration going on. Somebody had explosives. Did no damage, except it frightened the horses. Driver had one arm, they said, and couldn't hold them back. Turned over the cart and the old lady was thrown out, and the driver was dragged half a mile. Got tangled in the harness and couldn't free hisself. Both dead, Carrie my lover. I'm some sorry – as if you didn't have enough troubles! But tell you what, my handsome – you stop down the barn as long as you want, and I'll let you have a bit of food and clothes when I can.'

She went to Penzance and they let her see Ernie. He was stricken with grief, too upset to care what happened to him any more. He just kept saying, 'My fault, that's what it is. All my fault. Deserve everything I get, I do,' over and over again. Carrie could get no sense out of him.

When the time came he went into the police court like a cow waiting for slaughter, and answered their questions in a monotone, as though he no longer cared what happened to him. Even so, he was not prepared for what happened. The police courts were taking a firm line with agitators, especially those who had injured policemen. Witnesses argued that the missile was 'thrown at the head with an intention to kill'. Carrie could not believe it. Ernie – committed for trial at the St Austell Assizes, on a charge of attempted murder. That would be penal servitude for years, or worse: a man had been sentenced to penal servitude for life only a year before, for shooting at a policeman.

She wanted to speak to Ernie, but they would not permit it, simply bundled him into a prison-cart (a sort of motor-lorry) and took him away in handcuffs to the County Jail at Bodmin. Carrie stood in the street, with Blossom in her arms, looking helplessly after him. Whatever was she to do now?

Even the few days between his arrest and his trial had cost her dearly. She had taken a room in Penzance to be near Ernie. There was nowhere to cook, or wash, and that had meant going to the bath-house, and buying food from the street-stalls and the bakehouses. At the time she had not counted the cost, so long as she and Blossom were warm and fed, and she could follow the trial. And now it would all be to do again in St Austell, and there would be fares to find besides. Wherever was she to find the money? She stood on the steps outside the police court, so overwhelmed with despair that she hardly noticed when a man from the *Graphic Messenger* came and set up his camera and took a photograph of her for the papers.

Still, she could not stand here for ever. It would be a fortnight or more before Ernie's case came to trial. Attempted murder! She repeated the words to herself, but her brain refused to accept it. But there was still Blossom to think of.

She went back, at first, to Crowdie and the barn, but although it was dry and warm – warmer than Bert Hoskins' bedroom, in fact – she heard something the second night which made her determined to move out of it, if only for Blossom's sake. Rats. She could remember when she was a girl and a man over at Trewithen had died in a barn of a seizure. It was days before they found him, and when they did, his face was half-eaten away. While she had breath in her body and a penny in her purse, Blossom should be protected from that.

But there was still Miss Limmon. She had half promised. She had been kind. And surely, now that things had taken such a terrible turn, she would do something? Carrie went up to Albert Villas the next day.

She could tell something was the matter from the first moment Ellie opened the door. The girl's eyes opened wide with alarm.

'My life, Carrie, whatever in the world are you doing here?'

Carrie hoisted Blossom more firmly on her shoulder and explained. 'Said she'd see what she could do, and told me to come back in week or two,' she finished lamely.

Ellie shook her head. 'I should save your breath, my handsome. In some taking, she was, when she read about that police trial in the papers. Picture of you in it, and all. Wanted to know if I'd known your Ernie was a wanted criminal when you came here before, and of course I said "no", but I don't think she believed me. Carrying on about how she couldn't have you under her roof, any price – and how she'd have something to say to you when she saw you for daring to come here. No, I wouldn't even ask her, if I were you, my lover. Do better to leave it a bit, and the fuss has all died down. She's got a good heart, underneath it all, and she'd give you something for the child, maybe. But for a job, I think you can forget it.'

Carrie closed her eyes against the tears of weariness and despair. 'Well, what am I going to do? Be the workhouse, that's what. Never thought it would come to that.'

Ellie looked at her for a moment. 'If I were you, my handsome,' she said, 'I'd go down see Dolly, talk it over with her. She'd have the child, I know, and then you could find somewhere perhaps.'

Carrie thought for a moment, and she then nodded, and walked slowly away.

She spent a couple of days looking, but there was no work to be had. Too many people had seen her photograph in the paper, and no one wanted a woman whose husband was in prison – though some were kind enough to pretend it was because they couldn't take a woman with a child. It was possible, she thought wearily. She might do better without Blossom, perhaps. Well, job or no job, she'd have to get the child looked after. She couldn't walk the streets day after day with the child on her arm. And if she was going to St Austell Assizes, she would certainly need someone then.

On the Friday she went down to Fairmaids Lane.

CHAPTER SIX

Dolly never read the papers, but Tommy heard most things down at the tavern, and she had heard with horror all about the trial. She was upstairs mending nets when the tap on the door came, but as soon as she heard it she knew who it was.

'Carrie!' She would hardly have recognised her friend; the face so pinched and worn with worry, eyes and hair limp and lifeless under the black straw hat. 'Come in, do. We've been waiting for you.'

'Waiting?' A glimmer of hope in the voice. 'For me?'

'For the pair of you. Ellie came in here yesterday. Miss Limmon is sending her off somewhere, seemingly to help out in a family out Crowlas where the maid's been took sick – and she came in to say goodbye. She said as she'd seen you, and told you to come here. I told her she did right. You can count on me and welcome.'

'Then you'll have Blossom? I can pay you a bit, Dolly, I'm not looking for favours. I got a bit put by.' Carrie sat down on a chair, suddenly – as if a weight had fallen on her, instead of lifted – and began to cry.

'There!' Dolly said. 'Course I will. And don't you worry about money till you've found a position.' She looked searchingly at the worn face and the arms, a little too thin under the faded blouse. 'And you, my handsome. Where are you? Got a place to stay yourself, have you?'

It was foolish, stupid. They hadn't but two bedrooms in the house, and they were already stretched to bursting. And goodness knows what Tommy would say – a woman whose husband was accused of attempted murder! But she couldn't stand back and see Carrie and the child in the workhouse. Let people say what they liked about the father, it wasn't the child's fault.

Carrie was looking at her, tears standing in her eyes. 'Dolly! You haven't got room.'

Dolly avoided her eyes. 'We'll make room.'

'It wouldn't be for long,' Carrie said. 'Dismiss the case, I'm sure they will, and then we can find a place of our own. Or Katie'll be back in a month or so. She'd give me something, I'm sure she would.'

But her face told the story of the despair she was feeling. Dolly turned away and put the kettle on the hob, and stirred the soup of fish heads and onions which was bubbling on the fire. Another potato, and they could stretch that to feed another. Though what they should do when the winter came and the fishing stopped, goodness alone knew. She measured tea-leaves into the pot and refused to think of it. 'Sufficient unto the day.'

'Miss Limmon won't have me,' Carrie said softly.

'Not just now, any road.' Dolly said. 'She might think of it later, when the scandal's died. Might be quicker'n you think. There's been another fellow up for shooting a policeman in the leg, so Tommy was saying. They charged him with attempted murder too, but they've dropped it to "unlawful wounding". Do the same for Ernie, see if they don't!'

She wasn't at all sure about that, but Carrie's face lifted at once. 'And that was a gun, too,' she said. 'Lot worse than a stone, that is.'

'There you are then, see,' Dolly said. 'And if they change their mind a bit, Miss Limmon might think different.' There was a lot more she might have added. Ellie had come in yesterday with tales of how Old Button-eyes was fair torturing herself over turning Carrie away. She wanted to help Carrie, but at the same time she didn't want her, with this scandal hanging over her. Ellie thought it was partly that Miss Limmon didn't want the baby: but Dolly remembered M. Philippe, and had her own ideas. Didn't want a rival, more like. Though, looking at the pale, worn creature sitting forlornly at the table, it was hard to imagine that Carrie could be a threat to anyone. 'Here,' pushing the cup across the table, 'have some tea. And a bit of hevva cake. Put some colour in your cheeks.' The hevva cake had been for Tommy's tea, but this was an emergency, Dolly felt.

Carrie lifted the cup to her lips. 'I can't just come here, Dolly. You're pressed enough as it is. Got to go up to this trial, and even then it isn't as if I had a job somewhere to come back to. I've asked all day, and there's no-one willing. Heard about Ernie I suppose, and bad mud sticks. If I was earning a bit, I could bring something home, and earn my keep.'

She was already calling it 'home' Dolly noticed. She said aloud, 'Well, we'll talk to Tommy when he comes in. But you can stay here tonight, any road. You have a drop of soup, put Blossom down in our bed, and go out for a walk. I'll see what he says.'

304

But when Tommy came in he was less put about than she expected. 'Had a hard time, they clayers,' he said. 'And that Ernie was a good man, from what they say. Attempted murder! Never was for a moment! But Carrie must be frightened half to death. Yes, you help them out, Dolly girl – never know when we might be glad to have someone do the same for us. And as to earning, she could give you a hand with the fish when the trial's over, if she's a mind. You got your hands full, with Little Ell, and Carrie could help with the filleting. Every little bit helps, this time of year – the fishing is always bad after October. And she could sell too, come to that. She's got a nice way with her, always had. And if Ellie's right, Miss Limmon would give her a fat order, just to salve her conscience.'

Dolly brought him the hevva cake – Carrie hadn't touched it. 'You're a good man, Tommy Williams,' she said. 'How will I make it up to you?'

He caught her arm. 'We'll think of something.'

'Well, you'll have to be quiet then,' she said, 'with strangers in the front room.'

'Trying to put me off the idea, are you?' he said, and then, more seriously, 'We could make her a bed up in the net-loft, I suppose. Give us all a bit of privacy. It's a bit draughty, and it niffs a bit, but it's clean and dry enough and if we shifted up the nets there'd be room enough and to spare. She'll have to find a place of her own in the end, of course.'

'The loft'd be handsome,' Carrie said, when they told her. 'I'll look for a place. Soon as ever the scandal's died. And maybe, if you're right, Ernie'll be home in a year or two . . .' Her voice quivered and she blinked hard for a minute. Then she said, more calmly, 'I got a shilling or two put by, anyway, Dolly – and I'll have a bit extra come in when they've sold those bits up to St Blurzey. I can give you something, even if it's only a bob or two a week.'

It was more than Dolly expected. 'Well, I'll put it by,' she said. Carrie would be happier if she was paying something. 'Few shillings extra will come in handy in the winter, I won't pretend they won't.'

'I'll be gone by then,' Carrie said. 'Soon as ever I get the chance. Supposing I aren't caught up in Tommy's nets and taken round the fairs for a mermaid.' It wasn't much of jest, but already the despair had gone from her eyes and her face was like the old Carrie, living and dancing. 'And once the trial's over, I'll give a hand with the fish for a week or two, if you'll show me how. Might as well be useful.'

'Well, then, we'll all be gainers,' Dolly smiled. No point in saying what she was thinking. Carrie would never get her 'chance' now, not till Ernie had done his time, and maybe not even then. A week in the fish, and you reeked of it. Nobody would ever have you anywhere else again.

★

'Will that be all, Miss Limmon?'

Emily nodded her head sharply. It was by no means all, in fact. She would have liked a hot supper tray sent up, and a second warming pan in her bed, but there would be no-one to do it tonight. It was her own fault, sending that Ellie to Crowlas.

It was partly a kindness. The maid up there had a sister with spotted fever, and of course she had to be sent home. Couldn't have that in the house! Spread like wildfire, the fever cart at the door, and that awful fever hospital where you couldn't even see in the windows because the doctors were so worried about infection. She'd have to be very careful at Albert Villas when Ellie came back. Leave it for a good long time – you couldn't afford to have germs in. She'd never forgotten the business of King Edward and his appendicitis. You couldn't be too careful.

A lot of people wouldn't have lent their staff, under the circumstances. But Ellie had no objection to going – it was a nice house and the children were pleasant enough, as children went – and Emily had been secretly glad to see the back of the girl. Not that there was anything wrong with Ellie – she'd learned to be quite efficient over the years – but her presence was a kind of silent reproach.

Well, she couldn't have had Carrie back, not with her husband in prison. Photographs in the paper, and headlines too. Of course she couldn't. No-one could possibly have expected her to. She had been prepared to make a place for Carrie, out of the kindness of her heart, when she thought the girl was suffering because of the clay-strike. And Philippe would have approved.

But this was different. The clayers had all gone back to work now, so if it wasn't for that awful young man and his violence, Carrie would have had money coming in and be settled back in her own home weeks ago. No, she had absolutely nothing to reproach herself with. It was just that she didn't care to have Ellie looking at her like that. The whole unfortunate business was far better forgotten.

And then this afternoon James Tavy, of all people, had raised the subject: and in her own drawing room, too. He had come to deal with some papers, and began to talk – as he had taken to doing lately – about his own life and affairs. Some fellow called Morrison was paying, apparently, for him to represent Ernie Clarance at the Assizes.

'Morrison speaks most highly of the young man,' Tavy said. 'Impressed with his transparent sincerity. I shall be going up to see him, shortly. I understand you . . . ah . . . knew the family?'

'The wife was a maid here, once,' Emily said shortly. 'She was harmless enough. As for the boy – I can't say I'm altogether surprised. I met him only once – creating a disturbance in the back lane then, shouting and throwing things about. A most undesirable type. I had occasion to speak to him severely. Myself and M. Diavezour.'

Tavy looked at her shrewdly. 'Ah, yes. M. Diavezour. Have you . . . ah . . . spoken to him lately?' Tavy seemed a little embarrassed at the indelicacy of his own question. He hurried on, as if to explain, 'He had . . . ah . . . things to discuss with you, I think.'

She smiled, feeling herself colour a little. 'Mr Diavezour has been wonderful. So helpful and supportive. Like yourself, Mr Tavy,' she added, hastily. No point in allowing the man to suppose that she had a partiality. Although she did. Of course she did. Her heart gave a little flutter at the thought. 'Asking on behalf of a friend of his' – as if she didn't perfectly well see through his little ruse! Well she had let him know, plainly enough, that his attentions would be welcome.

'He writes that he will be in town again shortly,' Tavy said. 'I expect him daily – there are still matters of the Trezayle estate to be finally settled.'

Emily nodded. She had thought that she recognised a certain pair of darker brown sails when she had glanced – ever so casually, of course – over towards the incoming boats on this morning's tide. As she always did.

When Tavy had gone, she sat down at the writing desk and penned a note to Philippe, urging him to call. She could make a pretence at least, of asking him what to do about Carrie. And, it would give him an opportunity to speak a little more . . . intimately, if he wished.

But here it was, late in the evening, and no Philippe had appeared. And she was stuck in the house with a cold supper-tray and the maid had the evening off. Emily was not in the happiest of tempers.

As if on cue, the maid appeared at the bedroom door.

'Myrtle? I thought you had gone?'

'Well, so I was going, Miss Limmon, only there's a man at the door, asking for you most particularly. It's that French gentleman, ma'am. I told him as how you were gone upstairs for the night, but he was that insistent. Said he must speak to you, if it was only a minute.'

Emily flushed, her irritation forgotten. 'I see. Well, tell him I will come down.' So he had come. But unaccompanied and at this hour? Whatever would the neighbours say? He could not mean, surely, to speak to her tonight? It was most indelicate. All very well in France perhaps, but not here. And she could not entertain him alone, at this time of night. 'You had better stay for a moment, Myrtle. I won't keep you longer than I can help.'

'Yes Miss Limmon.' And the girl was gone. Looking put out, too.

Emily sighed with vexation. It was bad enough having Philippe arrive like this when she could not entertain him. And then to have Myrtle flounce and sigh because she was asked to stay back for half an hour! It was like that anti-union man said in the papers. People seemed to be expected to live their lives these days for the convenience of the working class. Look at her own servants. First Carrie, then Ellie and her reproachful looks, and now this. She dabbed a little carmine on her lips and went down to see Philippe. She was smiling.

Ten minutes later, though, the smile had vanished. How could he! It had been her own fault of course, mentioning the wretched girl. And Philippe had been very charming, in fact, as he always was. But there had been no question of a proposal. The minute she had mentioned Carrie, all he had wanted to talk about was that wretched child and her criminal husband – simply because he had seen her photograph in the *Graphic Messenger*. He had read the note, picked up the paper in the town, and come hot-foot to Albert Villas to find news of her.

She had had to tell him, outright, that she had turned the girl away. He had understood, of course. Naturally. But it was Ellie all over again. That look of disappointment and reproach. It was ridiculous. The girl's husband was up on a serious charge. She had no idea where Carrie was: and no, Ellie wasn't here either, so it wasn't possible to ask her. And he had gone away, without the hint of a personal conversation between them, and only the vaguest of promises to come back soon.

Altogether, it was the least successful meeting with Philippe Diavezour that Emily had ever had.

The Assizes seemed to pass in a daze. Carrie went up for the trial, unable to eat or sleep until it was over.

In fact, Ernie got off lightly: six months for unlawful wounding, inciting to riot, and assaulting a police officer. Dolly was right about the charges. Mr Morrison, of all people, had got to hear of the trial – from Ralph Whittaker more than likely – and sent down a lawyer to speak for Ernie. Carrie didn't warm to him much, he was a thin, hawk-faced man called Tavy with eyes like razors, but he got the charges reduced in no time. He told the court that although Ernie had been throwing stones, and that was an offence, he had never intended to hit what he called 'the person' of the police officer – and that there was 'reasonable doubt' that he was even responsible for the man's injuries. 'I submit that two glass objects were found, one of which was nowhere near the target, and the defendant clearly states that he threw only one, which was aimed at the lantern. And the police agree that the lantern was on the gatepost at the time of the incident, and not in the officer's hand. Isn't that so?'

The police witness agreed that it was.

'And there were two of you in the hallway at the time?' Tavy persisted, turning to Ernie.

'Yes.'

'Where is the companion of yours now?' the prosecutor wanted to know.

Ernie shook his head. 'Dunno. Ran off next morning, same as me. Said he was going abroad if he could.'

'So you have no witness to your statement.'

'No sir.'

'That is very convenient, Mr Clarance,' the man said, and a little ripple of laughter ran around the court. 'But even had you not thrown the missile in question, you must have been aware that you might have caused permanent damage. The officer might well have been much closer to the lantern, if not actually holding it. It is sheer chance that the consequences were not more serious. What do you say to that?'

Ernie raised his head, which had been bowed all through the proceedings and looked at the man who had spoken. 'I as good as killed my da and Linny May,' he said hopelessly. 'Isn't that serious enough?'

It caused a murmur of sympathy in the court, and the newspaper writers scribbled busily. When the judge came to pass sentence he said that he took into account 'the mitigation pleaded by the defendant's counsel, and the defendant's own sincere and evident remorse.' There was a lot more, too, full of 'heretofores' and 'whereinunders', which Carrie only half understood. The outcome, however, she understood perfectly. Ernie was in prison, and Da and Linny May were in their graves.

They had not even been to the funeral. Somehow the force of that didn't strike Carrie until the trial was over. But it was true. It had taken ten days and more to trace Ernie, and by that time Mr Whittaker had arranged everything. Only Da had known where Carrie and Ernie were, and he was dead. Mr Whittaker had refused to know, just as he had refused to hear Vince's plans, and Linny May told everyone that they were 'probably gone to America'. It had only been pieced together when the police found Bill Giles, and talked to the postwoman who remembered Da sending a letter to Penvarris.

That idea struck Ernie worst of all. 'Put them in their grave and never saw them to it!'

Carrie, though, had little time to mourn. There was the question of money, for one thing. What with the rent and food and fares and the money she gave Dolly, she had only fifty-two shillings remaining. More than two guineas squandered in less than a fortnight. Besides, Ernie was to be taken up to the County Jail at Bodmin, and she would have to find more money somehow, to go and see him once in a way at least.

She did get a few shillings from the furniture. It would have cost a fortune to send, and there was nowhere to put it if it came. Besides, most things had been damaged beyond repair when the cart turned over. She arranged with Mr Whittaker to use the broken pieces for firing, and got the rest sent to a sale-room.

After the trial, she took Tommy at his word and tried her hand at the fish. The boys, Drew and Billy especially, laughed at her efforts, and to start they *were* laughable. She didn't know a plaice from a flatfish, and though she had been skilled in the kitchen it took her longer to fillet one cod than it took Dolly to bone five.

And she hated it. Hated the floundering, gaping bodies in the fish-baskets of a morning. Hated the blood and scales and guts and oil that ran in your fingers and squelched under your boots. Hated the stench which oozed little by little into your skin and hair and breathed out through your very pores. Hated the days she was called on down at the palace when a big catch came in, packing fish into the brine-bins till the salt and scales leeched into your soul. But she persevered. And gradually, she learned.

Learned how to break out and wash the 'bulked' pichards from the salt. Learned how to stack a hogshead with neat circles of fishes lying cheek by jowl like spokes in a wheel. How to tell a good pickle by the shine. How dorys grunt when they are caught, and 'poor cod' must be eaten the day it is caught or it tastes of nothing. How pressed pilchards groan and shriek and 'cry for more' as the swim bladders break, all at once, under the pressing-screws. How Fairmaids Lane got its name: from the 'fumados' – the smoked fish which were shipped, regular as clockwork, to Italy, for the Catholics there to eat of a Friday.

There were things too, she must learn *not* to do. Not to whistle when the boats went out, for fear of a wind. Not to move the stale bread from Tommy's pockets – it was there for the Bucca, and Christian though he was, he never went to sea without it. Never to talk of 'white chokers' while the men were about – though why vicars and ministers should bring such bad luck to God-fearing men she could never fathom. It was the same with rabbits: 'Furliners' they called them, so as not even to say the name. Supposed to be terrible bad luck to mention them, and worse to see them on your way to a catch. 'I can see the sense in that,' Carrie said to Dolly when she heard. 'See a rabbit when you're supposed to be a mile out from Land's End and you would be in trouble.' But Dolly did not even smile. 'Furliners' were no laughing matter in that house.

And if there were shoals of fish about, it was important not to look at the sea. Especially pilchards. And if there weren't pilchards, which there weren't these days, it was apt to be her fault for looking. 'Pilchards can smell a woman's glance at a hundred yards,' Tommy would say, and tell how they used to lock up the womenfolk, one time, so they wouldn't frighten the fish.

But most of all she learned to sell. Walking the streets at first, hawking fish from a basket, just like that picture of Dolly which Rawlings had painted all those years ago. Then, gradually, as the year drew on and the weather worsened, she began to work the houses. Tommy said to call on Miss Limmon, and he was right. Soon as she knew it was Carrie on the street she always sent out to buy something, though she had never been a fish-lover as a rule. Even sent out a few extra pence too, once, 'for the baby', though Carrie gave them to Dolly to buy a bit extra for the larder.

Blossom was happy. Thriving. Dolly's girl was company for her, and Dolly was good with them − though she was expecting again, Carrie knew. What would happen after the new baby came she could not bear to think. But perhaps, after all, if the fish-palace didn't close down and go over to ice, as people were saying, she might yet be skilled enough to earn a proper job on the fish-floor. It was all she could hope for. She knew that now, and did not need Dolly to tell her. The smell of blood and oil had become part of her, like her smile, and brought the seagulls whirling over her wherever she went.

Even Ernie noticed it, when she went one afternoon to see him. It was an awkward meeting − if you could call it a meeting, with a grille and an iron door between them. It was a long weary journey up to Bodmin, and the fare had made another hole in the dwindling store of money in the bottom of her little box. But Ernie had been grateful, devouring her with his eyes, like a starving man gazing at food.

They talked awkwardly for a while. Ernie had had a letter from Mr Whittaker, and one from Morrison. She told him about Blossom and the fish.

'Here,' he said suddenly, when they had exchanged all the news they could think of and were eyeing each other in silence. 'Take off your hat and scarf, Carrie, and let me see you, properly.'

She was wearing both over her head, as the women with jouster baskets often did: the scarf tied over the straw boater to keep it anchored to your head, and to keep your hair out of the fish-oil and slime in the basket on your shoulders. She had put them on so automatically, and never noticed that she had done it.

She took the scarf off, and the hat, and as she did so her looped hair escaped from its braids and fell loose around her face. It smelt of fish.

'Now look,' she said, half laughing. 'Got to get back to Penzance and my hair's all over the place. Should have left well alone. Lost half me pins now, and I'll never keep my hat on with my hair like this!'

But Ernie didn't seem to care. Not even about the smell. 'Pretty as ever,' he said. And then, urgently, 'You will wait for me, won't you, Carrie?'

'Where would I go?' she said, and then the time was over. The journey home seemed longer than ever, and she sat hunched on the wooden seat, hearing Ernie's words, over and over, like an echo.

She got out and walked slowly – not straight home, but out onto the fields and cliffs. She needed to think. Poor Ernie, cooped up like that – and Vince, who was more to blame than anyone, freer than air. It was a long time before she was ready to go back to Newlyn, and even then she did not go straight to the house. She wanted to be busy, and though it would have been nice to see Blossom, she was not quite ready yet to face Dolly's questions about Ernie and how prison life was treating him.

She went to the harbour. Drew was there already, sitting on the low wall filleting fish, and she sat down beside him. Her hat, lacking its hatpins, had been sliding defiantly sideways every time she turned her head, and she pulled it off altogether with an exasperated sigh and put it down beside her, slipping her shawl over her head to cover her tousled locks. Like some old peasant in a painting, she thought crossly. She took up her filleting knife with a sigh.

'Been someone here,' Drew said. 'Looking for you.'

'For me?' Carrie was surprised. 'One of my customers, was it?'

'Carriage folk, by the looks,' Drew said.

Carrie put down the fish and pushed up her sleeves. She was already covered in fish-blood to the elbow. 'Carriage folk?' Could it be Katie, back from Plymouth, who had somehow learned that she was here, and come wanting to let bygones be bygones? Her heart gave a little bound. 'Did she say her name?'

Drew grinned. 'Wasn't a her, it was a him. Here he is again.'

She turned round and saw him. A touch of grey in the hair. The face more lined, more bronzed, more beautiful. Older now, but elegant in a smart cut suit. Holding her terrible battered straw hat. M. Philippe, his eyes misted and gentle, and his voice between laughter and crying, saying in a terrible parody of his own accent, 'And this time, Mamzelle, I 'ave not treaden upon your 'at!'

PART SIX : 1913

CHAPTER ONE

He had found her!

He had searched like a man demented. Emily Limmon's note first alerted him, and then he had picked up the paper and seen the photograph. He had known her at once, and felt a great upwelling of pity and tenderness. What a fool he had been ever to let her go. And that dreadful Assizes trial. He had read the account of that, too, in the paper. 'Mrs Clarance is now living in the Penzance area.' He had started to look for her at once. And now, he had found her.

She had altered. Her face and figure were still lovely, but even in the few short weeks since the photograph was taken, care and want had begun to etch their mark on her face and form. It turned his heart to see her like this, in an apron of coarse sacking, with her sleeves and hem tattered and stained with the muddy filth of the fish market. Housemaid she might have been at Albert Villas, but Carrie was always neat and clean.

She must have felt it too, because the joy went out of her eyes as she sensed his glance, and she hung her head, trying in vain to clean her hands on her fish-smeared apron.

'M. Philippe! However did you find me here?'

He did not tell her. Suddenly it seemed an unseemly tale, and he was embarrassed by it. She was a married woman, after all – the cheap ring was still bright on her finger – and he had no right to behave as he had done. Rushing in, desperate to find her, acting before he thought.

As soon as he saw the newspaper account he had attempted to call on Tavy. According to the papers, it was Tavy who had represented Ernie Clarance in the trial, and if anyone knew where Carrie could be found, surely he was the one. But there was nothing to be gained from there. First

Tavy was in Bodmin, at the Assizes, and then in London on business for Emily Limmon: and his clerk knew nothing.

Next he had called on Emily Limmon. She had hardly wanted to discuss the matter – more interested in discussing 'his friend's intentions' – and Philippe had been close to losing patience with her. In the end, though, she had told him something. 'She came here looking for a job, Monsieur, and I would have made a place for her of *course*, but when I heard the charges against her husband, obviously it was impossible . . .'

After that it had become almost an obsession with him. Carrie, reduced to knocking on doors and begging for a job, with a child to care for and a husband in prison – the idea haunted his dreams. He could not even ask Ellie for news – she wasn't there, 'on loan' to a family out of town whose own maid was ill.

He had looked everywhere. Neglected his ships – sent them out to fish without him, and did not care that they called him a 'land-skipper', and whispered that he was getting too grand for the sea. There were still things to attend to from Adeline's estate, and with Ramon still in prison – three months in the local lock-up for disturbing the peace – even they could see that he had all the excuse he needed to remain in Penzance.

He began to hunt for Carrie. Not obviously: that might have caused her more upset and embarrassment, but quietly, persistently. Called on all Adeline's acquaintances that he could reasonably visit, to sip English tea, which he hated, listen to the gossip, and ask idly about available servants as though he were thinking of taking staff at Trezayle House himself. Accepted invitations from other landowners, which had been coming to him ever since Adeline's death, and which up to now he had refused. Dusted off his frock-coat and his society manners, and allowed himself to be lionised by substantial squires and their even more substantial wives. Drank their port, danced with their women, listened to their opinions on cricket and brought the conversation by slow degrees to the news he was hoping to hear. But he learned nothing, beyond what the papers had already told him. Ernie's trial, and sentence, even the death of his father – that was the talk of the town. But there was no news of Carrie herself.

He was itching for Tavy to get back.

He went back to Penvarris and walked on the cliffs. He talked to the Terrace folk, and learned from Bert Hoskins that 'there always was something sly about that Carrie – and her husband too', and from others that they didn't know where she'd gone now, but it was a sorry shame.

'And who are you when you're home?' Bert Hoskins demanded. 'Aren't you that fellow used to walk her on the cliffs?' And Philippe had been obliged to mutter something about being a friend to the family she had worked for, and he set off back across the fields. Everything reminded him of Carrie. The wall where Loeiz had found her hat. The stile where they had stood and talked. The cliffs where they had walked. What a waste. What a stupid, sinful sorry waste of possible happiness.

And then, at last, he did what he should have done in the first place: went back to the Harbour Tavern and sought out Tommy Williams. And struck gold.

'Yes, of course. Staying with us, she is, and trying to give a bit of a hand with the fish. Quick learner too – she can fillet a turbot quicker 'n some who've been learning it for years, and she's only been at it a month or two. Find her down at the fish market, most days, if she isn't out with the baskets.' Tommy looked at him quizzically. 'Don't tell me that woman up Albert Terrace is thinking to offer her a place after all?'

Philippe shook his head. 'No, but that was where I had expected to find her – somewhere like that, in service. I thought she was a housemaid.'

Tommy smiled. 'So she was, but it's not everyone'll have a woman with a child – let alone one with a husband locked away for violence. No, she's had to come to us, poor soul. It'll be the end of her in service, more than like. If she did get an interview now, the woman would take one whiff of her, and there'd be an end of it. Need to get away from the fish, to get away from the fish – there's the pity of it. Still she's a good girl and we're glad to have her – our four boys have taken to her grand, and Dolly's that fond of young Blossom!'

But, Philippe thought, you do not find it easy, these extra people in your house. I read it in your eyes. Aloud he said, 'Could she not find a room in Penzance or Newlyn? It must be difficult with eight people in a house.' He remembered the tiny terraced cottages in Fairmaids Lane where Dolly had spoken to him.

'Nine of us,' Tommy said. 'Be ten, too, before so long. But Carrie does what she can – and she gives Dolly eighteenpence a week, regular, though how she does it, the dear knows. So we get by. And like I say, she's a dab hand with the fish. No, that's where you'll find her, if you're looking.'

And that was where he had found her, at last.

'How did you come to find me here?' she was saying again.

He said, with an attempt at lightness, looking at that ring on her fourth finger, 'I was passing.'

But she knew better. 'Drew said you were looking for me,' she said, with a glance at the grinning urchin beside her. 'You wanted me, Monsieur?'

Oh yes, he wanted her. Wanted her more than anything he had ever desired in his life. Wanted her with every pore and nerve of his body. But he could hardly say so. He had thought no further than a wild, irrational desire to see her and know that she was safe. Now that he had found her, what was he to say? He thought quickly.

There was a silver florin in his pocket. He felt for it, and held it out to her. 'I heard you had a child,' he said. 'I wished to help.'

She was affronted. Her face flushed. 'Monsieur! I am not a beggar.'

He had been clumsy, but he did not take back the coin. An idea struck him, and he smiled. 'Ah,' he said, 'but you misunderstand. This is an old Breton custom.'

He saw the answering smile pluck at her lips. She met his eyes and her own were laughing. 'Ah, Monsieur Philippe!'

He held out the coin. 'Friends?'

'Friends,' she said, and then, looking down in dismay at her fishwife's clothing, 'Though I'm ashamed for you to see me like this.'

He smiled. 'My dear . . .' he was going to say 'Carrie', but he amended it. 'My dear Mrs Clarance, I have been at sea these twenty years. I am not frightened by a little fish.' But the hand which he took in his and closed around the coin was reeking with blood and oil, and even as he pressed the fingers over the coin he was making a resolution.

She was married. She was a mother. She was not his. But Tommy was right – working here, she could never hope for an indoor job again. Somehow, he must find a way to get her 'out of the fish'.

Dolly was at her wits' end by the time Carrie and Drew got home. It had been a dreadful day.

She was all behind, for one thing. The two babies – hers and Carrie's – seemed to be into everything. She was getting heavy and slow – tired too, more tired than she ever remembered when she was carrying any of the other five. Twice today she had let the fire go out, and had to rekindle it. Blossom and Little Ell got filthy playing with coal-dust while her back was turned, and then they got into the store-cupboard and started eating the candles. In the end she had made a sort of cage for them under the table, by fencing them in behind one of Tommy's nets. It made the kitchen stink of tar and oak-cutch, and the babies squalled their hands off, but at least it kept them out of trouble.

All the same, she felt close to tears once or twice. And when she went out for a drop of milk and heard about the plans to close the fish-floor, it almost finished her off entirely.

'Closing? Shutting up for good?'

'Before Christmas, as I heard it,' the woman said, filling Dolly's jug with buttermilk. 'Not the fish for it, these days, that's what they say.'

Dolly shook her head forlornly. That was true enough – not a single large shoal to speak of since that day Carrie had come and found her down the pressing-floor. There had been rumours of the business closing, many a time. But what would they do without the few shillings coming in from working on the fish-floor, and winter coming?

'What about the brine-tanks?' she said, but without hope. 'Spent a fortune putting them in, they did.'

'All ice, isn't it, now?' the woman said. 'Get the fish in and frozen, it can be up to London on the table before the haddock knows it's caught. No market for tinned and salted now. Mind, I dearly love a drop of marinated pilchard myself, though my mother always used to do her own, in a great earthenware bussa.'

'Yes,' Dolly said, but when she got home the babies had torn a great hole in the net and upset the ash-bucket. She cleared it up and then sat down at the table and buried her head in her hands.

That was where Carrie found her when she came in.

'My dear Dolly, whatever is it?'

Dolly looked up, wiping her cheeks with the back of her hand. 'Oh, it's nothing, Carrie my lover, it's just . . .' And out it all came, the work, the worry, the money. 'I'm not saying anything about you, my handsome, you've been good as gold. But, with this fish-parlour closing, I'm fair mazed to know how we'll make do this winter, and that's a fact.'

Carrie put down three parcels on the table. 'Well, there's this, that's a start. Make up a bit of tea tonight, any road.'

Dolly looked up, startled. If there was food to buy she usually bought it herself – whatever she could find cheap in the market, to supplement the fish Tommy brought home.

'If I'd known you were feeling so low, I'd have fetched home a bit more,' Carrie said. 'M. Philippe saw me in the fishmarket and gave me two shillings. For Blossom, he said, but I went down and had my boots mended – they were letting water something chronic. A pair of new soles will see me through the winter, and it's more help to Blossom if I'm not catching my death of cold, or coming home limping with chilblains.'

Dolly was on her feet, opening the parcels. 'Half a dozen eggs, a knuckle-end for soup and a bag of broken biscuits. And here's me as good as saying we can't manage with all of us! Two meals, we've got here – three, good as, because there's a pan of sprats waiting to fry and we can have that tomorrow, with all this. Scrambled eggs – what do you say to that? And broken biscuits after! Some handsome tea we shall have tonight!' Somehow the sight of the few simple items of food had lifted her spirits hugely, and her mouth was watering at the thought of the treat in store.

But Carrie was looking thoughtful. 'Can't go on, though, can it, Dolly? If there's no work down the parlour and the fishing gets scarce there won't be enough here for you, let alone me as well.'

Dolly was wishing she had held her tongue. 'Well,' she said, 'without you we'd be one and six a week worse off, let alone what you earn selling fish.' That was true, though what Carrie brought in went straight out again keeping Carrie and Blossom, when you came right down to it.

Carrie said, 'Wasn't supposed to be for ever, though, was it? Ernie won't be out for months. I never thought about what a burden I was being to you and Tommy, and that's a fact.'

Dolly looked at her helplessly. 'Where you going to go, though, Carrie? That's the thing.'

Carrie turned scarlet. 'There's the parish, I suppose.'

Dolly rounded on her. 'Have you up the workhouse, and a baby to keep? Over my dead body, Carrie Clarance. No, long as there's food on the table, and a roof over our heads, we won't see you driven to that, my lover, and there's an end of it.'

'There's outside relief, these days,' Carrie said doubtfully.

'I shouldn't have said!' Dolly felt embarrassed. 'We'll manage somehow, see if we don't.'

'I suppose,' Carrie said slowly, 'I could go and see Miss Limmon again.'

Dolly shook her head. 'No point. Though . . . No, I don't suppose . . .'

'What?'

Dolly took out the basin and began cracking the eggs into it, avoiding Carrie's eyes. 'It's only . . . well, there was that friend of yours up to Trevarnon. Katie, was she called? You always were going to go up and see her when she came back from Plymouth. Wouldn't do no harm, I suppose?' She added buttermilk to the mixture and beat the eggs to a froth. 'She belonged to take a bit of fish from us, anyway, when she was home – so it wouldn't do any harm, would it? Might bring in a few pennies that way, if nothing else came of it. Though I suppose a lady like that wouldn't want to see a fish-woman, personal.' Let alone hire her, she thought to herself.

But Carrie was looking thoughtful. 'I could, I suppose. I've wondered about it, once or twice. We had a bit of a misunderstanding, once, but she can't do more than bite my head off, can she?'

Dolly shrugged. 'She didn't seem that sort to me. Worth asking, Carrie. Couldn't ask for a job up there, of course – if Miss Limmon was afraid of the scandal, it would be ten times worse for the Trevarnons. But you never know, she might know of something.'

'Yes, you're right. Don't know why I didn't go up there before, Dolly. I'll do it tomorrow.'

Dolly put down the fork she was whisking with. 'You can't! Go up there whiffing of fish and ask to see the lady of the house? Write to her, I was thinking.' Already she was regretting mentioning it. You never could tell what Carrie would take it into her head to do next. Why had she said anything? Only because the fish-house is closing, she thought dully, and I can see us living on fresh air before the winter is out.

Carrie had washed her hands and was setting the knuckle-end in a saucepan to make stock. 'They eat fish, you just said so, even up to Trevarnon,' she said. 'I'll go up tomorrow with a basket, and try to see Katie. See what she says. Now, what about putting on the pan for those eggs? Handsome, they'll be.'

And they were.

For all her stout words, Carrie was nervous when it came to it. The night before, talking bravely in Dolly's kitchen, it had seemed a simple idea: go to Trevarnon, find Katie, and ask for a bit of help in finding a job. That business over the picture had been a long time ago. Katie had forgotten it, more than likely. And she must know a power of people, with farms and all sorts. Of course, there were a lot of folk looking, with all sorts of men striking, and the slump in tin, but there must be something. Anything would do – skivvying, looking after the pigs, anything, as long as it put a roof over her head and kept Blossom fed. Anything that kept them out of the workhouse.

But this morning, standing at the great wrought-iron gates on their granite gateposts, and looking at the avenue winding up between the trees, it didn't seem so simple at all. Katie might have started on the Terrace, but she was a world away now. And hadn't she as good as let Carrie know that she didn't want to be 'associated with working folk', as Ernie would say? Carrie was more conscious than ever of her appearance.

She had done her best with it. Brought in a great bucket of salt water and soaked her bedraggled blouse and skirt-tails. Went three times to the street-pump for water to wash the worst out of her hair and skin. Her clothes had been hung, steaming, by the fire all night, and even now they were not quite dry, and hung damply about her in the thin November wind. It was a pity about her hems, but not all the sewing in the world could quite repair the ravages of mud and blood, wear and weather.

She remembered Linny May's motto 'one to wear and one to wash', but even that had become impossible as Blossom grew, and old skirts and petticoats had been pressed into service and cut down into dresses and a coat for the child. And there was only a pound or two left of her precious hoard. What would become of them, she wondered, when that was gone?

Carrie Clarance, you are beginning to sound like the 'pale maid' in that song of Linny May's, she thought to herself crossly. You aren't out 'homeless and alone' in the wind and storm yet. And if you stop shilly-shallying about at the gates, and go and see Katie like you meant to do, perhaps you won't be, either. She squared her shoulders, settled the fish-basket more comfortably on her back, and strode up the path towards the house.

Even then she hesitated. She couldn't, after all, go up the steps to that forbidding front door as she had done last time. Not with a basket full of dead turbot on her back. She would go to the back door, speak to the cook perhaps, and ask for Mrs Trevarnon after.

She made her way carefully towards the stables, and found a small flight of steps leading down to a cobbled courtyard with a trough and pump. The back door, clearly. She was straightening her skirts, preparing herself to go down and lift the heavy knocker, when a voice interrupted her thoughts.

'What do you want? Are you looking for somebody? We don't have hawkers.'

She whirled around. For a moment she almost believed it was Katie. Katie gone blonde. The same tumbling curls, the same cornflower eyes, something in the set of the head and the lift of the shoulders. But of course, it could not be – Katie was a woman in her twenties now, like herself. This was Katie as she had been fourteen years ago, that morning of the storm. Pegging baby-clothes onto the line while a black broomstick of an aunt grumbled from the doorway. Too old, though, to be Katie's child, though she was dressed like gentry. Best wool, from the smart navy skirt and jacket down to the neat stockinged feet in their gleaming soft-leather boots.

'Who are you?' Carrie said, too startled to remember manners.

'Shouldn't I be asking you that?' the girl said. She had a little defiant flick of the head, a boldness in her cool gaze. Less like Katie than she had first seemed.

'I'm sorry,' Carrie said. 'My name is Carrie. I came to see Mrs Trevarnon . . .'

The girl's face had broken into a wide, delighted smile. 'You're Carrie! Katie will be so sorry to have missed you. She's gone out with Uncle George and the children to buy a pony – David is keen to have one, and it will be his birthday soon.'

Out! So she had missed her! Again! Perhaps it was as well. What could Carrie have in common with a woman who bought her children ponies for presents? Carrie was often hard pressed to it to buy Blossom enough to eat.

'You're lucky to find me,' the girl was saying. 'I might have gone with them, only I wanted to ride.'

'You ride a horse, too?' Carrie asked dully.

The girl laughed. 'A horse? No, I have a bicycle. Katie says it's unladylike, but Uncle George says we shall all have wheels by and by. Oh,' she pulled off her glove and offered a small white hand, 'I'm Rosa, by the way. Rosa Warren. I remember you from the Terrace. You used to give me a bit of your saffron bun, sometimes, when you came home on a Thursday.'

Carrie stared. Rosa! Katie's sister – the baby whose clothes Katie had been hanging out! How long ago and far off it all seemed, and yet she was surprised to find Rosa grown into a young woman.

'Katie will be vexed that she has missed you again,' Rosa said. 'She was sorry to miss you last time.'

'She was?' Carrie's heart gave a great leap. Perhaps, after all . . . ?

'Very sorry,' the girl said. 'Especially after – what happened to your husband.'

Was that a message? Carrie dropped her eyes. 'You heard about that, then?'

'Oh, yes,' Rosa said. 'Thrilling, I thought it was. Standing up for his rights. Like Mrs Pankhurst and the Suffragettes. Shouldn't you like to be like them – prepared to go to prison for your principles? Katie says I'm soft to talk like this, but Uncle George says there is sense in it. He's quite a Liberal – he's not really my uncle of course, but I call him that. But don't you agree? Shouldn't you like to be a Suffragette above anything?'

Carrie shook her head. 'Don't talk to me about politics,' she said. 'Principles are all very fine, but they don't put pennies in your pocket. What I should like above anything else is to find a job – a proper job where I could keep myself and not have to sleep in a net-loft, and live in a house with a friend, where I'm in the way day and night, taking the bread out of their mouths and getting under their feet so there isn't room to turn around . . .' She broke off, astounded by her own outburst. 'I'm sorry, it's just . . . with my husband in prison and everything, it doesn't seem so "thrilling" to me, somehow, that's all.'

Rosa looked at her thoughtfully. 'I see. Is that what you wanted to see Katie for? See if there might be a job here?'

It was what she had hoped, secretly, but put baldly like that Carrie was ashamed to own it. 'No,' she said, 'not that so much. I wondered if she might know an opening. There's plenty won't have a woman with a child

– and when you've been down the fish market there's no way people will take you on, leastwise, not unless someone puts in a word. Let alone with a husband in prison . . . I know she isn't . . . might not be so keen on being asked favours like this, but . . . well, you see how it is.'

Rosa nodded. 'I see. Well, you want to come up to the house and wait? Have a cup of tea, at least. Cook will make us one.'

Looking at Rosa in her smart clothes and her expensive boots, Carrie was suddenly struck by the enormity of it all. 'I can't,' she said simply. 'Not with this fish.'

'No,' Rosa said. 'I suppose you can't. Tell you what, though . . .' She brightened up as she spoke, as though an idea had occurred to her. 'You wait here.' She disappeared down the steps at an unladylike run, and went into the house. Carrie could hear her voice calling, 'Cook! Cook!'

Carrie waited. The wind was chill and her damp blouse was cold and clammy on her skin. Seconds stretched into minutes. She shuffled from foot to foot, half ready to give up and go away. At last Rosa reappeared, with a large, plump, good-natured looking woman at her side.

'I'm Cook,' the woman said. 'Rosa says as how you've fish to sell.' She peered into the basket with an expert eye. 'Nice bit of turbot you've got there. Fresh, is it?'

'Caught last night,' Carrie said. 'Won't get fresher. Twopence a pound. Twice that, it would cost you in the town.'

The woman looked at her shrewdly. 'Well, I daresay Mr George would fancy a bit of turbot with his dinner.'

'With' his dinner, Carrie thought. In Dolly's house turbot was a luxury they could rarely afford to eat, unless it was the heads and tails made into soup.

'I'll take it, then,' the cook said.

Carrie smiled. Selling the fish was something. Big house too, she might make a shilling to take home. 'How much?'

'Whatever you've got,' the cook said. 'We've got an ice-house now, and what we don't eat we can keep.'

'But I got a stone of fish here,' Carrie said in amazement.

'Then it's a stone I'll buy,' the cook said, as though it were the most ordinary thing in the world to buy enough fish for a hotel. 'The master has company coming, and I daresay we'll find a use for it – good fish like this, and cheap too. And from what young Rosa says, I figure the mistress would be pleased to do you a service, besides – so we're all the gainers.' She counted out the money, two and fourpence, and went off for a platter to take the fish.

Rosa who had been watching with a broad grin, said, 'And I'll tell Katie that you called. Where can she find you – supposing she wants more fish, for example? She might give you a regular order, at least.'

Carrie gave the address in Fairmaids Lane. A regular order. That would be something, even if she couldn't take home near enough a half-crown every week. If Katie would put in a word for her at a few houses, perhaps she could even start her own fish-round she thought, wildly. Cost her a bit, of course, to buy the fish – but even a farthing a pound profit . . .

She was doing the calculations all the way home.

CHAPTER TWO

Emily sat at her writing desk and hugged herself miserably. It had been dreadful. Dreadful! To be humiliated in that fashion twice in a lifetime. By Philippe, of all people. Well, the afternoon had taught her something. He was not at all the sort of person she had supposed him to be.

He was a foreigner, after all, she consoled herself. One could hardly expect him to behave like an Englishman. But the reflection did little to comfort her. She had made a fool of herself in front of him, and that she would find very difficult to forgive.

There had been no sign of any problem when he first came in. Unannounced of course, as he always was, simply arriving at the door and sending up word by the maidservants, and expecting to be invited in. It was her own fault, really, she had encouraged him. Written and urged him to call on her, indeed. Her cheeks flushed slightly at the thought of how much encouragement there had actually been. Well, she knew better now!

He had come in, all flamboyant charm, as usual, to set her heart a-flutter, and she had made a point of asking his advice on money matters. She had done that a great deal, recently. One thing she had learned from Father was how a man liked to be flattered by someone asking his opinion about finance. She scarcely needed his advice (she had long ago decided how to invest her money), but she had hoped it would encourage him to speak out – as she had been waiting so long for him to do – on that other matter he had once, obliquely, alluded to.

She had been particularly hopeful, today. Partly because he had been absent from the house for so long. Bringing himself around to it, she had told herself, and when she had seen him today she was quite convinced of it. He was so fidgety, so uncharacteristically anxious and embarrassed, that she knew he was on the point of saying something personal.

She felt her heart beat a little faster, and her cheeks flush at the very thought. He had as good as asked for permission to come courting, and she had given it to him. Admittedly, last time he called, he had said not a word on the subject, but that was because he was anxious for Carrie – taking his cue from her own note, in fact. There was nothing of that, this time. He would have asked directly, as he did before. And she would have been able to tell him the news. A fish-girl, hawking dead cod around the street. But he did not ask. So it could be nothing to do with that.

It was a pity, really. Philippe had always been – well, soft-hearted towards the girl. But if he knew that she was a fish-wife, he would see her for what she was, and at the same time stop worrying about her and be encouraged to say . . . what she was waiting for him to say.

She felt a little breathless at the audacity of her thoughts. But still he said nothing, just talked about neutral subjects with that fidgety air. In the end she asked him, asked him outright, though she squirmed now on her chair to think of it.

'Is there something you wished to say, Philippe?' Oh, her treacherous heart! Thumping like a traction engine as she spoke the words. For she had hoped – more than hoped, half believed, that she already knew what it was.

And he replied, uncomfortably, twisting his fingers together and avoiding her gaze, 'Emily, there *is* something particular I wished to ask you.'

There was meaning in it, she could tell from the heightened colour in his cheek, the softening of his tone. She coloured. She could feel the blood in her face. She had waited so long for this. 'Something particular, Monsieur?' Did it sound coquettish, as she hoped? And did he see in her blushes the attractive flush of maidenly confusion, or merely the blotchy redness of middle age?

He looked at her. 'Very particular. It is something I do not ask lightly, but if you would agree, it would mean a great deal to me. And you would not regret it, I assure you.'

She smiled, her best arch and alluring smile. It made her blush again to recall it, that silly schoolgirlish simper, and the foolish fatuous words. 'I cannot think what you mean, Monsieur.'

He had leaned towards her, all intensity. 'It is something, I think, that you were asked to do once before – and half promised, before . . . before circumstance altered.'

She knew what he meant, or supposed that she did. He had known for a long time the whole story of her 'engagement' and the fiancé who went to America. She had taken care that he did hear it, and from her own lips. She said carefully, 'I think I know what you are speaking of. Sometimes a thing is better done later, and not in the first flush of emotions.'

There! She had done it. As good as told him that his attentions were not unwelcome and that, if he only asked her, she would willingly consent to be his wife.

He leaned back in his chair, smiling. 'You will do it then? You will find a post here for Carrie in spite of her husband? I should take it uncommonly kindly, Emily, if you did.' He rambled on, talking about Carrie's hardships.

She stared. It took a moment or two for the realisation to sink in, and then like a fool she had let him know it. 'That was it? That was what you wanted to ask me?'

And his face, puzzled, surprised, saying gently, 'But of course. What did you suppose?' Then, most humiliating of all, the dawning of understanding in his eyes. 'Did you think . . .' He paused. 'Did you think I wanted something for myself? You did not – did you? – suppose that it was myself I spoke of when I told you of my friend . . . of Mr Tavy's . . . attentions?'

Tavy! She had scarcely thought of him as a man at all. Tavy! She could have sunk through her chair with confusion. So she said, with a brittle laugh, 'La, sir, why should I suppose any such thing?' Had she really said 'La', like something out of a novel? But he knew what she had truly been thinking, she could read in it his face. He looked dismayed, aghast almost, before he forced a smile to his lips. She felt a prickle of embarrassment roll over her from the soles of her feet to the roots of her swept-up hair.

He was still smiling. 'I knew I could rely on your kindness, Emily. I remember that incident with the cream jug – you could not bear, even then, to see injustice done. And it is not Carrie's fault, after all, that this misfortune has come upon her . . .'

Suddenly she could bear it no longer, and she burst out in a rage of disappointment and humiliation, 'Well, I shall do nothing for her! Nothing, do you hear? If she is unfortunate, she has brought it on herself. Two of a kind, I daresay – him with his speeches, and her with her quick tongue. She knew what he was like long ago: I might have told her myself, the day I found them creating a disturbance in the lane.' And you were as bad, she thought bitterly, looking at Philippe's handsome face as it flushed a sullen red. Kissing a servant girl in the street, and giving her presents to boot. I could have seen you then for what you were. But I allowed myself to be deflected. What a fool I was. Even then you had eyes only for her. And she knew it – always flaunting the fact that she had known you from a girl. As though there were some sort of special secret between you.

'I will do nothing for her,' she said again. 'Nothing. Do you understand?' She spoke with such force that she was almost trembling.

Philippe got to his feet. 'Emily, you are overwrought. I am sorry to have disturbed you.' He was walking to the door, and she was willing him through it. Back to his boat, back to France, anywhere, so that she did not have to set eyes on him again, knowing what he knew.

He stopped, one hand on the door-jamb. 'You are a good woman, Emily. I am sorry to have caused you pain. But if there is something, anything, that you could do, I know that I can rely on you.'

And then he was gone, and she was alone, sitting at the writing-desk and rocking to and fro in mental agony. How could she have been such a fool? Revealing her weaknesses in that way. What could she possibly do now?

She sat there, huddled into herself for more than an hour, until the blood had drained from her fevered cheeks and her tormented brain had settled into rational thought. And then it came to her. A small, insistent thought. A way perhaps, to salvage a little pride.

She would not have Carrie, of course. After this afternoon it would be impossible to allow the girl into the house for a single second. But perhaps, after all there was a way . . . ?

She opened her desk and looked at the newspaper cuttings she had so carefully filed away. Yes, there it was. 'The defence was conducted by Mr Tavy and paid for by Mr Morrison, a noted Liberal from Penzance.'

She took out pen and paper, sketching the letter in her mind. 'Read of the case . . . used to be a maidservant here . . . small contribution of ten shillings to be spent upon the child . . . small *anonymous* contribution to be spent on the child, from someone who cannot bear to see injustice done.' That was better. It gave her a kind of moral upper hand. And if Philippe ever came to hear of it, he would know who the donor was. She was after all 'a good woman' – he had said so himself, even if she was never to be a good wife.

Drat Philippe. He must have known she would never sleep if she supposed that Carrie and her child were starving on the streets. And besides, it was always possible that news of her little gesture would reach . . . Mr Tavy.

Rather a personable man, when she came to think of it. Such a support, during these last difficult times. And a widower, too.

She dipped the pen into the ink and began to write. 'Dear Mr Morrison . . .'

The envelope arrived at Fairmaids Lane on Friday, 28 November. The post-boy brought it, panting down the lane on his bicycle with the rain streaming from his cape and handlebars, and the mud splashing up to his eyeballs from the puddles on the rutted road.

Dolly left the net she was mending and went to fetch the letter in, aware of the women in the street watching from doorways. Wasn't a lot of mail in Fairmaids Lane, unless it was from the landlord, or the Government, or from relatives away up country, or in America. But then, everyone knew more or less what day that letter would come. People would go round to hear it, likely as not, over a pot of tea and the steaming cutch for the nets.

An unexpected letter often meant trouble – a death more than likely, or the return of some distant cousin from the Empire asking to visit and stretch the budget of the household to breaking point. Something unlooked for. Dolly took the envelope with shaking hands.

But this was not for her. It was addressed to Carrie. She thought for a moment of going down to the harbour – a letter was too important a matter to be allowed to wait – but Carrie was out with the fish-baskets, selling up at Newbridge. Dolly stood for a little while, torn between curiosity and good manners, but at last she put the letter behind the clock. She hid it out of sight, but it still seemed to loom out at her all the afternoon.

When Carrie and Drew came home she was so bursting to know what was in it that she snatched up the envelope and held it out before Carrie even had time to take her bonnet off.

Carrie turned pale, and took the letter timidly, as though it might bite her. 'Trouble for Ernie!' she said. She sat down at the table staring at the envelope in her hands.

'Well go on,' Drew said at last. 'The worst thing is not knowing. Anyhow,' he said, peering at it more closely, 'it can't be Ernie – there's a Penzance postmark.'

So there was. Dolly should have noticed that herself. Carrie looked a little relieved, and slit the envelope with a knife. 'Scented paper,' she said in surprise.

Good thick paper, with a strong, slanted, educated hand. Only a few lines. And the address printed. Dolly could see no more than that. 'Well,' she prompted, hugging herself with impatience, 'what does it say?'

'My dear Carrie . . .'

'Only hear that!' Drew said. 'It's that gentrified friend of yours up to Trevarnon, see if it isn't.'

'Can't be,' Dolly said. 'Why would she post a letter instead of sending the coachman down with it? Stands to reason.'

''Tis though,' Carrie said. 'Thought I knew the writing! Requests the pleasure of your company,' Carrie read aloud. 'May I suggest supper on Sunday. And signed "Katie Trevarnon".'

Dolly stared at her. 'Well, there's a thing.'

Carrie put down the note on the table. 'Nice of her,' she said, but her voice was brittle, dry and hard as old lobster-shells.

'Will you go?' Dolly said.

Carrie gazed at her, 'How can I! Drinking tea in a drawing room, with servants, and her in her silks and satins and me in a fishwife's skirt! No. Can't go, of course.' Her voice shook.

Dolly nodded and turned away. She understood. That letter had shown Carrie what a big gap there was between her and her former friend.

'I was really hoping for a bit of help from Katie,' Carrie said, miserably, folding up the letter with mechanical fingers. 'I went round today and looked at a room in Penzance, but they wanted one and six a week, and coals extra – and that's without the food and paying someone to look after Blossom. I might have managed, if I'd have found a position, but now . . . Still, can't be helped. I'll think of something, Dolly, see if I don't . . .'

Dolly stared at the letter. 'Here!' she said. 'What's this on the back?'

For a moment Carrie stared at her in bewilderment, and then, slowly she turned over the paper and looked at the scrawl on the back. It was in huge untidy capital letters, all written backwards. 'You . . . should . . . tay, no, try . . . it,' Dolly read aloud, blankly.

And then, all at once, Carrie laughed.

'What is it?'

Carrie turned to her, eyes suddenly alight. 'It's a message – from Katie. I wrote the same thing to her once – backwards, just like this. She's telling me it's all right – nothing's changed. She's still the old Katie.' She was looking down at the foolish scrawl and Dolly could see the tears running down her nose. Tears of relief, she realised.

There was relief in Carrie's voice too. Relief and a sudden wild hope. 'I can go,' she said. 'It'll be all right. But whatever am I to wear?'

Suddenly, Dolly too caught the mood. 'We'll think of something,' she said. Perhaps, after all, everything *would* be all right.

They raided half the lane to put it together. A new blouse that the woman opposite had had for a wedding, and hardly worn since. A skirt that Ellie had sent down from the fever-house belonging to the girl that died. Dolly had worn it once or twice and it was wide on Carrie, but they fixed it in with a few pins and it looked a treat – a bit bunched at the waist and a bit short at the hem, but handsome compared to her own bedraggled garment. Dolly herself had a good bonnet and apron for Sundays which she could lend. Carrie had none. She blushed to recall that once she had owned clothes decent enough to go to chapel, but she had never been back, except for buryings, since that day she had watched the dancing dust while her father lay dead.

'There!' Dolly said on Sunday evening as the dressing was completed. 'Prettier than a picture. Think you were a shop-girl, they would, in that. And hardly a whiff of fish.'

'I rinsed my hair three times,' Carrie said. 'With carbolic, too.' She had needed to. There had been a catch of 'poor cod' the day before, and that was a fish had to be cleaned and cooked in twelve hours or it tasted of nothing, so she had worked for hours without a pause, and the scales had got everywhere. But today there was no filleting.

'Wonder did Katie know there was no fishing Sundays?' she wondered aloud.

'Shouldn't wonder,' Dolly said. 'There's been enough about it in the papers, one way and another. All that argy-bargy with St Ives and the up-country fishermen who do land a catch Sunday. And well enough if she did – give you a bit of time to clean up proper. Only a pity it's raining so – get drenched you will, walking up there in all this weather. Put a bit of sacking over you, keep the worst off.'

And she did, although she tried to hold it away from her, because the sack smelt of seaweed. She took it off at the gates of Trevarnon and hid it in the hedge, just as she had once hidden her bonnet. But without her sacking, she was open to the elements, and there was a long drive at Trevarnon. By the time she reached the door she was drenched through. But it was the front door this time, she decided. She was a guest, even if she was a dank and dripping one.

Katie herself answered it. It didn't occur to Carrie until much later that Katie must have planned that on purpose, not to embarrass her with a maid or a manservant.

'My dear Carrie! What are you doing, and in all this rain too? I sent the carriage for you ten minutes ago!'

And rain, seaweed, fish and oil notwithstanding, Katie put her arms around her and gave her a warm hug. It was too much. Carrie stood in the polished hallway, among the statues and paintings and polished wood, dripping puddles onto the deep-pile rug, weeping like a child.

'You're perished,' Katie said. 'My dear Carrie, however have you let things get to this state? Why didn't you come to me before?'

Carrie gulped. 'I did. I tried. But I didn't like to make a thing about it – not when you didn't answer my letters.'

Katie looked startled. 'What letters?'

'When I was first at Buglers and I wrote and asked you to go and see about the painting,' Carrie sobbed. 'I know I shouldn't have, but . . .'

Katie interrupted her. 'The painting?' She put out her hands and took Carrie's worn fingers in her own. 'My dear Carrie, I never got any letters. They must have got lost somehow, in the post.'

Carrie looked at her doubtfully. 'That true?'

'Of course it is. My dear girl, have you been worrying about that all this time? Of course if you'd asked me to go and see about something I would have done it. I wondered why you suddenly stopped writing. Thought it was because I'd married an architect, and you didn't like to write any more, or your husband didn't want you to, or something.'

Carrie thought about Ernie and his insistence that he didn't want charity. 'Could be that, too,' she said slowly. 'I gave them him to post. Oh, Katie!' And she burst into a new flood of sobbing, though whether it was relief, or guilt, or simple weariness she could not herself have said.

Katie patted her shoulder. 'Well, you're here now. That's what matters. And what you need before anything is a cup of cocoa and a good hot bath.'

Carrie sniffed, and wiped her eyes, ashamed of herself. 'There's never time for that,' she said, though she felt warmed through by the very suggestion. 'Take for ever to heat the water.'

Katie smiled. It was astonishing. Suddenly the years had fallen away and they were girls together sharing secrets in the terrace. 'You don't know George. If there's a new invention, he has to have it. Wait till you see this. Come this way.'

'I'll take my boots off,' Carrie said, suddenly confident. 'I'm wet leaking.'

And she did so before following Katie into the house. It was like fairyland. She had seen comfort of course, at the Tuckers'. Solid, respectable comfort, and a dressing-room with a hip bath and big china bowls and dressing stands, and towels hanging to warm by the fire. But this was different. A proper bath, in its own room, with carved iron legs, and little red roses in the glaze. There was a big gas-thing over it which lit with a little burst when Katie put a flame to it, and would heat enough water for a bath in minutes, Katie said. A huge towel, fluffier than a tom-cat, already warming on the gas-pipe. Soap that smelt of roses, and a mat on the floor that said 'Bath' in big letters in cross-stitch worked into the weave. Just for standing on, Katie said. Imagine having a mat just for getting out of the bath on.

And a big glass bottle with a stopper – 'Rosemary shampoo,' Katie said. 'I have it made up at the chemist's. I thought you might like to wash your hair – since you are so soaked through.'

Since you smell of fish, was what she meant, but she was too good a friend, and too polite to say so. 'You're very good,' Carrie managed, though she was too choked to say more.

'You and your mother were good to me when I needed it,' Katie said. 'It's a debt paid, that's all it is. Now, I'll get Mabel to bring up a cup of cocoa, and run your bath, and then we'll leave you in peace for a bit. I'll find you something to put on when you're dry – your things are soaked. I'll be in that room opposite. It's my sitting room and we shan't be disturbed.'

'What about my cocoa?' It was months since Carrie had tasted cocoa.

'Drink it in the bath. That'll warm you through.'

Cocoa in the bath. Better than a princess, Carrie thought. Bet Queen Alexandra herself didn't often get to drink cocoa in the bath. And such a bath! Perfumed water, and a soft cloth for washing with, embroidered on the corner too. Hot water, gallons of it, that came out of a tap when you turned it. She lay and soaked and wallowed and gloried in it, washing cod and herring out of her pores, until her fingers crinkled and she had almost turned into a fish herself.

And then out, to find the clothes that Katie had sent for her. And to think she had doubted her friend's willingness to help! A good grey skirt and jacket – a little worn, but good cloth and decent. She slipped it on, revelling in the warmth of it. She glanced at herself in the long mirror on its frame. It was a bit short for her, but apart from that she looked like something on a fashion plate: you would hardly recognise the figure that had come in, for all that her hair was only towelled dry, and brushed into rough order with the silver-backed brush set on the wash-stand. Easy to look like a lady if you lived like this, she thought.

She went across the hallway to the room where Katie was waiting. A room lined with books and pictures and full of flowers. Where did they come from, in November? Katie was sitting by the fire, a book in her hand.

'Have you done, Carrie? That looks a bit warmer.'

'I . . . I don't know where my clothes are to,' Carrie said.

Katie looked uncomfortable. 'They were rather wet,' she said. 'But that uniform is yours to keep if you can use it. No, don't start fussing, Carrie! It's an old debt, I told you. And besides, it used to be my uniform once, when I was in service, and I shan't need it now!' She reached up and rang a bell-pull by the fireplace. 'Mabel shall bring us that supper I promised you, and you can tell me all about this help you need.'

It was hard to think about your problems when there were real beef patties and pickles and sandwiches and cake and tea – and you could drink as much as you liked without worrying would be there be enough for tomorrow. Never mind how much milk you used, there was a whole jugful for the two of them, and sugar and cream besides. And there was

Katie's news to hear. All about her first marriage, to the architect in Truro, and her children, and then how she had come back at last, as a widow, to marry Mr George. She was so natural and friendly that the years between seemed forgotten, and when Carrie had eaten as much as she dared she did tell Katie all about it – Fairmaids Lane, and the fish, and how she needed a position.

'Wouldn't need to be much,' she finished. 'Just enough to pay for that room in St James Street, and someone to look after Blossom. With the money from the furniture, I've got two pound and a few shillings – that'd see us for food for a long time.' She didn't say what she was thinking, that there were many long weeks before Ernie would be out, and even then, few people would take a jail-bird. But for now, it was enough to worry about the winter months to come.

'Well,' Katie said, 'we can do something for you at least. I could find you a place here . . .'

'I couldn't ask you that,' Carrie said. She meant, she would be embarrassed, working as a servant here, especially after today. But Katie seemed to read her thoughts.

'Better than that though – come February, I know someone who wants a housekeeper. Live in – and wouldn't mind a child, if you could keep an eye on her own little boy. They want a couple really, so there'd be a place for your Ernie when he came out, if he wanted.'

That was real kindness. Ever since Ernie had been put into prison, Carrie had been lying awake nights, wondering who would ever have him when he came out. She said doubtfully, 'But would they . . . ?'

Katie smiled. 'Oh, I think they would if I recommended you. They're farming folk, manage our farm over at St Ives.' Work on our land, she meant, and wouldn't turn down someone that came recommended from Trevarnon. Well, Carrie thought, if they did give her a chance, she would see that they never regretted it.

Katie went on, 'Wouldn't be a fortune, Carrie, but it would be five shillings a week and all found.'

Five shillings! And no rent or food to buy. It *was* a fortune. 'Katie!' After her first outbreak of relief, she had worried about what to call her friend – 'Mrs Trevarnon' seemed too formal, and 'Katie' too forward – but now the word burst from her lips. 'Katie, that would be . . .' But she couldn't find a word to express the marvel of it.

'If I put a word in, I'm sure she'll take you. Not till February, that's the problem. What are we to do with you till then? You could come here . . .'

'It's all right,' Carrie said. Two pounds and a few shillings, she still had that. Her 'insurance'. She could take that room in St James Street, earn herself a bit from the fish market, maybe – Dolly would go on having Blossom in the day. It was possible, if there was a position at the end of it. Besides, the woman would be happier to let the room to her now – she was a bit cleaner. If only she could keep that way till tomorrow.

She thought about that problem until it was time to leave. A solution occurred to her. 'Katie, I'd best be off before it gets any colder. My old things be dry, will they?' she said. Perhaps she could change before she went home, and keep her new things decent.

Katie looked troubled. 'I thought,' she said slowly, 'perhaps with a new outfit you might like us to . . . burn them?'

'Burn! They're borrowed, half of them!'

Katie rang the bell quickly, and sent the maid for 'Mrs Clarance's things'. The girl looked startled. She really was going to burn them, Carrie realised. She had asked for them just in time! It was the first time Katie had really shown the difference between Carrie's world and her own.

But the clothes were rescued, and brought. They weren't dry, and Mabel handled them with care. Good thing they didn't see the sack, Carrie thought. She went into the bathroom and changed, and was struck again by the strength of the fish odour which clung to the folds. When she came back she tried to keep her fishiness at a distance, holding out an embarrassed hand as she tried to express her thanks.

'You'll come to see us again,' Katie said. 'When George and the children are here.' She had asked her tonight on purpose, Carrie realised, to spare any embarrassment.

'Oh, Katie, you're some good,' she said for the tenth time, trying to grasp the magnitude of it all.

'One more thing,' Katie said, with an odd, wicked smile. 'There is something here I think you ought to have. It's yours, I'm sure. I always thought so, and after what you said tonight I'm sure of it.' She rang the bell. 'Mabel, bring Mrs Clarance the picture. The one leaning against the wall in the box-room.'

CHAPTER THREE

Carrie couldn't believe her eyes. *Girl with a Hairbrush*. There it was, in all its embarrassing glory. She clapped her hand across her mouth and felt the burning blush rush up her face and down to her toes themselves.

'My lor, Katie!' she said, sitting down again heavily, as though shame had taken the stiffening out of her very knees. 'Wherever did you get that? I thought you said you never got my letter?'

Katie, to her horror, was laughing gently, a mischievous glee in her eyes. 'I didn't, either. But when you started talking about a painting, I guessed that this was the one. George bought it, years ago – long before he married me. He is a bit of a collector, you know, and he thought very highly of Rawlings' work. It *is* you, isn't it? It's no good denying it, you wouldn't turn redder than the carpet-runner if it wasn't. I knew it was as soon as I laid eyes on it – I remember you telling me that you had modelled for a picture to pay a doctor for your poor father. And I've seen you with your hair brushed down like that scores of times when we lived in the Terrace – remember the morning I was hanging out washing? Though you had more clothes on then!'

Carrie raised her eyes slowly, and dropped them again. 'Oh, my lor!' she said again. 'And your husband buying it, and looking at me like that. Oh my dear life!'

'Carrie!' Katie's voice was gentle with concern. 'There's nothing in the world to be ashamed of in that. He bought a beautiful picture, that's all – he hasn't seen you more than half a dozen times in his life. Never crossed his mind it might be you. But I knew.'

'And you let him hang it up, and look at it?' Carrie said, in anguish. It was ridiculous, of course. What else did people buy a picture for?

But Katie was shaking her head. 'No,' she said, 'I never did. I told him I

337

thought it was you, and said why you did it, and we've never hung the picture since. But when I knew you were coming I looked it out. I thought you deserved to have it, Carrie, if anybody did.'

Carrie looked at her friend, the colour draining from her cheeks. 'But I couldn't. It's worth no end.'

'It isn't worth much stood in the attic,' Katie said. 'No, George agrees with me. You ought to have the picture.'

Carrie shook her head. 'You should have sold it.'

'Who to?' Katie said. 'If we'd put it on the market round here Mr Tucker would have had it for sure, and you wouldn't have wanted that, I know. He was always looking out for anything by Rawlings – George met him once or twice at auctions, and he was always asking. I think he was actually after that particular picture. Somebody was – we had an auctioneer asking us if we had that very picture, only a month or two ago. That was for somebody local, so it was probably Edward Tucker.'

'Couldn't have been,' Carrie said. 'The Tuckers are dead.'

'Oh, of course.' Katie was horrified at her own thoughtlessness. 'I read about it in the paper. What a perfectly dreadful business. But there's this about it. If it wasn't Mr Tucker wanting the picture, it means that somebody else was. And they wouldn't know you – so you could sell it and never worry. I'll get Mabel to wrap it up for you – and those clothes, if you like.'

But Carrie shook her head again. 'I can't take it, Katie. You've done enough. Looking out for a job for me, or giving me clothes, that's one thing. But this is worth pounds. Fourteen guineas, or more.'

Katie stopped, with her hand on the bell-pull, and looked at her shrewdly. 'Fourteen guineas? That's very precise. You know a little bit about art, do you?'

Carrie found herself flushing scarlet again. She had never told a soul about Philippe's gift, and how she had sold it in Truro. 'I heard it fetched that, near enough, from the gallery,' she said. 'I went down to try and buy it, but I couldn't afford it, of course.'

She hoped that would close the matter, but Katie's gaze was thoughtful. 'Buy it, you say?'

Carrie nodded ruefully. 'Didn't realise, you see. He paid me a guinea, I thought it would cost . . . well, not much more.'

Katie got up. 'Well, so it does. One guinea. You won't let me give you the picture, so I'm offering to sell it to you. One guinea. My final offer.'

Carrie looked at her in amazement, but Katie seemed to be serious.

'Don't be daft, Katie, it's worth ever so much more than that.'

Her friend looked at her steadily. 'Not to me, Carrie. The picture doesn't hang in this house. And I'll not sell it, except to you. Now, you posed for that picture to earn a guinea to save your father. Spend that guinea now, to help your daughter.'

Put like that, it was hard to resist. Carrie felt the lump in her throat. Katie was as good as giving her thirteen guineas, perhaps more – the picture would be easy to sell. She couldn't speak, she only nodded dumbly and stretched out a hand.

Katie squeezed it. 'Well then,' she said briskly, 'now that's settled, I'll send for the coachman. It's raining fit for Noah out there, and I'm not having you soaked to the skin twice in an evening. Besides, you'd best keep that picture dry.' She raised a hand to the bell-pull again.

'I can't take it now,' Carrie said. 'It'll get all over fish. Can I collect it tomorrow? And the dress too, perhaps. I'll get that room in the morning, supposing it hasn't been taken.' She could, she realised. She really could. She would go up to Bodmin and see Ernie, and sell the painting at the same time. There was no-one up there to know her, and she should get a good price, especially if she went in her new clothes, all smart and tidy. 'I'll bring the guinea up, same time. Won't disturb you, in case you're entertaining. I'll come to the kitchen.'

Katie looked as if she might argue, but in the end she simply smiled. 'I'll send it down,' she said. 'Rosa is going to town tomorrow, at noon. The coachman can bring it on. St James Street, you said?'

'Fifty-nine,' Carrie agreed. 'But the room might be taken. Still,' she added, 'if I don't find that room I'll find another.' With thirteen guineas she could afford to. A bigger one perhaps, with a stove to cook on, and a tap in the yard, and maybe carpet on the floor. 'I'll be there, twelve o'clock on the dot. And thank you a million times, Katie. It's better than I deserved.'

'You and your family were good friends to me,' Katie said again, and then she did ring the bell.

It wasn't even a carriage that the coachman brought to the door; it was a motor-car, with leather seats and carbide lights, and a little step you climbed on when you opened the door. Carrie had never even seen inside a motor-car before, let alone been in one, but she climbed in, borrowed fishy clothes and all, and rode home to Fairmaids Lane feeling as glamorous as Isadora Duncan!

Emily Limmon too, had a visitor that evening.

She had not at all been expecting anyone. Since that dreadful business with Philippe she had avoided company. But Ellie was back, and she had planned an evening based on having the servants heat enough water for a bath in front of the fire in her dressing room, and retiring straight to bed from that draughty exertion with a tray of hot milk and crumpets.

But no sooner had she arranged to have all the kettles and pans filled and set to warm on the stove, with the maids scampering upstairs with stone hot-water-bottles and extra scuttles of coal, than there was a knock on the door. Mr Tavy presenting his compliments, Ellie reported.

'Mr Tavy!' The words were out before Emily could prevent them. After what Philippe had said, how could she possibly entertain Mr Tavy ever again, and at this hour of the evening too?

'Yes ma'am, Mr Tavy,' Ellie went on. 'He says, please excuse him for the unexpectedness of his visit and the lateness of the hour, but he's got a Mr Morrison with him, and he wishes to speak to Miss Limmon on a matter of great importance and urgency.' The girl recited the words as though they were a litany.

Morrison? For a moment the name meant nothing to her, but then she remembered. The gentleman she had written to. She folded her lips disapprovingly. This was certainly a most inconvenient and unconventional time of night to come calling, and bringing a total stranger. The chemist's wife next door would be sure to have seen the conveyance, and who knew what she might suspect? And after what Philippe had said too. The thought afforded her a little unexpected flutter of the pulse.

After all, she thought, it was I who wrote the letter, and it would seem ill-natured to turn him away now, in this weather. The gentleman was not altogether unknown to her, and Mr Tavy had been to the house many times. Besides, since his carriage was standing at the door in any case, any damage to her reputation was already done.

There was something else, too. Whatever her disappointment over Philippe, there was a little consolation to be derived from the recollection that there really had been a 'friend' who was interested in her company. And he was waiting, downstairs in the hall.

It would not do to capitulate too easily. 'It should be important and urgent, to bring him here in this fashion,' she said sharply. 'Well, I suppose you had better light the lamps and show them into the parlour, Ellie. There is no fire, but they can hardly carp at that, arriving unannounced and in the evening too. Tell them I will join them shortly.'

She would have liked, really, to take a little time over her appearance, but despite her bravado there was still the chemist's wife to consider, and every moment that the carriage stood at the door would be bruited among her acquaintances, so it was only a matter of two minutes or so before she went down, duly brushed and buttoned, to greet the two gentlemen in the chilly lamplight of the parlour.

'Mr Morrison? Mr Tavy?' Her voice was deliberately frosty, and she didn't offer her hand, but Morrison seized it at once. He was a butterball of a man, dressed in gaiters and a faded black museum piece of a cut-away jacket, with shrewd little eyes that twinkled behind wire spectacles. Absurd. He looked like an illustration for Mr Pickwick. By his side Tavy seemed taller and more angular than ever.

'My dear Miss Limmon, I am sorry to intrude upon your hospitality so.' The room was cold, but his manner was warm. Warm enough to bring a little glow to his cheeks. His eyes, too, were shrewd, and looking her too with an intensity she had never previously noticed. But rather *nice* eyes, Emily thought.

'You wanted to see me?' Her voice was a little softer, though she had not intended it to be so.

It was Morrison who answered. 'It is about that money you sent for poor Clarance . . .'

'Clarence? Clarence who?'

'Ernest Clarance, the unfortunate clay-worker. You were kind . . . no, munificent enough to send ten shillings for his family.'

'Oh yes.' She was about to add that for her part, the less she heard of him the better, but she realised that Tavy was looking at her with genuine admiration. Munificent. It had an agreeable ring. 'His wife worked for me at one time.'

'I am convinced, you know, that he didn't do it,' Morrison said.

Emily contrived to disguise her disdain. 'Didn't do it? But the poor constable was taken to the cottage hospital. Quite dazed, for days.'

'Didn't throw the stone – the ink-bottle in question.' That was Tavy.

'There were two, you understand, and he only threw the one. He had a companion, so he claims. I know the other boy. Much more the type to take a cockshy,' Morrison explained.

'I see,' Emily said, knowing that she didn't.

'I knew I could rely on your understanding,' Tavy said. 'That's why we wanted to ask you for your help.'

He's going to ask for money, she thought, but Tavy went on, 'Mr Morrison has a piece to write. There has been a lot of interest in the case – especially in an article of mine a week or two back. Well, the *Graphic Messenger* discovered another photograph of the couple in its archives – apparently it was taken at the clay-pit some time ago. They want a piece, urgently, so that they can use the picture and make a real illustrated article – and as you know, perhaps, Mr Morrison has quite a reputation as a socialist journalist. He asked me if I would introduce you.'

She was beginning to wish she had asked Ellie to make up the fire. 'What do you want of me?'

Morrison said, urgently, 'I want a different approach. Something to stir the heartstrings. I know the lad, of course, met him several times, and I've some stirring information about the boy's father. But it's the wife and family. That's what I'm after, something about them, and their sufferings. And then you sent this little contribution, and Tavy mentioned to me that Carrie Clarance had worked for you at one time. I thought perhaps you might help me.'

Tavy broke in. 'It is an inconvenient time of the evening, I know, but there is a particular urgency. The column must be wired to the paper by tomorrow morning or it will miss the presses. So I took the liberty of bringing him, and imposing on your hospitality. Mr Morrison was particularly touched by your gesture. And, if you will allow me to say so, Miss Limmon . . . Emily . . . so also was I.'

She felt the pink in her cheeks. She had been seeking M. Philippe's good opinion, but if these two gentlemen were also prepared to think well of her, it was an unexpected bonus. Especially, now she came to think of it, Mr Tavy. Such a cultivated man.

And he had called her 'Emily'. She said, greatly daring, 'Of course, James. Anything I can do for a friend of yours. Ellie shall make up the fire.' Let the chemist's wife say what she will! She reached out a hand and rang the bell.

'On second thoughts,' she said, when the maid arrived hot and breathless, 'you can bring the supper tray in here. Enough for three. A pot of tea, perhaps, instead of the warm milk, and you can bring down some hot coals and start the fire. Mr Morrison and I have one or two things to talk about.' And then, remembering her new role as the champion of the working man, she said, 'And when we have finished here, Ellie, you may go to bed. Clearing the tray can wait till morning.'

Tavy gave her an encouraging smile. It was flattering, having him seek her out like this – a professional man like him, too. And he did have such nice eyes. English eyes, not a bit like those of treacherous foreigners. Eyes you could trust.

'Now,' she said, and as the heat of the fire took the chill from the room she felt herself melting with it, and her voice lost its Antarctic edge, 'let me see . . .'

Carrie was half-inclined to pinch herself when she woke, to make sure it was not all a dream. But, no, it seemed not. Dolly was as excited as she was, and kept saying, 'Only think of that!' over and over.

Carrie didn't go with Drew to meet the boats, or down to the fishmarket filleting. Instead, as soon as it was a decent hour, she went straight back to St James Street and arranged for a room – not the bare attic she had first looked at, but a proper big downstairs room, with sash windows looking over the street and a fire big enough to cook on. There was a scullery and a wash-house in the backyard, with a pump over the sink, 'for the use of residents', and a privy and washing lines and a zinc safe besides. Carrie had to blink hard when she heard the price – two and three a week, coals and candles included – but a lot of landladies wouldn't have people with babies, and with Katie's kindness she could afford it.

She gave the woman a shilling on account, and went back to Fairmaids Lane to pack her few belongings.

On the way she met Philippe.

He was leaning on the harbour wall, but he straightened up as she approached; almost, she thought, as if he had been waiting for her.

'Carrie!' He fell into step beside her. 'Dolly said you were gone into town. I was afraid I had missed you.'

So he *had* been looking for her. 'You almost did,' she said, and she found herself talking to him again, as she always did, telling him everything – all about Katie, the new rooms, the February job. 'And you'll never guess,' she said, looking at him sideways under the brim of her bonnet. 'What do you think she and Mister George had in the attic? That picture! The one you gave me.'

He looked at her sharply. 'They have it?'

She smiled. 'They've sold it,' she said, 'or as good as.' She clasped her hands and hugged them against her apron, half willing him to ask who the buyer was, and half bursting to tell him before he asked.

But he seemed preoccupied. 'Sold it! It cannot have been at auction then. There was a man instructed particularly to look out for it.' He gave a little bitter laugh. 'Well, I suppose it cannot be helped. I hope at least they got a good price. Not less than thirty guineas.'

She stared at him in surprise. 'You? We thought it was Mr Tucker wanted it.'

He looked at her then, and his face softened to a smile. 'I thought so too – was even ready to go to London when his pictures were auctioned. But it wasn't in the sale catalogue, so there was no point.'

There was a pause. The morning seemed suddenly still, and his words hung in the air as if the world was waiting for something.

She said, slowly, 'You wanted the picture so much?'

He stopped walking and turned her to face him. 'The picture? No. That wasn't what I wanted. I wanted the original. But I can't have that, can I? So the picture will have to do. Don't let them sell it, Carrie. Not to anyone else. Make them sell it to me. Or tell me who has bought it and I will go to them, and better the price they paid.'

She dropped her eyes, as if looking into his was too painful. 'It wouldn't be hard to better it,' she said. 'The price agreed was one guinea. Katie is selling it to me.'

He caught her hands, right there in the public street, and she had to snatch them away although the flush in her cheeks must have told him that she did not want to do so.

'Oh, Monsieur Philippe,' she said, in misery. 'I ought to say you could have the picture – you paid for it once, after all. But I've gone and said I'll have these rooms in St James Street – I've given the woman a shilling and all – and I can't do it without I sell the picture and make a bit of money.'

'Sell it to me, then,' he said, catching her hands again. This time she did not withdraw them. 'Thirty guineas, I told you.'

She turned her head from him. 'I can't do that,' she said. 'You've paid for it once already. Anyway, I shouldn't have liked to ask that much. Fifteen, more like.'

He pressed her fingers. 'Then you undersell yourself. Beauty like that is priceless. No, Carrie, listen to me. I want the picture, you want to sell it. You argue that I paid for the picture once. Fourteen guineas – you know that, but it is worth thirty, at least. Very well, I will pay you sixteen guineas for your picture. Then I have paid only the market price, you have the money you require, and I have the picture I purchased in the first place.'

She dragged her eyes up to meet his. 'You twist logic,' she said.

His eyes danced with mischief. 'Ah, but I drive a hard bargain. From any other seller I should have paid double. And if you sell it elsewhere I shall trace it, I promise you, Carrie – and I should have to pay again. Truly, you will save me time and trouble, as well as fourteen guineas – and make a guinea more than you hoped for into the bargain.'

She tried to disengage her fingers but he would not let her. 'Is it a bargain, Carrie?'

She smiled. 'Yes.'

'Then I will meet you in St James Street as soon as ever the picture is delivered. Twelve o'clock, you said? What number are these rooms?'

She gave him the address and he took his leave, and walked down the street whistling. It was not until he had gone that she realised the enormity of it. She had agreed to sell a portrait of herself, half naked, and to a man she knew. A man she had kissed. A man who revelled in it. Yet she was not ashamed – that was the worst of it. It was *pleasing* to know that the picture would be in his hands, that it would be his eyes which looked at her – at her, Carrie herself, and not an unknown *Girl with a Hairbrush*. What was it he had said? 'What I want is the original'. And the surprising thing was that it was no surprise at all. He wanted her. She had always known it, just as she had always known that she had wanted him. It was as if his words had given her permission to recognise the fact.

She got to St James Street before noon, but her surprises were not over. The woman greeted her and Blossom with positive enthusiasm, and when Carrie offered her the one and three that was owing, the woman only laughed. 'Rent's all paid, three months in advance,' she said, giving Carrie a little playful push. 'As if you didn't know! And there's a parcel for you too. Came in a motor-car, no less.' She looked at Carrie appraisingly. 'Seems as if I misjudged you after all. Friends in high places, even if you have got a baby and no husband to show for it. Well, I shan't be worrying about my rent, that's one thing certain. I've lit the fire and put a bit of new soap in by the wash-stand. Anything else you want, just let me know.'

It was astonishing, Carrie thought, what a difference a little money could make. One call from Katie's coachman, and the woman was falling over herself to be helpful. Last night she could barely bring herself to be civil. It was good of Katie, too, to try to pay the rent. She would make sure the money was repaid, of course – Katie had done enough.

But for now she could do nothing but rejoice. She was here, safe and sound with Blossom, in a comfortable room, with a roof over her head, the rent paid, clean clothes in the bedroom and money in her pocket. Twenty-four hours ago none of it would have seemed possible.

She unpacked her few possessions, fetched clean water from the tap into the china washbowl, stripped herself to the skin and had a good wash. Scented soap, too, not the coarse homemade variety. Then she dressed herself afresh in Katie's clean grey uniform. It made her feel like a new woman – as if she could tip away the cares and worries of the past weeks together with the dirty washing-water. She bathed Blossom as well, and the child laughed and chattered and rubbed the soap to make bubbles, and then lay down in the middle of the bed and fell asleep instantly, as though she too knew that it was possible to relax. There was a knock on the door.

'Gentleman to see you,' the woman said, with a knowing leer. She stood aside to let the visitor in.

It was Philippe, of course, come for his picture. Carrie was aghast. This might be a sitting room – there was an easy chair and a small table by the fireplace – but it was also her bedroom. The woman, though, had gone out and shut the door.

'Sixteen guineas,' he said, placing the money carefully on the wash-stand.

Carrie, too embarrassed for words, said nothing, only picked up the picture, and rewrapped it hastily in the paper it had been delivered in. The woman in the hall would make something of that portrait if she ever saw it. She held it out to him. 'Here you are.'

He took it without speaking, and laid it carefully on the table. 'You have forgotten,' he said. 'There is an old Breton custom . . .'

And she found herself being taken into his arms, and his lips were on hers. She should have resisted but she did not. She answered him warmth for warmth.

He kissed her again. And again. All the years of separation were in those kisses, and it was warm, and sweet and wonderful. More than that, her breath came quicker, and her heart was thumping. When he released her a little and looked down into her face she looked into his eyes and knew that his breath and his heart were quickened too.

'Carrie,' he said miserably. 'What are we to do?'

And then she did turn from him. 'Nothing,' she said. 'No, we mustn't.'

He let her go then. 'I'm sorry. That was unforgivable.'

She put her own arms around him. 'No, don't be sorry.' There were tears in her eyes, she could feel them. 'An old Breton custom.'

He held her for a moment and then gently took her hands, pressed them together, and kissed her fingers. She was acutely aware of how roughened and raw they were, but he lingered over them, pressing his lips to them, kissing the damaged skin tenderly, passionately.

'I must go,' he said, and she nodded 'yes', but their eyes were locked, and his movement was towards her, not away. His lips fastened on hers again.

Blossom stirred. They stepped back, and the spell was broken.

'I'll see you again,' he said, taking up his package, and his words were not a question. 'I'll see myself out.'

It was as well he did. Carrie sat for a long time in the easy chair, her body still as stone but her mind and blood racing. The child's cry roused her. Blossom was fretting, 'Hungry, Mummy!' in a thin unhappy whimper. They had eaten nothing since breakfast, Carrie realised, and it was almost five. She caught up her basket and picked up the coins from the wash-stand.

Bread and butter, milk and jam, cold meat and eggs even, or a bought pie from the pie-seller. Forget about the kiss that burned on her lips and the blood that boiled in her veins. Think about the food, and the baby. And she would send something down to Dolly and the boys. She could afford any of it now.

CHAPTER FOUR

Dolly took it wonderfully. She wasn't jealous, or carping, as some women would have been. She was simply, uncomplicatedly glad for Carrie and relieved for herself. And she didn't resent it, either, when Carrie tried to share her good fortune – accepted with delight the little tidbits that Carrie sent down, and insisted on saving a really nice bit of fish for Carrie on Fridays, although the winter catches were poor.

'Shame if we can't look out for each other,' she said. 'And I'm some glad you've fallen on your feet, my lover. Tell you the truth I was beginning to wonder how we'd manage with this baby coming. Now, if you want to look out for a bit of work, till this job comes up, I'll have Blossom in the day and welcome. Glad of the bit of extra money, too, and no mistake.'

So it was arranged. There wasn't a lot of work to be had, and Carrie wasn't skilled. And she was married with a child – so there was no hope of work in a shop, a factory, or an office, even if she had been smart enough, which she probably wasn't, even in her good new grey. But she did find a position helping out in a kitchen, where the assistant cook had 'fallen over stairs' and broken her arm. Miss Limmon, of all people, had heard of it and given her a character.

It was hard work, but it was a holiday compared to fish filleting, and it was pleasant remembering old skills, unused since the days in the doctor's kitchen long ago. Carrie had forgotten the art of stuffing blackcock and partridge, making timbales of beef and fricassées of chicken, and at her first attempt at making stone cream she was so heavy-handed with the arrowroot that the pudding set like a clay-brick, and it was all to do again. The chief cook let her take it home, though, wrapped in a tea-cloth, and when she went to fetch Blossom they all ate it, sweet and rich and

347

almondy. Drew had so much he made himself sick, because he wasn't used to 'rich things' as Dolly said. So the job was pleasant enough.

Besides, she had two afternoons a week off, and often the morning besides if she wasn't wanted. She was only standing in, paid by the day, and there was no point in paying her to stand idle, so the woman said. Carrie did not care. Things had fallen wonderfully into place, like a dream, and like a dream there seemed to be no reality in it. She had leisure for the first time since she was a girl.

If she was not working there was plenty to do. She could walk around the markets and take her time choosing the cheapest and best, there were clothes for Blossom to knit and sew – and with her precious guineas she could buy new wool instead of running back old cardigans. One of these days, too, she would take the train and go and see Ernie, really she would. But in the meantime she was content to stay at home. There, in the privacy of her room, she could cook or sew or mend and think about Philippe.

He had came back, as he promised. Not once, but time and again. The woman who owned the house smiled knowingly every time he came and went, and even Dolly asked meaningfully after him, but Carrie no longer cared.

She loved him. She had always known it, from those days long back on the cliffs, when she had been a mere child, and everything – age, background, nationality – stood between them. She had adored him then, and she adored him now. Not as she loved Ernie – not that steady, dull, dependable affection born of shared responsibility, friendship and care, but another thing altogether. A wild, irresponsible happiness. A leap of the blood.

She had not meant it to happen. Even now she could not quite believe it. She, Carrie Clarance, a respectable married woman, in love with – in bed with! – another man. And she did not care.

'On thing leads to another,' Father used to say. That was how it had been. The kiss that became a caress. The hands that moved from shoulders to breasts, from breasts to buttons. But it did not feel wrong. Not though she tried to think of Ernie and the hurt it would cost him. This was sin, she thought – not the inability to tell right from wrong, but this: when wrong *was* right, and anything else was impossible.

She was not even unhappy. Philippe made her laugh. Even as his fingers touched her skin and turned her to molten gold, he could make her laugh. Like when he teasingly insisted that she pose for him, hairbrush in hand, and her hair falling over her face, as she was in the picture.

'More beautiful than ever,' he murmured, taking the brush from her and brushing her hair with firm gentle strokes that made her spine tingle. And they came together, deep and inevitable as the sea.

Even then, she had to learn to love him; there had been too many fumbling, clumsy nights after the Tinner's Arms. But he taught her, and she learned willingly, understanding for the first time the radiance that had lighted her mother's worn face some winter evenings when her father had come back early from the pit, and Carrie had come home to find them sitting together in the flickering firelight of the Terrace kitchen.

She felt like that now. As if she had come home.

'What will you do tomorrow, little Carrie?' he said, murmuring into her hair as she refastened the grey skirt around her. It was a bitter December afternoon. 'Will you come with me and see Trezayle House?'

'I'd better see Ernie,' she said. 'Haven't been for three weeks. Wrote and told him, of course, all about the job and everything, but he'll be wondering.' She wanted to weep suddenly. Ernie belonged to the other world, the real world of hunger and cold and grey. 'Keep saying I'll go up. Time I did it.'

'Will you tell him?' Philippe said.

She looked at him in horror.

'You must tell him. Surely you can see that? You must tell him. You belong with me, Carrie.'

She said, and the words tasted bitter, 'However can I do that? Me a married woman.'

He sat her down on the bed, pressing his hands on her shoulders. 'This is marriage, Carrie. What we have. Come to Trezayle House and live with me.'

'Whatever would people say?' she said, thinking of Crowdie, and Mr Whittaker and Dolly and all the others. And Ernie. She could already see the hurt in his eyes.

But Philippe's face was hurt, too. 'Who cares what they say? But you could become my wife, Carrie. There are ways. And if you worry so much about gossips and their tongues, we could go to France. To Ploumenach. I have a house, quite a big house, and no-one would know you there.' He laughed, a bitter little laugh. 'They would talk of course, but they would do the same if you were a brand-new bride. They would talk about any woman of mine, if she were a Breton saint. But they talk in Breton. You would not understand them, and I would not care. It need not worry us. And if you liked, I would give up the sea for good and come back to the land.'

'You have land in France?' She had known that his parents had a farm, ever since those first snatched conversations on the cliff, but she had imagined them somehow as a substantial tenant farmers, like Crowdie.

'A lot of land,' he said. 'I have tenants, of course, but the old *manoir* is still standing.'

'A manor!'

He laughed. 'Not like an English manor, Carrie – not like the one belonging to your friend at Trevarnon. But a big stone house, more like Trezayle House, with a dovecote and stables and sheds for the harvest.'

She twisted around to look at him more fully. 'Who lives there now?'

'There is a *matez* – a housekeeper, you would say. But, otherwise it is empty. I keep a room or two but I have not lived in most of it since . . .'

'Since your wife died?' she finished for him. She remembered the pain that the memory had always caused him. Strangely, it did not seem to pain him now.

'My first wife,' he said. 'But I could live there again, with you.'

'I am not Eved.'

'No, you are Carrie, and that is better still. That is over, Carrie, this is reality. Say you will come with me. Ramon and Jacques will bring the boat back from Ireland soon and when they do, I must decide. It is already late in the year, and I must go back to Brittany or stay.'

She shook her head. 'What about Blossom?'

'Blossom of course. She must come with us. She is your daughter. It would be wonderful for her. Plenty to eat, good food, sunshine more than here. Marie, my *matez*, always longed for children. She would be spoiled and grow strong running among the daisies.'

He knew how to twist her heart. 'And Ernie?' she said.

'You must tell him,' Philippe insisted. 'If you do not tell him, it makes us – guilty, somehow.'

She turned her head away. They *were* guilty. 'But he is in prison,' she said helplessly. 'He has suffering enough.'

Philippe leaned forward and kissed her hair. 'He must know some time,' he said softly. 'Don't leave it too long. Now, will you visit St Just with me tomorrow?' He smiled, and his eyes mocked her gently. 'We could go to Pendeen if you like. I always dreamed of building you a house there.'

She laughed. 'Oh very well.' She got to her feet. 'But not tomorrow. Tomorrow I must go and see Ernie.' She waited for him to repeat 'tell him', but he said nothing.

'Your next free day,' he said, and she gave her promise, although she had been half intending to go to Trevarnon. She had sent up the owing guinea, but there was still the question of the rent.

She watched him go, loving the lithe power of him, the vigour of his step, like a wound spring waiting to recoil. When she turned back, the landlady was waiting for her.

'Nice gentleman friend you've got there,' she said, with that half-disapproving, half-leering, meaningful smile. 'You're luckier than some. Thought so from the first moment, when he came in and paid your rent. Foreign, is he?'

As though she were a trollop, Carrie thought, her cheeks blazing. No wonder the woman looked so knowing. *He* had paid the rent. Good thing she hadn't gone up thanking Katie, she would have looked a proper fool. For a moment she was tempted to rush to the safety of her own room, to hide her face in the pillow and cover her blushes. But the damage was done. She squared her shoulders and raised her head defiantly.

'Yes,' she answered, her voice as cool and level as she could keep it, 'foreign. My husband knows him. By the way, I shall be visiting Bodmin tomorrow to see Mr Clarance. He is in prison, for supporting the Union cause.' It was true, more or less. Ernie did know about Philippe, and his problems did spring from his Union meetings.

The woman looked taken aback, but she said with a little sneer, 'What about paying your rooms then? And visiting you of an afternoon?'

The worst of it was, the woman was right. Carrie was back in the waking world, the world of right and wrong. But enough of the dream was left to make her say, with a little ghost of a smile which she could not suppress, 'Oh, that! As you say, he is foreign. Their habits are different from ours. Ask him, he'll tell you the same. An old Breton custom.'

It was wonderful seeing Carrie. Seeing her properly that is. Ernie seemed to dream of nothing else, and he would wake day after day believing she was beside him, or down at the pit scraping the clay-blocks, only a whistle away. But now here she was, in the flesh.

Looking a treat, too. He had tried to imagine it, from her letters: the grey uniform, the new boots. That gentrified friend of hers had given her a painting that wasn't wanted, she said, and it had made no end when she sold it. Well, it looked like it, and all. There were roses in her cheeks, and a bounce in her step, and Ernie could see the admiring looks of the warders when she came in. Made him proud to see her.

He had things to tell her, as well. Exciting things. 'You won't believe it, Carrie, Morrison wrote and told me himself. Miss Limmon, of all people, sending ten whole shillings! It's waiting for you in the office. And he wrote an article about us as well. Mind, it's more about Miss Limmon than anything, and how good she always was to you. Make you laugh, if it wasn't so daft. See it, did you?'

Carrie shook her head. She never took the papers. 'Well, here it is, he sent me a copy.' He held it out towards her and she read it, burying her head in the page.

He had expected her to laugh, or burst out with some angry response, or do an imitation of 'Old Lemon-pips'. But she just gave the paper back to him. 'Very nice,' she said.

She seemed awkward, as if there were something worrying her, and she avoided his eyes as he took the paper. No wonder, perhaps – Morrison's piece held her up like a sideshow, the struggling woman with a child forced to work in the fishmarket, and he remembered how upset she had been about the 'humiliation' of Da. He should have thought of it.

'Thing is,' he said, 'it might have done a bit of good, after all. Vince and that Jeannie of his saw it, up to Plymouth, and they've written me a letter. Think I should show it to Morrison, do you?'

He offered her the paper, but she shook her head. 'Read it to me,' she said. 'I'm that mazed with the train and everything, I don't seem able to concentrate somehow.'

He read it. It was better really, because he could leave out some bits. It was Jeannie'd made Vince write the letter, that was as clear as daylight. Vince had got her into trouble again – no wonder he'd dropped her quicker than a hot cake, for fear of what Feyther would say – and then, when she'd gone to Plymouth to have the baby, he'd come running and asked her to marry him, knowing she'd got money put by. He didn't read all that to Carrie, she was down enough on Vince as it was.

'It's this bit,' he said, 'listen. "I've agreed to Vince's proposal, and we are going to go to America. I'm paying for the tickets. But I told him I'd only buy them on condition he wrote and told you what he told me. So here it is. I shan't post this till Tuesday" – that's more'n a week ago – "so by the time you get this, we shall be long gone. But it might be some use to you, anyway, and I couldn't hold my head up without we sent it. Signed Jeannie Whittaker, Mrs." ' He looked at Carrie. 'Always said that girl had a mind of her own. And here's the most important thing. Letter from Vince. "It wasn't you that stood up to the policeman, that night, it was me. And you never hit him. Couldn't hit a waggon-side at twenty paces, you couldn't. It was me, I felt it hit him and saw him go down. So don't you go giving yourself airs and calling yourself 'the clayman's Mr Pankhurst' like that fellow does in the paper." There, Carrie what do you think of that?'

'That's very good,' she said. But her heart wasn't in it.

'Think I should send it Morrison?'

'Why not?'

'Wouldn't do Vince any harm. They'd never bring him all the way back

352

from America. And they've written to Vince's Feyther, too, saying the same. So if I don't send it, likely he will. What d'you think? Send it to Morrison? Or maybe Tavy? Might make a difference – Tavy always said we needed a confession from Vince. Court never believed me that there were two of us. And here he's as good as said it was him that did it and not me at all. There might still be a chance. So, what shall I do? Send it to Tavy, do you think?'

'Why not?' She was only half listening. That train journey must have left her feeling terrible.

He said, 'I will then,' and there was a pause.

'Ernie?'

'Yes?'

'There's something . . .' She looked up at him, and he smiled at her.

'What is it, my handsome? Isn't much I can do in here, but you tell me, and I'll write to Morrison, see if he can help you out. Man like that behind you, you can't go far wrong.'

His eyes met hers and she smiled back at him. She looked a bit down, he thought. 'Oh, it's nothing.'

But he was not convinced. 'Blossom all right?'

She nodded. 'Blossoming.' Their old joke.

'Can't wait to see her. It's some long time, Carrie girl, but we'll get through it, see if we don't. And maybe, if I send this letter to Morrison . . . But what was it you wanted to tell me?'

She stood up, shaking her head and smiling. 'Nothing. I've got a headache, that's all. You keep your spirits up, Ernie, and don't worry about us. We've been very lucky. I've got a good room, and a good clean job. Katie's been as good as gold . . . and M. Philippe comes in to see after us sometimes, too.'

Ernie nodded. 'Does he now? That's good of him. Miss Limmon's doing, I'll be bound. Perhaps I've judged her a bit harsh, after all. Well, you thank him for me. And keep your pecker up, Carrie. I don't know what I should do in here, if I didn't know you were waiting for me. Listened to you in the first place, I never would have been here, and that's a fact.'

She smiled at him again, that smile that could always turn his heart over. 'Well, never you mind about that. You just take care of yourself,' and then it was time to leave.

He sat down, first time they let him have pen and paper, and wrote to Mr Morrison. After a little thought he enclosed the letter from Vince.

Carrie's first free day after that was Saturday, and Philippe came for her in Adeline's old carriage, dug out of storage for the occasion. He had intended to drive it himself, but the coachman, older and more mummified than ever, got wind of it and insisted on doing the job, donning his faded black coat and high hat with the enthusiasm of a man half his age.

It occurred to Philippe that Carrie might be amused by the trappings of Adeline's inheritance; the carriage, the house – things he had turned his back on long ago and no longer regarded. He was rewarded: she was as innocently delighted as a child, even by the drive in the carriage.

'Used to think Miss Limmon was some old fuss-pot, messing around with her muff and gloves, on purpose to be seen in the brougham,' she said, as they bowled along. 'Know how she feels!'

And when they turned up the drive to Trezayle House, her enthusiasm was almost embarrassing. 'Only think!' she kept saying. 'Miss Adeline's house, where Miss Limmon used to come, and here's me driving up to the front door like a guest.'

'You are a guest, Carrie,' he said. 'But you could be more than that, if you choose. Ride in a carriage every day.'

'Don't be daft,' she said. She had refused to discuss the future, ever since she had gone up to Bodmin to see Ernie, but her eyes were shining as the coachman extended his hand to help her down from the carriage-step. Maria, pressed into service for the afternoon, opened the door and led the way into the drawing room. There was a fire in the grate and a light tea had been set on a table, with a pair of chairs beside it, although most of the furniture was in store, and a lot of the rest was covered by dustsheets.

'My lor,' Carrie said, tucking into the tongue sandwiches, 'it is a big house, isn't it? I thought it would be something like Albert Villas, but it's more like Trevarnon House, this is.'

'Not above half the size,' Philippe said. 'Twenty-odd rooms in Trevarnon, I heard you say, and we have only nine. But yes, a big enough house. Too big for a man to live in alone.'

She looked at him, challenging him with a grin. 'Miss Adeline did it, and she was a lot littler than you!'

He laughed aloud. It was this, her freshness and directness, which was more than half her charm. With her he was a child again too, seeing things with her topsy-turvy logic. A hundred women would have fluttered at his remark, taken his meaning. He caught her glance, and saw the mischief in it. She had understood well enough what he meant. He said so. 'You understand me perfectly well, Carrie.'

She dropped her eyes, the mischief gone. 'Yes.'

'And?'

She glanced at him, sighed, looked away. 'I don't know. When I'm with you it seems so right, and when I saw Ernie . . . I don't know. Anyway,' she got up, and came over to take his hand, tugging him to his feet, 'I thought we had come to look at the house.'

'So we have,' he said lightly, and allowed himself to be led out, into the echoing hall. He took her over the place, seeing it with new eyes as she gasped in astonishment at the bedrooms, the landings, the attics, the dining room, the breakfast room, the writing room, and finally the kitchen where Maria was washing the tea-things in the sink and looked astonished and embarrassed at being caught at it.

'And this is all yours?' she said, as they went upstairs again, past the shrouded grandfather clock. 'What are you going to do with it?'

'I shall live here, if you'll come with me. Otherwise – I don't know. Sell it, I suppose. Though what use a house like this would be to anyone, I don't know. Once you might have found a mine-owner to buy it, but the industry is dying. And there is no money in fish or flowers. People are moving to the cities, now.'

'I should think anyone would want a lovely house like this,' Carrie said. 'Big enough for a school, or a hospital!'

'Hardly!' he said, laughing. 'But, as I say, too big for me alone. If you won't come with me, Carrie, I shall go back to Brittany and put this house up for sale. Sad, really, the end of the Trezayles. But I can't go on having two houses in two countries both falling into disrepair. They will end up like Willie Polzeal's cottage.'

'Who's Willie Polzeal?'

'My grandfather's boatman,' he said. 'Died years ago. Used to live in the ruined cottage down on the cliffs – you know. Left it to Grandfather when he died. I used to dream, once, of building you a house there. A house of our own.'

She looked at him, her eyes bright. 'Can we go down there?'

'What, now? It's December. It's getting dark. It's blowing a gale and it will probably rain before long.'

'It'll do that whether we go or not. It's not far, is it?'

'Not really.' He could not deny her anything, and her enthusiasm was infectious. 'If you lived here,' he said slyly, 'we could go there as often as you liked.'

She grinned up at him. 'Let's go now, anyway.'

So they walked, arm in arm in the teeth of the wind. It was a long walk, and the cold brought a glow to her cheeks. He felt the warm pressure of her body and knew that he loved her and wanted her beyond anything.

'There it is.' They were on the clifftop, with the ruins of the cottage in front of them. There was little of it left, now, even less than the last time he had come. Farmers had raided the building for stones, and there were only a few broken walls, with tufts of spiky grass growing from the ruined windowsills, and the chimney-stack.

'Be careful,' he said, as she bent her head to enter the roofless room through the empty arch of the door. 'It may be dangerous.'

She looked at the floor with its missing flagstones; someone had been digging underneath them. 'What's been going on here?'

He laughed. 'This was a smuggler's cottage. The children, I suppose, hoping to find treasure.'

'Was there treasure?'

He chuckled. 'Not buried here, at any rate. Grandfather was too shrewd for that. Took everything to France. I remember him telling me about the customs men. "Called themselves the preventative men," he used to say, "but they never prevented Willie and me!" You'd have liked my grandfather. And he would have loved you!'

She smiled. 'But there was no treasure.'

He was seized by mischief. 'Yes,' he said. 'There is, look. I've found it. Treasure.'

She was by his side at once. 'Where?'

He seized her. 'Here!' he said, and rained kisses on her face. 'This is all the treasure I want.'

And she yielded to him, there in the broken ruins of the cottage, with the winds of Cornwall ruffling their hair, and the soft rain falling, and in their ears the deep rhythmic surge of the sea.

Afterwards they walked back to Trezayle hand in hand. The brougham was waiting.

'Will you come?' he said, urgently, as the carriage stopped in St James Street and the landlady peeped at them from behind her curtains. 'Will you come and live with me, where you belong?'

She looked at him long and hard. 'I want to. Oh, I want to. But it's so hard. There's Ernie . . .'

'The boat will be here on Wednesday,' he said. 'I must tell the men.'

'On Wednesday then, I promise. I'll give you your answer on Wednesday.'

And she would have slipped out of the carriage and indoors, but he laid a hand on her arm. He could not bear to let her go like this. Supposing, on Wednesday, she should say no. What then? He would lose her, and this time it would be for ever. He could not bear it. He must do something. He wanted a sign, something to bind them together.

He slipped his hand deep into his pocket, and found a coin. 'Here,' he said. 'You wanted treasure. You shall have it. A tiny treasure for you. A

French coin. It's called a franc. A little memento. A present from me. Spend it, when you come to France with me. And look . . .' He took a slip of paper and wrote his name on it, and the address of the *manoir*. He folded it carefully around the coin and gave it to her. 'There. That shall be your home one day, if you say yes.'

He saw her into the room, and she slipped the paper into her marquetry box, reverently, like a talisman. The action gave him hope.

CHAPTER FIVE

Carrie did not sleep that night. Or the next. She went to work mechanically, and afterwards could not remember cleaning, drawing and roasting the duck and boiling and straining the giblets, though she must have done it, because there was the salmis on its potato base and with its orange garnish, and the lady of the house even sent down to the kitchen to compliment the cook.

She went over her problem again and again. Philippe? Every atom of her, body and soul wanted to go with him – perhaps not to Trezayle House, there were too many eyes to see, too many tongues to wag, too many people who remembered Mother, and Father, and whose poor opinion would have grieved them. But to Brittany perhaps, where no-one knew her, and where she could start again, a new life in a new land.

Or Ernie. Poor loyal, honest, stupid, clumsy Ernie, who was her lawful wedded husband until death do us part. She went back to making Toledo soup and beat the living daylights out of the egg yolks to make the yellow garnish. But it did nothing to relieve her feelings.

On Monday there were two letters delivered to St James Street. Two. Carrie began to feel as if she were on one of those mechanical staircases they had shown at the Earl's Court exhibition, so she'd heard, with events moving faster and faster, without her doing anything at all herself.

One letter was from Trevarnon, asking Carrie and Blossom to the house for a 'pre-Christmas tea, some evening this week to suit'. The man was waiting for an answer and Carrie sent back to accept for the next evening, when she wasn't working. It would be good to see Katie again, and it would fill the terrible space between now and Wednesday.

Wednesday. She had to make up her mind.

The other message was a request, though it read like a command, to go to Albert Villas. 'Miss E. Limmon would be obliged if Mrs Clarance could present herself at the above address early on Tuesday evening, at her convenience.' It would be all the same, she told herself crossly, if she had been working that evening. At her convenience indeed! But she had received the promised ten shillings, and Old Button-eyes deserved a heartfelt thank you for that at least. Poor Old Lemon-pips. How she had hankered after her French sea-captain. Carrie had the grace to feel a little sorry for Emily Limmon.

She went to Albert Villas first, on the way to Trevarnon. She was let in by a flustered Ellie. 'I hope you aren't mad at me, Carrie,' she whispered, as she led the way to the parlour. 'It was me told Miss Limmon where you were and all about you. Never dreamt she'd have it in the papers.'

It took Carrie a moment or two to take it in. Of course. Ernie had been full of it, some article that Morrison had written. She had looked at it briefly without taking in a word.

'It doesn't signify, Ellie,' she said with a smile. Whatever it was, it hadn't done any harm, at least up to now. And Ernie had seemed quite pleased. Something about a letter from Vince Whittaker. She went into the room.

'This is Carrie, James,' Miss Limmon was saying. 'Carrie, this is Mr Tavy, and Mr Morrison. They have been good enough to take an interest in your husband's case.'

So Mr Tavy was 'James', Carrie noted with an inward smile, even as she said aloud, 'Yes Miss Limmon. I know Mr Tavy, he was at the trial. Good evening. And to you, Mr Morrison.'

They were as different as chalk and cheese. Tavy was as thin as a boryer, and you could have used Morrison as a biscuit barrel. But they had been good to Ernie. She said, 'Ernie showed me your article.'

Morrison waved a fat hand. 'It created a certain interest. In fact, that was what I hoped to speak to you about. Did your husband show you the letter?'

'Yes, from Vince Whittaker.'

Tavy broke in. 'You realise it might be significant? The young man admits his own guilt and exonerates your husband. Proves that he is innocent.'

'No-one would take a bit of notice of anything Vince Whittaker said,' Carrie said bitterly. 'Nothing but trouble since he came to St Blurzey, though his pa's nice, mind.'

Mr Morrison bowed and smiled, in a way which reminded Carrie of the old minister who used to come to Penvarris schoolroom and ask questions on scripture.

Tavy said, 'Presumption of guilt, that's what it was. And a man should be presumed innocent. Glad to take it up, glad to, especially for a young man like your husband. Now this is what it comes to. Your husband tells me you could put your hand on a few pounds now, if the need arose.'

It was a shock. Why would Ernie need money? But she said, 'Yes.'

'Commuted, you see,' the man said. 'We might get it commuted to a fine. If all goes well. I wanted to be sure you could meet the occasion, although your husband assured me that you were not in want, now.'

She shook her head. 'We're grand now, me and Blossom.'

He smiled thinly. 'The power of the press, eh? Well, I am glad to hear it. Mr Morrison here was prepared to take a leaf from dear Miss Limmon, prepared to reach into his own purse to alleviate your distress. If that was necessary.'

Why had she said 'yes' so quickly? She might have had the fine paid for her. But she had cooked her goose now. 'Miss Limmon was very good,' Carrie said. 'I wanted to thank her.'

'Tut, girl, it was nothing,' Miss Limmon said. It was the first time she had spoken since introducing Carrie, and her words were rewarded by warm smiles from both the gentlemen. But it was 'James' that Miss Limmon was smiling back at, Carrie noticed. She hadn't seen Miss Limmon smile like that since M. Philippe came calling. I wonder if she's wearing her lacy camisole, she thought irreverently, and the thought gave her courage.

'Well,' Miss Limmon said, 'if you have money for the fine, well and good. James shall go ahead with his appeal. Won't you, James? Mr Morrison has been good enough to agree to meet the fee.'

That would teach her, Carrie thought, to jump to conclusions. 'You're very good,' she said, again.

Tavy got to his feet. 'Thank you for coming, Carrie. It is a pleasure to see you so well.'

And that appeared to be that. After all that it was a relief to pick up Blossom from downstairs where Mrs Rowe was making a fuss of her, and take her up to Trevarnon.

It was a cold night, but Katie's welcome could not have been warmer. There was a huge fire in the hearth, and a great table loaded with tea. Katie's husband was there too, and all the children – from Rosa down to the youngest Trevarnons.

'A nursery tea,' Katie said, and so it was. Boiled eggs and bread and butter, and jelly and sandwiches and cake. Blossom was at her most enchanting, toddling everywhere with her big wistful eyes and her shy smile, and the older children took to her at once. Rosa found a little tin monkey with a drum, and they spent a long time winding it up over and over, so that it marched along beating its drumsticks, while Blossom gurgled with delight.

There was a great parcel, too. 'A bit of Christmas,' Katie said. 'Nothing grand.' But it was grand. Hand-me-down clothes for Blossom, of a quality and cloth that Carrie could never have matched: a skirt and blouse for herself, and even a vest and shirt for Ernie; and on top, a big bag of Christmas treats, oranges and apples, nuts and sugar-plums, a tin of peaches and a slab of corned beef. A feast. Carrie made a mental note to get down to Dolly's and order the best and biggest turbot of the catch for delivery to Trevarnon.

She looked around at the scene. Blossom, sitting by the fire, singing to a rag doll which one of the children had looked out for her, well-fed, warm and happy. This could be hers too, she thought, if she went with Philippe. A big house, a big fire, warmth and family.

'And how is Ernie bearing up?' Katie said, coming to sit beside her on the padded couch.

Carrie looked at her friend. 'Do you think,' she asked slowly, 'if there is a chance of happiness, that you should take it, and never mind the cost?'

Katie looked at her. 'Generally,' she said. 'As long as the cost isn't to other people.'

Carrie sighed. 'That's the trouble,' she said. 'It usually is, isn't it?' Katie was gazing at her thoughtfully, and Carrie changed the subject quickly. 'Like tonight, for instance. Mr Morrison sent to ask if I could pay a fine for Ernie, if it came to it. Well, course I could, and will – but if I do that, and it's a big fine, I could be struggling for Blossom.'

Katie nodded. 'Yes, it's a problem, I can see that. And if there is anything I can do, you have only to ask. But in the end, Carrie, you have to follow your heart. It's all anyone can do.'

And then Rosa came to join the conversation, and they talked about other things until it was time to go home.

Wednesday. She had promised him an answer on Wednesday. The hours were hanging on Philippe's hands like dead eels, heavy, long and lifeless. He would have to wait, he knew, until she had finished preparing dinner for the household where she worked, and then collected Blossom from the fishmarket. The day seemed to drag endlessly.

He went down to the boat, but its stuffy fishiness turned his stomach, and he lost his patience with Jacques and Ramon.

'Are you sailing with us, maître?' Jacques said, looking with a sailor's disdain at the smart landsman's suit and starched collar. 'You aren't dressed for the sea.'

'Damn your impudence,' Philippe growled. 'I'll dress as I choose. I know how to equip myself for the sea, I should hope.' There were sea-boots, jerseys and oilskins in his locker. 'But we don't sail till midnight. Get off ashore and drink yourselves stupid if you must, but be back here at eleven, for the tide. And get yourself arrested again, Ramon, and you sail with me no more.'

They went ashore grumbling and bickering, and he prowled the deck for a little, unable to settle. Eventually he went up to the harbour wall, and positioned himself where she would be certain to see him.

And, at last, she came. Blossom was with her, trailing at her skirts, but he had only to look at Carrie's face to know that she had been as anxious, as agonised as he had.

'Well?' he said, stepping forward into the lamplight.

She hesitated for a moment, and then stepped forward into his arms.

'Then you will live with me?'

She raised her face. 'Brittany, Philippe. It must be Brittany. Here I couldn't bear it. It's too close to home.'

He pressed her fiercely to him. 'America, Africa, if you say so. Anywhere. As long as we are together. So will you come, now?' His heart was thumping so that he could scarcely breathe. She was coming. Would be his. He could have danced for joy.

But she was shaking her head. 'I must go home first. I have things to collect. Things to do. And I should write. To my job, to Katie . . .'

He tilted her head up to look into her eyes. 'We will write together. How long will you be?'

'An hour, no more. And I have Blossom to feed.'

He nodded. 'I will come with you.'

They walked together up the darkened streets. It was not late, but it was cold, with a brisk breeze blowing. A broad reach, Philippe thought, his mind already on the voyage ahead.

He helped her pack, saw her put her precious possessions into two pillowcases, watched her as she opened a little marquetry box and counted out ten pounds into a spill of paper. 'For Mr Morrison. For the fine if necessary,' she wrote in her wayward curling hand, and he walked to Albert Villas himself to deliver it by hand to Ellie, while Carrie fed the child and wrapped her warm.

He was worried for her. About her clothes, for one thing. He had boasted to Jaques of his own sea-boots, but Carrie had none, and the deck of a pitching vessel was no place for a woman in skirts and petticoats. She had no oilskins either, and there was nothing he could offer the child. They would have to stay below, in the bunks, though the fish-smell was strong in the cabin, and the motion of the boat always worse when you were not in the open air. It would be a miserable passage, with a rising wind, and Jacques and Ramon would not be happy either, with a woman and child aboard. But it was one night and day only. Tomorrow they would be back safe, and then – he admitted it to himself – then their problems really would begin.

She was ready and waiting by the time he got back, and he took the child and one of her bundles and set off into the street. Blossom was singing, 'Baa baa bla shee' and beating time with a spoon, but Carrie was pale, and trembling.

'I'm afraid,' she said, in a voice so humble that it melted him.

'I have thought of that,' he said, and explained about the bunks.

She shook her head. 'Oh yes, I am terrified of the sea, but it isn't what I mean. I'm just – afraid.'

He helped her onto the boat, aware for the first time of how strange it was to her. The way she gave a little yelp of fright when the deck moved under her as she stepped aboard: the way she struggled to keep her feet against the motion, although the boat was only in harbour, riding a slight swell. It would be a long night for her, out under the stars with the seas milky with foam and no land in sight.

'Come down below,' he said, 'and get used to it a little.' If she were below, he thought to himself, it would give him longer to handle Ramon and Jacques when they returned. And the child, perhaps, could be settled before they left harbour. She was sitting now on a locker-top and gazing around her, her eyes wide with wonder. Some children had been known to sleep a whole voyage with the rocking of the ship, so they said.

'You will need to tie a blanket, like this, so that you don't fall from the bunk if the waves are rough,' he said, showing Carrie how to secure a lee-sheet. He could see the fear in her eyes, and he did not add that before the night was out, that same blanket would be drenched with water pouring from the hatches. Time enough for that fear when they were out to sea. And he would slacken sail, run before the wind where he could, anything to keep the boat as stable as possible. There would be no fishing tonight.

He looked down at her, and she smiled, strained but brave. He felt a rush of tenderness. He would protect her. He could. He could not help the wind and the cold and the wet, but he would make it up to her over the years. She would never regret this, never.

She stretched out her arms and he went to her, losing himself in her kiss. It was worth it, he thought, worth anything. He stretched over her, burying his hands in her hair and his head in her shoulder.

Outside there was a sharp, shrill cry. A splash.

'What's that?' Carrie was bolt upright. 'Oh, my God. Blossom.'

He was up the steps before she was on her feet. He looked around. The child was gone. He went to the side. There in the inky, cold blackness, a flash of white, a gurgling splash.

He went in. Swift as an arrow over the side. Cold. So cold it tore the breath from his lungs and for a moment he too was floundering. Water in his boots, dragging him down. He struggled up, clawing at the quayside. A white bundle flashing before him, going down for the third time. He snatched, lifted, hoisted.

Blossom was inert, whooping with water. He shook her, squeezing the sea from her lungs. She spat vomit, gulped, hiccoughed, breathed. The boat lunged at him, riding on the swell. He braced himself against it, holding Blossom clear, feeling her trembling, shuddering with cold, the little heart slowing against his neck. And then the boat was on him, crushing him, and Carrie was on the deck, her voice a piercing shriek of panic.

'Help!!!'

Suddenly the world was full of running. Hands reached down for the child, for him. Someone threw a lifebelt and he grasped at it blindly, fighting the red pain from his shattered arm. And then he was numb, dragged, chill to the heart but lying somewhere, and his boots were not pulling him down, and they put a blanket over him, and Carrie was sobbing and there was something . . . brandy . . . something . . . and he was floating, floating . . .

Ernie got off the train at Penzance station, whistling. He still couldn't believe it. Too good to be true.

It was only at three o'clock he had heard it for certain himself. He had known it was possible, of course. Tavy had come to see him, on purpose to tell him there was a good chance of having his sentence 'commuted' – turned into a sort of fine, it turned out to mean. Morrison was going to London with Vince's letter, and had got onto politicians, judges, Lord knows what. Prime Minister himself, more than like – Ernie wouldn't put it past him.

And it had turned out better than anyone could have hoped. A free pardon. And here he was, on his way back to Carrie and Blossom. Couldn't wait to see their faces – Carrie knew about this commuting the sentence business, but she had no idea they had let him go altogether. He thought of sending a telegram, but that cost money, and in any case it would be a treat to see her face when she saw him home, a free man. And it was all the Union's doing. He always said the Union wouldn't let you down.

He asked his way to St James Street. The woman who opened the door looked at him coldly. 'And who might you be?' she said when he asked for Carrie.

'I'm her husband,' he said. The woman looked abashed.

'Oh,' she said. 'Well, that's different then, I suppose. Well, they're not in. Not any of them. Gone off down Newlyn to the harbour, I heard them say.'

Ernie frowned. 'Off down see Dolly, I'll be bound. Wonder why, this time of night?'

The woman shrugged. 'Went off with all sorts of stuff. And sent money up to some house in Victoria Road. That's all I know.'

He grinned. 'Mr Morrison. Doing it for me, she was. Morrison said she might have to raise some, to pay a fine. Must be going to pawn things, or sell them. Isn't that just like her? Well, I aren't going to hang around here. I'll go down and surprise them.'

He set off at a sprint.

He didn't hear Carrie's desperate cry, but as he came to the harbour he heard the shouts and the confusion, and saw the lights and lanterns, and movement on the quay.

'What is it?' he stopped to enquire from a tall bald-headed man who was running up with a rope.

'Child fallen in the harbour,' the man shouted over his shoulder. 'Some Frenchman jumped in to save it. They've got him out, but he looks in a poor way. Child's all right, though it'll need to be got warm, sharpish, before it gets its death of cold.'

'Can I help?' Ernie said, running onto the quay beside him.

And then, suddenly, there was Carrie, and it was Blossom she was carrying, cold and dripping. Her face was ashen in the lamp-light, streaked with tears, and he stripped off his jacket and put it round her, and took them in his arms, his wife and daughter, and led them gently away.

'What you doing here?' Carrie said. Her face was lined with shock.

'Morrison's doing,' he said shortly. 'I'll tell you later. Now come on home and let's get that child in the warm before it's too late.'

She came with him then, but she was still saying, 'What about *him*?'

'He'll be all right,' Ernie said. 'They're sending a motor-ambulance. Nothing we can do for him. But if we don't have that child in dry clothes this minute, he'll have jumped in after her all in vain.'

Carrie looked at him a half-second, and thrust the child into his arms and turned away, running, as if jolted into action by his words. 'I've got some,' she called over her shoulder. 'You go on. I'll catch you.'

There was urgency in her voice now. The shock had passed, he thought with relief, and she was living in the real world again. He strode off, cradling Blossom against his chest, stripping off her wet clothing and holding her against him, wrapping her in the jacket as he walked.

Carrie came alongside, carrying a pillowcase stuffed with things. 'Here.' She found a cardigan and they put it on the child, there in the street under the lamp. Another cardigan for her legs, and a woollen blanket around her shoulders. The child stopped juddering and settled into a rhythmic shiver, her little teeth chattering. He held her against him again, using the heat of his own body to warm hers.

'Come on,' he said, and set off running. Carrie followed him.

It took them an hour. More. In the room with a good fire blazing, rubbing the little hands and legs, wrapping a firebrick in a blanket to make a warm nest, coaxing heated milk and honey between her lips. But at last there was warmth in the little limbs and colour in the face, and Blossom stopped whimpering and sank into a deep, exhausted sleep.

Only then did they stop and take stock. 'Where were you going with all this?' he said, when he had explained his unforeseen arrival.

Carrie flushed. 'It was . . . well. It doesn't matter now.'

He smiled. 'Going to pawn them, were you? Getting money for Morrison? Well, we won't be needing it. Mind you, Carrie, you didn't ought to have pawned everything, even if it came to it. You should have kept something back, for yourself.' He reached out a hand for her. 'Come here, girl.'

She was beside him. He had dreamed of this moment a thousand times, not just in prison but long before, when she was in the front room in Buglers and he was alone in the upstairs bed. She did not pull away from him.

It was urgent and clumsy, but it was triumphant, wonderful. And he had moved her, too, for once. He knew because he saw her face in the firelight, and there were tears standing on her cheeks.

CHAPTER SIX

She came to see him in hospital. He had known she would, somehow, though Jacques and Ramon had pieced together the story for him, how the child's father had come and taken his wife and daughter away while Philippe was unconscious on the quayside.

His shoulder was crushed, and the whole side of his body broken and bruised. A wonder he didn't shatter all his ribs, the matron said. But he would make a recovery. A fortnight or so, and he should be well enough to travel. The men would sail the boat, though, and he would be a mere passenger.

'Be a long time before you're fit to go to sea no more,' the woman said. 'Just don't go jumping overboard another time. But you can travel, just this once. Provided you stay in your bed all the journey.'

She didn't know much about bunks at sea, but he nodded, and said nothing. He told Carrie though, when she came in to see him.

'Day before Christmas,' he said. It hurt to talk, but he had to let her know. 'Tide is at ten. It's not too late, Carrie. You can come. You can still come.'

But she said nothing.

'Ernie's back?' he managed, through the pain.

She nodded. 'Thinks you're a blooming hero. Never stops talking about it, how you jumped in to save Blossom. Never once stopped to ask how she came to fall in, in the first place.' She turned her face to him, and the light had gone out of it, totally, like a snuffed candle. 'It was my fault, Philippe. I should have had an eye on her, and all I was thinking of was myself. If it hadn't been for you . . .'

He said, with difficulty, 'If it hadn't been for me, you wouldn't have been there. We are in this together, Carrie. You can't blame yourself.'

367

'But I did nothing,' she said. 'Stood and shouted, while other people saved my baby. And saved you.'

He looked at her from one blackened eye. 'Can you swim?'

She shook her head.

'Well then.' She managed a smile, and he tried again. 'Don't forget. The twenty-fourth. I'll wait for you. Till the tide turns.'

'And if I don't come?'

He shook his head, winced with the pain. 'I won't come back.' He couldn't bear it. It had been so close, so nearly his.

But he had lost her. He could see it in her face.

She wished, almost, that he hadn't told her. The twenty-fourth. It rang in her head like a bell. It was impossible, of course, quite impossible. The incident with Blossom had shown her that. It was the child she had to think of, the child even now turning in her bed, still recovering slowly from the chill she had taken.

But she couldn't put it from her mind. Not even when she was wanted every day in the kitchen for mincepies, and candied chestnuts, plum tarts and baked hams and row on row of cakes and tarts and confectionery, ready for Christmas. Not even when Mr Morrison sent back her ten pounds with another two shillings 'from Miss Limmon' to buy something for Blossom, and she could walk the lighted streets dreaming of dolls and dresses and sugar-plums, even if she did settle for a pair of new boots and a woollen coat for the child. Not even in the mornings early, when she felt sometimes a little unwell and off her food, in a way she remembered once before. Not even then.

The twenty-fourth. He had never mentioned it since, though she had been to his bedside once or twice with Ernie Ernie had passed it on to Mr Morrison and there were write-ups in the paper. The *Graphic Messenger* sent a man down to take photographs, but the hospital wouldn't let him in, and neither would Carrie at St James Street, so he had to be satisfied with a picture of the boat and the harbour, with Philippe's three crewmen grinning cheerfully from the quayside.

The twenty-fourth. It dawned, cold and overcast with a leaden sky, heavy as her heart. She worked in the morning, her last morning. The cook with the broken arm was recovered and coming in to work on Boxing Day. Ernie was out, trying to earn a few pence carrying parcels. But it wasn't easy these days. Once upon a time you could have picked up a few coppers holding the horses, or lighting the way home with a lantern. But there were too many cars and bicycles, and gas lamps in the street. You were lucky if you could get a bit of porterage, and that was heavy work.

Three o'clock, when she got home. She had some homemade sweets – mis-shapes brought home from the kitchen – and she wrapped them carefully in blue sugar paper and took them down to Dolly and the children. Dolly gave her tea, and a slice of 'Christmas roll', a piece of pastry with sugar and dried fruit baked inside it. Blossom and Little Ell had 'helped', rolling balls of dough into grey balls between sticky fingers. Blossom insisted on giving hers to Carrie.

Half past four.

She went home and cooked tea for Blossom. Homemade soup, and she lingered over the cooking, making it stretch as far as possible. The child ate it, every scrap, and then sang a 'Kiss-miss carol' that had neither tune nor words. She was improving now, getting stronger again every day.

Ten past six. Time to put Blossom to bed.

Carrie turned to the mending, waiting for Ernie to come home. He was late, and tired. Walked all the way to Pendeen, he said, carrying a parcel, and the woman only gave him a few pence. But he insisted on doing it. It was his place, he said, to support his family. He couldn't sit by and see Carrie working and himself not bringing in a penny. It wasn't fitting. And she could hardly ask him to stay home with the baby, although that would have put a shilling a week in their pockets, on its own. Ernie had his soup and sat down by the fire, exhausted.

Five to eight. The minutes seemed to drag past now. She knitted and sewed until her fingers ached, but a glance at the clock showed her that only ten minutes had inched past. He would be on the ship now. She could imagine it, having been there. He would be stepping aboard, pacing the deck, going down into the cabin.

Ten past nine. That was better. A whole hour and a quarter since the last time she looked. She put on the kettle and made a cup of tea, but she did not drink it. She sat, holding the cup and staring into the fire. Ernie, in the chair, stirred and snored.

Twenty to ten. 'I won't come back.' That's what he had said. Lying there with the crushed shoulder and the bruised face that were all her fault. 'Won't come back.' She thought of him, here in this room, lying on this bed. Down at Trezayle. Out at the cottage on the cliff. Once, long ago, holding out her ruined bonnet. 'I have treaden upon your 'at.'

Three minutes to ten. She looked at Ernie, at Blossom in the cot. The child's new warm clothes were wrapped, ready for Christmas. All at once she got up and scooped up the parcel, then seized her coat and the child, and ran out into the street. Ernie did not stir.

She was running hard now, down the roads bright with Christmas, down Market Jew Street and down towards the front. Blossom woke and looked at her, little eyes wide with surprise. 'Mummie go out?' Carrie ran on.

Across the promenade and round the darkened streets towards the bridge and Newlyn. She turned into the harbour and stood panting. There was the wall, the mooring. And there, out across the water was a dark ship, sailing, her sail already filling across the long dark empty road of the moonlit sea.

Carrie stood for a long moment watching. Then she turned and walked back, slowly, through the town. It was beginning to snow.

When she got to St James Street, Ernie was still sleeping. She put Blossom into the blankets, and walked softly to the table by the bed. The marquetry box winked up at her and she held it, slowly.

Ernie, in his chair, opened one eye. 'Carrie?' He saw her, smiled, and slumped back into sleep.

She opened the box. Philippe's coin, with the note wrapped around it. And her father's message. 'Silence is golden.'

Then, with a sigh, she took off her blouse and skirt and slipped, silently, into bed.

EPILOGUE: 1915

Ernie eased himself a little further into his foxhole, and waved to the two men to follow him. They wriggled nearer, scrabbling in the sand. He rolled over and began taking out the explosives, the fuses, the detonators.

He had been one of the first volunteers. Needed to be. The army didn't ask about your record, and they were glad to have miners, especially the engineers. Royal Engineers. Ernie knew more about explosives than half the instructors on the training course, the men used to say. Katie had been good as her word, mind – fixed Carrie up with that job, and found something for him, too, but it was only labouring. Man needed more than that, with a wife and two children to support.

Two children. Still made him smile, that. Sturdy little fellow the boy was, and eyes as blue as claypools. Frank. Strange name for a boy, that: he'd wanted 'James' after Mr Tavy, but Carrie had been insistent. 'What's it mean?' he wanted to know, and she just laughed and said it was a coin.

'Just be thankful I didn't want to call it August,' she said. 'I called the last one May.'

But he hadn't cared really, so long as the child was all right, and Carrie too. It had been easier for her, this time, all round. Like as if she'd got the hang of it, he said, and she had almost laughed.

She hadn't liked it, though, when he came for a soldier – not even though he looked smarter than paint in his uniform, and he'd got his stripe up in no time. Good leader of men, they said he was, and had their eye on him for sergeant.

He rolled over again, burying the explosive charge deep into the soft soil. Undermining they called it, close to the enemy lines. Skilled work. He liked it. And better here, in the Middle East, than floundering in the mud somewhere in France, half afraid of a gas attack every second minute.

There was sun here, and sand, and a job to do and respect from the others when you did it well. There were worse lives.

'Look out!'

The explosion came from somewhere to his left. It buried him over his head in sand, and at his side there was a warm sticky sensation. He put down his hand and it came away red. Funny, the rest of the world seemed to be green . . . grey . . . black . . .

He did not hear the second shell, the one that killed him.

Carrie stood for a long, long time looking at the notice. Ernest Clarance, killed in action. She turned away, a lump in her throat.

Had she loved him? Yes, perhaps she had. Not as Mother had loved Father. Not even as Ma Clarance had loved Da. But in her way, as a mother loves a naughty child. She would weep for Ernie.

She was at St Ives now, housekeeper to the farmer's wife. A good life. Blossom, growing sturdy and healthy romping among the fields, and chasing seagulls from the early crops. Frank, 'a present from me', blue-eyed and placid, already with his father's smile. But no Ernie. Never again.

She walked back through a world that was strangely, ominously empty. There were new buds on the honeysuckle, and a solitary bee kissed the first flowers in the lane. A new spring.

She went into the house, upstairs to the bright attic room with its chintz curtains and the little latticed windows which was hers as housekeeper. The box was on the table by her bed.

The piece of paper was still in it, neatly folded as he had given it to her. She drew it out. *Philippe Trezayle, dit Diavezour, Manoir de Ploumenou, Ploumenach, Brittany.*

One day, not now, but one day soon, when her tears for Ernie Clarance had ended, she would write. The certainty of it gave her a little thrill of pleasure, even today. Would he get it? In war-torn France did letters arrive? And was he still there, in that *manoir*, with his *manez*, or was he somewhere else? In the navy, or fighting in the fields at Flanders? Dead, perhaps, or wounded. And if he *was* there, what would he do when he received her letter?

She did not know. She could only write. And then she would have to wait and see.